A
PERFECT DEATH

Also by Kate Ellis

Wesley Peterson series:
The Merchant's House
The Armada Boy
An Unhallowed Grave
The Funeral Boat
The Bone Garden
A Painted Doom
The Skeleton Room
The Plague Maiden
A Cursed Inheritance
The Marriage Hearse
The Shining Skull
The Blood Pit

Joe Plantagenet series:
Seeking the Dead
Playing With Bones

For more information regarding Kate Ellis
log on to Kate's website: www.kateellis.co.uk

Kate Ellis

A
PERFECT DEATH

PIATKUS

PIATKUS

First published in Great Britain in 2009 by Piatkus Books

Copyright © 2009 by Kate Ellis

The moral right of the author has been asserted

A CIP catalogue record for this book
is available from the British Library

ISBN 978-0-7499-0910-9

Typeset in Times by Action Publishing Technology Ltd, Gloucester
Printed and bound in Great Britain by CPI Mackays, Chatham, ME5 8TD

Papers used by Piatkus are natural, renewable and recyclable
products sourced from well-managed forests and certified
in accordance with the rules of the Forest Stewardship Council.

Mixed Sources
Product group from well-managed
forests and other controlled sources
www.fsc.org Cert no. SGS-COC-004081
© 1996 Forest Stewardship Council

Piatkus Books
An imprint of
Little, Brown Book Group
100 Victoria Embankment
London EC4Y 0DY

An Hachette UK Company

www.hachette.co.uk
www.piatkus.co.uk

For Cal and John

Prologue

'This is the place.'

Something in those whispered words made the young woman shudder.

'Some people would call it a place of execution but I call it a place of purification.'

'You're scaring me,' she whispered. She had come this far to learn the truth and she wasn't going to give up now, even though all her senses were screaming that something wasn't right.

Her companion was moving fast, leaning slightly with the weight of the holdall. Not for the first time she wondered what was in it. They had almost reached the hedgerow at the end of the field and she could just see the river through the gaps in the trees, oily dark, swelling and shifting in the moonlight.

She could hear the water lapping drowsily against the shore but the sound of her companion's voice in the darkness ahead broke the river's sleepy spell. 'It happened around here.'

'What did?'

'Her execution. This is where she was burned to death.'

Suddenly she knew that going there had been a dreadful mistake. But it was too late now for escape. Her companion had begun to walk towards her, determined and mechanical. And in that lonely spot there was nobody around to hear her scream.

It hadn't rained for ten days and the ground was tinder dry. Perfect kindling for a fire, she thought with terrifying foresight. She felt a sharp blow to the side of her head and stumbled, stunned and helpless, to the ground, grabbing at her attacker's clothing. Then she felt her arms being pinned roughly behind her back and something being wound around her wrists: something hard, a strap or a belt. Finding a sudden strength, she tried to lash out but another blow landed and everything went dark.

As the cold liquid splashed about her some of it landed on her face and brought her back to consciousness for a few moments. She coughed with the stench. Now she knew what the holdall had contained. Petrol.

There was a sound like rushing wind as the vapour caught alight and when the flames began to lick at her limbs her body jerked with shock as agony overwhelmed her.

Her screams died away on the salty air. And through the flames she could just make out her executioner's face, masked with a grubby handkerchief to block out the heat and the stench of burning flesh, as the fire consumed her like a voracious animal.

Then came the silence. The silence of the dead.

1

Legends. All we have is legends. But in every legend there is a grain – or perhaps more than a grain – of truth.

I first read the story in a book of Devon tales. I took little notice back then but, when I began to help Yves with his work, I remembered that story and began to delve further.

The legend of the burning girl – or the burning bride – had been recorded over the years by various local storytellers and historians. A lord, so the story goes, went to the Crusades and returned with a bride he'd rescued from the flames as she was about to be burned as a heretic. The only crusade that appears to fit is that in the Languedoc against the Albigensians, as there are no accounts of anyone actually being burned for heresy during the campaigns in the Middle East.

Legends. How they confuse and mislead. And yet I am sure I'm getting near the truth. I even know the name of the burning girl. Jeanne de Minerve. Jeanne the Heretic. I sympathise with Jeanne because I too am a heretic of sorts: a seeker after truth who won't be fobbed off with what I'm told.

> *(From papers found in the possession of Professor Yves Demancour)*

Wesley and Pam Peterson had no idea that they were being watched as they sat at the restaurant table. The watcher sat in the shadows of the Calvary Garden smoking a cigarette on the stone steps of the central cross while, somewhere on the other side of the square, the small, dark haired singer – a devotee of Edith Piaf – assured her audience that she regretted nothing, her voice quivering with passion.

Pam raised her hand and pushed her straight brown hair off her face before looking round. It seemed that every cobble of the ancient Place Marcou was utilised, crammed with the tables and chairs of a dozen rival restaurants, and the strings of lights around the square gave the place a festive look as an army of waiters in black T-shirts scurried around with trays held high.

'How was the pudding?' There was a note of anxiety in Wesley's voice.

Pam patted her stomach, took a long sip of red wine and slumped back in her seat with a blissful smile on her face.

Wesley leaned forward. 'What do you fancy doing now?' He hesitated for a second, looking into her eyes. 'Early night?'

Her hand came to rest on his. 'Sounds good.' Then the smile turned into an apologetic grin. 'Mind you, I've eaten far too much, so how about a quick walk round the walls first, eh?'

'OK. If you want,' said Wesley with an understanding smile. A romantic walk before returning to the hotel was fine by him.

It was dusk but the air was still comfortably warm. For a precious week Wesley and Pam had had the freedom to do as they pleased without jobs or children to consider. At first, having lost the habit of spontaneity, they had hesitated to make the most of it, like caged birds suddenly shown an open door to the outside world. It had

4

taken two days in the Languedoc sun with no decisions to make, apart from which restaurant to choose, before they began to relax and enjoy the old walled city of Carcassonne.

As soon as the bill was settled, they stood up, their chairs scraping on the cobbles. Pam slipped her hand into Wesley's and as they strolled out of the square the singer moved on to "Chanson d'Amour".

'This is the life,' he heard Pam mutter to no one in particular as they started to weave their way through the narrow streets hand in hand, past the tables of what seemed like a thousand restaurants. When they reached the paved square in front of the cathedral of Saint Nazaire, they rested on a stone bench for a few leisurely minutes, staring up at the leering gargoyles, before wandering on towards the walls.

Once they had passed through the shadowy gateways of the Tour Saint Nazaire, they found themselves on the wide gravel path between the concentric walls. Wesley squeezed Pam's hand and she smiled up at him. Before the holiday she'd seemed a little preoccupied, as though there'd been something on her mind ... something she was reluctant to share with him. But that might have been his imagination. She might have just been tired after a long term of teaching.

Although it was quieter here between the walls than in Carcassonne's bustling streets and squares, a lot of tourists were still out and about taking the evening air. But, once they had passed the Porte Narbonnaise, they suddenly found themselves alone watching the swifts and bats swooping and wheeling between the towers in their nightly show of prowess. Wesley felt Pam's hand slip around his waist and he was overwhelmed by a sudden wave of happiness. This really was the life – reality could wait.

5

Then a sudden sound made him turn his head and he thought he caught a glimpse of something in the corner of his retina: a slight movement in the shadows of a doorway leading into one of the outer towers, which was topped by a cone of slates. But he told himself that it was probably his imagination. A place like this, with its history of sieges and bloody battles, was bound to retain echoes of suffering in its warm, glowing stones. That was how ghost stories began.

As they strolled on, Pam stopped every now and then to shake the sandy gravel out of her sandals. They passed a French couple with two young children trotting obedi-ently by their mother's side and Wesley saw Pam shoot them an envious look. If Michael had been there with them he would have been asking constant questions and Amelia would have been whining about some imagined discomfort. But tonight this wasn't their problem. The children were back in Devon with Wesley's sister. And the world of police and crime couldn't touch them. Not even Gerry Heffernan's influence could stretch this far.

It was growing darker as they reached the Porte de Rodez and the towers around them glowed golden in the newly lit floodlights.

Pam broke away from her husband and climbed the steps up to the parapet walk, where she paused to stare out over the Ville Basse, Carcassonne's newer, sprawl-ing city spread out below them like a sea of twinkling lights. Wesley stood at the foot of the steps feeling content and slightly tipsy with the wine he'd had at dinner. Perfectly at peace with the world. And totally unaware that something was about to shatter his leisurely idyll.

'Wesley.'

A man's voice spoke his name almost in a whisper and Wesley's heart began to beat a little faster as the tranquil spell was suddenly broken. He swung round and saw a tall figure standing a few yards away but in the deep shadows cast by the city walls he found it hard to make out the newcomer's features.

'Wesley Peterson? It is you, isn't it?'

Wesley held his breath as the figure stepped forward: a man around his own age wearing faded jeans, a washed-out black T-shirt and a tattered ethnic scarf around his neck. His mousy hair was long and in his left hand he carried a guitar case.

'You don't recognise me, do you, mate?'

Wesley stared at the half-familiar face – at the freckled snub nose and the wide mouth fixed in a semi-permanent crooked smile – and long-distant memories of his early days at university gradually began to stir in his brain. 'It's not Ian, is it? Ian Rowe?'

The man's smile widened and suddenly Wesley knew he was right. But Rowe looked different: thinner and more careworn. The Ian Rowe he'd known back at university was well built, verging on the plump, with a penchant for bright shirts and partying. That Ian Rowe had dropped out of his archaeology course at the end of his second year after failing his exams. And the detective in Wesley couldn't help wondering what had happened to him in the intervening years. And how he came to be here in the south of France just as he and Pam were having a cosy few days *à deux*.

He nodded towards Pam, who was standing on the ramparts, watching them with curiosity. 'I recognise your girlfriend . . . wasn't she at . . .?'

'Yeah. Pam was studying English. And we're married.'

'How very grown up,' Rowe said with a hint of bitterness. 'But you always were grown up, weren't you, Wesley Peterson?

7

Wesley didn't answer. He caught a whiff of cigarette smoke and stepped back. Somehow he didn't want to prolong this conversation. It had brought a stain of reality to their Gallic fantasy.

But Rowe wasn't going to let him escape that easily. 'Ever hear from that Neil you used to hang round with?'

'Yes, I see him quite often. He's working for the Devon County Archaeological Unit.'

A bitter sneer twisted Rowe's mouth. 'What about you?'

Wesley hesitated for a second. 'I joined the police. I'm a detective inspector in Tradmouth.' He harboured the uncharitable hope that the revelation might discourage further conversation. Some instinct told him that Rowe's life since university might not always have been lived on the right side of the law.

He was rather surprised when the man's lips curled upwards into a knowing smile. 'I did know about your surprising choice of career, as a matter of fact.'

'How?'

'Someone told me when I was back in England a while ago.'

'Who?'

Rowe shrugged. 'Can't remember. I spotted you earlier in the Place Marcou. Almost like fate, I suppose.'

The way he said the words made Wesley feel a little uneasy. 'You followed us?'

'Well, I couldn't let the opportunity pass, could I? Tradmouth. That's near Morbay, isn't it?'

'Morbay's on our patch, yes.' He glanced in Pam's direction; she was coming down the steps, heading towards them.

Rowe suddenly grasped Wesley's arm. 'Look, I need a bit of advice. Someone I know could be in a bit of bother. I'm worried about her and when I saw you I thought . . .'

8

'Wes, are you going to be long?' he heard Pam say pointedly.

But Rowe seemed to take her words as encouragement. 'Why don't you introduce us?'

Wesley turned to Pam. 'Pam, this is Ian Rowe. He was on my course.'

'Failed his exams and dropped out. Nice to see you, Pam.'

Pam blustered, as though she feared she'd misread the situation. 'Sorry. I didn't realise you were ... Are you on holiday or ...?'

'Sadly not. Got a job washing up in the Auberge de la Cité. Just temporary while I look for something better.'

'Do you get back to England much?' she said. Wesley guessed that the question was motivated by a mixture of politeness and curiosity.

Rowe's expression clouded. 'Not much. In fact I haven't been back since my mum died six months back.'

'Oh, I'm sorry,' Pam rapidly rearranged her features into a mask of sympathy.

'Don't worry, Pam. One of those things.' Rowe looked at his watch. 'Shit,' he said under his breath. 'If I don't get a move on, I'll be late for my shift.' He turned to Wesley. 'Look, Wes, can we meet up tomorrow?'

Wesley glanced at Pam. His instincts told him that he might be treading on dangerous ground if he agreed to any disruption to their holiday plans. But her expression was neutral.

'We're going to the tournament but we've nothing else planned,' he heard himself saying. He was becoming rather intrigued by Ian Rowe. He wanted to know what had brought him there ... and why he was so anxious to obtain his advice.

'The tournament finishes at three thirty sharp so I'll

9

meet you afterwards in the Place Saint Nazaire. In front of the cathedral. OK?' Rowe said quickly, leaving no room for objections. 'Look, I've really got to go.'

He turned and ran up the steps, disappearing beneath the arch of the Porte de Rodez. Wesley and Pam stood there for a few moments in silence.

'Well, he certainly seems worried about something,' Pam said softly as they began to walk back towards the hotel.

'Apparently someone told him I'd joined the police and now he wants my advice – don't ask me what about.' He decided not to mention that Rowe had followed them from the Place Marcou, waiting for an opportunity to get him alone.

'Are you going to meet him?'

'Not if you don't want me to,' Wesley said quickly.

Pam gave the matter some thought. 'I suppose it wouldn't do any harm to find out what's bothering him.' She smiled and took his hand. 'Now how about that early night you mentioned?'

DCI Gerry Heffernan glanced at the calendar on his office wall. Three more days and Wesley would return. The sun would shine in the heavens, all crime in South Devon would cease and muggers would start helping old ladies across the road without pinching their pensions. Or, failing that, he would have an extra pair of hands to rely on. DS Rachel Tracey was doing a fair job of filling in during Wesley's absence but Gerry was a creature of habit and, to him, things just weren't the same without his DI.

He sat at his desk playing with his pen, wondering why he'd been landed with this problem first thing on a Wednesday morning, just when CID was short handed. But he tried to convince himself that he was being unduly

10

pessimistic. Someone setting themselves alight in a field might well be a particularly unpleasant case of suicide – not something that need occupy CID's resources for too long.

He began to read the report on his desk. Just outside Queenswear a farmer, unable to sleep for worrying about falling milk prices, had looked out of an upstairs window and spotted the blaze shortly after midnight. But the firemen who'd answered his call had been in for a shock. The fire was in a field that had recently been sold off by the farmer to be used for new housing and, when the flames were extinguished, the firemen made a grim discovery – the burned remains of a human body.

The first police officer on the scene had been sick. And then he had the presence of mind to call in the scene of crime team. With a deep sigh, Gerry stood up and strolled out into the CID office. His eyes were drawn to the window. The first floor of the police station afforded a good view of the river and, as it was a fine summer's day, the yachts were out there already, enjoying the sunshine and the excellent sailing conditions. Gerry felt a twinge of envy. He'd much rather be sailing round the headland on the *Rosie May* on a morning like this than standing in a field looking at some poor bugger's charred remains.

He saw that Rachel Tracey was waiting for him, her blonde hair tied back in a businesslike ponytail and her handbag slung over her shoulder, ready for the off. She had a keen expression on her face, like a border collie who'd just spotted a straggling herd of sheep badly in need of rounding up. She looked as if she was eager to examine the burned corpse in the field even if her boss wasn't.

'You all right there, Rach?' The question was rhetorical. He could see for himself that Rachel was all right.

She was taking to the role of acting detective inspector like a seagull to a chimney pot. When Wesley returned from holiday, she would be a detective sergeant again. But Gerry was reluctant to press too hard for her promotion as he didn't want to lose Rachel to uniform . . . or, worse still, traffic. She was a valuable asset – a jewel to be prized and kept away from the avaricious eyes of others. Besides, Gerry was used to her and he liked what he knew.

Rachel drove as usual – Gerry Heffernan saved his navigational skills for the water and, besides, Rachel, having been brought up on a local farm, knew the area as only a native can. Gerry, originally from Liverpool, had married a local girl but he still considered himself an outsider, even after twenty-six years in Tradmouth. Rachel's family, however, had farmed the Devon land for centuries and she steered the car down single-track lanes with a confidence that made her boss turn pale. He sat in the passenger seat, enjoying the trip over the river on the clanking car ferry, but when they reached dry land he closed his eyes tight. Wesley's driving, he thought to himself, was far more cautious.

When they came to a sudden halt Gerry's eyes flicked open. The fields here rolled into one another, the green landscape undulating like a swelling sea, punctuated by copses, ancient hedgerows and the occasional mellow house or agricultural building. It was rich land with lush grass and red, fertile soil. A herd of Jersey cows grazed studiously in the field beyond the gate.

'Grandal Farm. This is the place,' Rachel said.

'Where is everyone?'

Rachel didn't answer for a few seconds. Then she started the engine and drove further up the lane. Around the bend a patrol car and Dr Colin Bowman's Volvo squatted in a wide passing place. Rachel said nothing.

Never, in all the time Gerry had known her, had she ever admitted she was wrong.

'Here goes,' Gerry Heffernan mumbled as he extricated his bulky body from his seat belt and climbed out of the car.

He could see a group of people in the distance, mostly clad in white overalls. They were crowded near a small copse of trees at the far end of the field. There was a bright flash from the photographer's camera as they approached and Gerry could make out the pathologist, Colin Bowman, at the centre of the group, stooping over something on the ground. Gerry had an ominous feeling that he was about to see something frightful. He bit his lip and carried on, fixing a smile of greeting to his lips. But he noticed that Rachel's expression was serious, as though she knew exactly what was coming.

He walked over the uneven surface of the newly mown field ahead of Rachel and, as he approached, Colin Bowman moved forward to greet him, his body shielding the thing on the ground from view.

'Gerry, good to see you,' he said.

'What's the story then?' Gerry had just caught a fleeting glimpse of something blackened and twisted lying there on the ground and suddenly he didn't feel in the mood for Colin's usual social chit-chat.

'I'm afraid it's a nasty one, Gerry,' said Colin. 'But I'll be able to tell you more when I've had a proper look back at the mortuary.'

'Could it be suicide?'

Colin shook his head. 'I don't think so.'

Gerry hesitated. 'I assume the poor bugger was dead when he was set alight?'

'I rather suspect it's a she actually but it's not easy to tell.' Colin sighed, deep in thought. 'I'll have to check the lungs to see whether any smoke was inhaled but . . .'

Gerry sensed there was something Colin was keeping back. 'What is it? What's the matter?'

Colin was silent for a few moments. 'The arms aren't in the classic pugilistic position so there's a possibility that she was tied up before being burned alive. The SOCOs have found the charred remains of a buckle so it's possible that her arms were secured by a belt or ... However, I won't be able to say for sure until ...'

'So it looks like we've got a murder on our hands?'

Colin Bowman looked at him, suddenly solemn. 'Yes. And it's a particularly nasty one.'

Pam was smiling as the tournament came to a close. Recently smiles had been rare, Wesley thought as he put his arm around her shoulders. The mounted knights rode past acknowledging the cheers of the crowd, but as the horses' hoofs clattered on the hard ground a mobile phone in the row began to ring, returning them rudely to the twenty-first century.

They walked out of the arena hand in hand, following the other chattering spectators. They had five minutes before their appointment with Ian Rowe and the Place Saint Nazaire was only round the corner so they strolled slowly, enjoying the warmth of the sun.

'Perhaps he'll be able to recommend somewhere for dinner tonight,' Pam said hopefully. Wesley didn't reply. He guessed the last thing on Ian Rowe's mind would be small talk and restaurant recommendations. And, from what he remembered of Rowe during his time at university, he wasn't the sort he'd choose to pass the time of day with on a precious holiday either. He'd listen to whatever Rowe had to say then he'd make his excuses.

The Place Saint Nazaire was busy but they spotted Rowe right away. He was waiting for them, sitting on the stone bench Wesley and Pam had occupied briefly the

14

night before, strumming a guitar, the instrument case open on the ground in front of him. Wesley could see some coins in the guitar case.

They fought their way past camera-wielding tourists and a party of pubescent French schoolchildren, alternately chattering and making a massive effort to appear cool in front of their peers. As Wesley drew closer to Rowe, he could hear him singing – something by the Beatles. "Yesterday". Somehow the song seemed appropriate. Rowe's voice was pleasant – not good enough for a professional performance, perhaps, but easy to listen to and in tune. Wesley felt in his pocket and pulled out a euro coin, then he stood for a while listening, just out of Rowe's line of vision.

When the song was finished, the small audience of tourists started to drift away, some throwing coins which landed in the guitar case with a succession of dull thuds. Wesley noticed that Rowe's face looked gaunt in the bright sunlight, as though he could do with a good meal.

'Very good,' he said with a smile as he threw the coin into the case. He sat down on the bench beside Rowe but Pam remained standing, as though preparing to make a quick getaway. Wesley sensed she didn't want to waste time and neither did he, so he came straight to the point.

'Last night you said you wanted some advice.'

Rowe looked round nervously, as though afraid of eavesdroppers. 'Never had you down as a cop, Wesley Peterson. Do they give you a hard time . . . being black?'

'It's been known . . . but that's their problem, not mine. You said you were worried about a friend of yours.' He could sense Pam behind him, prickling with impatience.

Ian lowered his voice. 'Yeah. She lives in Neston and works in Morbay so when I found out you were working near there . . .'

The sudden look of anxiety in Rowe's eyes told Wesley that his worry was genuine.

'Let's just start at the beginning. Who is she and why are you worried about her?'

'Her name's Nadia Lucas. I met her when I dropped out of uni. I worked with her at Sir—' He stopped in mid sentence. 'But that's another story – I'm still sorting that one out,' he added, slightly mysteriously. 'Anyway, Nadia turned up over here about eighteen months ago working for this professor at Toulouse University. Then about nine months ago he moved on to Morbay Uni and Nadia went with him. Weird little bloke,' Rowe added with an unpleasant grin.

'So?'

'I keep in touch with Nadia by phone and e-mail and recently she's been going on about her mum's death – really heavy stuff. She says she's getting close to the truth, whatever that is. I've been trying to contact her for the past few days but she hasn't replied. It's not like her and I'm worried.'

'She might have gone away. Her computer might be down; phone out of order.'

'She would have said if she was going away and she works at Morbay University – plenty of computers there and they can't all be down. Like I said, it's not like her.'

Wesley sighed. This had all the hallmarks of a wild goose chase. The woman was probably busy – or just sick of corresponding with Ian Rowe.

'I'm due to go back there myself soon – bit of personal business – but I thought you'd have ways of checking people out and . . . Off the record, like. Just to make sure she's OK.'

Wesley took a deep breath. So far everything Rowe had said was irritatingly vague. Pam had wandered off and he could see that she was making for the cathedral.

She'd had enough. And Wesley knew how she felt. He had a creeping suspicion that this man was wasting his time, disturbing his precious holiday when he didn't even have any evidence to hand.

'Tell you what, Ian, why don't you get any relevant e-mails printed off and once I'm home I'll make a few discreet enquiries if I have time. Unless you have evidence that a crime's been committed, that's the best I can offer, I'm afraid. How well do you know this Nadia?' he asked, trying to keep the impatience he felt out of his voice. He scanned the square but there was no sign of Pam. She was probably inside the cathedral now, he thought, and suddenly he wanted to be in there with her.

Rowe strummed a chord on his guitar, as though he needed time to consider his answer. 'Pretty well. She was good to me when I needed a bit of care and attention, so I reckon I owe her.'

'And is she the sort to over-dramatise ... to make things up?'

'She has what they call "issues". Her mum vanished when she was little and it was assumed she'd killed herself. She was brought up by her dad but he died a couple of years ago – cancer. A while ago she told me she'd just found some letter hidden amongst her dad's belongings and she's been going on about trying to find out what really happened to her mum ever since. Look, all I'm asking is that you make sure she's OK.'

Wesley said nothing for a few seconds. Rowe sounded sincere. But perhaps he always sounded like that. Some of the best con men he'd come across in the course of his career had been remarkably convincing.

'So how come you're here in France, Ian?'

'I like it here. And the weather's a whole lot better than in dear old England. Plenty of tourists. Plenty of work.'

17

'What exactly have you been up to since you dropped out of uni?' He'd noted Rowe's evasion when he'd spoken of how he'd met Nadia. There was something he was holding back.

An enigmatic smile appeared on Ian's lips. 'This and that. Bit of driving. Bit of waiting on and washing up. Bit of singing. Anything that brings in a few euros.' He paused and the smile widened. 'But I might not have to worry about money for long. Ever heard of Saissac?'

'We went there the day after we arrived. What about it?'

'Interesting place. Lovely views of the Pyrenees.'

'Yes.' Wesley remembered the dramatic ruins towering above the small village. The wind had been strong and Pam hadn't wanted to hang around there for long.

'Some workmen discovered treasure there during restoration work in 1979 ... it's on display in the local museum.'

'We saw it.'

'You know all about the Cathars, I take it?'

'You can't avoid them round here. Or all the conspiracy theories ... mostly rubbish, I imagine.'

Rowe tapped the side of his nose and picked up his guitar case, emptying the coins into a canvas bag which he slung across his shoulder. 'Not bad,' he muttered to himself as he placed the guitar lovingly in its battered case. He looked Wesley in the eye. 'I've got to go. I'll see you tomorrow – ten thirty here. I'll get copies of those e-mails printed out for you. Don't be late ... I'm on the lunchtime shift at the restaurant and the chef there's a bastard.'

Wesley watched him disappear into the crowd of tourists, resentful of Rowe's presumption. Why should he disrupt his holiday at the behest of a casual acquaintance? But, on the other hand, something about Rowe intrigued him. He stood up and walked to the cathedral to join Pam.

As his eyes adjusted to the gloom of the great church, he spotted her. She was studying a stained-glass window depicting the Tree of Life, lost in her own thoughts. It was time to make it up to her. Time to forget about Ian Rowe, frightened women and the world outside.

'Any idea who she was?' Colin Bowman looked at Gerry Heffernan enquiringly across the charred corpse on the mortuary table. His glasses had slipped down his nose, giving him a studious appearance. He pushed them back up with his forearm, avoiding touching his face with his gloved hand.

'Your guess is as good as mine, Colin. I reckon our best bet is dental records.'

'Sorry, Gerry. As far as I can see she's had no fillings. Obviously looked after her teeth, which is very inconsiderate of her.'

'It is a she, is it?' The thing on the stainless-steel table bore little resemblance to a human being apart from the vague shape. It was blackened and twisted and the charred flesh had almost peeled away from the skull, displaying a row of smoke-stained, grinning teeth.

Colin paused and looked at the body like an artist assessing his handiwork. 'Oh, yes, I think we can be sure it's a she.'

'Age?'

'The wisdom teeth are through but there's not that much wear on the molars. If I had to hazard a guess I'd say she was in her twenties. But that is just a guess. The PM and X-rays might give us more information but . . .'

'Height?'

'Five five, five six.'

'Shoe size?'

19

Colin studied the feet. The fire had fused what looked like peep-toed sandals to the blackened flesh. 'Average, I should think. Size five or six.'

'That gives us something to go on, I suppose.'

'I've had a look at the lungs,' Colin said with a sigh. 'She was almost certainly alive when she was set alight. The fire officers reckon some sort of accelerant was used.'

'So some bastard doused her in petrol and set her alight?'

Colin didn't reply. The very thought was unpalatable.

'It's definitely murder then? It can't have been suicide?'

Colin nodded earnestly. 'As I'm sure that her arms were secured behind her back and no petrol container was found by the body, accident or suicide seem rather unlikely. Somebody burned this poor woman alive. And I'm sure you'll agree, Gerry, that someone capable of that is highly dangerous.'

Gerry looked round. Rachel Tracey was standing against the wall, her eyes focused on Colin's trolley of instruments rather than the thing on the table.

'Rach.'

She jumped. 'What, sir?'

'There's no need for you to hang around here. You get off and see if Missing Persons have come up with anyone who fits the bill.'

Colin saw the relief on her face and knew that she wanted to be out of that room with its lingering stench of burning flesh.

'Fancy a cup of Earl Grey when we've finished here, Gerry?' he asked as soon as Rachel had gone.

But the answer was a shake of the head.

Rachel lost no time in leaving Tradmouth Hospital

mortuary and hurrying down the narrow streets back to the police station near by.

And half an hour after she started sifting through the missing persons reports on her desk, she came up with a name. Missing woman aged twenty-five. Five feet five and a half inches tall and size six shoes.

She only hoped she'd got it right. This was her moment. Her chance to shine.

Only two days of the holiday left. Wesley wished it was longer as he and Pam walked arm in arm down the Rue Saint Sernin, satisfied after a long lie-in, a spot of morning passion and a rather good breakfast.

Wesley was starting to wonder whether he'd been wise to agree to another meeting with Ian Rowe. He had a nasty suspicion that Rowe might use the opportunity to extract money from him; that all the stuff about Nadia might be a juicy bit of bait guaranteed to hook a former archaeology student turned detective and reel him in.

He hadn't trusted Ian Rowe back at university. In fact he and Neil had tended to avoid him whenever possible. He'd felt uncomfortable in Rowe's company all those years ago ... maybe even out of his depth. Rowe had possessed that aura of danger that often attracts the opposite sex. He had partied hard and indulged in illegal substances while Wesley and Neil had spent most of their time with like-minded friends in the quieter pubs, immersing themselves in history and muddy excavations. Wesley wasn't particularly looking forward to his appointment with Rowe. But he had promised and Wesley had always been one to keep his word.

Besides, Pam wanted to do some shopping in his absence – presents for home.

After they'd parted, Wesley made his way to the Place Saint Nazaire. He waited half an hour ... then a little longer, just in case.

Then, at eleven thirty, he abandoned his wait. Ian Rowe hadn't turned up. And Wesley wondered why.

2

The royal visit to Tradmouth began on Saturday the eighteenth of June 1205 and King John stayed at Townton Hall as the guest of Walter Fitzallen until the following Wednesday.

In contemporary records Walter Fitzallen's pride concerning his royal visitor is almost palpable, although King John can't have been an easy guest for the lord of a Devon manor, however prosperous and enterprising, to entertain.

One can imagine the adjustment of finery as the local gentry assembled on the quayside to watch the royal ship's stately progress up the River Trad and the excitement in the Fitzallen household as the servants rushed to and fro with fine linen and food to impress their royal visitor and his retinue. There would be lavish feasts in the smoky great hall with its central hearth as Walter attempted to prove that the gentry of Devon, so distant from the centre of government, were more than a match for their counterparts at court.

It is recorded that Stephen de Grendalle was present when the King stepped ashore and I am curious about the relationship between Walter Fitzallen and de Grendalle with his extensive estates over the River Trad at Queenswear. Was there rivalry between the men, I wonder? And did the roots of the coming tragedy lie in this royal visit? Such events, after all, can bring out the worst in men.

(From papers found in the possession of Professor Yves Demancour)

Rachel Tracey placed the photograph and its accompanying missing persons form on Gerry Heffernan's cluttered desk.

The young woman on the photograph was bottle blonde with sharp features and her thin lips were drawn together in a sneering smile.

The chief inspector studied the image for a while before looking up at Rachel. 'She fits the bill, I suppose. How long has she been missing?'

'Her mother hasn't seen her for a week but she reported her missing three days ago.'

'She lives at home?'

Rachel nodded. 'On the Tradmouth estate.'

'Family?'

'Two younger sisters. No father to speak of. Mother thought she was with her boyfriend at first but there's been no reply from her mobile and she's usually good about keeping in touch.'

He studied the form again. 'She's twenty-five, according to this. She might think it's time to cut the apron strings. Has the mother spoken to the boyfriend?'

'Yes, but he says he hasn't seen her.'

'Does she believe him?'

'Not sure. I got the impression she doesn't approve of him but she didn't say why.'

'Might be worth having another word.' He looked Rachel in the eye. 'Did you tell her about the body?'

Rachel shook her head. 'I didn't want to alarm her.'

'Yeah, you did right.' He stared at the photograph,

24

wondering whether this could really be the face he had seen charred and peeling from the bone like a piece of overcooked meat. It was an uncomfortable thought. And the thought that this girl had a mother and family who'd have to be informed of the manner of her death was even worse. But the woman in the field was somebody's daughter, somebody's sister, wife or friend. Someone was going to have to suffer eventually. 'Any other possibilities?'

Rachel shook her head. 'No local ones. But if she was brought here from somewhere else ...'

He knew Rachel had a point. If the young woman had been brought by car to that field on the outskirts of Queenswear, she could have come from anywhere in the country. Someone might have chosen South Devon as a handy place to dispose of a body and confuse the police. How Gerry Heffernan hated it when criminals used their brains.

'I don't suppose some farm worker trudging up the lane saw a car parked there and happened to note down the registration number?' he said hopefully.

Rachel smiled apologetically at his optimism and shook her head again.

'I suppose DNA is our best hope.' Heffernan sighed. 'It has the smell of a punishment killing to me. What's the betting she's offended some bastard of a pimp or made waves for some drug dealer.' He felt a wave of anger surge inside him. And he knew that if they ever got their hands on the killer, he'd have to exercise iron self-control during the interviewing process.

'If you're right, sir, we might never be able to give her a name,' Rachel said almost in a whisper.

They both sat in silence for a while. They knew only too well that Devon wasn't immune to the horrors of the outside world. Gerry wondered whether it ever had been.

Rachel stood up. 'I'll go and have a word with this
...' She picked up the form on the boss's desk. 'Donna
Grogen's mother.'

Gerry looked up and gave her a sad smile. 'Rather you
than me.'

Dr Neil Watson had never felt at home in offices. In
fact he felt as uncomfortable as a polar bear in the
Sahara, sitting there in the spacious Morbay offices of
Tradford Developments. He fingered the collar of his
shirt, tight as a noose around his neck, as the office
door opened.

The man who emerged was in his mid forties, tall and
with the heavy build of a habitual rugby player. He had
pre-empted nature by cropping his receding hair almost
to the scalp and he wore a diamond earring in his left ear
that looked incongruous with his dark suit, striped shirt
and tie.

He approached Neil with outstretched hand. 'Jon
Bright. Dr Watson, I presume?' He smirked. 'Not
brought Sherlock with you, eh?'

Neil tried to smile but only managed an insincere
grimace. The powers that be in the County
Archaeological Unit had issued their orders – he wasn't
to rub this man up the wrong way. There was money in
the deal. He had to make an effort.

'Sorry to keep you waiting. My receptionist's gone
AWOL. Didn't turn up for work a few days ago and
we've not heard from her since. No sense of responsibility, these girls today.'

Neil said nothing.

Jon Bright opened a filing cabinet to the right of the
reception desk. 'Now where did she put the correspondence?' He pulled out a file triumphantly. 'This is it. I'll
say one thing for Donna, she's not bad at filing. Sorry I

26

can't offer you tea. My secretary's gone to the dentist's and I'm not sure where the milk's kept.'

'That's OK,' Neil said quickly. Tea was the last thing on his mind.

'Anyway, let's go into my office and get down to business.' He sighed. 'I suppose I'd better tell you that I've had the police on the blower this morning. Someone's decided to commit suicide on the site so the place is going to be out of bounds for a while ... cordoned off for forensic examination.'

Neil assumed a solemn expression. 'That's awful. Do they know who it is or why ...?'

'If they do, they didn't choose to share the information with me. I'm wondering whether it's one of these activists I've been having trouble with – the bloody Pure Sons of the West. One of the bastards might have decided to top himself and make life awkward for Tradford Developments at the same time. The grand gesture.'

Neil thought that Bright's theory was highly unlikely. Environmentalists don't usually opt for self-destruction. But he remained silent.

'This archaeological assessment of the Queenswear site. How long will it take? Time is money, you know.'

Neil took a deep breath. He'd already taken a dislike to Bright with his ready clichés and his artificial bonhomie. 'That depends what we find. From what I've already discovered, it seems to be an interesting site, archaeologically speaking. There are records of a medieval manorial complex on the site ... a family called de Grendalle held the property from Judhael who held Neston from the King.'

He noticed that Bright's hard blue eyes were beginning to glaze over but he carried on. 'The de Grendalles are first mentioned in the Domesday Book, you know. The house fell into disuse in the Tudor period when a new house was built quarter of a mile away; they must have been into recycling back then because they used a lot of materials from the old place to construct the new one. What's left of the new manor house is now used as a farmhouse, altered drastically over the centuries, of course.'

'So what's this got to do with my development?'

'If the original manorial site is considered to be of archaeological importance, it needs to be thoroughly investigated. Actually there was an excavation there back in the early nineteen eighties but it came to a sudden halt for some reason ... I haven't managed to find out why. But we need to do a proper investigation. It's a legal requirement, as you know.' He leaned forward. 'Look, you might be able to do yourself a bit of good here, Mr Bright. Some developers have made a big thing of working with the archaeological team ... even put on exhibitions of the finds for the local community. It's done their reputation in the area no end of good.' He sat back in his chair. That covered just about everything. Carrot and stick.

'So you can't give me a timescale?'

'It all depends what we find down there, Mr Bright. But I assure you, we won't take any longer than necessary.'

Bright looked as if he didn't believe him, but smiled all the same – with his mouth if not with his eyes.

'I'll see what I can find about the nineteen eighties dig. Perhaps their findings will help to hurry things up a bit.' Neil offered this verbal olive branch, aware that he'd heard rumours that there'd been something strange about this previous excavation: something that might even take him some time to sort out. But he wasn't letting Bright know this.

There were some professional mysteries he was keeping to himself.

'You're not going to look for him at that restaurant. You can't.' Pam Peterson stood blocking the way.

'We can go there for lunch if you like,' said Wesley.

'So you can sneak off into the kitchens and start asking questions. Ian Rowe's unreliable. He couldn't be bothered to turn up. End of story.'

'But he said he was worried about that friend of his . . . Nadia. I'd like to have a quick look at those e-mails he mentioned, just to make sure there's nothing to panic about. It won't take long. I promise.' Wesley almost wished he'd just disappeared off on his own and not bothered telling Pam of the nagging worry he'd felt since Rowe hadn't turned up at their rendezvous. He'd tried to convince himself that there was some simple explanation. Rowe had been waylaid somehow and, not having Wesley's mobile number, he'd been unable to let him know. This was the sensible explanation. But a persistent voice in Wesley's head was telling him it was the wrong one.

Pam looked exasperated but then she touched his hand. 'OK, I know you won't be happy until you've checked it out. But just remember you're not at work now.'

For a moment the image of Gerry Heffernan flashed into Wesley's mind, sitting at one of the nearby restaurant tables, tucking into a large meal and a vat of wine. If Gerry had been there he'd probably have told him to forget all about Ian Rowe and concentrate on enjoying his holiday.

'Come on.' He took hold of Pam's hand and led her towards the door of the Auberge de la Cité. The tables were set inside and the place looked inviting. Pam walked ahead as they crossed the threshold.

The meal was more than satisfactory – the chef had done something interesting with sea bass, followed by a textbook crème brulée – and after they had coffee, Wesley waylaid the young waitress who'd served them. He'd noticed that her English was good so he wouldn't be forced to trawl the murky depths of his schoolboy French in order to communicate. This was a delicate matter and the last thing he wanted was a misunderstanding.

She was small and slim with short dark hair and large brown eyes. As he went through the rituals of Gallic politeness, she stood there attentively, expecting a question about some tourist site or the opening hours of the Château Comptal. And from the change of expression on her face, it was clear that Wesley's first question was quite unexpected.

'Do you know Ian Rowe?' he asked. 'I believe he works in the kitchens here.'

'Yes, I know him.' The way she said the words made it sound as if she regretted the acquaintance.

'Is he in work today?'

She shook her head. 'He should be but he has not come in. The *patron* he ring his number but he is not there. Why do you ask?'

Wesley decided it would be better if he came up with something approaching the truth. 'I was at university with him.'

'Oxford? You were at Oxford?'

He was surprised. But then it would be just like Rowe to embellish his educational achievements. 'No. We were at Exeter actually.'

She gave Wesley a wary look, as though she suspected him of lying. 'Ian has a doctorate from Oxford. He told me. He worked as Sir Martin Crace's assistant for a while and he is taking time off to travel.'

Wesley was tempted to enlighten her but he had second thoughts. Who was to say that Rowe hadn't made a fresh start after dropping out of Exeter? Who was to say he wasn't telling the truth? Either that or Ian Rowe was a boastful fantasist, which was probably more likely. However, the mention of Sir Martin Crace puzzled him. Crace was high profile, an entrepreneur who'd made his millions in the pharmaceutical industry then turned philanthropist; a regular guest at 10 Downing Street and Buckingham Palace and one of the nation's Great and Good. A connection like that could easily be disproved. But, in Wesley's experience, that sort of thing never bothered fantasists.

'We arranged to meet this morning and he didn't turn up.'

The young waitress shrugged. It really wasn't her problem.

'Do you know where he lives?' Wesley said automatically, suddenly aware that he was slipping into policeman mode. And one glance at Pam sitting beside him absentmindedly excavating the sugar bowl told him he had to stop.

'He and two of the waiters share a house in the Ville Basse.'

'Are the others here now? Can I speak to them?' He glanced at Pam again and knew he'd just said the wrong thing. He was on holiday. The last thing he needed was to make it a holiday of the busman's kind. Besides, they only had one day left.

'They are in tonight. You come back tonight.'

'Can you give me his address?'

She hesitated for a moment then scribbled an address on one of the restaurant's cards. 'If you see him you tell him that chef is angry with him. OK?'

'I'll tell him,' Wesley said with a reassuring smile.

31

She was about to go when another question came into his head. 'Has he ever mentioned a girl called Nadia?'

The waitress shook her head and walked away quickly, as though the subject of Rowe was beginning to bore her.

Wesley gave Pam an apologetic smile. 'Sorry about that.'

She pouted, putting on the pretence of anger. 'I should think so too. So Ian Rowe's also been putting it about that he's got a doctorate from Oxford?'

'When he was thrown out of Exeter for failing his exams.'

'The man's a bloody liar.'

'I reckon he always was a bit of a fantasist, even when we knew him. And he's claiming he used to be Sir Martin Crace's assistant.'

Pam snorted. 'How likely is that? Like you say, he's a fantasist.' She thought for a moment. 'Mind you, it doesn't mean he didn't have some sort of menial post in Crace's organisation. Washing up in his kitchens or general dogsbody.'

Wesley looked at Pam in admiration. It was obvious when you thought about it. The best lies have a kernel of truth in them. 'At least we've got Rowe's address.'

'And you want to pay him a call?' she said. It was hard to read the expression on her face – to know whether she approved or disapproved of this new development.

She fell silent for a few seconds then she looked him in the eye. 'Well, to tell you the truth, I'm a bit intrigued myself.'

After leaving a generous tip, Wesley took hold of Pam's hand and they walked out of the restaurant. As they reached the door, he turned and saw that the waitress was watching them leave, a worried look on her face.

*

Donna Grogen worked on the reception desk in the offices of Tradford Developments – or in Admin, as her mother put it proudly. She commuted to Morbay each day and her boss, Mr Bright, thought very highly of her. There was no reason in the world that she should disappear without telling anyone.

Donna's mother, Carla, was a large woman with bottle blonde hair and she sat surrounded by used tissues like some exotic bird that had started to shed its plumage. Rachel Tracey listened sympathetically to the proud mother's recital of Donna's virtues, wondering how she could bring up the possibility that Donna might be lying dead in the mortuary, burned beyond recognition. But Rachel knew she couldn't put it off indefinitely. She'd been faced with this situation so many times before but it never seemed to get any easier.

Rachel cleared her throat. 'Mrs Grogen, there's no easy way to say this but the body of a young woman's been found in a field near Queenswear ... on land owned by Tradford Developments.'

She looked at Carla. The woman's hand had gone to her mouth as though she was trying to stifle a scream.

'I'm sorry I have to ask this but can you tell me whether Donna had any dental work done? Any fillings?'

Carla shook her head. 'She looks after her teeth ... always has.'

This was bad news. Rachel had rather been hoping to hear that Donna had been partial to boiled sweets and fizzy drinks and had a mouthful of silver-grey amalgam.

'Is it her? Is it my Donna? Can I see her?' Carla's eyes were starting to fill with tears.

'I'm afraid that won't be possible. We might have to ask you to provide a DNA sample. It's a simple procedure ...'

'Oh, my God.' The hand was clamped to the mouth

33

again and Rachel looked away. She couldn't stand the grief in the woman's eyes.

'If my Donna's dead, I know who killed her,' the mother said after a few seconds. 'It's that Chas. That's who it is. I told her she was stupid. I told her to have nothing to do with him when he got involved with those Pure Sons of Devon or whatever they call themselves, but would she listen?'

Rachel sat forward. 'Who's Chas?' she asked gently. 'And where can we find him?'

The house Ian Rowe shared with his colleagues at the Auberge de la Cité stood on a dark claustrophobic street between the old Cité and the Basse Ville, just beyond the old bridge and off the tourist trail. It was a terraced house of indeterminate age, dark, with flaking paint on the door and shutters and a small heap of dog mess near the front step. Most of the houses in the narrow road had their shutters closed and the only sign of life was a garage at the end where three men in oily overalls sat outside smoking and staring at Wesley and Pam as if they were an exotic sideshow come there to relieve the boredom of their day.

Wesley looked up. The sky was brilliant blue but the sun's rays didn't reach the Rue de Montfort. Here life was always dark.

It was Pam who rang the yellowing plastic doorbell. Wesley, careful to avoid the dog mess, stepped back and looked at the upstairs windows. The shutters were open but there was no twitching of the grubby lace curtains that hid the rooms within. It looked as though the house was empty. They'd come at the wrong time.

But, just as they were about to abandon their quest, the door opened a crack.

'*Qu'est-ce que c'est?*'

Pam said in her best schoolgirl French that they were old friends of Ian Rowe and asked where they could find him. Wesley knew she'd been rehearsing this ever since they made the decision to look for him but he was still impressed.

There was a rapid and incomprehensible reply, then the door opened to reveal a young man in a dazzling white T-shirt. He was dark haired, unshaven and handsome as a male model in a Sunday supplement and he looked at Pam appreciatively, undressing her slim figure with his eyes. When he noticed Wesley standing behind her he scowled and muttered something under his breath that Wesley guessed was either racist or insulting or both.

Pam gave the man a charming smile before asking if they could come in. The man's English was good and her agonising over French tenses and vocabulary had probably been unnecessary. But the fact that she had made the effort, Wesley told himself, might well have made some difference to their reception.

The man shrugged and stood to one side, glancing at his reflection in a dusty mirror hanging in the hallway. 'You can come in but you will not find him and I do not know where he is. This morning he receive a letter. Then he packs a bag and he goes.'

'He was supposed to be meeting me this morning,' said Wesley. 'My name's Wesley Peterson. I don't suppose he mentioned it?' It was a long shot but it was worth a try.

The guarded expression on the man's face suddenly changed. 'You are Wesley?'

'Yes. Did he leave a message for me?'

'You wait.' The man hurried away down the hallway and disappeared into a back room, returning a minute or so later clutching a brown envelope. 'He leave this. He ask me to post it but ...'

Wesley took it from him and saw that it was addressed to Wesley Peterson, The Police Station, Tradmouth, Devon, Angleterre. He resisted the temptation to tear it open there and then and stuffed it in his pocket. 'May we see his room?' he asked.

The man looked him up and down. 'Why?'

'He told us he was worried about someone and he asked us to contact her for him when we got back to England. We need to see if he's left us her address.'

The man considered this for a few moments and Wesley wondered what their next move should be if the answer proved to be no. But he had no need to worry.

'Up the stairs, first on the right.' He addressed Pam, ignoring Wesley.

'What's in the envelope?' Pam whispered as they made their way up the steep staircase with its threadbare carpet.

'Give us a chance,' he said with a grin. He had the impression she was starting to enjoy herself.

Pam pushed the door open and stepped over the threshold. Ian Rowe's room was shabby and what furniture there was looked as though it belonged in a junk shop. The bare floorboards were unvarnished and the lace curtains at the window were filthy. However, the bed was made and the place was neat. When Pam opened the massive armoire in the corner of the room, she found that it was almost empty apart from some items of clothing that had seen better days hanging forlornly from wire hangers.

'Looks like pretty boy was telling the truth. He's gone,' Pam said, disappointed.

Wesley frowned. 'But why the sudden departure?'

'Perhaps he's heard from this woman, Nadia. Perhaps he's gone to look for her himself. Come on, what's in that envelope?'

Pam watched impatiently as Wesley slit the envelope open and drew out three sheets of paper. He laid them on the bed, side by side, and began to read.

They were print-outs of e-mails and they were all from one person . . . Nadia. Rowe had kept his promise.

There were no e-mail addresses on the print-outs, just names – from Nadia to Ian. He read through the first. 'Ian, you should be careful. I know M seems all sweetness and light but he has powerful friends and a lot to lose. Don't antagonise him. If I were you, I'd just drop the whole thing. And how do you intend to prove it anyway?'

Pam read over his shoulder. 'M? Could that be Sir Martin Crace? He told that waitress he used to work for him. And he fits the bill – powerful friends and all sweetness and light on the surface.'

Wesley didn't answer. He read the next one.

'You have a right to know the truth but please be careful. I've been talking to Yves about my research. He's being very secretive and I think he's hiding something – just a hunch. Maybe it's something to do with that thing I told you about – his dirty little secret. I still don't know what this "treasure" is – he won't tell me but he seems very excited about it. He says he'll tell me soon and I'll just have to be patient. My research has gone crazy and it's like Jeanne de Minerve has taken over my life. I try to keep it scholarly and stick to the facts but when I write the emotions take over. Yves said it won't do at all but the dry academic approach doesn't seem to do the subject justice somehow. Perhaps I should be writing it as a novel. What do you think? I'm not getting far with the other matter. The man says it might take time.'

Wesley picked up the third e-mail, dated a few days ago.

37

'Ian. I don't know what to do. The man contacted me after I'd spoken to you on the phone. He thought he'd found a witness but it didn't turn out to be much help and I really can't afford him any more so I'm going to go it alone. I'm following a few leads of my own and I've been speaking to some people who knew her. Maybe I'm getting obsessed with what happened to mum like you said but I've got to know the truth. I know something's not right. Don't say I'm paranoid but I'm sure there's no way she killed herself and I'll prove it. I know you're waiting to hear from M but why don't you come back anyway? I need you. If I'm right, there might be someone who doesn't want the truth to come out. I'm following another lead tomorrow. I feel I'm close now but I'm not getting my hopes up. It might come to nothing. I'll tell you all about it when you call me. Nadia.'

'Looks as if he was telling the truth about Nadia's mother,' Wesley said quietly. 'But where has he gone?'

'I'll ask our friend downstairs if he knows any more,' Pam volunteered before hurrying from the room.

After a quick search of the wardrobe and drawers, Wesley spotted a small cork notice board hanging on the wall in the corner of the room with various scraps of paper pinned to it: brief shopping lists and work rotas. There was a sheet of paper with a name and address scribbled on it. Professor Yves Demancour, Department of History, Morbay University. Wesley unpinned it from the board, folded it carefully and placed it in his pocket. Nobody in this house was likely to miss it.

He met up with Pam downstairs in the hall and, as soon as he appeared, the man she had been talking to disappeared into a back room.

Once they were outside in the street, she touched his arm. 'That creep's called Thierry.' From the look on her face Wesley guessed that Thierry had tried it on and that she had responded by bristling with feminist indignation. He felt rather relieved that she had found the handsome Thierry's advances so offensive.

'Has he any idea where Rowe could have gone?'

'No, and I reckon Thierry's too interested in Thierry to notice what's going on around him. That man really loves himself.'

'Anything else?' Wesley asked before Pam began to warm to the subject of Thierry.

'He said Rowe went to an internet café last night – must be where he got the e-mails printed off. And the letter he received this morning had a typewritten address and a British stamp. As soon as he read it he said he had to go and he left the envelope with Thierry to post on to you. What do you think we should do next?'

Wesley took hold of her hand. Recently he'd sensed that the demands of work and family had been putting a strain on their relationship. But perhaps their stay in Carcassonne, intended to give them some time to relax together, was succeeding in some unexpected ways.

Gerry Heffernan scratched his head before pushing open the glass door. Tradford Developments must be doing well, he thought, if they could afford offices like this. But then property prices in this part of Devon were high. And some people were always keen to poke their snouts into an overflowing trough.

He knew he might be getting this all wrong. Donna Grogen had probably gone off somewhere with some flighty friend or unsuitable man. His theory about the burning girl being some prostitute punished by her pimp for some imagined misdemeanour was far more likely: you read it in the papers and saw it on TV all the time. And such things weren't confined to the rougher areas of big cities. They flourished like a poisonous fungus in respectable suburbs, in small towns and pretty rural areas. And the innocents, often girls who were promised a better life in a faraway land that never materialised, were always the victims.

Such matters had been on his mind a lot since his daughter, Rosie, recently graduated from music college, had volunteered to help out at a women's refuge in Neston, killing time before she began her teacher training. At first she'd come home with some heartbreaking stories. But after a while the stories had stopped and now she kept her knowledge locked up inside, which wasn't like Rosie, who was usually so open about her feelings. Gerry almost wished she'd give up the refuge but she was a grown woman now, he acknowledged sadly. Things had been a lot easier when she was a little girl.

When he stepped into Tradford Developments' reception area there was nobody there at the desk to greet him. He'd harboured a fleeting hope that he might arrive there to find that Donna had turned up at work, but it seemed that he'd hoped in vain. They had DNA from the burned body and Rachel had just obtained a sample from Donna's mother so, if there was a match, they'd soon know for sure. But in the meantime the case was still open.

Jon Bright was expecting him and he emerged from an office beside the pale wood reception desk with a smile fixed firmly to his face.

'Chief Inspector. Do come into the office and take a seat. Coffee?'

Gerry Heffernan answered in the affirmative. He needed something to kick-start his brain cells. As he made himself comfortable, a middle-aged secretary brought in the drinks. Gerry thanked her, making a mental note to ask her about Donna. She looked the type who'd know all the office gossip.

'I understand you want to speak to me about Donna. It's very worrying that there's been no word of her. Of course I'll help in any way I can.' Jon Bright's features formed into the concerned frown Gerry had seen on many a politician anxious to assure the public that they really cared.

'You know about the incident up near Queenswear ... on land you've recently acquired?'

'Yes. I was informed by one of your uniformed colleagues earlier. Tragic. But I don't see what it has to do with me if someone chooses to set fire to themselves on my land.' He hesitated. 'You've been enquiring about Donna ... you surely don't think ...'

'According to Donna's mother, she's been mixed up with a young man who has – how can I put it? – strong opinions about local developments. His name's Chas Ventisard. Ever met him?'

Jon Bright shook his head.

'Did Donna ever mention him to you?'

'No. But then she wouldn't, would she? We're hardly on those sort of terms, Chief Inspector.'

'Ever heard of an organisation called the Pure Sons of the West? I say organisation, and their web site claims they've got lots of support, but for all I know it could be a couple of blokes in a pub sounding off when they've had a few lagers too many.'

Gerry Heffernan saw that the colour had drained from Jon Bright's face. He'd heard of the Pure Sons of the West all right.

'Yes,' he said almost in a whisper. 'I've heard of them.' He sat back in his leather swivel chair and arched his fingers. Gerry watched him. Whatever was on his mind was something important.

'Did you know that Donna's boyfriend Chas was one of them?'

Bright shook his head vigorously. 'No, I didn't. If I'd known I would have had a word with her. Not that I ever took what they said too seriously. I've come across that sort of thing before. It's an occupational hazard for a developer ... especially when the site's regarded as sensitive. It was just an idle threat.'

'What was?'

Bright didn't answer.

Gerry leaned forward. 'So these Pure Sons of the West have been threatening you?'

Bright looked a little embarrassed. 'Not me directly. My wife's received a couple of stupid letters from them but we didn't take it seriously. And we certainly didn't think it was worth bothering the police about.'

'So they've actually threatened your wife?'

'She didn't take it seriously. She didn't want the police involved.'

Gerry was losing patience. 'Well, we are involved now. Your receptionist's missing and the burned corpse of a young woman was found on a plot of land you intend to develop. And by the way, our pathologist says it wasn't suicide.' He paused for dramatic effect before dropping his bombshell. 'He says the victim was alive when she was set alight so it's a particularly nasty case of murder, Mr Bright. And I want to catch the bastard responsible. I need to know all about these threats your wife's been getting.'

Jon Bright's mouth had fallen open, displaying a row of even white teeth of the sort only available from an expensive cosmetic dentist. After a few seconds of silence he spoke, his voice unsteady.

'Look, I think there's something I should tell you.'

'I'm all ears. Go on.' There was no mistaking the fact

that Bright suddenly looked worried. Very worried.

'Those letters my wife received. They threatened to burn her to death.'

For once Gerry Heffernan was lost for words.

'Look, I didn't take it seriously. I thought they were just trying to scare me. They've done it before to other developers ... made stupid threats. They never carry them out. They're just a bunch of losers.'

'But a woman was burned to death on your land.'

Jon Bright's initial confidence had vanished. He looked terrified. 'You think someone mistook the dead woman for my wife?' he said almost in a whisper.

'I think you'd better tell me when you last saw Donna ... sir.'

3

Walter Fitzallen single-handedly transformed Tradmouth from a minor fishing community into an international port. He must have been a forceful man, dynamic as any modern entrepreneur, and it is said that power is the ulti-mate aphrodisiac.

I digress, however. Perhaps Fitzallen's power is luring me, turning me from my intended path even after all those centuries. It is Stephen de Grendalle's story that concerns me. Stephen's and Jeanne's.

Contemporary manorial records indicate that Stephen de Grendalle spent ten months in south-west France in 1209–10 'with the Earl of Leicester driving heretics out with force'. Presumably this means that he joined the crusade launched by Pope Innocent III against the Cathars of the Languedoc and led by Simon de Montfort, Earl of Leicester (a place he never visited), whose more famous son, also Simon, caused King John's son and successor, Henry III, so much trouble. King John's rela-tionship with Pope Innocent was hardly good and his sister, Joan, had married Raymond, Count of Toulouse, a supporter of the Cathars. Nevertheless some sources indicate that some of John's English subjects who were not inclined to fight in the Holy Land saw a trip to France to persecute the Cathars as an easier way to gain

44

salvation. Perhaps de Grendalle fell into this category. Or perhaps he truly believed in what he was doing. After eight hundred years, we can never know his true motives. However, we do know that the whole enterprise ended in tragedy and death.

(From papers found in the possession of Professor Yves Demancour)

Gerry Heffernan wished the DNA results would come through. If he knew for sure that the young woman who'd been burned to death on the site of Jon Bright's proposed development was Donna, Bright's missing receptionist, he'd be able to make a proper start. But he still had the uneasy feeling that Donna might be leading him up a blind alley. He could be getting it all wrong.

On the other hand the Pure Sons of the West had threatened to burn Bright's wife to death and it would surely be too much of a coincidence if the two things were unconnected.

He sat in his glass-fronted office at the side of the incident room, staring at the calendar on his wall. Wesley would be back in a couple of days. In his absence he had come to realise how much he relied on his logical way of thinking a case through. He had sensed a tension in the Peterson marriage so he'd encouraged Wesley to take a break in the French sunshine. He'd almost bullied his inspector into booking the flights to get away from the stresses of work. But now he was starting to regret this act of charity.

A sharp knock on his door made him jump. He looked up and saw Rachel Tracey through the glass. There was a keen and satisfied expression on her face, as though she had important news to impart. She pushed the door open and placed a sheet of paper on his desk.

'Good news, sir. Or at least it's good for someone.'

Gerry tilted his head, awaiting the verdict.

'The DNA results have come back. Whoever was burned to death in that field, it wasn't Donna Grogen. Looks like we're back to square one.'

'Not necessarily. I spoke to the property developer who's bought the field. Some clowns called the Pure Sons of the West have been threatening to burn his wife to death. I've got someone checking them out.'

Rachel sat down and leaned forward. 'I've heard of them. They're a fairly new organisation – if you can dignify them with that title – dedicated to purging the West Country of all second-home owners. They started in Cornwall but word has it they're spreading to Devon.'

'How come they haven't come to our attention?'

'They have in parts of Cornwall, like I said. Only so far round here they've confined themselves to ranting in a few selected pubs.'

'All mouth, you mean.'

'Something like that. In Cornwall they've issued veiled threats to burn down second homes but nothing's actually happened yet.'

'So threatening to burn Jon Bright's wife alive is rather a departure from the norm.'

'Especially if they've carried out the threat.'

'As far as we know, Bright's wife's still alive and kicking.'

Rachel raised her eyebrows. 'Arc we absolutely sure of that, sir? Her husband hasn't reported her missing but if he'd killed her, using these Pure Sons of the West as a scapegoat, he would keep quiet, wouldn't he?'

'You do have a suspicious mind, Rach.'

'Well, has anybody spoken to her?'

Gerry Heffernan had to agree that Rachel had a point. If it wasn't Donna Grogen who had died in that fire on the site of Jon Bright's proposed development, then it had to be someone. And Mrs Bright was as good a place as any to begin.

Some instinct made Wesley Peterson keep the print-outs of Nadia's e-mails in his pocket. For some reason he couldn't quite fathom, he didn't like the idea of leaving them lying round his hotel room. But Pam thought he was being too cautious. Conspiracy theories belonged in the pages of fiction. Nadia, whoever she was, was probably overimaginative and was seeking reassurance that her mother hadn't chosen to commit suicide. If they ever found out the truth, it was bound to be a disappointment, Pam had told him as she gave him a lingering kiss in their hotel bathroom.

It was their last afternoon. Tomorrow they'd fly back home and although Wesley wouldn't have admitted it to Pam, he was quite looking forward to seeing the children again and getting back to work. For one horrifying moment, he even realised that he was missing Gerry Heffernan.

They had decided to drive out in their hire car to Minerve, where, according to the guidebook of the region that Wesley had bought on their arrival, a hundred and forty Cathars had been burned for their faith in 1210. Pam always believed in seeing everything she could. And besides, the mention of a Jeanne de Minerve in Nadia's e-mails had intrigued them both.

Pam led the way up the narrow streets of the little walled town, its ancient stones and terracotta roofs glowing golden in the strong sunlight. As they made their way towards the candela, the only part of the Cathar castle that still stood defiant, the effort of walking in the heat made Wesley realise that the rich food, red wine and idleness of the past week had taken their toll on his body. He perched on a wall of tumbled grey stone with his arm round Pam, admiring the breathtaking view of the dramatic limestone gorges and thick wooded landscape. It must have once been an exceptional defensive position but now it was just stunningly beautiful. Yet somehow he still preferred Devon.

Pam wandered off to take some pictures so Wesley took the opportunity to reread Nadia's e-mails, alert for any clues and hints about her life and relationships. There were mentions of someone they referred to as M. Rowe had told the waitress at the restaurant that he had worked for Sir Martin Crace. At the time, Wesley had suspected this was a bit of name-dropping but it was always possible that Rowe had once had some tenuous link with the great man.

Everyone knew about Sir Martin Crace. He had developed drugs for the AIDS epidemic in Africa and paid personally for their distribution. With his wealth he had started a charitable foundation, building schools and hospitals in developing countries. The government consulted him about welfare policy yet he had famously refused a peerage and liked to be known as a man of the people. Rumour had it that the holy grail of many tabloid editors was to discover some dirt on Crace. But so far all their efforts had failed and he remained widely regarded as a secular saint and a national treasure in the making.

It was difficult to know what connection Ian Rowe could possibly have with this paragon of virtue. After glimpsing a little of the life Rowe led in Carcassonne, Wesley was sure they would move in entirely different circles.

Unless Nadia was the link. As he sat there he began to go through in his head everything he actually knew about Nadia. He knew that she lived in Neston and worked for a professor at Morbay University who had once worked in Toulouse. And he had found the address of a Professor

Yves Demancour at Morbay University in Rowe's house. Nadia had mentioned an Yves in her e-mails, an Yves who had a dirty little secret, and someone called Jeanne de Minerve who was taking over her life – presumably something to do with her research. But the e-mails gave little away, apart from the fact that she was sure her mother hadn't killed herself and that she was trying to discover the truth about her death. And that she suspected there might be someone who didn't want that truth to come out.

He glanced up at Pam. She had her guidebook out again. 'Did you know that on the twenty-second of July, twelve hundred and ten, a hundred and forty Cathars were burned to death on a huge pyre?'

'I do now,' said Wesley, putting the e-mails back into his pocket. 'No mention of a Jeanne?'

'No. No mention of a Jeanne.'

As they walked back to their car they passed a monument, a rough stone pierced with the shape of a dove. Wesley paused and read the words. Simple words in Occitan, the ancient language of the region. '*Als Catars*': to the Cathars. He turned away, suddenly feeling a chill despite the burning heat.

Neil Watson had had enough of his desk. He had read everything he could get his hands on about the site on the outskirts of Queenswear but now he wanted to have a look at what he was dealing with. The theory was all very well but it was the practical aspect of archaeology that made his pulse race a little faster.

But something was puzzling him. There were references in the records he had to an excavation of the site in the 1980s and normally he would consult the plans and findings of the previous dig before deciding what course of action to take. But he had a problem – rather a large one – because the records of the 1980s dig appeared to be missing. It was always possible that someone had put them in the wrong place, of course, but it still struck Neil as strange.

He forgot his troubles for a while and settled down with a juicy set of aerial photographs, taken a few years ago during a rare drought, in which the outline of a high status house and its outlying buildings could be seen quite clearly. To Neil it looked like a typical early medieval house with great hall, solar wing and kitchens. There were many such houses dotted around the country but those that still stood had usually been extended and improved over the centuries, so that it took a leap of imagination to envisage their original form with their central hearth and privacy only for the lord and lady, if they were lucky.

He stared at the dark outline against the parched green of the field. The outbuildings – the business end of the medieval house – were quite clearly visible along with various enclosures for the estate's animals. But there was one shape that rather intrigued Neil – a small round circle near the main house.

Then he smiled to himself. He knew what it was – in fact he'd dealt with one before, a few years ago, around the time Wesley was working in London as a detective sergeant in the Met's Arts and Antique Squad. If he wasn't mistaken it was a dovecot. But the intensity of the mark in the grass was puzzling.

He launched into another search for the records of the old dig. But there was still no sign of them. It was a bit of a mystery and yet he was sure it was one he could easily solve. The world of archaeology was a fairly small one.

Jon Bright might have dismissed the threats from the

Pure Sons of the West as posturing nonsense but now the situation had changed. A woman had been burned to death and the matter had suddenly become deadly serious. And, because of this, Gerry Heffernan decided that a few words of warning were called for.

He decided to take Rachel along with him because she had the knack of putting people at their ease, as well as an excellent ear for lies and evasions.

Gerry was rather surprised to discover that the Brights lived in a tastefully converted barn just outside the village of Stokeworthy. Somehow his imagination had conjured up a neo-Georgian mansion with a forest of pillars and a brace of BMW 4x4s parked on a sweeping gravel drive. But instead the drive was stone flagged and a bright-red Mini Cooper was stationed outside the detached garage.

For a moment Gerry thought the woman who answered the door, holding a sink plunger like a sceptre, was the cleaner, but when they identified themselves she introduced herself as Sheryl Bright. She was in her forties, still attractive, with mousy brown hair pulled back into a pony tail. Her jeans emphasised her long, slender legs but a large checked shirt concealed the rest of her figure.

She looked rather surprised to see them on her doorstep. Gerry, who always favoured the element of surprise, hadn't warned her of their visit. But she didn't look particularly worried, and he thought this was rather strange. If he lived in an isolated property and someone had threatened to burn him alive, he'd be in a locked room with a bottle of something strong, a phone and a shotgun, if one was available.

'Sorry about all this,' the woman said, as she led them to the drawing room. She turned, waved the sink plunger vaguely and gave the chief inspector a lopsided smile.

'Don't suppose you're any good at unblocking sinks?'

'I'll try anything once, love.' He gave her his widest grin. 'But first I'd like a chat. Your husband said you've been getting death threats.' He tilted his head to one side. 'You didn't think to contact us at all?'

She rolled her eyes. 'Oh, we didn't take them seriously. Jon's a property developer and in some people's eyes that makes him Satan's right-hand man. What they don't realise is that he intends to build affordable housing for local people. We didn't want to call out the police and waste their time. And isn't wasting police time a crime or something?'

'You wouldn't have been wasting our time, Mrs Bright,' Rachel chipped in. 'We take any kind of threat very seriously. You do know about the burned body that was found on your husband's land?'

'Of course. It's terrible. But it can't have anything to do with the threats I've been getting. They're from the Pure Sons of the West. Ever heard of them?'

'We have now.'

'Well, they're just a bunch of pathetic inadequates who have a few drinks too many and start spouting off. They've never actually done anything. All mouth and trousers, as my gran used to say.'

'They threatened to burn you alive then a woman is burned alive in Grandal Field. You're not worried?'

She took a deep breath. 'When you put it like that . . . But it can't be these Pure Sons of the West. It's not their style. They're harmless.'

'What makes you so sure?'

'It's common knowledge. They've never done anything but talk. You must know that from your records.'

'You can't think of anyone else who might have a grudge against you?'

She shook her head.

Gerry glanced at Rachel. He had to admire this woman's courage but he had an uneasy feeling that a little caution wouldn't come amiss.

'How did they threaten you? In a phone call or a letter or . . .?'

'I received two letters with Morbay postmarks. You know the sort of thing – words cut out of newspapers. How corny can you get?'

'You've still got them, I take it?' Gerry asked hopefully.

But Sheryl Bright shook her head. 'I put them on the fire. If you start taking that sort of thing seriously, they've won, haven't they. It was just someone playing games . . . and I wasn't going to join in.'

'Have you ever met any of these Pure Sons of the West?' It was Rachel who asked the question.

'No. Of course not,' she said quickly.

'You're sure of that?' Gerry asked.

Sheryl Bright nodded. But there was an uneasy look in her eyes. She wasn't a good actress and, from her reaction, Gerry began to suspect that she was more concerned than she cared to admit.

Gerry took the opportunity to look around the room. It was comfortable and stylish but there were magazines and papers strewn around and an empty coffee mug stood on the sideboard. Not show-house tidy, but at least it had a homely, lived-in feel. The walls were filled with watercolours of local scenes – good ones. The artist had talent.

'Nice pictures,' he said.

Sheryl gave a modest smile. 'Thanks. They're mine actually. I've got an exhibition soon in Neston.' She picked up a couple of cards from the sideboard and handed them to Gerry and Rachel. 'Do come along if you get the chance. The more the merrier.' She wiped her hands on her shirt. 'Can I offer you a cup of tea or . . .'

Gerry thanked her and said he'd love one. And he'd have a go at unblocking her sink when he'd finished. Having met both Brights, it seemed to him that they were an incongruous couple. Sometimes opposites attract but he was intrigued.

She disappeared into the kitchen and returned five minutes later with a tray of steaming mugs. When the tea had been drunk Gerry glanced at Rachel. He knew she'd understood the signal. Keep her talking while I'm in the kitchen. Find out all you can.

He stood up, took off his jacket to reveal the badly ironed shirt beneath and made a show of rolling up his sleeves. 'I'll have a go at that sink then, love. Give us your plunger.'

Sheryl had left the plunger on the coffee table. She picked it up and handed it to the chief inspector. As he made for the kitchen to do some impromptu plumbing, he was confident he could leave the real work to Rachel.

'What time's the flight?'

'Six thirty. We've got plenty of time.' Wesley looked round the hotel room, making sure they hadn't left anything behind.

Pam slipped her hand around his waist and stood on tiptoe to kiss his cheek. 'What do you want to do?'

'Not much. Unless you want to . . .'

'No. I'm not bothered. We can just have a last wander around if you like.'

This was what Wesley wanted to hear. He'd been afraid that Pam might want to take their hired car to some Cathar stronghold they'd missed out of their itinerary. A final stroll around the old city and a leisurely lunch would suit him fine.

She began to close her suitcase, muttering that she'd

54

bought too many souvenirs and presents. Wesley watched her as she sat down on the case in an effort to get it fastened. After a bit of a struggle she succeeded and a grin of triumph appeared on her face.

But Wesley's mind wasn't on luggage. 'You know when we looked in Ian Rowe's room ... did you notice a passport?'

Pam stopped what she was doing. 'No. I can't say I did. Anyway, it's hardly surprising. He'd packed up all the possessions he'd wanted to take and buggered off. He might have gone back to England to see this Nadia. When you get back maybe you can check her out.'

Wesley smiled to himself. It seemed that this little mystery was gnawing away at Pam's imagination. Perhaps now she might understand how he felt about his work.

'At least those e-mails tell us he wasn't lying.'

'It looks that way. But I didn't trust Rowe when we were students and I see no reason to change my opinion now.'

'Will you follow it up when we get back?' She wasn't letting the matter drop.

'Do you think I should?'

'You could have a word with that professor Nadia works for.'

'I don't know what'll be waiting on my desk when I get back to the office. It'd just be my luck if there's been a spate of bank robberies while I've been away.'

'Or serial killings.'

Wesley looked at her and saw that she was smiling. 'Don't joke about things like that. It happens.'

Pam kissed him again. Sometimes Wesley took things so seriously. 'Look, why don't we have lunch again at the Auberge de la Cité where Ian worked. Perhaps someone's heard from him by now.'

'Or we could have another word with his housemate, Thierry.' He looked her in the eye. 'Maybe not.'

Pam gave a small shudder and said nothing.

After leaving their bags behind the reception, they made their way to the Auberge de la Cité, where they ate a good lunch and had another word with the waitress, who told them that nobody had heard from Ian Rowe since the morning he'd disappeared.

After a final stroll around Carcassonne, they made their way to the airport. For his own peace of mind, Wesley resolved to carry out a discreet check to see whether a Nadia Lucas was working for a Professor Yves Demancour at Morbay University and, if so, whether she was alive and well. But he doubted whether his and Rowe's paths would ever cross again.

And somehow, he didn't mind in the least.

Owl Cottage was nothing special: slightly run down with pink washed walls in need of a coat of paint and a shabby glass front door circa 1960. Not thatched, with no roses round the door, it was ideal for the first-time buyer willing to do a bit of work. But it would still be way beyond the pockets of most locals.

The owner had bought it in the spring intending to do it up and add it to his portfolio of holiday lets: a cosy little retreat from urban life. But he'd been so busy running the business that he hadn't got round to organising the tradesmen and now he was planning to wait for the winter when work was scarce and prices were lower. Or alternatively he might bring in some of the Eastern Europeans who'd worked on his other houses. They were good. And, what's more, they were cheap.

Owl Cottage had been empty for a few months now – damp patches in the living room and an army of ants marching across the kitchen floor hardly being conducive to relaxed weekends away in the countryside. The place was a dump. But the owner had no objection to letting mates use it if they were desperate enough to put up with the basic living conditions.

But the mind of the hooded figure peeping through the letter box wasn't on the cottage's deficiencies as he opened the petrol can. Holding the letter box open, he sprinkled some petrol inside and then splashed some on the rag he was holding. Then he stood quite still for a moment breathing in the fumes before setting the rag alight with a cheap disposable lighter and pushing it through the letter box.

He scurried back and watched from the bushes as the golden flames began to leap and dance at the windows. And as soon as he was sure the fire had taken hold, he ran off into the night.

4

In Tradmouth's town records covering the twelfth and thirteenth centuries there are several accounts of ships laden with pilgrims setting sail from the port. Stephen de Grendalle might have sailed on one of these ships bound for the shrine of San Diego de Compostela in Northern Spain. There were carved cockleshells on his impressive tomb in Morre Abbey (alas, destroyed during Henry VIII's dissolution of the monasteries), which indicates that he must have made that particular pilgrimage at least once.

It is my theory that on one of these occasions, for reasons we can only guess at, he made a detour north to the Languedoc region of France. Perhaps he went with others, eager to fight in a crusade – any crusade – in order to win salvation for his soul. Only this particular crusade wasn't against the unbeliever. Rather it was against the Cathars or Albigensians, as they were sometimes known. This was against men and women who considered that they had discovered a purer, more perfect, form of faith without the corruption of worldly ritual.

And, from the evidence, it seems that this encounter with purity was to change Stephen de Grendalle's life for ever.

(From papers found in the possession of Professor Yves Demancour)

It seemed strange to be back in Devon. But good. Wesley hadn't realised how much he'd missed the children and the first thing he and Pam did was to call at Belsham Vicarage to see them.

Even though Wesley's sister Maritia had, as yet, no children of her own, she seemed to have coped admirably, taking time off work to look after her nephew and niece. Her patients and the surgery, she said, could get along without her for a few days. Besides, she assured her brother a little too brightly, she'd enjoyed the break from her busy routine. However, the strain on her face and the forced nature of her smile told him that the past week hadn't been as smooth and uneventful as she claimed.

It was a short drive home from Belsham with the children chattering in the back. Wesley's initial guilt at leaving them melted: they seemed to have enjoyed themselves during their absence. Perhaps a little part of him wished that they'd missed their parents more.

After sorting through the stack of post on the doormat, Pam went off with the children to put the kettle on, leaving Wesley staring at the telephone.

He resisted the temptation for a few minutes but eventually he picked up the receiver and dialled Gerry Heffernan's direct number.

'Wes, great to hear from you, mate. Good holiday?'

'Great, thanks. What's new?' Wesley had lowered his voice.

'You've missed all the excitement.'

'What excitement?' Wesley sat down on the chair in the hall, sneaking a look at the kitchen door. Pam was still fully occupied. But she'd soon be on at him to unpack so she could get the washing machine on. He hadn't got long.

'Some poor woman's been burned to death in a field on the outskirts of Queenswear. According to Forensic someone poured petrol on her and set her alight.' He paused. 'She was still alive when he did it. Colin thinks she was tied up.'

Wesley took a deep breath. 'Any suspects?'

'A few possibles. It was on the site of a proposed new development – they're going to build houses there and our theory is that the two things could be connected. The developer's a bloke called Jon Bright. His receptionist's gone missing and his wife's had anonymous letters threatening to burn her to death.'

'Sounds straightforward then. All we have to do is find out who sent the letters.'

'Oh, we know that already. It's an organisation called the Pure Sons of the West. Ever heard of them?'

'Can't say I have. I take it they've been brought in?'

'It's on my list.'

'Has the dead woman been identified?'

'That's the problem, Wes. At first we thought the victim might be this receptionist, Donna Grogen – her boyfriend's one of these Pure Sons of the West so there's a connection. But, according to DNA tests, it's not her.'

'Definitely?'

'Definitely. And Bright's wife doesn't seem particularly bothered by the death threats. Either that or she's putting a brave face on it. But I suspect she knows more than she's telling us.'

Wesley was distracted by shouts of 'daddy, daddy' as Michael emerged from the kitchen and hurtled towards him with outstretched arms.

Gerry heard the commotion. 'You'd better go. How soon can you come in to work?'

Wesley cradled the telephone receiver in his shoulder as he allowed himself to be dragged along the hall. 'First thing tomorrow but I'll have to square it with Pam. I'm supposed to be off for another couple of days, remember?'

60

'I'm sure you can use your charms,' the DCI said with a chuckle. 'See you first thing in the morning then.'

Neil Watson hated files and paperwork. He hated having to deal with all that crisp white paper when all he really wanted to do was scrape the earth away with a trowel to reveal hidden and wonderful things. Wonderful to him, at any rate – shards of broken pottery and the remnants of a few old walls would mean nothing to most people.

He sat in his Exeter flat staring at the pile of yellowing reports on his old dining table and sighed. The dig at Grandal Field was meant to start the next day but, as it was being treated as a crime scene, he hadn't yet had permission from the police. However, Wesley would be back home by now so he was sure it wouldn't be a problem. It was always an advantage to have friends in high – or not so high – places.

Thinking of Wesley reminded him of the text message he'd received from his friend a couple of days before. 'Remember Ian Rowe. Just met him here. Tell all when I get back.'

He remembered Ian Rowe all right. At university he had attended all the most drug-fuelled parties, hung around with a bunch of posing losers and taken scant interest in the study of archaeology. He had messed about on training excavations and Neil had always suspected that he'd only enrolled on the course because he couldn't think of anything else to do. Neil had felt a glow of self-righteous satisfaction when Rowe had failed his exams and been thrown off the course. Ian Rowe, in his opinion, had got everything he deserved.

Nevertheless, he was curious about Wesley's message. What, he wondered, had become of Rowe in the intervening years? Somehow he didn't expect it would be anything good.

He looked at his watch. Nine thirty. He might as well go through a few more files before he turned in for the night ... just to see if he could find any mention of the excavation on the Grandal Farm site in the 1980s.

Then suddenly he abandoned his files to search his battered bureau for his old address book. Professor Karl Maplin knew about most of the excavations in the area and, although semi-retired, still took an active interest in the world of local archaeology. Neil picked up the phone and dialled his number.

The conversation with Professor Maplin lasted almost an hour. Maplin lived alone and, once given the opportunity to talk with Neil about their favourite subject, interspersed with Maplin's usual smattering of gossip and scandal, there was no stopping him. But by the end of the call, Neil knew he had learned something that might put him on the right track.

An archaeologist called Dr Maggie March had been in charge of the Grandal Field dig. She had died tragically in a car accident shortly after the excavation ended. Then, strangely, her deputy had gone missing ... along with the records of the dig.

Neil poured himself a beer. This one needed some thought.

'The moment you fly off to foreign climes, all hell breaks loose. Good to see you back, Wes. Sit yourself down.'

Gerry Heffernan was grinning, showing a fine set of crooked teeth. Wesley had rarely seen anyone so pleased to see him. Something told him that things must be desperate.

On his way in he'd met Rachel Tracey, who'd looked as if she'd like to throw her arms round him and kiss him but was exercising iron self-control. He'd told himself it was his imagination. She had a new man in her life – a city banker who'd downsized to a Devon smallholding with disastrous results until Rachel, with generations of farming experience behind her, had taken him in hand. At one time Wesley had felt attracted to Rachel, although neither of them had acted on that invisible magnetism. But that was firmly in the past, he told himself. He had Pam and the kids.

'So what's all this about someone being set alight in a field?' Wesley began. Gerry had told him the bare facts on the phone last night but now he was after the details.

Once Gerry had supplied them, chapter and verse, and reiterated his suspicions that the Brights might be involved somehow, his face suddenly assumed a solemn expression.

'And something else has come in. Someone torched a cottage last night – run-down place according to the locals. The fire was spotted by a couple of lads on their way to the Sportsman's Arms and they raised the alarm. Luckily the fire engines got there in time to save quite a bit of the building. The place was waiting to be done up and the neighbours said it would probably be empty.' He paused for dramatic effect. 'But the firemen found a body inside. The poor sod was in the part of the house worst hit by the fire. If he'd been upstairs he might have stood a chance. The fire investigators reckon it's arson. The seat of the fire's in the hallway and there's traces of accelerant. They're doing more tests but . . .'

'So we're treating it as murder?'

'That's right and we've already got a suspect . . . or suspects.'

'So who is it?'

Gerry Heffernan sucked in air through his teeth. 'Go to your desk and switch on the Internet. Look up a site called "www.PureSonsoftheWest.com."'

Wesley had to smile to himself. Gerry wouldn't have a computer in his office. He was terrified of the things and claimed that if he ever touched one it would break immediately. He relied on the fact that his colleagues could journey into the world of high technology and report back.

'The same ones who threatened the developer's wife?'

'The very same.'

Wesley made for his desk and found the website. It was an amateurish effort but the message was clear. Second-home owners should get out of the West Country or there would be dire consequences – or 'revolutionary action' as the site put it. Wesley scrolled down to the next page. This was entitled 'latest news'.

'Last night,' it said, 'a cottage near Whitely caught fire. It belonged to an outsider who left it to rot while our own are homeless. The place was empty and neglected and there was no loss of life. How's that for justice?'

'Oh dear.' Wesley mouthed the words silently. It seemed they didn't know the place was occupied, and in any case they'd worded the announcement so that there was no admission of guilt. But even if they were responsible, it was unlikely that any court would convict them of premeditated murder. If he was a betting man, he would have put money on a manslaughter verdict.

As he returned to Gerry's office he looked at the huge notice board that filled one wall of the incident room. There were photographs of the charred corpse found in the field near Queenswear, only the shape making it recognisable as a human being. There was also a picture of a young woman with the name Donna Grogen scrawled beneath it in Gerry Heffernan's untidy hand, with the note 'no DNA match' scribbled beside the name as an afterthought.

There was also a posed photograph of a prosperous-looking middle-aged man. The name underneath was Jon Bright – local property developer and the new owner of the field where the burned body was discovered. His wife's name had been added to the display as well, along with the comment that she had been receiving death threats, but there was, as yet, no photograph of the unlucky lady.

Wesley studied the board for a while. It would take him some time to get up to speed with all the details of the case. Sometimes holidays just weren't worth the trouble. Not that he hadn't enjoyed Carcassonne ... at least until his meeting with Ian Rowe. He made a mental note to call Neil later to tell him all about the encounter.

'I think she's hiding something.'

Wesley swung round to see Rachel Tracey standing there.

'Who is?'

'Sheryl Bright – Jon Bright's wife. The boss and I went to see her yesterday. She receives an anonymous threat to burn her to death then, lo and behold, a woman's burned to death on the site where her husband's due to build twenty houses. Now does that sound like a coincidence to you or does it sound like mistaken identity?'

'What do we know about these Pure Sons of the West?'

'We know one of them's called Chas Ventisard. Donna Grogen is going out with him.'

Wesley smiled. 'So I've heard. Has this Ventisard got form?'

'Drunk and disorderly. Driving while banned.'

'We'd better pay him a visit.'

'Aren't you supposed to be ...?'

'On holiday? Sort of.'

'Bet Pam's not pleased about that,' she said, avoiding his eyes.

'As a matter of fact she was remarkably understanding,'

he said, looking at his watch. Pam's attitude had rather surprised him. Things were definitely looking up. 'I'll go with the boss to see this Ventisard character, then I'll get off home. Have we identified any more of these Pure Sons of the West?'

'Trish is working on it.'

DC Trish Walton, Rachel's housemate, was several desks away, talking on the phone and frowning with concentration as she made copious notes.

'Who's that?' Wesley nodded in the direction of a plump man in his thirties with thinning red hair. His was a face Wesley didn't recognise. He'd only been away for a week and it seemed that things in the office had changed in that short time.

Rachel lowered her voice. 'He's Steve's replacement. His name's Nick Tarnaby and he's been transferred from Neston. Boss doesn't think he's too bright.'

'And what do you think?'

Rachel shrugged. 'He seems a bit morose . . . hardly a bundle of laughs.'

'Perhaps he's got problems.'

'And if the boss takes a dislike to him his problems are going to multiply. Who was it who said that Gerry Heffernan doesn't suffer fools gladly?'

'Probably Gerry Heffernan.' Their eyes met and they exchanged a smile. 'Which reminds me, he's waiting for me.'

'He's asked me to have another word with Mrs Bright. I'm taking our new boy . . . got to show him the ropes,' said Rachel with a wink before returning to her desk.

Half an hour later Wesley was driving to the council estate on the fringe of Tradmouth with Gerry Heffernan lolling in the passenger seat. The DCI looked completely relaxed and there was a small beatific smile on his chubby face.

'You look pleased with yourself, Gerry,' Wesley commented. 'How's Joyce?'

'Fine, fine. I'm thinking of telling our Rosie about her this weekend.'

Wesley suppressed a smile. He'd never known a man before who was so terrified of his daughter that he'd omitted to mention the fact that he'd been seeing a lady friend for the past year or so. He reckoned Rosie would interpret it as a betrayal of her late mother's memory. Wesley, however, wasn't so sure. Gerry's son, Sam, had taken the news well. But Sam was an easygoing young man, unlike the talented and musical Rosie.

'Good luck. I'm sure she'll be fine about it. Joyce is a hard woman to dislike, isn't she?'

Gerry said nothing as Wesley brought the car to a halt in front of Chas Ventisard's front door. The house was freshly painted with clean net curtains and a neatly trimmed front garden. Something told Wesley that Chas lived with his mother.

And it was his mother who opened the door to them. Wesley had expected a show of defiance when they introduced themselves but Mrs Ventisard looked worried and stepped aside to let them in. Wesley found himself feeling a little sorry for her.

Chas was in. He did the evening shift at the poultry factory and he'd only just woken up, the anxious mother told them breathlessly. She wheezed a little; anxiety was never good for asthmatics.

'Did your son go out last night?' Gerry Heffernan asked, making the question sound innocent. 'Only someone said they saw him down the Shipwright's Arms.' Wesley knew it was a lie, of course, but they had to begin somewhere.

'They can't have done. He finished his shift at ten thirty and he came straight home. Got in around eleven.'

There was an honesty about her swift answer that made it sound convincing. Now all they had to do was to see if Chas came up with the same story.

Mrs Ventisard stood at the foot of the narrow stairs and called her son's name. A couple of minutes later the man himself appeared, dressed in boxer shorts and a grubby T-shirt, wiping the sleep from his eyes.

'What is it? You found Donna?' he said, suddenly alert. 'Is she all right?' As far as Wesley could tell there was genuine concern in his voice.

'Sorry,' Wesley answered. 'We haven't come about Donna. Have you heard about the fire last night. Holiday cottage near Whitely?'

A wariness appeared in Chas's eyes. 'It was on the radio. Late night news.'

'Someone died.'

Chas looked up, worried. 'I didn't know that. It's got nothing to do with me.'

'I believe you belong to an organisation known as the Pure Sons of the West.'

'So what? It's not illegal.'

'It is if you're going round burning down houses and killing people. Did you know they planned to burn down the cottage last night?'

Chas looked as though he was torn between denial and a desire to be seen to be in the know, at the centre of things. But eventually he seemed to plump for the first option. 'We didn't do nothing.'

'Your website talks about taking action. There's even a mention of last night's fire. How's that for justice, it said.'

'So? It doesn't say we had anything to do with starting it, does it?'

'Perhaps your mates decided to act without you.' Wesley watched Chas's face. He'd been right – Chas looked a little hurt at his last words. If there was action going, he wanted to belong. 'Can you tell us your movements last night?'

He replied without hesitation and his story was the same as his mother's. He had worked until ten thirty and he'd driven straight home and gone to bed. If he had ambitions to make his name in the field of terrorism, he wasn't showing much promise.

'We'll need the names of your mates.'

'They couldn't have set fire to that cottage. They made threats, like, but they wouldn't have torched the place if there was someone in the house. I know they wouldn't.'

'We'll still need their names.'

Chas pressed his lips together in a stubborn line. 'I'm not saying.'

The mother was standing with arms folded listening carefully to the exchange. For a second, Wesley thought she was about to clip her son around the ear in the old-fashioned way but instead she began to tell him in no uncertain terms that he shouldn't be shielding criminals, not if they went round murdering people. But her words were ignored. It seemed that Chas knew better. And besides, he was a lot bigger than her.

When Gerry announced that Chas was being taken in for questioning, Mrs Ventisard burst into tears. And through the sobs came the protestations that her Chas was a good lad, practically a saint. There was no way he was involved in anything illegal.

But mothers never see their children's little faults.

The firemen had reached the blaze in time to save most of Owl Cottage before the flames took hold of the upper floor. But the dead male had been on the ground floor, in the room next to the seat of the fire ... and the body was unrecognisable.

The remains had been transported in a plain black van to the mortuary to lie in a metal drawer. Like the woman in the field, this one wouldn't be identifiable by his next of kin. But they had to find something that would give the authorities a name. Somewhere to begin.

Then they had a stroke of luck.

When the firemen searched the property, a holdall was discovered in the corner of one of the bedrooms, a room which had been heavily smoke and water damaged but untouched by the flames. The thing stank of smoke and damp but a fire officer had brought it down with him and handed it over to the uniformed constable who was hanging about at the scene, showing a token police presence.

The constable was under strict instructions to call Tradmouth CID as soon as the fire crew gave the go-ahead for the building to be searched. But as things seemed to be moving slowly, the gift of the holdall was something to relieve the monotony. He put on a pair of plastic gloves and gently drew back the zip, wrinkling his nose at the acrid stench of smoke. The thing was full of clothes and he gently pushed them to one side to see if there was anything more interesting underneath.

He wasn't disappointed. Inside a thin cardboard file nestling at the bottom of the holdall he found some papers and a passport.

He pulled the passport out carefully. It was a UK passport although the embossed crest on the front had been worn away with use.

As soon as he opened it up, his radio crackled into life. But he ignored it for a second while he read the name inside the passport.

It was there printed beside the awkwardly posed photograph. A short name. Quite ordinary. Ian Rowe, whoever he was, had been bloody unlucky.

5

The Cathars (from the Greek katharos *meaning pure) believed in an all-powerful God of goodness and love but they considered that this perfection made Him unable to deal with the evils of the world. The evil world and the flesh, they believed, were ruled over by Lucifer, the Prince of Darkness. Pure souls, they said, were trapped within bodies that were 'tunics of flesh', little more than prisons. Salvation consisted of freeing the soul from this earthly prison and gaining the knowledge revealed to mankind by Christ, who was sent by God for this very purpose. Only the spiritual baptism of the* consolamentum *could bring this about and, failing this, the soul would pass to another body and wait to attain the knowledge that brings with it salvation.*

This rather attractive and gentle version of the Christian faith spread throughout that part of France known as the Languedoc and the local rulers, even if they weren't themselves Cathars, were remarkably tolerant of the faith embraced by their subjects. The Catholic Church, however, took a different point of view. Cathars were heretics of the worst kind. And heretics had to be destroyed.

I wonder how much Stephen de Grendalle subscribed to this opinion. I wonder what his motives were for joining the crusade against those apparently harmless people . . . and what brought about his dramatic change of heart.

(From papers found in the possession of Professor Yves Demancour)

Wesley Peterson felt the blood drain from his face. It was impossible. Surely there was no way the dead man in the cottage could be Ian Rowe.

However, he had to acknowledge that there had been no sign of a passport in his Carcassonne lodgings and that he would have had ample time to reach Devon. And Thierry had mentioned a letter with a British stamp that had arrived on the morning of his disappearance. Had this letter been the cause of Rowe's sudden flight? Or was it Nadia Lucas's pleas for help and her claim that she needed him?

But what on earth had he been doing in an isolated holiday cottage just outside Whitely? Like most things connected with Rowe, it was a mystery.

He sat at his desk staring at Rowe's passport. Officially he was still on leave and, until half an hour ago, he had had every intention of getting home early to keep on the right side of Pam. But this discovery had put paid to his plans.

He decided that the best course of action was to take Pam into his confidence. After all, she had met Ian Rowe too. She had become involved in the puzzle when they had made their perfunctory search of Rowe's room on the Rue de Montfort. She would want to know what was happening. And so, he imagined, would Neil.

His thoughts were interrupted by the sound of someone clearing their throat just behind him. He turned and saw DC Nick Tarnaby standing there. He looked awkward, almost embarrassed. Rachel had confided that Gerry

72

Heffernan didn't rate the man's intellectual abilities. But Wesley was willing to give him a chance.

'I've got this, sir. It was found in the cottage – in one of the upstairs rooms. What shall I do with it?'

Wesley caught a whiff of smoke and looked down at Nick Tarnaby's brightly polished shoes. On the floor beside them was a smoke-stained holdall.

'The passport was in it, sir.'

Wesley noticed that there was no flight label attached to the straps. If this belonged to Rowe, it was a safe bet that he had travelled by train and ferry from France.

'Thanks.' He looked at the DC, who was shifting from foot to foot awkwardly, as though anxious to answer a call of nature. 'Is that all?'

'There's something else. They've found a car parked just down the lane from the cottage. It's registered to a Nadia Lucas but there's no sign of the owner and the cottage is the only house in the vicinity and ... Well, there's no parking space outside the cottage and ...'

'So it could have been driven by the dead man.' Wesley finished the man's sentence for him. He was finding it hard to see him struggle.

'Yeah.'

'Thanks. Nick, isn't it?'

The new DC nodded, avoiding eye contact.

'We need to speak to the owner of the cottage to see if he or she can throw any light on what Rowe was doing there.'

Nick Tarnaby turned and hurried away, as though reluctant to prolong the conversation. Wesley watched his disappearing back, wondering why the man seemed so uncommunicative. Perhaps he was like that with everyone, he thought. Or perhaps there was another reason.

His mind began to race. Nadia Lucas's car was parked down the lane from the cottage so it looked as if Rowe had found her after all. But where was she now?

He picked up the phone and dialled his home number. It was the school holidays so there was a good chance Pam would be home. And he suspected that once he'd told her about Ian Rowe, she'd understand why he wouldn't be home early as he'd promised. But there was no reply. She was probably out somewhere with the children. He tried her mobile number but the phone was switched off: if she hadn't gone far she probably hadn't bothered to take it with her.

He stared at the telephone for a few seconds, lost in thought. Ian Rowe had vanished from his life over ten years ago but now, it seemed, he couldn't escape the man, alive or dead. Rowe had intruded upon his well-earned break in France and now he'd turned up back in Devon. Dead. Disrupting his life again.

The smoke-damaged holdall was sitting on the floor by his feet. The smell had made him cough at first but now he was getting used to it. He'd seen his colleagues wrinkling their noses as they passed near his desk but, as yet, nobody had said anything.

Gerry Heffernan, however, had never believed in mincing his words. He emerged from his office, holding his nose theatrically. 'Something stinks in here.'

'It's the holdall from Owl Cottage. Nick Tarnaby brought it in.'

Heffernan looked at his watch. 'You get home if you like, Wes. Me and Paul Johnson can deal with Chas Ventisard.'

'I was going to, Gerry, but something's cropped up.' He slid the passport across the desk towards the DCI. 'I haven't had a chance to tell you about my holiday yet.'

'Love to hear about it, Wes, but it'll have to keep. I can't leave Ventisard down in that interview room for — '

'No, Gerry, it's relevant, I promise you. Sit down. I'd better start at the beginning.'

Gerry Heffernan sat down heavily on the spare chair by Wesley's desk and glanced at his watch. Chas Ventisard had already been at the police station for an hour and the clock was ticking.

Wesley took a deep breath, wondering where to begin. 'When Pam and I were in Carcassonne we bumped into a bloke I knew from university, name of Ian Rowe. Well, I didn't actually know him that well. We didn't mix in the same circles if you see what I mean. He was into drugs and partying and he dropped out after his second year.'

Gerry nodded. 'Go on.'

'Well, Rowe recognised me and he'd found out somehow that I was a policeman. He told me he was worried about someone he knew called Nadia Lucas. He said she was trying to discover the truth about her mother's death and that there might be someone who didn't want that truth to come out. He said he hadn't been able to get in touch with her.'

'And?'

'Before I could find out more, he disappeared. But I did get copies of some e-mails Nadia had sent him and it looks as if he was telling the truth.' Wesley paused. 'And now he's turned up again.' He nodded towards the passport. 'That was found in the holdall, near the body. Look at the name.'

Heffernan opened the passport and swore softly under his breath. 'The photo? Is it him?'

Wesley nodded. 'And a car registered to Nadia Lucas was found parked near the cottage so it's likely that they met up. We'll have to find her.'

'We'll get someone round to her address,' said Gerry. He thought for a moment. 'The body was burned. It's unidentifiable unless we get DNA or dental records. I mean, someone could have swiped his passport and—'

'I've thought of that. I need to get down to the

mortuary to make sure it's him, don't I?'

'Might not be much use if the body's as burned as they say but you can have a go if you like. So what can you tell me about this . . .' He picked up the passport again and studied the name and photograph. 'Ian Rowe?'

Wesley went over everything he knew. It was good to put his knowledge into words. It helped to get things organised in his head. But as he spoke he started to realise how little he really knew about Rowe. There was still so much to discover.

'He mentioned a professor called Yves Demancour based at Morbay University. It seems this Nadia works for him.' He paused. 'And Rowe told his colleagues at the restaurant that he used to work for Sir Martin Crace.'

Gerry snorted. 'He was probably name-dropping. Trying to impress.'

Wesley shrugged. It was possible.

Gerry Heffernan stared at the malodorous holdall. 'Have you looked through his things yet?'

Wesley shook his head. The truth was he hadn't been able to face the task. But, realising he couldn't put it off any longer, he hauled the holdall onto his desk. It was heavy. And the disturbance increased the stench of acrid smoke.

As he opened it he saw that there were clothes inside. After clearing a space on his desk he took them out carefully. Two pairs of jeans. Three T-shirts. An assortment of socks and underpants and a pair of trainers. Ian Rowe had travelled fairly light.

Underneath the clothes lay a thin cardboard file. Wesley opened it carefully and discovered that it contained a letter typed on expensive headed paper bearing the name and address of Sir Martin Crace. The envelope was in the file too. British stamp, typewritten and addressed to the Rue de Montfort. From the date on the postmark this was probably the letter Rowe had

76

received on the morning of his disappearance.

Wesley put on a pair of plastic gloves and examined the letter. It was addressed to Mr Ian Rowe and signed by an E. Liversedge, PA to Sir Martin Crace.

The letter was short and to the point. It acknowledged a letter Rowe had sent and stated that Sir Martin was willing to meet Rowe at Bewton Hall on 3 August at 2 pm. Just two days away. It was an appointment Ian Rowe would be unable to keep.

'So he wasn't lying about Crace,' Wesley observed quietly, handing the letter to Gerry.

'There's nothing here to suggest they were bosom buddies, Wes. Quite the reverse. And Sir Martin's known for being a soft touch.' Heffernan frowned. 'I'm wondering, from what you've told me about Rowe, whether he hoped for a handout. Or maybe he intended to try a bit of blackmail.'

'Anything's possible.' Wesley looked at his watch. 'I'll give Colin Bowman a call. See if it's OK to go to the mortuary. And we need to talk to the owner of that cottage. If he or she says Ian was there with permission . . .'

'If it does turn out to be your mate—'

'He was no mate of mine,' Wesley said quickly.

Gerry Heffernan raised his eyebrows. 'If it does turn out to be this Ian Rowe, we'll have to have a word with Sir Martin Crace and all.' He tilted his head to one side. 'I've always wanted to meet him. Good bloke.'

Wesley grinned. 'You're not biased then?'

'He seems to have done a lot of good with his millions. Not like some.'

Wesley couldn't argue with that. But a cynical little voice inside him was saying that if people in the public eye seem too good to be true, it's probably because they are.

'Off you go then,' Gerry said, picking up the folder containing Crace's letter.

Wesley stood up. He'd attempt to identify the body, then he'd get off home.

Anybody listening to Chas Ventisard's account of the activities of the Pure Sons of the West would have assumed it was a charitable organisation. Its only aim, according to Chas, was to provide the hard-working young people of the South Hams with decent housing so that they could live near to their work, settle down and raise families in the sort of accommodation their grandparents would have taken for granted.

The enemies of these rosy-cheeked young pioneers were, of course, wealthy second-home owners – usually from London – who paid phenomenal sums for small houses and occupied them only at weekends or during holidays, thus pricing the locals out of the market.

As Gerry Heffernan and DC Paul Johnson listened to the arguments, they couldn't help feeling some sympathy. Paul was still stuck at home with his parents and there was little hope of Gerry's son, Sam, a newly qualified vet, getting a home of his own in the more picturesque parts of Tradmouth.

'The statements on your website seem pretty threatening,' Gerry said, leaning forward over the interview room table.

'Yeah, but that's just to put the wind up them. To make them move out.'

The DCI caught Paul's eye and leaned back. Paul was sitting awkwardly in a chair that was too small for his tall, lanky frame and the DCI took pity on him. But it wouldn't be long now. Chas Ventisard was soft as butter. He'd be easy to crack.

'What do you know about the threatening letters that were sent to Sheryl Bright?'

'Who's Sheryl Bright?' Chas asked, an expression of cherubic innocence on his face.

Gerry Heffernan glanced at Paul. 'She's married to the owner of Tradford Developments. He's going to build houses on the Grandal Field site. She received a couple of *billets doux* from your Pure Sons of the West threatening to burn her alive. Then a woman's found burned alive on the very site her husband's developing. Now does that sound like a case of mistaken identity to you? 'Cause it does to me. Someone wanted Mrs Bright dead but he – or they – killed the wrong woman. Doesn't look good for the Pure Sons of the West, does it? Not after that fire last night and all.'

Chas shifted in his chair, revealing a glimpse of pallid flesh between his T-shirt and his shorts. 'I don't know nothing about it. I swear. And the Sons didn't send them letters to that Bright woman. They wouldn't. We're a pressure group, that's all. We don't go round hurting people and that's God's honest truth.'

If Gerry hadn't seen the photos of the charred corpse in the field with his own eyes, he would have believed him. But there was always the chance that Chas wasn't privy to everything the others in the organisation believed or got up to. For the umpteenth time he wished that Sheryl Bright hadn't destroyed those letters.

'But you can see our problem, can't you, Chas? The Pure Sons of the West do the threatening so we're assuming that they've done the killing as well.'

'They didn't. I swear on my mother's—'

'Well, they mentioned that cottage near Whitely on their website almost as soon as it happened and they knew the owner wasn't from round here so they'd been doing their homework. Do they keep a list of second homes or . . .?'

He hesitated. 'Yeah. But they didn't do it. They wouldn't.'

'A man died.'

Chas's eyes widened in alarm. 'That's nothing to do with me. The Sons didn't do it. I didn't do it.'

'Come on, Chas, you might as well tell us the truth. We'll find out anyway from forensics and all that.'

Chas shook his head and Gerry knew he was getting nowhere.

He tried again. 'Maybe your fellow Pure Sons of the West can help us. If you give us their names we'll have a chat. Friendly like.' He gave Chas Ventisard his widest grin. Guaranteed to put him at his ease ... or to scare the living daylights out of him.

'No comment.'

'So tell us about Donna Grogen,' said Gerry, watching his face carefully. 'You and her were an item so you must have some idea why she's gone missing. We know from DNA tests that she isn't the woman who died at Grandal Field but we'd still like to know where she is.'

Chas's eyes widened for a moment and he shook his head vigorously. 'I don't know where she is. If I knew anything, I'd tell you.'

'So what do you think has happened to her?'

'Dunno. She was acting a bit weird before she went off. I asked her if there was someone else but she told me to piss off.' Chas Ventisard looked Gerry Heffernan in the eye. 'That's all I know and that's all I'm saying until you get me a solicitor.'

And those were the last words he said for the remainder of the interview.

Gerry always hated it when a suspect exercised his right to silence.

It was impossible to tell whether the charred human form on the stainless steel table was Ian Rowe. But the height and build were about right.

Of course someone might have nicked Rowe's passport and decided to use his name but the more Wesley thought about it, the more unlikely that seemed.

He thanked Colin Bowman, anxious to get away. He felt no inclination to accept Colin's invitation to join him in his office for a pot of Earl Grey. The truth was, he felt slightly sick.

As soon as he'd left the hospital, he took his mobile phone from his pocket and tried his home number. Pam hadn't yet heard the news of Rowe's probable fate and he felt she ought to know. But there was still no answer.

He stood on the pavement in the High Street, the slow-moving crowd of summer tourists parting around him. He wanted to talk to someone, someone who'd actually met the dead man. And as Pam was unavailable, there was one obvious choice. He punched out Neil Watson's number and waited.

Neil answered after three rings. And he sounded delighted to hear Wesley's voice. 'Wes, mate. I was just going to ring you. I got your text. That's really weird about Ian Rowe. You've not set eyes on him for twelve years then he turns up out of the blue when you're on holiday. Weird,' he repeated. In his mind's eye Wesley could see him shaking his head in disbelief.

'Where are you at the moment?'

'Queenswear. Having a look at the Grandal Field site. Part of it's still taped off by your lot as a crime scene but I didn't think there was any harm in a bit of forward planning.'

'I'll come and join you. It's about time I had a look at the place for myself.'

'Know who that poor woman was yet?'

'Not yet,' he said apologetically. The identification of the victim burned alive in Grandal Field was taking far

81

too long, in his opinion. 'I'll be with you in half an hour. That OK?'

Wesley hadn't taken into account the queue for the car ferry. It was easy sometimes to forget about the holiday season and the difference it made to the lives of Tradmouth's residents. It was forty-five minutes before he managed to locate the field and park up behind Neil's distinctive yellow Mini.

He found Neil walking around the empty field, scribbling notes on a pad and taking photographs with a small digital camera. Every so often he'd squat down and pick something up from the ground, examine it closely and put it back down where he'd found it. He was so engrossed in what he was doing that he was unaware of Wesley's arrival.

Wesley watched his friend for a while before shouting to him, then he saw Neil swing round, a broad smile of greeting spreading across his face. 'Hi, mate. Just having a look. I've got a load of students coming tomorrow to do some field walking. Then we're doing more geophysics.'

Wesley smiled to himself. It was typical of Neil to place archaeological concerns above everything else. 'I've got some news,' he said.

It seemed that Neil hadn't heard. 'I can't get over you meeting Ian Rowe. Talk about small world. Not that I could stand him. What's he doing now?'

Wesley hesitated. Then he decided he'd better get it over with. 'Actually he's lying in the mortuary at Tradmouth Hospital.'

Neil's mouth fell open. 'But ... but I thought you'd met him in France. I thought ...'

'Well, I did but ... It's a long story.'

Neil looked at his watch. 'Fancy a drink? There's a decent pub up the road.'

Wesley knew he should say no. But, on the other hand, if he delayed his journey back he might avoid the rush-hour traffic on the car ferry. 'OK. I'd better give Pam a ring first.'

Neil nodded. 'How was the holiday anyway?'

'Good. Apart from Ian Rowe.'

Wesley managed to speak to Pam this time and, when the call was finished, Neil looked at him, puzzled.

'You didn't mention Rowe. Does she know yet?'

Wesley shook his head. 'She met Rowe in Carcassonne. I intended to tell her right away but now I think I should really tell her face to face ... pick the right moment.'

'But he wasn't exactly a friend, was he?'

Wesley had to acknowledge that Neil was right. Pam had been on little more than nodding terms with Ian Rowe and, although she'd be shocked at the news of his death, she'd hardly be grief-stricken. But before he talked to her, he wanted to get things straight in his head. And a chat with Neil would help him do just that.

The pub was ideal. Low-beamed and cosy, it served a good pint but, as both men were driving, they made do with shandy instead. Wesley didn't have to be a detective to know that most of the clientele were tourists. In the winter the landlord struggled to keep going. What he made in the summer would tide him over for the whole year.

They found a corner table, tucked away from the main bar. It was quiet here. Wesley sat down and took a long drink. He was thirsty.

Neil looked round. 'Wonder how the new housing development will affect this place. Might not be good for the tourist trade but I suppose there'll be regulars all year round. Swings and roundabouts.'

'How big's the development going to be?'

'Twenty houses. Half detached, half what they call cottage-style town houses.'

'And I expect they'll go for a good price.'

'I've heard he plans to flog them for half a million apiece. But planning permission was given on the understanding that ten per cent of them should be what they describe as affordable.'

Wesley almost choked on his shandy. 'Affordable to whom? Russian billionaires?'

'You've got a point there,' Neil answered with a smirk. 'Somehow I can't see Jon Bright letting two of his money boxes go to the peasantry for a knock-down price.' He took another swig of shandy. 'If he was going to be that generous, I might have bought one myself. Now tell us about Ian Rowe.'

Wesley gave him an account of the bare facts. How Ian Rowe had accosted him as he and Pam were having a romantic evening stroll along the ramparts of Carcassonne. How they had arranged to meet the next day and how Rowe was worried about someone he knew – a woman called Nadia. Rowe had arranged another meeting the next morning but he hadn't turned up. However, Wesley had obtained copies of e-mails sent by Nadia which seemed to confirm Rowe's story and throw up some intriguing possibilities. As he spoke it helped to clarify things in his mind. Nadia should really be the focus of his investigations. The car near Owl Cottage belonged to her so presumably Rowe had seen her on his return to Devon. Or maybe things weren't that straightforward.

Neil frowned. 'This Nadia woman might have contacted him. If he found out she was in danger of some kind he might have come rushing back.'

Wesley sighed. Neil could well be right. Perhaps Nadia was the reason for Rowe's sudden return and not the letter from Sir Martin Crace that he'd received on the day of his disappearance. 'What do you remember about Ian Rowe?'

'I remember he used to fancy himself. And he was more into mind-altering substances than archaeology. He dropped out after he failed his second-year exams, didn't he?'

Wesley nodded. Neil's recollection of Rowe's departure from university was as vague as his own. By that time they were moving in entirely different circles.

'I remember he was a bloody pain when we did that fieldwork in Somerset. He was supposed to be recording our trench and he was doing doodles of cartoon characters instead.' Neil sounded quite indignant.

'His heart certainly wasn't in archaeology, I'll give you that.' He paused, collecting his thoughts. 'It looks as if he might have had some connection with Sir Martin Crace.'

Neil raised his eyebrows. 'What sort of connection?'

'I don't know. But he claimed that he once worked for Crace and he did receive a letter from Crace's PA on the day he left Carcassonne. We found it amongst his belongings. He had an appointment to see Crace the day after tomorrow – which I intend to keep for him.'

'We *are* moving in high circles. Ask him if he'll make a large donation to the archaeological unit while you're there, will you?' He frowned. 'Somehow I can't see a loser like Ian Rowe hobnobbing with someone like Martin Crace. Can you?'

'No doubt all will be revealed.' He felt the subject of Ian Rowe was exhausted for now. Neil didn't know any more about the man than he did. Which was as he'd expected. But a part of him had been clinging to the hope that Neil could remember something relevant about the dead man or his friends that had passed him by. 'When are you starting the dig?'

'As soon as the field walking and the geophysics are done. The site was dug before, back in the nineteen eighties. But I can't find the reports.'

'Probably filed in the wrong place.'

He saw Neil shrug. Filing, he imagined, wasn't his strong point. 'The director of the dig was a Dr Maggie March. She was killed in a car accident shortly after the dig was completed.'

'But there must be someone else you can ask.'

'March's second in command – a woman called Wendy Haskel – went missing the day after March died. Rumour has it that her clothes were found on the beach at Littlebury. Suicide probably.'

Wesley raised his eyebrows. 'Oh dear, not a lucky dig, was it?'

'You could say that. I've had everyone looking high and low for the site reports but there's no sign of them so it looks like I'll have to start from scratch.' A sly smile appeared on his lips. 'Still, that should hold things up a bit for Mr Bright. What is it they say about clouds and silver linings? It's a lovely spot. Sloping down towards the river; views of the water through the trees. Pity it's got to be concreted over. I've done some preliminary research. The estate belonged to a family called de Grendalle back in the middle ages – hence the name Grandal Field, I suppose. From the geophysics, it looks as if there's a whole manorial complex under there – high-status site.'

'Have you tried to trace the other people who took part in the nineteen eighties dig?'

'Funny you should say that. I rang Professor Maplin last night. You remember Karl Maplin?'

Wesley nodded. He remembered Professor Maplin

from his student days. He'd been a gossipy little man, quite fun to be with unless you were on the receiving end. 'Of course I do. How is he?'

'Same as ever – loves to dish the dirt. He's semi-retired now, of course, but he still does some teaching and digs when he can. He told me he can't remember much about Dr March's dig here. It was only really remarkable, he said, for what happened afterwards – March's accident and her deputy's disappearance.'

Wesley looked at his watch. 'I'd better get back.'

Neil stood up. 'Me too. Duty calls. I've got to make Jon Bright's life a misery by telling him that the geophysics and the aerial photos indicate that it could be a really important site and that could mean major delays to the development.'

Wesley had to smile. Neil's attitude towards the world of commerce was adversarial, to say the least.

'Bit of a shock about Rowe,' Neil said quietly as they strolled outside, making for Wesley's car. 'Let me know how you get on with Sir Martin Crace, won't you?'

'Will do.' Wesley unlocked the car door and turned to face his friend. 'And good luck with the dig. From what I hear about Jon Bright, you're going to need it. By the way, have you heard of a group called the Pure Sons of the West?'

'I've heard of them. Keep threatening to take action against second-home owners but, as far as I can see, they're all talk.'

'They've been sending threatening letters to Jon Bright's wife.'

Neil gave a low whistle.

'Keep in touch,' Wesley said as he climbed into the driver's seat.

Neil suddenly looked worried. 'They might see us digging and think we're connected with the developers.

You don't think my team could be in danger?'

'Just don't ask for police protection. We're stretched as it is,' said Wesley with a grin before driving off.

Jem Burrows knew that Chas Ventisard had been taken in for questioning but he was certain that he wouldn't talk.

Jem sat surrounded by computer equipment like a spider in the centre of a web of wires and cables. From his bedroom he had command of all useful knowledge at the click of a mouse. With a bit of searching on line he could even discover the names and home addresses of the second-home owners – the ones who turned up at weekends in their 4x4s with their luxury ready meals bought at distant supermarkets. The ones who clogged up the M4 on summer Friday evenings to get to their expensively bought piece of paradise.

He knew who they were and where they lived. That was a start.

Since he'd finished his degree in Media Studies at Morbay University, Jem had moved back to live with his mother and his two younger brothers. He hadn't had much choice in the matter. Not with things as they were.

Chas Ventisard had imagined that mentioning the Whitely fire on the website would send a warning shot across the enemies' bows. But there had been someone in the house. And because of that, it might look bad for the Sons. It might make them look like murderers. Jem had always known Chas was a liability.

Would a new denial rectify the situation? Probably not. The damage had been done and now the police might start taking a serious interest. And that was the last thing Jem Burrows wanted.

Wesley hadn't bothered to drop in at the police station on

his way home. He was still supposed to be on leave, after all. But, even so, he just couldn't get Ian Rowe out of his head.

As soon as he arrived home he broke the news to Pam and, as he expected, she was shocked but not particularly upset. She was quiet as they ate supper and he knew that she was reliving their encounter with Rowe in Carcassonne, seeing if she could, with hindsight, recognise any signs or clues to what had happened.

'So what the hell was Rowe doing in Whitely?' she asked as soon as they'd got the domestic drudgery out of the way and settled the children in bed.

'No idea. But he was driving Nadia Lucas's car.'

'Perhaps she lent it to him. Have you spoken to her yet?'

'Some uniforms went round to the address we traced from her car registration but there was no answer.' Wesley put his arm round her shoulders. 'We found a letter from Sir Martin Crace's PA in his holdall.'

'So he wasn't lying about knowing Crace?'

'I wouldn't go that far. The letter confirmed that he had an appointment but it was quite formal. Certainly no indication that Rowe and Crace were bosom buddies – or even that they knew each other. The meeting was fixed for the day after tomorrow at Bewton Hall.'

'Crace's home. I saw it once in one of those magazines at the doctor's – fabulous place. If Ian was actually invited to the house surely it means he was telling the truth.'

'I think Crace uses it as his headquarters.'

Pam looked disappointed. Another theory shot down in flames.

Wesley stood up. 'Those copies of Nadia's e-mails are somewhere in that case I haven't unpacked yet. I want to read through them again.'

Pam looked him in the eye. 'Is this fire being treated as suspicious then? Could Ian have been murdered?'

Wesley shrugged. 'The fire investigators say it was started deliberately but we don't know the cause of death yet. We'll have to wait and see.'

Colin Bowman's initial assumption was that he was in the living room when the fire started and he couldn't escape. The probability was that he died of smoke inhalation before the flames reached his body. But that was before the post mortem. Tomorrow things might change.

When he found the e-mails, he and Pam sat re-reading them. But they only served to confirm that he needed to find Nadia Lucas – sooner rather than later.

There was still no answer at Nadia Lucas's address and Rachel Tracey had been given the job of contacting Professor Yves Demancour, the man Nadia worked for. But the professor was proving as elusive as his assistant. He wasn't in his office – it was the university vacation, after all, and academic staff often used that time to pursue their own research. The departmental secretary seemed reluctant to give out his home address but Rachel was never one to take no for an answer. And she had the advantage of having the full force of the law behind her.

No sooner had she written down the address than Wesley Peterson entered the office. Rachel greeted him with a smile, resigned to the fact that her moment of glory was over for a while. With the DI back she was relegated to DS again – a cross between a go-between and a dogsbody.

'Hi,' Wesley said. 'What's new?'

'Still no sign of Nadia Lucas but I've got an address for Professor Demancour.'

'Great. Has the owner of Owl Cottage been traced yet?'

Rachel gave him a martyred look. 'Nick's doing it. But he hasn't got back to me yet.'

'I'll go and chivvy him along. Then perhaps we can pay the professor a visit.'

Rachel looked up and smiled. A trip out of the office was just what she needed.

Informing the unhappy cottage owner that his property was badly damaged by a combination of fire and water from the firemen's hoses would normally have been uniform's job. But as there had been a suspicious fatality, Gerry Heffernan had felt it was CID's responsibility.

Wesley walked over to the desk where Nick Tarnaby was sitting surrounded by witness statements and other miscellaneous paperwork. He looked as though he was about to be buried in the stuff. Wesley often felt that way but he had never let it build up to this extent.

Tarnaby looked up warily as Wesley approached.

'Rachel says you've been trying to trace the owner of the cottage that burned down.' Wesley looked at him expectantly. The technique usually worked but not in this case.

Tarnaby's freckled face flushed red. 'Er, sorry, sir. Not had time. I'll ... er ... get on to it right away.'

'Yes. You do that.' Wesley tried to hide his annoyance. This was information he needed fast. Unless Ian Rowe had broken in and was squatting at the property, it was highly likely the owner knew him – and how he came to be there. 'As soon as possible, please. Everything else can wait.' He knew that Gerry Heffernan would have given Tarnaby an earful. He was being too polite. But he couldn't help it.

Tarnaby didn't answer and Wesley wondered whether he should ask Paul Johnson or Trish Walton to do the job instead. But he decided to give the man another chance. If he hadn't produced a name and address by the time he and Rachel got back from seeing Professor Demancour, he'd think again.

Rachel was waiting by her desk, her bag slung over her shoulder. She was dressed for the warm weather in a short linen skirt and a short-sleeved white blouse. She looked businesslike and beautiful. But Wesley put the thought out of his head.

'The phone number the university gave me for Demancour seems to be unobtainable. Maybe he's been cut off for not paying the bill.' She gave Wesley a conspiratorial grin. 'Looks like we'll just have to surprise him.'

'The boss always believes in the element of surprise,' Wesley said as they reached the car park. 'In fact he swears by it.'

'He would. Has Nick traced the owner of Owl Cottage?'

Wesley shook his head. Rachel was getting in the driving seat, which suited him fine. He wasn't in the mood for tackling the Morbay traffic.

'I know he's new but he seems pretty useless,' Rachel said as she let the hand brake off. 'I never thought I'd miss Steve but . . .'

Wesley said nothing for a few seconds. The mention of Steve Carstairs's name had shaken him. It had brought back memories he'd rather forget – memories of how he hadn't liked the racist and obstructive Steve. And memories of how Steve had died what everyone assumed was a hero's death. 'If he's that bad, Gerry will have him transferred.'

'Traffic perhaps. I can just see him handing out parking tickets.'

'You've had no more thoughts about applying for promotion?'

'And end up sorting out traffic flow in Regatta Week? I

think I'll stick to CID for now. Barty reckons you should-n't go chasing money if it's going to make you unhappy and I think he's right.'

Wesley nodded. Barty Carter, the latest man in Rachel's life, had spent many years chasing money so he should know what he was talking about.

Rachel decided not to take the car ferry, not while the place was infested with tourists, as she put it. She took the A roads through Neston and then on to the outskirts of Morbay. But even avoiding the ferries, the traffic was thick and slow – rather like Nick Tarnaby, Rachel quipped. Wesley made no comment. He was still willing to give the man a chance.

Professor Yves Demancour lived on the far side of Morbay in a hilly, leafy district favoured by prosperous Victorians as a place to build their stucco seaside villas. Many of these villas had distant views of the sea and at least two thirds had been converted into hotels, flats or nursing homes. However they still stood firmly on the right side of town. The professor had chosen well.

The address given them by the university turned out to be a white stucco detached villa sitting behind a high laurel hedge. From the bell pushes beside the front door, there appeared to be seven flats in the building, so if the professor wasn't at home, Wesley thought, there was always a chance that one of the neighbours might know where he was.

Wesley rang the bell of flat number three. After a few seconds the entry phone crackled into life and when they announced themselves the lock on the front door was released, allowing them to make their way up a sweeping staircase.

Demancour was waiting for them in the open doorway. He was a slightly built man, of average height with slicked-back dark hair, slightly thinning on top. He stooped a little and his eyes were warm and dark brown. If Wesley had read a description of the man on paper, he would have considered it unpromising. But in the flesh there was something attractive about him, something he wouldn't be able to put into words. Charisma perhaps. Or maybe plain, old-fashioned sex appeal. He glanced at Rachel and noted the appreciative look on her face.

Demancour's manners were impeccable. He invited them to sit and offered coffee – which was refused – before sitting opposite them with an attentive expression on his face. Wesley felt optimistic. Yves Demancour didn't look like a man with a lot to hide. But then he recalled Nadia's e-mails to Ian Rowe. 'He's very secretive and I think he's hiding something.' And he couldn't forget the mention of the dirty little secret. It was possible that the man sitting before him was dangerous so he wasn't taking any chances.

'Professor, we're sorry to intrude like this but we're making investigations into the whereabouts of a Nadia Lucas. I believe she knew a man called Ian Rowe.'

Demancour's eyes widened a little then he rearranged his features. 'May I ask why?'

Wesley took a deep breath. The body hadn't been identified as yet but he was as sure as he could be that it was Rowe. He decided to take a chance. 'We have reason to believe that Mr Rowe was killed in a house fire in Whitely, not far from Tradmouth.' He watched the professor's reaction carefully but saw only a conventional frown of concern flicker over his face.

'I am very sorry to hear that. I only saw him a couple of times, of course but he knew Nadia well. I think they used to be lovers but she never . . . .'

'And Nadia works for you?'

'She is my assistant. She helps with my research.'

Wesley saw him give Rachel a charming smile.

94

'Nadia's been keeping in contact with Ian Rowe,' he said. 'She sent him an e-mail suggesting that you were hiding something. And she mentioned that she was trying to find out about her mother's death.' He watched Demancour's reaction carefully.

But the professor merely looked surprised. 'I can't think what she means. What should I be hiding? And she has never said anything to me about her mother's death. I cannot think that this has anything to do with me.'

Wesley had to hand it to him – he sounded very convincing.

'What kind of research does Nadia do for you?'

'I have a great interest in the history of the Languedoc region of France in the thirteenth century.'

'The Cathars?'

The professor turned his gaze to Wesley. He looked surprised, and rather impressed. 'You are familiar with the history of that region, Inspector?' The expression of surprise faded, to be replaced by one of amused cynicism. 'Or have you just been reading cheap fiction and conspiracy theories?'

Wesley shook his head. 'As a matter of fact I've just come back from Carcassonne. My wife and I spent a week there and we met Ian Rowe. He was living there and working in a restaurant. He recognised me. I was at university with him. I studied archaeology at Exeter.'

'Nadia never mentioned that Rowe had an archaeology degree.' He sounded rather hurt.

'He hadn't. He dropped out after his second year. Usual case of a misspent youth, I'm afraid.'

'And you?'

Wesley shuffled his feet modestly. 'I stuck the course.'

'And with this degree in archaeology you became a detective.' He raised his finger and smiled. 'I will have to watch what I say, no?'

'Does the name Jeanne de Minerve mean anything to you?'

Demancour smiled. 'This is easy, Inspector. In 1210, when the crusade led by Simon de Montfort against the Cathars in Languedoc was at its height, many so-called heretics were burned in the town of Minerve, which was a Cathar stronghold. A Stephen de Grendalle joined the crusade. He held estates not far away from here.'

'Near Queenswear?'

'That's right. How did you ...?'

'A friend of mine is excavating a site round there. He mentioned the name.'

Demancour nodded. 'I have not discovered why de Grendalle chose to join the crusade against the Cathars but it is on record that he sailed to San Diego de Compostela from Tradmouth in 1209 and made his way to southern France where he took part in the siege of Carcassonne. He was then in the force that laid siege to the town of Minerve in 1210. Raymond Tresorer was a knight in the household of Guillaume de Minerve. He was burned for his faith in that year. He had a daughter called Jeanne.'

'He was a Cathar?'

Demancour nodded. 'It seems so. As was his daughter. It is said she escaped the flames somehow and married Stephen de Grendalle, who brought her back with him to his estates here in Devon. She was called Jeanne, known as Jeanne de Minerve and there are many stories about her. Legends. Hearsay. As yet, I have found some written evidence but not a great deal ... only tantalising fragments. Solid evidence of her life story is my holy grail, Inspector,' he said with a smile. Then he paused. 'You say Ian Rowe is dead. He died in a house fire?'

'I'm afraid so. The body hasn't been formally identified yet but his passport and other belongings were found at the scene and ...'

'That is truly terrible.' Demancour bowed his head for a moment, a gesture of respect. Although the Ian Rowe Wesley had known briefly hardly seemed likely to inspire respect in a man like the professor.

'Rowe had your name and address in his room in Carcassonne.' Wesley watched Demancour's face carefully.

'I do not know why this should be. Perhaps it was something to do with Nadia. I myself have had little to do with him.'

'I realise that but anything you can tell me about him would be helpful.'

Demancour shrugged. 'I know very little. When we were out in the Languedoc he would come to meet her sometimes. They used to work together. That is how they met.'

'Where did they work?'

'They both worked for Sir Martin Crace. You have heard of him?'

Wesley and Rachel exchanged glances. Then they nodded.

'What kind of work did they do?' Rachel asked.

'Nadia once worked for Sir Martin's PA but I am not sure what position Ian Rowe held. A driver perhaps, or maybe he worked in the gardens. Or the kitchens?'

'Not Crace's PA then?'

The amused smirk appeared again. 'I think not. I had the impression from Nadia that Rowe was – how do they put it? – a free spirit.'

'Do you know where can we find Nadia? We need to speak to her urgently.'

'You have tried her address?'

'Yes, but there's no answer.'

'Then I cannot help you. I have not seen her for a week.'

'Did she say she was going away?'

'No. You do not suspect her of any crime?'

'Oh no, not in the least,' Wesley said quickly. 'I just want to talk to her, that's all. Do you have her mobile number?'

Demancour frowned then spread his hands apologetically. 'I'm afraid I do not have it with me. There is a list of contact numbers back in her office back at the university. It will be there.'

The professor stood up, flashing a charming smile in Rachel's direction. 'I'm sorry that I cannot help. Nadia has seemed troubled recently . . . preoccupied. But, alas, she has not confided in me.'

'Are you worried about her?'

The answer was a small, reluctant nod.

'Thank you, sir,' said Wesley formally.

As they walked down the front path to the car, Wesley glanced back and saw Professor Yves Demancour standing in his window watching them. It was hard to read the expression on his face. But it might have been fear.

Gerry Heffernan thought Chas Ventisard was worth another interview. Even though he had obviously decided to play dumb.

'It would help us if we spoke to some of your mates. If what you say is true, they'll back up your story, won't they? And once they do, you'll be out of here. How about giving me some names?' Gerry was at his most reasonable, trying his hardest to ooze charm but not quite managing it.

He looked at the young solicitor sitting by Ventisard's side and gave him what he considered to be a conspiratorial smile. In his opinion the lad looked about twelve but he seemed to be taking his responsibility for his client's defence extremely seriously.

'We'll find out sooner or later, Chas. You might as well tell us. Save us all a lot of trouble.' Gerry could tell by his expression that he was tiring of the game. He wanted to be out of there.

'OK. But I swear that none of us burned that cottage.'

'So you keep saying. But you keep a list of second homes and you use some pretty inflammatory language on that website of yours.'

'I told you, that's only to put the wind up the enemy. Know what I mean? Psychological warfare. That's what it is. Psychological warfare.'

The phrase sat uncomfortably on Chas's lips and he suspected that the words had been spoken by someone further up the organisation. Someone with a bit more intelligence and education than Chas Ventisard.

'OK, OK, Chas. I believe you. Thousands wouldn't. But you'll have to sign a statement.'

'Then can I go?'

'We'd like some names first. I just want to talk to your mates. It doesn't mean I'm going to arrest them,' he said. 'Just a friendly chat.'

Chas Ventisard looked at the DCI suspiciously. Then, realising he had little choice, he began to mumble. 'Jem Burrows is the main man. But he doesn't agree with violence. We're a peaceful organisation.'

'Yeah. Course you are.' Gerry Heffernan's mouth turned upwards into a dangerous grin. 'Where can I find this Jem Burrows?'

Chas glanced sideways at his solicitor. 'I've given you a name like you asked. I'm no Judas. You can find him yourself.'

Gerry Heffernan had to be satisfied with this morsel. It would have been too much to hope for chapter and verse on every Pure Son of the West who ever dreamed up some half-baked threats in the public bar of their local. He had a name and Jem Burrows wouldn't be difficult to find. With any luck, he might have a record. Easily traced.

He left the interview room and made for the CID office. There was a lot to do and he had wasted enough time on Chas Ventisard. He found it hard to believe that Chas and his cronies would actually have had the guts to set fire to Owl Cottage. They were all talk, and hinting at involvement on the website had probably been an opportunistic act – one they'd swiftly regretted.

As soon as he reached the CID office, Trish Walton came bounding up to him, as though she'd been on the lookout for his arrival.

'I've just been talking to the owner of Owl Cottage, sir.'

Heffernan stopped. This was the news he'd been waiting for.

'His name's Jack Plesance and he lives near Birmingham. He's coming straight down.'

'Did he know Ian Rowe was—?'

'Yes. He said he could have the cottage for a week while he sorted something out.'

'Did you find out anything else? How he came to know him or . . .?'

Trish looked apologetic. 'Sorry.'

Gerry said nothing. No doubt he'd learn all about Jack Plesance's connection with Ian Rowe soon enough. Patience – or so his mother had always told him – was a virtue.

As Trish was about to return to her desk, Gerry had a sudden thought. 'Was it you who chased this up, Trish?'

As she nodded, she looked slightly embarrassed.

'I asked Nick to do it. What's up with him? Has he lost the use of his brains or what?' He was aware that he was growing angry. And that wasn't good for his blood pressure. He took a deep, calming breath.

'He had something to do, sir.'

The DCI looked at the new boy's desk. It was heaped with paperwork. And the seat was empty. 'Where is he?'

'I'm not sure.'

Trish was covering for him, he could tell. She'd never have made a living as an actress. Good job she'd stuck to police work.

'Tell him I want a word when he gets back.'

He looked at his watch, wondering how long it would be before Wesley returned from visiting Professor Demancour. He would have liked to see the man for himself. But even he couldn't be everywhere at once.

After he had instructed Paul Johnson to find an address for Jem Burrows he walked over to the open window and looked out over the river. The waterway was teeming with craft and from time to time he caught a few words of amplified commentary from the sleek pleasure boats that cruised up and down the river, packed with tourists. He had heard it all before so it only took the odd word to give him the gist of what was being said. The guide was telling the passengers how ships assembled in the River Trad before sailing off to the Crusades and how Tradmouth was a thriving port during the Middle Ages when great wooden cogs traded with Bordeaux and returned to the town with their cargoes of French wine. But that was a long time ago.

The sound of Paul Johnson's voice roused him from his reverie. 'I've got Jem Burrows's address, sir. And he's got a record. He was convicted of selling fake DVDs last year. Flogged them in local markets. Got a two-year suspended sentence.'

'So he's got a lot to lose if he gets into trouble again.'

'Two years of his life. Well, a year with full remission.' Paul had always been a little pedantic.

'Go and have a quiet word, will you? Take Trish.'

101

Gerry assumed that it was the prospect of Trish's company that had brought a smile to Paul's face rather than an encounter with Jem Burrows.

He strolled back to his office. He needed to think. And he wished Wesley was there to help him do it.

Wesley Peterson sat in the passenger seat looking out of the window at the passing scenery as Rachel drove to Nadia's address. Uniform had had no luck but, as Neston was on the way back, Wesley thought it would do no harm to try again.

After a while Rachel broke the amicable silence. 'Aren't you still supposed to be on leave?'

'I'm supposed to be.'

'Is Pam happy with that?'

Wesley didn't answer for a few seconds. 'It's the school holidays. Pam tends to be happy in the school holidays and stressed in term time. It's an occupational hazard of being a teacher.'

'But surely she'd like you at home.'

'I'll take some more leave when this is all cleared up. She understands. And she did know Ian Rowe . . . sort of.'

'Did she like him?'

'Not much.'

'So we're sure the man in the cottage is Rowe?'

'Everything points that way. His passport was in the holdall upstairs. The owner of Owl Cottage has been contacted and he said that Rowe phoned him to ask if he could use the cottage while he sorted out some business in Devon. There seems to be little doubt that it's him. Nobody else it could be, really. Maybe we'll know more once we've talked to Nadia Lucas. She obviously lent Rowe her car so it's odds-on she saw him when he arrived here.'

'They must be close. I'd be choosy about who I lent my car to. When's the post mortem?'

'First thing tomorrow. Colin couldn't fit it in any sooner. There's a lot of death about, apparently.'

'So what's new?' Rachel muttered under her breath.

Rachel brought the car to a halt outside a small Victorian terraced house on the edge of Neston. 'This is it,' she said. 'This is the address we have for Nadia Lucas. What did you think of Professor Demancour, by the way?'

'I'm not sure,' said Wesley honestly. He hadn't quite known what to make of the professor. It had been hard to tell whether he was lying or not.

'Neither am I. I'm not sure what was going on behind all that show of co-operation and all that Gallic charm.' She grinned. 'Not that I approve of racial stereotypes, of course.'

'I reckon he knows more than he told us so he might be worth another visit. Let's hope we have more luck than uniform and find Nadia at home this time. It'll be interesting to see how she reacts to the news of Ian's death.'

'Mmm. Do you want to tell her or shall I?'

'I'll do it,' he said quickly. He wanted to choose his own words when the time came.

He locked the car and walked slowly to the front door. The house was neat and freshly painted and there were red geraniums tumbling from a window box. The Roman blinds at the windows looked expensive. It seemed that Nadia Lucas was considerably better off than Ian Rowe, who had scratched a living busking and washing up in restaurants. Not for the first time, Wesley found himself wondering about their exact relationship.

Wesley knocked on the door, impatient now to see the woman who'd sent those tantalising e-mails to Rowe. After a few moments the door opened to reveal a striking woman, probably around his own age, with short

103

dark hair. She wore a striped top and long peasant skirt – a fashion *de rigueur* in the self-consciously New Age town of Neston.

As soon as Wesley held up his warrant card and identified himself, the woman's expression hardened. He wondered why.

'I presume you've come about the break-in. About time too. I was fobbed off last time – they just gave me a crime number so I could claim on the insurance and a card with the number of Victim Support but—'

Wesley stopped her in full flow. 'I'm sorry. We haven't come about a break-in. Are you Nadia Lucas?'

'No. She's not here. I haven't seen her for a while. I've been away for a couple of days and I've only just got back.'

'But she does live here? We were given this address.'

'Yes, she lives here. We share. But, like I said, I've not seen her.'

'And you are?'

'Caroline Tay,' she answered, a hint of suspicion in her voice.

'Do you mind if we come in – just for a chat?' Rachel asked, giving the woman an unthreatening smile.

Wesley saw her hesitate for a few moments before standing aside to let them in, as though afraid that letting the police into the house would be inviting bad luck.

When they were in the front room, with its stripped wood floor and its richly coloured Indian throws, Caroline Tay invited them to sit.

'We're looking for Nadia because a friend of hers has been killed,' Wesley began. He thought he'd better make it clear from the start that Nadia wasn't in any sort of trouble – at least not trouble of the legal kind.

Caroline's eye's widened in alarm. 'Killed. Was it an accident or ...?'

'We're still not sure of the circumstances.'

'Who is this friend?'

'A man called Ian Rowe. Have you heard of him?' Wesley watched the woman's face carefully.

'No. I don't think she ever mentioned an Ian. But then we've only been sharing for a few months. There's still a lot I don't know about Nadia.'

'He was driving her car.'

Caroline shrugged. 'Perhaps she lent it to him. I don't know.'

'Do you work with her?'

'Sort of. I work at the university and she answered an advert I put on the noticeboard for someone to share and help with the mortgage. Couldn't manage it on my own. Nadia and I get on OK but we're not bosom buddies. She's quiet and fairly tidy and she's out a lot of the time—'

Wesley interrupted before Caroline could continue her eulogy. 'We found some e-mails Nadia sent to the dead man and we think she might be able to help us.' He didn't feel inclined to tell her about his own involvement. Keep things simple.

Caroline Tay took a deep breath. 'The truth is I am a bit concerned. Nadia hasn't been home for a few days and her mobile's switched off.'

'Can we have her number?' Wesley asked quickly.

'Of course. I'll write it down for you.' She hesitated. 'Like I said, I've been away for a couple of days and I thought she'd be here when I got back but there's no sign of her.'

Wesley's eyes met Rachel's.

'She usually lets me know if she's going to be away but . . . Nothing.'

'And you're worried?' Rachel said gently.

The answer was a nod.

6

We can't get a clear picture of what kind of man Stephen de Grendalle was from contemporary documents. All such sources tell us are the bare facts and, as an academic, I am well aware that I should stick to dry realities. Imagination is for novelists. But imagination is something I cannot control. Perhaps I should write this story in novel form. Perhaps that is the only way I'll be able to express the truth as I see it ... and bring the people behind the sterile words to life.

We don't know how Stephen came to meet Jeanne. Records indicate that she was amongst those sentenced to be burned alive at Minerve but there is no explanation of how Stephen rescued her from such a fate. Did he see her and fall in love at once, I wonder? And what ruse did he devise to secure her release?

Of course we cannot know after all these centuries but I see it in my dreams: the parade of prisoners; the young man struck by beauty; the subterfuge as he spirits her away from mortal danger. No romantic novel could do it justice.

So why did it end as it did?

(From papers found in the possession of Professor Yves Demancour)

The excavation of the Grandal Field site was due to start that day and Neil Watson found it hard to sleep.

The light was filtering through his bedroom curtains. He looked at the alarm clock and saw that it was six thirty. It was time to get up and drive all the way down to Queenswear, even though he would have sold his soul for another couple of hours in bed.

He turned over, wrapping the duvet closely around his body. Five more minutes. And as he lay there in the morning silence memories of Ian Rowe began to play like a video in his head. Ian Rowe sitting at the back of the lecture room doodling and gazing out of the window. Ian Rowe in their hall of residence gathering a group of idle cronies around him while Neil, Wesley and their like-minded friends tended to keep their distance. Ian Rowe out of his head on some illegal substance in the Students' Union bar while Neil and Wesley sat in the corner downing pints of beer discussing the rights and wrongs of Heinrich Schliemann's excavation of Troy. After the first year Neil and Wesley had moved out of hall to share a rented house with three other students and, from that time onwards, they'd had little to do with Rowe and his entourage of wasters. They hadn't been particularly surprised when Rowe had been chucked out of university and after that he'd just become a distant memory.

The thing that surprised Neil most was the way Rowe had sought Wesley's help in Carcassonne. Their acquaintance had been sketchy to say the least. Wesley had said that he'd been keen to ask his advice because somehow he'd discovered that he was a policeman, which meant Rowe must have had serious worries about something. Then, before Wesley could learn the whole story, Rowe had left France and returned to Devon where he had died in a house blaze. The whole affair was rather baffling.

Neil threw off the duvet. If he didn't set off soon he'd hit the worst of the morning traffic. As he pulled on his clothes, he made a mental list of all the people he knew who might have had some contact with Rowe since he left university. It was an extremely short list. Most of Neil's friends and acquaintances were unlikely to have kept in touch. However, there was something hidden in the recesses of his memory. And the more he tried to retrieve it, the more it drove him mad.

It wasn't until he was half way to Queenswear that it finally came to him. He had been having a drink with Una Gibson – now Dr Gibson – a few months ago and she had mentioned Ian Rowe. She had seen him somewhere: they had met and had a brief conversation. He tried to remember what she'd told him but he probably hadn't been paying much attention at the time.

But Una might remember. When he reached Queenswear, he'd give her a ring.

Gerry Heffernan had told Wesley to meet him at the hospital. He could have a bit of a lie-in, the DCI had said benevolently with a Santa Claus smile. As the affair of Ian Rowe had disrupted his leave, he was owed some free time.

But as the post mortem on the man in the cottage was booked for ten, Wesley's lie-in wasn't a long one, especially with a couple of lively children leaping on the bed, intent on disturbing his precious peace.

Pam gave him a sympathetic smile. Since the holiday she'd seemed far more relaxed. Perhaps the small taste of detection they'd shared in Carcassonne had given her a new understanding of his work, he thought. Whatever the reason, he found it rather gratifying.

He gave her a lingering goodbye kiss and set off for Tradmouth Hospital. As he walked down the steep, narrow street towards the centre of the town, his stomach began to churn. He would never get used to seeing human bodies cut open. His parents were doctors, as was his sister, but Wesley had concluded long ago that he must be a throwback to some squeamish ancestor.

Gerry Heffernan was waiting for him outside the plastic swing doors leading to the mortuary and, considering his workload, he looked remarkably cheerful.

'How did you get on with Professor Demancour yesterday?'

'He said that both Rowe and Nadia used to work for Sir Martin Crace but other than that he didn't tell us much we didn't know already. We called at Nadia's address on the way back. She wasn't there but we spoke to her housemate who seems a bit worried about her. She hasn't seen her for a few days and her mobile's switched off.'

'So she's done a runner?'

'It's possible. Rachel's giving the housemate another call this morning to see if Nadia's turned up.'

'Good.'

'How's Joyce?' Wesley asked as they walked down the corridor to Colin Bowman's office, sensing that the DCI needed a break from discussing the case.

'Fine. We went out for an Italian last night. New place near the boat float. Very good. And not expensive. You should try it.'

Before Wesley could reply, Colin Bowman emerged from his office and greeted them like old friends as usual. Wesley had rarely encountered such a sociable and hospitable man. It was just a pity that his patients were in no position to appreciate his cheerful nature.

The corpse discovered in the burned cottage was waiting for them in the post mortem room. There was a lingering smell of burned flesh in the air, blending rather unpleasantly with the floral scent of air freshener, and Wesley put his hand to his nose.

'I take it we still haven't got a name for the woman from Grandal Field?' Colin asked as he gently folded the sheet back to reveal the corpse in its full horror.

'Not yet. We've been through all our missing persons but none seem to fit. I'm working on the theory that she's probably some poor lass from Eastern Europe – victim of sex traffickers punished by some bastard of a pimp.'

Colin sighed. 'It's a wicked world, Gerry. And I'm afraid my findings don't help very much. She'd had no dental treatment. Unlike our friend here. He'd had a couple of fillings so at least that gives us somewhere to start.'

Wesley looked down at the body of the man from Owl Cottage. The features were burned beyond recognition. Had he noticed fillings in Ian Rowe's mouth? The answer was no, but then he hadn't been looking.

'We'll try and trace Ian Rowe's dental records. Shouldn't be difficult,' said Gerry with what sounded like confidence.

'I understand the fire was started deliberately,' said Colin.

'According to the fire investigators. But luckily it was put out before it spread to the whole building. The upstairs was smoke and water damaged but the firemen found a holdall in the bedroom. There was a passport in it, amongst other things. Name of Ian Rowe. And we know the owner of the cottage told Rowe he could use it for a few days. Told him to let himself in with the key under the doormat apparently – some people don't give a toss about security. Also, the body's the right sort of height and build so everything points to this being Ian Rowe.' Gerry paused for effect. 'You knew him, didn't you Wes?'

Wesley's eyes had been focused on a steel trolley at the other end of the room but he glanced at the body in front of him. 'Yes. I was at uni with him.'

Colin Bowman arranged his features into an expression of sympathy, the one he used for grieving relatives. 'Oh, Wesley, I didn't realise. I'm so sorry. You sure you're all right with this?'

'Quite sure.' There was determination in Wesley's words. He was going to see this through.

Colin didn't talk much as he carried out the post mortem. From time to time he looked up at Wesley to see his reaction. But Wesley's gaze was focused elsewhere.

'Well, gentlemen,' he said as he took off his green surgical gown. 'I can tell you for certain that he probably died from smoke inhalation.' He raised a finger as though he was about to impart some important news. 'But there's a slight fracture to the skull, probably caused by our old friend the proverbial blunt instrument. He could well have been unconscious before the fire started.' Colin smiled. 'You look as if you need a cup of tea, Wesley. Sorry I've nothing stronger. Earl Grey and biscuits?'

'That'll do nicely,' said Gerry Heffernan, making for the door.

The excavation had begun and the chugging JCB was scraping the surface soil off the first of Neil's planned trenches. The sun was out and so far it was going well, Neil thought, as he watched the machine back up slowly to shave the earth of another section.

But there was always something to spoil the day, and this time it was the arrival of a brand new Range Rover at the gateway to the site. The thing had tinted windows and, as it rolled its stately way across the rough terrain,

Neil couldn't make out who was driving. But he knew who it was all right. He had seen Jon Bright getting in and out of his gas-guzzling vehicle on a number of occasions.

Neil watched as the car came to a halt uncomfortably close to the edge of his trench. For a split second he wished the trench was deeper and that Bright would accidentally apply the accelerator instead of the brake, making the great beast hurtle forward into the abyss. It would have made his day to see Bright stuck and embarrassed. But the trench was only a foot or so deep as yet so it wasn't going to happen.

The car door opened and Bright climbed out. The suit he was wearing looked expensive – it would have taken a humble archaeologist months to earn enough to pay for it. But Neil felt no envy. How could you envy someone like Bright?

'Dr Watson. How's it going?'

Neil stood in front of his trench with his arms folded, as though preparing to defend it from attackers. 'We're just putting the first trench in.'

'What about the . . .?' Bright nodded towards the area of charred grass in the corner of the field. It was still cordoned off with blue and white police tape.

'We can't touch it just yet. Which is a pity. There's a circular anomaly in that section I'd like to have a look at.'

'How long—?'

'No idea,' Neil replied quickly. 'The police said they'd give me the go-ahead but they're taking their time. I've been instructed not to disturb that area. There might still be forensic evidence, apparently. They said something about sending someone over . . .'

Bright frowned. Neil thought he looked worried.

'Well, if that's all, I'd better get on,' Neil said. He

knew he probably sounded rude but somehow he didn't really care what this man thought of him.

As Bright shifted from foot to foot with irritation, Neil could almost read his thoughts: it was his land and what right did this scruffy archaeologist have to treat him like an unwanted intruder? Bright bristled for a few moments before deciding that there was nothing to gain from holding up the dig any further. Time was money. He climbed back into the car, slammed the door angrily and drove away.

As Neil watched his disappearing tail lights, his mobile phone began to ring.

'Have you been trying to call me?' said the female voice on the other end.

It looked as if he had caught up with Una Gibson at last. Now it was just a case of standing in the middle of a field and shouting over the noise of the JCB engine while he tried to steer the conversation round to what Una knew about Ian Rowe. But then Neil had always relished a challenge.

When he returned from the mortuary Gerry Heffernan stood for a while, staring out of the office window at the glistening river, pondering the problem that had landed in CID's lap over the past few days. He wondered whether they would discover anything useful that afternoon when they kept Ian Rowe's appointment with Sir Martin Crace. Gerry found that, as the meeting loomed nearer, he was rather looking forward to it.

'Gerry, we've got a visitor.'

He looked round and saw Wesley standing by Rachel's desk. He had been rather subdued since Rowe's post mortem but now his eyes glowed with excitement and there was a keen look on his face; the look of a huntsman who had just spotted his quarry. There had been a development in the case. Gerry had known him long enough to recognise the signs.

'Who is it?'

'The owner of the cottage. His name's Jack Plesance. He's waiting down in Reception.'

'He might be able to tell us more about the dead man. A bit of a mystery man, our friend Rowe.'

Wesley was about to reply when Rachel hurried in and, from the look on her face, he knew she too had news.

As usual she came straight to the point. 'I gave Nadia Lucas's housemate another call to see if she'd turned up but she still hasn't heard from her. I asked her if she wants to report Nadia officially missing but she seems a bit reluctant. She says she'd feel stupid if she's just gone off for a few days to see friends.'

'So when exactly did she last see her?' Heffernan asked.

'Last Tuesday. Nadia told her she was going out but she didn't give any indication that she was going away.'

'Does she know if Nadia has any family or ...?'

'Her parents are both dead and she's never mentioned any brothers or sisters.'

Gerry looked at Wesley who was standing beside him with a concerned frown on his face.

'So she disappeared last Tuesday?'

Rachel nodded.

'That's the day before that poor lass was found burned in that field.' He looked Wesley in the eye.

'There's no evidence to suppose ... And it's highly likely that she met Rowe to hand over the car when he arrived in England.'

'I suppose you're right. Go and see this housemate again, Rach. Find out everything you can about this Nadia Lucas.'

As Rachel hurried away he saw Paul Johnson hovering in the doorway as though he had something else to tell them. Gerry looked up at him. 'Hi, Paul. Anything new come in?'

'Yes, sir. Morbay nick's been on the phone. A woman's been reported missing. She disappeared last Monday and she sort of fits the description of that woman who was burned to death in the field.'

'And she's not been reported missing until now? Someone's taken their time.'

Paul Johnson cleared his throat. 'The woman who did the reporting's asking for police protection.'

Gerry glanced at Wesley, who was watching Paul expectantly.

'She's from Lithuania. The sergeant at Morbay nick who phoned me said she was scared stiff – in a right old state. She's called Yelena and it's her friend who's missing – name of Anya.' He swallowed hard. Paul was never good at concealing his feelings. 'It's a nasty one, sir. They paid someone to bring them to London to work as waitresses. Only when they arrived they were bundled into a van and taken to Morbay. Not that they knew it was Morbay – could have been anywhere. They were locked in this house and not allowed out. Injected with drugs and you can guess the rest. Last week this Anya vanished. Yelena managed to escape from the house this morning and she was found collapsed and half naked near the sea front by a female community support officer. She was petrified and she kept gabbling away in Lithuanian. It wasn't till they managed to get a translator that the story came out.'

The two men sat in stunned silence for a while. Gerry had thought all along that the burning had the feel of a punishment killing – the action of men who tempted women over to the country with the irresistible bait of

115

honest jobs and undreamed-of prosperity, only to use them like lumps of meat once they had them in their power. Anya had probably done something to offend her tormentors – perhaps she'd tried to escape. And if they'd caught up with Yelena she'd no doubt have met with the same fate. Only she'd been lucky. She'd made it to safety.

'Where's Yelena now?'

'She's in a women's refuge.'

Gerry gave a weary sigh. Refuges did their best but if Yelena's captors were really determined – if she could blow the lid on their operation – she might not be out of trouble just yet.

'If this Anya is our body in the field, Gerry,' Wesley said. 'It means you were right all along.'

But Gerry Heffernan derived no satisfaction from his instincts being proved correct. 'Well, if I am, it means our two murders aren't connected and we can concentrate on Ian Rowe,' he said quietly. 'Poor lass.' He stood up. 'Get an exact description of this Anya, will you, Paul? We'd better make sure, eh.'

'Sad,' said Wesley when Paul had closed the door behind him.

'Mmm.'

'Is your Rosie still helping at that refuge in Neston?'

The mention of Rosie in connection with the world of darkness and violence suddenly made Gerry feel uncomfortable. 'Yeah. She does two afternoons a week. But it's mainly women fleeing from domestic violence. I don't think they've had a case like this . . . yet.'

'If this Yelena's moved to Rosie's refuge in Neston, it might make her harder to find.'

'And easier for us to keep an eye on her. I'll get onto Morbay nick and suggest it . . . or somewhere even further from Morbay. As soon as we get the chance we'll visit this Lithuanian lass. But we've got to go and be nice to Sir Martin Crace first.' He looked up at Wesley and grinned. 'I'll leave the small talk to you, eh.'

'What about the Pure Sons of the West?'

'What about them?'

'Someone's been threatening to burn Sheryl Bright alive so we still have to follow the mistaken identity theory. And it's not impossible that they had something to do with the fire at Owl Cottage.

'Paul and Trish didn't get to see Jem Burrows yesterday but they're going to try again this morning. He'll probably deny everything but we can bring him in and put a bit of pressure on.'

Gerry rubbed his hands together. 'Right. Jack Plesance is waiting for us downstairs. Time to have a word with him.'

'Let's hope he'll throw some light on exactly what Rowe was up to,' said Wesley quietly.

Gerry stood up and gave him a sympathetic look. 'Hard to lose a mate,' he said.

'He wasn't my mate,' Wesley replied, almost in a whisper.

Jack Plesance was waiting for them in Reception, pacing up and down nervously. He was a wiry man, probably in his late forties or early fifties, and he rather reminded Wesley of a terrier. He had grizzled hair and a pointed face and he didn't smile as he shook hands with the two policemen. But then, if your cottage has been burned down, there's probably very little to smile about.

Wesley led the way into one of the more comfortable interview rooms on the ground floor and ordered tea – the decent stuff in china mugs, not the bilgewater that spurted out of the drinks machines. Plesance looked as though he could do with some sort of pick-me-up.

'Now then, Mr Plesance.' Gerry Heffernan leaned forward and attempted a sympathetic smile which didn't quite work. 'Sorry about your property.'

'The house doesn't matter. I've just been having nightmares thinking of Ian in there,' Plesance said softly. He turned his face away as though he was too embarrassed to express his feelings.

Wesley caught Gerry's eye. It was time to drop the bombshell. 'His post mortem was carried out this morning.' He saw Plesance wince. 'And the results were a bit surprising. It seems that Ian Rowe died as a result of the fire. And the evidence suggests that he was murdered.'

This got the reaction Wesley had anticipated. Jack Plesance's small grey eyes widened in shock. 'Fucking hell. I mean ... oh God. I don't believe it.'

'We think whoever killed him knocked him unconscious first, set the place alight and left him to die.'

For a while Jack Plesance was speechless. Wesley concluded that either the man was an extremely good actor, or he could be wiped off their list of suspects.

'How long have you owned the cottage?'

Plesance straightened his back and took a deep breath. 'I've had it for about a year. I own a few places down here – holiday lets. Owl Cottage was a good buy. It needed some work doing and I was going to make a start on the renovations this summer when I could get down for a week or two.'

'Why Devon?'

Plesance hesitated for a moment before answering. 'I've got family down here.'

'I see.'

'I mean family are important, aren't they?'

Wesley looked at him curiously. There was something slightly sad in the way he'd said the words. Perhaps there was an estranged wife down here he was desperate to stay in contact with . . . children he hardly saw. He didn't feel inclined to enquire further so he moved on to the next question.

'What is it you do?'

'I'm a property developer. I do up places and sell them, mainly in the Midlands. Then there's the holiday lets down here.'

'Beats working,' said Gerry with what sounded like envy.

'It can be quite hard work, believe me.'

'But you hadn't got round to renovating Owl Cottage?'

'I've been so busy with my other properties it slid down my list of priorities. You know how it is.'

Gerry glanced at Wesley then cleared his throat. 'So you were charging Ian Rowe for the privilege of staying in your property?'

Plesance shook his head. 'As a matter of fact I wasn't. The place was hardly in a state to let out. I said he could stay there for a few days while he was in the area. That's all. Favour for a mate.'

'I take it the cottage is insured.'

Plesance nodded. He was a businessman. He wasn't stupid enough to take the risk of leaving an empty property uninsured, especially with the likes of the Pure Sons of the West around.

'So what happened? How did Rowe get in touch with you?'

'He phoned me. Said he was ringing from Plymouth. He'd just arrived on the ferry and he had some business here. He wanted somewhere to hole up for a while, as he put it. He asked if the cottage was free.'

'And you let him know where the key was. Very generous,' said Gerry, slightly incredulous. 'He's an old friend, is he?'

'I've known him for a while, yes.'

'How did you meet?' Wesley asked, curious.

'I worked for Sir Martin Crace. I'd trained as a surveyor and for ten years I had a job dealing with Sir Martin's property portfolio. Then when my dad died a couple of years ago I decided to move back up to Birmingham and start my own business. I met Ian when he was working as Sir Martin's driver and we shared a flat in Dukesbridge for a while.'

Wesley said nothing. At least this solved one little mystery. Rowe had been a driver – not Sir Martin's PA as he'd claimed. It made Wesley wonder how much of what Rowe had told him had been fantasy or exaggeration.

'You stayed in touch?'

'Yeah. He'd call me from France from time to time and he'd let me know if he was in the country. And we met up when I was on holiday in France. He was living in Toulouse then, working in some café. Bit of a free spirit was Ian.'

Wesley nodded. Professor Demancour had described Ian Rowe as a free spirit too.

'When exactly did you last speak to him?'

Plesance thought for a moment and recited the date Rowe had left Carcassonne. Rowe must, Wesley thought, have set off for Devon when he received Crace's letter and called Plesance up to arrange his accommodation as soon as he reached Plymouth.

'Did you know someone called Nadia Lucas?'

'Nadia? Oh yes. She was a clever girl. Too clever for what she was doing.'

'She was a secretary, I understand.'

'That's right. I couldn't understand it really. She'd been at some university doing research – a doctorate, is it?'

120

Wesley nodded. 'Go on.'

'She said something about her funding running out but . . .'

'You didn't believe her?'

Plesance shrugged. 'What do I know about that sort of thing? She could have been telling the truth for all I know. Anyway, she worked for Crace for a while, typing his letters and doing his filing. Then she left and got a job with some French professor. I don't know how she put up with the bitch but—'

Wesley looked at Gerry. 'The bitch?'

'Eva Liversedge. Crace's PA and prize cow. No wonder Nadia left. She was a nice girl, Nadia. But a bit odd, if you know what I mean.'

Gerry Heffernan leaned forward. 'We don't know what you mean. Why don't you tell us?'

'She was very quiet.'

'It's not illegal,' said Gerry.

'That's it really. She was just a bit odd. But nice.'

'You've spoken to her recently?'

Plesance shook his head.

'We've been trying to find her but she seems to have disappeared. She went off last week and nobody knows where she is. Any ideas?'

Plesance shrugged. 'Can't help. Sorry.'

'Did Ian mention her to you?'

'He might have said something about not being able to get in touch with her but, to tell you the truth, I was only half listening. I didn't know her well.'

'Was she close to Ian?'

'Yeah, she seemed to be. I don't know what it was between them. Could have been sexual, of course, but I didn't think so at the time. They did a lot of whispering in corners, if you know what I mean.'

'But you didn't know what the whispering was about?'

121

'Search me. If she was telling him secrets, he never shared them with me.'

'And what kind of secrets do you think a girl like Nadia would have?' Heffernan asked.

'I always assumed it was man trouble,' Plesance said after a few moments' thought. 'Nadia had kissed quite a few frogs in her time from what I heard.' He grinned. 'Maybe that's why she's disappeared. Perhaps her prince has turned up at last.'

'Let's hope so,' Wesley muttered under his breath. Perhaps they were worrying for nothing. But then Nadia had told Ian Rowe that she was worried about something. And she'd been trying to find out the truth about her mother's death.

He and Gerry had read through Nadia's e-mails several times since the discovery of Rowe's body and they raised more questions than they answered. There had been a mention of 'that man' who had contacted her to tell her that he thought he'd found a witness. A witness to what? Perhaps Jack Plesance might know.

'Were you the man who contacted her to say he thought he'd found a witness?' He was fishing but he thought it was worth a try.

But Plesance shook his head. 'I've no idea what you're talking about. I never contacted Nadia. Why should I?'

'You worked with her.'

'I worked with a lot of people. Like I said, I didn't know her well.'

Gerry Heffernan gave Wesley a discreet nudge. This was all they were going to learn from Jack Plesance for now. But that didn't mean he wouldn't be worth another try. People often changed their stories, after all.

Jem Burrows – known to his mother as Jamie – lived with his parents in a suburb of Morbay. Not the best suburb but not the worst either. When he'd been at Morbay University he'd shared a run-down house with some mates. But after graduation he hadn't managed to find himself the glittering career he'd been expecting and money had soon become a problem.

Now he lived back at home, vying for space with his younger brothers. Being twenty-four, Jem had been given the box room to himself while his brothers shared. The room was big enough to house his array of computer equipment but sometimes he felt like punching the walls.

Jem's financial contribution to the household income came from a combination of gardening and bar work during the tourist season, but his parents, once so proud of his academic achievements, were wise enough not to push the matter. When he'd tried to show a little enterprise, going into business with a mate selling fake DVDs, the whole thing had backfired and he'd received a two-year suspended sentence. He had been wary of the police ever since. But he was sure he could deal with these two. They had nothing on him.

It was Paul Johnson who spoke first. 'Your name has come up in our enquiries, sir. We're investigating an organisation called the Pure Sons of the West.'

Jem kept his face a neutral mask, trying hard to show no signs of fear or guilt.

'It's a pressure group. It's not illegal.' This was the party line and he was sticking to it.

'It is when you go around threatening people,' Paul observed calmly.

'I can see that, but we don't do that sort of thing.'

'The Pure Sons of the West mentioned the fire near Whitely on their website. A man was killed.'

'That was nothing to do with us. One of my colleagues heard about the fire on the radio and it was put on the website. We keep a register of empty properties that are

123

only used at weekends or for holidays and Owl Cottage was one of them. We didn't have anything to do with starting the fire and you can't prove we did.' He looked Paul in the eye. 'Can you?'

'So you're denying it?'

'Of course I'm denying it. It's got nothing to do with me . . . or the Pure Sons of the West.'

'Where were you around eleven o'clock the night before last?'

'I went out for a drink. I got back home around eleven. I can give you the names of the people I was with and the pub's just down the road. Nowhere near Whitely.' He smirked, challenging them to prove otherwise.

'What about the woman who was burned to death near Queenswear?' said Trish. 'On the site of the proposed Grandal Field housing development.'

Jem paused. He needed to think about this one, to consider his answers carefully. 'What about her?'

'Where were you last Tuesday?'

He made a great show of concentration, trying to remember. 'I think I was at home. I'd have been using the computer. I'm sure your technical people'd be able to confirm that.'

'Your organisation has been sending threatening letters to the wife of a property developer. A Mrs Sheryl Bright. You said you'd burn her to death.'

Jem suppressed a brief flicker of panic. He looked at Trish Walton and saw that she was watching him like a cat watches a mouse. He'd have to be very careful indeed. 'Not me. I never threatened anyone. Have you seen the letters?' He knew he sounded confident. But was it too confident?

'No but—'

'Then how do you know they exist? Has this Mrs Bright still got them?'

'Apparently not but—'

'In that case, you've got no evidence against me. You're just on a fishing expedition, aren't you? Admit it. This woman probably made it all up to discredit us. We're a thorn in her husband's side. Did she tell you that? I bet she didn't. It's in his interests to silence us. If it wasn't for us, the likes of him would concrete over the whole of Devon. And the bloody planning authorities wouldn't lift a finger to stop them.'

'Do you know Mrs Sheryl Bright?' asked Paul.

'I know of her.'

'Have you ever met her?'

'I don't mix in those sort of circles, Detective Constable. The Brights aren't the sort who'd invite the likes of me round for cocktails.'

He hoped the vehemence of these last words would give them the ring of truth. And it seemed, judging by the expressions of slight disappointment on the officers' faces, that they'd swallowed the story whole. But he still had to take care.

Jem Burrows knew he was clever. But even the brightest and best sometimes slip up sooner or later.

Sheryl Bright hugged a silk cushion close, like a comforting teddy bear, and stared at the TV absentmindedly, picking at some paint that had become caught in her cuticles. The host of some inane quiz show was herding contestants from place to place like a hyperactive sheep dog but Sheryl wasn't really watching. She had other things on her mind.

When her husband entered the room, she looked up, her eyes anxious.

'What is it?' he asked, looking her in the eye. 'What's wrong?'

'They've sent another note. Pushed through the door this time.'

'You didn't see anyone?'

'No. I'd have told you if I had.' She looked away.

'What did the letter say?'

'Just that I'd be next. I'm getting worried now, Jon. I work here in my studio and I'm here on my own most of the time. I thought it was a joke at first but now . . .' She hesitated. 'What if they really mean it?'

Bright took a deep breath. 'OK. Where's the note? At least the police might be able to tell something from it . . . trace the bastards somehow. There could be finger-prints or . . .'

She shuddered, close to tears. 'I'm sorry, Jon. I couldn't stand having it in the house. I burned it. I know it was the wrong thing to do but—'

'You stupid cow,' said Jon Bright. He left the room, slamming the door behind him.

7

The site of Stephen de Grendalle's manor house is to be found on land belonging to Grandal Farm – named, I imagine, after the de Grendalle family who once held sway there.

I close my eyes and see Stephen and Jeanne hurrying through the French countryside to the coast after her rescue from a fiery death. He must have deserted from Simon de Montfort's crusading army. How love can give us courage.

In 1153 Henry II of England had married Eleanor of Aquitaine, thus bringing the great port of Bordeaux under English rule. Tradmouth's deep harbour made it an ideal port for trade with that fine French town. Barrels of good red wine were rolled ashore on Tradmouth's waterfront and the town's merchants grew fat and prosperous, building themselves fine houses and donating money to the church to buy their way into heaven. The boom continued in 1204 when Normandy was lost and the importance of ports on the western Channel grew even further.

De Grendalle and Jeanne must have entered Bordeaux hand in hand, looking for a captain willing to carry them back to Tradmouth with his valuable cargo. De Grendalle would probably have paid the ship's master

well for the voyage that would take Jeanne to a new life.
And ultimately to her death.

(From papers found in the possession of Professor
Yves Demancour)

Wesley Peterson was rarely cowed by wealth and social superiority, but even he felt a frisson of apprehension about coming face to face with Sir Martin Crace. He was a National Treasure. And National Treasures are untouchable and have to be treated with great respect. Even Gerry Heffernan looked subdued and Gerry was certainly no respecter of high positions. He'd always thought that, in the unlikely event of Her Majesty herself concealing a major crime, Gerry would have her hauled down to the interview room at Tradmouth police station in the state coach without a second thought.

Security at Bewton Hall, just outside the town of Dukesbridge, was low key but obviously present. Famous and wealthy men sometimes attract the desperate and delusional after all, and the likes of Sir Martin couldn't be too careful.

The black sign with gold lettering bearing the name of the hall was as discreet as Crace's security. Wesley drove past the entrance to the estate twice before he realised where it was and, when he swung the car into the drive, he was met by a barrier and two large men dressed from head to toe in black. He lowered the car window and one of them – a man with a shaved head and a thin, humourless mouth – leaned in, politely threatening. He was the type Wesley would normally leave some well-built uniformed colleagues to deal with, preferably with the aid of a baton and a CS canister.

'Afternoon . . . sir,' the man said with just a faint trace of a sneer. To him, a black man and a large unkempt Scouser in a car probably meant potential trouble.

128

Wesley recited their names and produced his warrant card and Gerry did likewise. 'We're here to see Sir Martin Crace. And before you ask, he isn't expecting us.'

A smug expression appeared on the security man's face. 'Sorry ... sir. Sir Martin doesn't see anyone without an appointment. I'll have to radio in and tell him you're here.'

Gerry Heffernan leaned across. 'We'd rather you didn't, mate.'

'No can do,' said the large man, fingering the black walkie talkie he'd just detached from his belt.

'Bugger off or we'll do you for obstruction,' Gerry shouted out of his open window. 'Fancy a few hours in the cells, do you?'

This seemed to work. The man shot a killing look at Wesley and stepped to one side, fingering his walkie talkie while Wesley revved the engine and shot past him, fuming. It wasn't often people got to him but this man had succeeded.

'When I was first mate on board ship, I had to deal with his sort all the time,' Gerry said as they swept up the drive. 'They need a firm hand, that's all.'

Wesley knew that the DCI's days in the merchant navy had given him valuable experience in dealing with the unpleasant, the fighting drunk and the downright bolshie. There were times when he thought his own upbringing – parents both doctors, private school education and university – had been far too genteel.

The drive was long, no doubt made that way in times gone by to impress visitors with the massive size of the owner's estate. It must have worked back then and it still worked now. Wesley carried on driving past woodland, fields and banks of rhododendrons. At one point they passed a small cottage tucked away at the edge of a

129

copse. The place had a look of neglect, which surprised Wesley as the rest of the estate seemed so well kept, and he wondered who lived there. One of the gorillas on the gate, maybe. Or some faithful retired retainer. The place looked too unloved to house one of Sir Martin's relations or a member of his more senior staff. But it could be the home of a lowly under-gardener – or even a driver such as Ian Rowe had been.

But all thoughts of the cottage went out of his head as the main house came into view. Suddenly the rural landscape yielded to an array of formal gardens, neat and well tended. And the house that loomed in front of them was even grander than he'd expected.

'Nice place,' said Wesley as he brought the car to a halt on the gravel circle in front of the portico.

The chief inspector didn't reply. Wesley saw that he was staring, dumbstruck, at the building in front of him.

'Georgian, I should think,' Wesley said. 'Lovely proportions.'

Bewton Hall's proportions were indeed impressive. Two wings sprouted from a central section fronted by a magnificent classical portico with five graceful pillars. A study in perfect symmetry.

'Do we use the tradesmen's entrance or what?' Gerry asked as they got out of the car.

Wesley said nothing. He wasn't really sure. All the confidence he had felt a few minutes earlier now began to drain away. But he supposed that was the point of buildings like Bewton Hall – to impress social equals and to intimidate social inferiors.

But he strode up the steps to the grand front door. There was no way they were going to be relegated to the tradesmen's entrance if he had anything to do with it. There was an old-fashioned bell push at the side of the door and Wesley pressed it hard. He could hear a jangling inside the house. The thing worked – he'd been half afraid that it wouldn't.

It seemed an age before the door was opened by a tall woman dressed in black. She had short brown hair and it was hard to guess her age. But she looked like a senior member of the domestic staff – a housekeeper perhaps. When Wesley introduced himself and his boss, she stood aside to let them in.

'I'll let Eva know you're here, gentlemen,' she said calmly as though a visit from the police was a routine event.

'And you are?'

'Jane Verity. I'm Sir Martin's housekeeper. If you'll excuse me.'

The woman disappeared up the graceful staircase – the sort of staircase many women dreamed of sweeping down in a Scarlett O'Hara gown. But Jane Verity showed no such romantic inclinations.

Gerry sat down heavily on a delicate-looking Regency sofa which, fortunately, held up under his weight. Wesley winced at the potential disaster, then he sat down beside him, very carefully.

It was a full five minutes before another woman appeared on the stairs. She was small with steel-grey hair, sharply chiselled features and intelligent grey eyes and she introduced herself as Eva Liversedge, Sir Martin's PA. Jack Plesance had described her as a prize cow and Wesley thought he could see why. In spite of her diminutive size, she looked formidable. Even Gerry Heffernan would think twice before arguing with the likes of Eva Liversedge.

'I believe you wish to see Sir Martin?' There was something in her voice that suggested they'd have a long wait.

Wesley answered in the affirmative and the two

officers showed their warrant cards, not that Eva Liversedge looked particularly impressed. There was a distinct sneer in her voice as she told them that Sir Martin was a busy man. And the sneer almost turned into a snarl when Ian Rowe's name was mentioned.

In the end it was Gerry Heffernan who almost lost his patience. He had never, to Wesley's knowledge, uttered the clichéd words 'This is a murder inquiry, madam', but he spoke them now, glancing at Wesley as though he expected him to issue a groan.

The cliché, however, seemed to work like a magic spell. For the first time Eva Liversedge looked uncertain of herself, and she said she'd have a word with Sir Martin.

'You do that, love,' Gerry said to her disappearing back, emboldened by his success. Wesley thought this was pushing his luck but he remained silent.

Ten minutes later they were being shown into Sir Martin's inner sanctum. His panelled office on the first floor overlooked the gardens and was the size of a tennis court. The man himself sat behind a monumental mahogany desk at the far end of the room and they had to cross what seemed like an acre of antique Turkish rug to get to him. This, Wesley guessed, was calculated to give the great man a psychological advantage. But he wasn't falling for that one.

Most of the population knew what Sir Martin Crace looked like – his face was familiar from TV and newspapers. But in the flesh he looked smaller, less impressive. He had a shock of white hair and his tanned face was less lined than Wesley had expected. He was in his early fifties – they knew that much from looking him up on Google – but his flesh showed no sign of sagging. Whether this was because of cosmetic surgery or a fortunate genetic inheritance, Wesley couldn't tell. But Sir

Martin looked good. Fit and glowing with health – and something else . . . intelligence.

The great man stood up as they approached, a charming smile fixed on his lips. 'Gentlemen, please sit down. Coffee? Tea?' His finger hovered over the intercom on his desk.

'Tea for me,' said Gerry Heffernan cheerfully. 'The cup that cheers and all that.'

'Tea would be fine. Thank you,' said Wesley formally. If Gerry was going to accept the offer of refreshment, he thought, he might as well benefit too.

Once Sir Martin had ordered the tea, he looked at the two men expectantly. 'Now then, gentlemen. What can I do for you?' He oozed openness and co-operation – the upright citizen with nothing to hide doing all he could to help the police.

It was Wesley who spoke. As he was a privately educated graduate, he knew the DCI usually left it up to him to deal with the upper echelons of society. 'We're very sorry to bother you, sir, but we're investigating the death of a man called Ian Rowe. I believe he had an appointment to see you today.'

Sir Martin arranged his features into a suitably solemn expression. 'That's right. He'd arranged an appointment through Eva. I'm very sorry to hear he's dead. How did he . . . er . . .?'

'His body was found in a burning cottage near the village of Whitely. The post mortem found that he was knocked unconscious and died of smoke inhalation. We think whoever attacked him set the place alight, which means we're treating it as a case of murder.' Wesley watched Sir Martin's face closely but there was no crack in the mask of polite concern.

'That's shocking. I did hear about the fire on the local news but they didn't say who . . .'

'We haven't released his name to the press yet. The next of kin have to be informed first and we're still in the process of tracing them.'

'Of course. If there's anything I can do to help.' He picked up a gold pen and began to turn it over in his fingers.

The tea arrived on a silver tray and when Eva had handed out the cups she retreated back to her office.

'You knew Ian Rowe well?' Wesley asked as soon as she was out of earshot.

'I would hardly say I knew him well, Inspector. He worked for me for a while. He was my driver.'

'Was he a good employee?' Wesley asked, suspecting that Sir Martin would be reluctant to speak ill of the dead. Perhaps he should have asked his questions before breaking the grim news. But it was too late now for regrets.

Sir Martin hesitated for a few moments and Wesley watched his face, suspecting that he was trying to choose his words carefully. 'I'm afraid I had to let him go, Inspector. He became unreliable, you see, and in my position I need reliable staff. He began to turn up late and on one occasion Eva said that she smelt alcohol on his breath. That's when he was asked to leave.'

Wesley glanced at Gerry who was listening intently. At least it seemed that Sir Martin was being honest with them.

'Do you know what happened to him after he left your employment?' Wesley asked.

'I believe he went to France. But that's all I know.'

'A woman called Nadia Lucas used to work here.' Gerry finally broke his silence.

Again Sir Martin's expression gave nothing away. 'That's right. She worked for Eva for about a year, I believe, but then she decided to resume her academic career. I believe she went to work for a professor . . . in Toulouse, I think.'

'Were Nadia and Ian Rowe close? Is he the reason why she went and got a job in France?'

Sir Martin gave Gerry a patient smile. 'I wasn't aware of a close relationship between them but I suppose it's possible, even though I wouldn't have thought it likely. I'm a busy man and I don't take much interest in gossip about my employees' private lives unless their work is affected.'

'Of course,' said Wesley quickly. 'Do you know why Ian Rowe wanted to see you today?'

'I'm sorry, I've no idea. But as he'd worked for me, I felt obliged to give him an appointment.' Sir Martin smiled. 'I rather suspected he would ask for a handout. My charitable activities are well known, Inspector, and people assume that I'm a soft touch.'

'Would you have given him anything if he'd asked for it?' Gerry asked, genuinely curious.

'That depends. If he'd genuinely fallen on hard times through no fault of his own . . . if he'd been a victim of circumstance, then . . . It would have been a loan, of course.'

'Of course,' echoed Wesley. Sir Martin Crace hadn't become a multimillionaire by throwing his money down drains.

'When did you last see Ian Rowe?'

'I haven't seen him since he worked for me.'

Something about his answer made Wesley uneasy, but he wasn't sure why. Perhaps it was just his suspicious mind.

'And Nadia Lucas – when did you last see Nadia Lucas?'

There was a slight hesitation, barely noticeable – unless you were looking for it, as Wesley was. 'After she left my employment I never saw her again.'

'Did Eva see her again?'

'You'll have to ask her.'

'What was your relationship with Nadia?'

This made Sir Martin sit up. 'I don't know what you're implying but—'

'I'm not implying anything, sir. I merely asked what — '

'I assure you, Inspector, there was nothing improper. She was an efficient employee and I had no reason to be dissatisfied with her work. That's all. And before you ask, I know nothing about her private life. As I said, I don't pry into ... Look, why don't you ask Nadia herself? She'll tell you ...'

'We would, sir. Only she's disappeared. Strange, that. Ian Rowe's murdered and Nadia Lucas disappears and the link between them is that they both worked for you.'

Sir Martin looked slightly exasperated. 'Look, Inspector, if two of my employees meet while they're working here and keep in touch, I can hardly be held responsible for what they get up to, can I? They're adults, after all.'

Wesley knew the man was right. But somehow, he couldn't let the matter rest. Sir Martin was the link between Nadia and Ian. Ian had made an appointment to see Sir Martin before he died and all his instincts told him that this was relevant. But, rather than risk upsetting a National Treasure, he knew he had to leave it be for the time being.

He smiled at Sir Martin, who was still fidgeting with his gold pen, impatient for the interview to end. He sensed that no more information about Ian Rowe or Nadia Lucas would be forthcoming so he thought he'd ask a question of his own, quite unconnected to the case. 'We passed a cottage on the way in. It was next to a copse of trees to the left of the drive. Looked rather uncared for. I was just wondering who lived there.'

Sir Martin visibly relaxed. 'My aunt, Bertha Trent, lives there – well, I call her an aunt but she's actually my mother's cousin. A couple of years ago she returned to this country from Zimbabwe and turned up here one day out of the blue. In fact I'd never actually met her until then but I knew of her existence, of course – bit of a family legend.' He smiled. 'She offered to catalogue some books and antiques for me in return for the cottage – she said she wanted to keep working even though she's over retirement age. Her face is disfigured thanks to an unfortunate incident when she was defending her farm from the violence of Robert Mugabe's regime. But she shows remarkable courage – never complains.'

Wesley nodded sympathetically but he was losing interest. The woman in the cottage was another of Sir Martin's charity cases. Nothing to do with Ian Rowe or Nadia Lucas.

'Bertha's rather an eccentric lady,' Sir Martin continued. 'And very independent so I don't see much of her. I've offered to do some work on the cottage but she says she likes it how it is.' He shrugged. 'If it suits her, that's fine by me.'

Wesley stood up and Gerry Heffernan struggled to his feet.

'I think that's all for now, sir. Thank you for sparing us some of your valuable time.'

After they'd shaken hands and taken the long walk across the Turkish carpet to the door, Gerry Heffernan whispered in Wesley's ear. 'Thank you for your valuable time, sir. Crawler.'

Wesley grinned. 'Let's have a word with Eva before we go. I bet she knows everything that goes on around here – and more.'

They found Eva Liversedge in her spacious office off the corridor leading to her boss's inner sanctum. Like his vast office, it was oak panelled with a sumptuous red Turkish carpet and her desk was a miniature version of Sir Martin's. When they entered she was typing onto a computer. She looked up and smiled with her lips – but not with her eyes.

'Can I help you, gentlemen?' she asked, tilting her head politely to one side.

Gerry Heffernan didn't stand on ceremony. He crossed the room and sat himself down on one of the chairs in front of the woman's desk, wriggling his backside to make himself comfortable. Wesley knew this meant that he intended to stay where he was until he was satisfied with the answers she gave to their questions.

'We'd like to ask you about Ian Rowe,' Wesley said, taking a seat beside the DCI. 'You made an appointment for him to see Sir Martin, I believe.'

'That's right.' She pressed her lips tightly together.

'And did you have any idea what he wanted to talk to Sir Martin about?'

'No idea at all, I'm afraid.'

Wesley caught Gerry's eye. Somehow he found the woman's answer hard to believe. Surely someone of Sir Martin's standing wouldn't see just anyone without having some notion of what they wished to discuss. He had hardly been on friendly terms with Ian Rowe – in fact Rowe had left his employment under a cloud – so he owed his former driver nothing.

'Presumably you asked him why he wanted to see your boss?' Heffernan said. 'Secretaries like you usually keep unwanted visitors away – the dragon guarding the gate and all that.'

Wesley watched Eva Liversedge's face. She didn't look pleased. Perhaps it was because the DCI had called her a dragon . . . or perhaps it was because he'd lowered her status to secretary.

But Gerry continued, undeterred. 'I shouldn't have thought the likes of Rowe would have been allowed into the inner sanctum without you giving him the third degree first.'

'You have to understand that Sir Martin isn't like other very rich men. He actually cares about people. I'm here to assist him not to . . .' She cleared her throat. 'Guard his gate, as you put it.'

She gave Gerry Heffernan a hostile scowl and he gave her a grin in return.

'What can you tell us about Ian Rowe?' Wesley asked, attempting to smooth things over.

'He was a driver. I'd tell him when he was needed to drive Sir Martin but, apart from that, I had little to do with him. I'm afraid he didn't prove to be very reliable. If it had been up to me he wouldn't have lasted as long as he did here but Sir Martin believes in giving everyone a chance.'

'So what happened? Why did he leave?' He wanted to hear her version of events.

'As I said, he was unreliable. He was supposed to be on call to take Sir Martin wherever he had to go but on two occasions he couldn't be found. When I smelled alcohol on his breath that was that. I summoned him here to the office and told him that his services were no longer required.'

She suddenly looked uncomfortable. There was something she was holding back.

'How did he react when you told him?'

There was a long silence. And the answer, when it finally came, proved as interesting as Wesley had anticipated.

'Ian Rowe was a nasty, violent man, Detective Inspector.'

Gerry leaned forward. 'How do you mean, love?'

'He . . . he hit me. And called me . . . Well, I'd rather not repeat his words if you don't mind.'

'Were you badly hurt?' Wesley asked.

She shook her head. 'He didn't hit me hard. I had a bruise on my cheek. The main injury was psychological. The shock, you understand.'

'Of course,' Wesley said sympathetically. 'It must have been very trying for you, thinking you were about to face him again.'

'Yes.'

'I take it Sir Martin was aware of what happened between you and Rowe?'

'Sir Martin is sometimes too forgiving for his own good,' she replied. ·

Wesley caught Gerry's eye again. 'You mean that people sometimes take advantage of his good nature? Does it happen often?'

'Not if I can help it,' the woman said quickly. Wesley suspected that Sir Martin Crace sometimes wasn't made aware of all the requests that came in for his time and money. Eva looked after him well. But somehow Ian Rowe's message had got through.

'But you passed on Ian Rowe's request for an appointment?'

Eva's mouth formed itself into a thin, disapproving line. 'There was a letter. Sir Martin came into my office and went through that day's post as he usually does. He saw Rowe's letter and told me to make an appointment. If it had been up to me—'

'He wouldn't have stood a chance.' Gerry finished off her sentence for her.

'Quite.'

'What about Nadia Lucas?'

Eva Liversedge looked up. 'What about her?'

140

'Tell us about her.'

'She worked as my assistant for about a year. She was an intelligent young woman. An academic, although she was having trouble getting funding for her higher degree. The job here was a stopgap – she made that quite clear and Sir Martin was happy about it. He likes to help out people who are going through difficult times financially. Nadia needed work and he was more than happy to give her a position here.'

'How did she get the job? Did she know Sir Martin or . . .?'

'She wrote in. I select suitable applications for Sir Martin's consideration. Nadia's was one of them.'

'And Ian Rowe?'

'Likewise. He wrote in. He claimed to be an un-employed archaeology graduate and said he was willing to work in any capacity. If he'd proved reliable in his driving post, no doubt Sir Martin would have found him something more . . . Sir Martin likes to help people. Give them a chance. That's why it was so shocking when Rowe proved to be so perfidious, Detective Inspector. It was an abuse of trust.'

'Yes,' said Wesley. 'I can see that. Tell me about Rowe's relationship with Nadia Lucas.'

'I'm not sure. They used to spend time together, I know that much. Whispering in corners, walking in the grounds.'

'Were they lovers?'

'I didn't get that impression. More like close friends. Confidantes.'

'Or conspirators?' Wesley suggested.

'I had no evidence of that.'

Gerry leaned further forward, as though he was anxious to get his question in. 'When did you last have any contact with Nadia, love?'

'I haven't seen her since she left Sir Martin's employment.'

'We're rather worried about Nadia. In fact she appears to be missing,' said Wesley, watching Eva's face for a reaction.

But the woman's expression remained neutral apart from a tiny, hardly perceptible, raising of her perfectly plucked eyebrows. 'I'm sorry to hear that but I know nothing about it. I'm afraid I can't help you.'

Wesley stood up, confident that they'd learned all they were going to learn from Eva Liversedge. However, Gerry Heffernan had one more question. 'Was Nadia pally with anyone else who worked here? Anyone she might have kept in touch with?'

'Not that I know of, Chief Inspector,' Eva said with stiff formality. 'Now if that's all . . .'

They knew when they were being dismissed. All Wesley's instincts told him there was more to learn but as he caught Gerry's eye, the older man gave a small, almost imperceptible shake of the head. They had pushed things far enough. For now.

As they drove back down the drive, Wesley noticed Gerry staring out of the window as they passed the run-down cottage nestling amongst the trees. Why was he suddenly and incongruously reminded of a fairy story he'd read to Michael before his trip to France – Hansel and Gretel? He smiled to himself. The idea of all that gingerbread probably meant he was feeling hungry, he thought, as they continued on down the drive towards the gatehouse.

Hansel and Gretel – Ian Rowe and Nadia Lucas being lured into Sir Martin Crace's glittering, seemingly generous world. A world of sweets and gingerbread for the lucky chosen few. He was about to say something to Gerry but he stopped himself. He was getting too imaginative.

*

Dr Una Gibson had been known as Boudicca in her student days because of her mane of auburn hair and her imposing figure. She looked every inch the warrior queen – until she opened her mouth. She had a soft, soothing voice with a faint trace of an Edinburgh accent that Neil Watson could have listened to for hours.

She wore combat trousers and a tight T-shirt that rode up to reveal a glimpse of pale midriff as she walked across the field, trying not to get in the way of the members of Neil's team, who were walking in straight lines, carrying bleeping geophysics machines, their faces earnest as they concentrated on their task. Neil stood and watched Una appreciatively, a sheepish smile fixed on his face.

'You made it then?'

'Obviously.'

Neil felt his cheeks burning. It had been a silly question. And Boudicca had never suffered fools gladly.

She looked at her watch. 'I haven't got long, I'm afraid. I've got to be at Morbay University at three thirty.'

Una, as an up-and-coming authority on ancient bones, tended to be increasingly in demand in academic circles these days. Neil tried to look suitably grateful and thanked her for sparing the time to see him.

'No problem,' she said. 'It was on my way and I fancied a quick look round the site. How's Wesley?' Whenever he saw her she always asked about Wesley. He sensed there was some attraction there which had lain dormant over the years. Never spoken of but always simmering beneath her cool exterior. Or that might be his imagination – she might just be enquiring about an old friend from university days.

'Actually he's the reason why I wanted to talk to you.'

143

Una frowned. 'Not bad news? He is OK?'

'He's fine.'

'It's just that you looked so serious.'

'Sorry.' He grinned. 'I told you he'd met Ian Rowe in France.'

'Yes. And you said there was something else.'

Neil nodded, wondering how to tackle the subject of death. But then Una, like himself, had only known Rowe slightly so she probably wouldn't be too grief-stricken at the news of his death. He decided to come straight to the point. 'He's dead. He died in that fire. It's been on the news. That cottage near Whitely . . .'

'I heard about that. It's awful.' She took a deep breath. 'They said the police were treating the death as suspicious but they didn't say who . . .'

'They don't give out the name until the next of kin have been told.'

'But Wes told you?'

Neil nodded and they stood in silence for a few moments, as if they were paying their respects. Although neither had had much respect for Ian Rowe in life.

It was Neil who spoke first. 'Didn't you tell me you met him a while ago?'

'That's right. I bumped into him in Exeter about six months back. He said he was working in France but he'd come back for his mum's funeral or something. Not that he seemed particularly grief-stricken. I was doing the sympathy bit but he seemed . . .' She searched for the appropriate word. 'Rather cocky. Pleased with himself. Said that he'd worked for Sir Martin Crace for a while but now he'd moved on.'

'So you had the impression he'd fallen on his feet?'

'Oh, aye. From the way he was talking you'd have thought he'd been Crace's right-hand man. But he always was a bullshitter if I remember rightly. I never used to

144

believe half of what he said.' She thought for a few moments. 'He spoke very highly of Crace – said he was good to work for. But that's what you'd expect, isn't it?'

'Suppose so.' As far as Martin Crace was concerned, everyone seemed to be in absolute agreement. Crace was one of the good guys. Which automatically made Neil suspicious. 'Did he say anything else?'

She raised a finger. 'He asked after a few people we knew at uni. I told him Wes had joined the police – he didn't seem impressed. I remember he said something about a girl he knew who was working for some professor with connections in southern France and he said that he'd found out something that might make him rich, but he was probably bullshitting.'

'Probably,' Neil agreed.

'And he asked me what I knew about the Cathars. I said sod all. Silly conspiracy theories and buried treasure aren't exactly my thing.'

'And what did he say to that?'

'Nothing much. Oh, I remember something else he said. He told me his mum had known Crace well ... implied that's how he got the job. That might have been bullshit too, of course.'

She glanced at her watch. 'I've got a hot date with some Anglo-Saxon bones. You can give me a quick guided tour then I'd better be off.'

After a swift tour of the site he walked Una to the gate. She leaned forward and kissed him on the cheek, telling him to take care. And to call her if any interesting bones turned up on the dig.

She was about to return to her car when Neil remembered something else he wanted to ask her. 'Have you ever heard of an archaeologist called Dr Maggie March? She excavated this site in the nineteen eighties.'

Una turned and shrugged. 'It's a bit before my time.

145

I'll ask around the university if you like.'

'Thanks. It's just that nobody can find any record of her excavation here.'

'She's bound to have left something. It's just a question of knowing where to look. The reports probably got attached to the back of something else or put in the wrong file. I'd get someone to have another look if I were you.'

'Professor Maplin says they'd gone missing.'

Una rolled her eyes. 'Maplin's a bitchy old woman and I doubt if filing's his strong suit. I shouldn't worry. Something's bound to turn up.'

He watched her battered Land Rover drive off down the lane and took his mobile phone out of his pocket. Glad to see that he'd got a signal at last, he punched out the number of the archaeological unit. If the records of the 1980s dig still existed, surely someone would have tracked them down by now. He'd asked them to look in all the most unexpected places, after all.

But the answer was still the same. There was no sign of any records of that particular excavation – not even a mention in other files. It was as though the dig at Grandal Field had never happened.

The telephone on Wesley's desk was ringing as he walked into the CID office. He sprinted over, picked up the receiver and uttered a breathless greeting, thinking to himself that he should really get more exercise.

'Inspector Peterson? It's Caroline Tay here.'

Wesley's mind suddenly went blank. Then, after a few embarrassing moments, he remembered. Caroline Tay was Nadia Lucas's housemate. Perhaps she was calling to say that Nadia had returned.

'What can I do for you, Ms Tay?' he said as he sat down and made himself comfortable. He glanced across at the next desk where Rachel Tracey was going through some witness statements. She gave him a coy smile and looked away.

'I don't know if it's important,' said Caroline on the other end of the line. 'I don't want to waste your time but I've had a visitor. Someone asking for Nadia.'

'Someone you recognised?'

'No. That's just it. It was a man and he just asked if Nadia was in. I told him I didn't know where she was. I said she'd gone off without telling anyone.'

'And what did he say?'

'He seemed a bit annoyed. Asked me if I'd any idea where she could be but I said I hadn't a clue. When I asked him for his name and if he wanted to leave a message for Nadia, he said not to bother. Said he'd deal with it. Then he got into his car and drove off. Like I said, he seemed a bit annoyed.'

'So you didn't get a name?'

'No. But I can describe him. He was white, five ten, aged about fifty. He was a bit overweight and he had greasy dark hair and a snub nose. He was dressed in a dark suit that had seen better days and his tie was stained. And he wore a wedding ring. And his breath smelled of garlic.'

Wesley smiled to himself. He wished all his witnesses were so observant. 'You didn't get the car registration, by any chance?'

'Sorry. I tried to see it but there was a van in the way. However, the man's car was dark blue, I could see that much. And a saloon – a Mondeo or a Vectra or something like that,' Caroline Tay said with breathtaking efficiency. This woman might be the perfect witness but Wesley suspected that a date with her would be like chatting up a robot. He thanked her and said he'd send someone to take a statement.

He looked round the room. Everyone in there seemed busy, dealing with forms, talking on the phone or typing industriously into their computers. Only the new boy, DC Nick Tarnaby, looked as if he was a loose end, staring out of the window at the view of the river, apparently in a world of his own while the paperwork piled up on his desk. Wesley felt a twinge of vindictiveness. If there was one thing that annoyed him it was people who didn't pull their weight.

He caught Rachel's eye. 'I've just been speaking to Nadia's housemate, Caroline Tay.'

Rachel nodded. She remembered Caroline. And, from the expression on her face, the slight raising of her eyebrows, Wesley guessed that she hadn't particularly taken to her.

'It seems that Nadia's had a visitor. Middle-aged man who didn't leave his name. Can you go and have another chat to Caroline, see what she can tell you?' He jerked his head in Nick Tarnaby's direction. 'Take Nick with you.'

Tarnaby looked up, shaken from his daydreams.

'And then get him to go through any CCTV footage in the vicinity – let's see if we can find a registration number for this mysterious visitor's car.'

'Is there any more news of that missing Lithuanian girl?' Rachel asked with a sudden frown.

'Her friend's being interviewed at Morbay but I'd like a word with her myself.'

'Think she could be the Grandal Field victim?'

'It's a possibility.' He thought for a moment. 'Tell you what, Rach, when you're at Caroline Tay's try to get a sample of Nadia Lucas's DNA – her toothbrush or hairs from her hairbrush. And see if there's a photo of her.'

'OK. Will do.' Rachel stood and swung her handbag over her shoulder. She looked keen to get out of the office and into the fresh air. Wesley felt a bit like that himself. He saw her look at Nick Tarnaby. 'Come on. We're off to Neston.'

Tarnaby stared at Rachel as though she'd made an unreasonable demand.

'In your own time, Nick,' she said in a rare flourish of sarcasm.

Nick Tarnaby reluctantly began to follow Rachel out. If he wasn't careful, Wesley thought, he would be the recipient of one of Gerry Heffernan's verbal kicks up the backside. And Wesley hoped it would be sooner rather than later. Perhaps he would have a quiet word.

As Rachel reached the office door, she turned and said something to Tarnaby, like a dog walker telling her pet to hurry up and come to heel. Wesley smiled to himself. If anyone would sort Tarnaby out it'd be Rachel.

He sat down at his desk and brought up the Pure Sons of the West website on his computer. He had an uneasy feeling about this particular organisation. They were big on threats and boasts but when he and Gerry had started to dig beneath the surface, they'd found little there apart from a ragged group of bar-room dissidents.

He stared at the screen, wondering whether the dramatic death by fire of the woman in the field and the burning of Jack Plesance's property had come as happy coincidences for the Pure Sons of the West. They'd mentioned Owl Cottage on their website, careful not to claim responsibility directly and denying all connection when they found out about the fatality, which meant they hardly registered in the Richter scale of terrorism.

However, Wesley still wanted to keep an eye on them. They had allegedly made threats against Sheryl Bright. And they had talked of taking action against second-home owners. The Pure Sons of the West were there,

149

lodged in the back of his mind. He didn't believe in coincidences.

He heard Gerry Heffernan's voice calling his name and he glanced at his watch. Six o'clock and he was feeling hungry. Pam would be giving the kids their evening meal and wondering what time she'd see him that night. He stood up and walked slowly to the DCI's office, passing the huge noticeboard that almost took up one wall of the CID office. He could hardly bear to look at the image of the two charred corpses, their blackened lips drawn back to reveal smoke-stained, grimacing teeth. It was hard to believe that one of them had been Ian Rowe and the thought made Wesley feel slightly ill. Ashes to ashes. The funeral service had it spot on.

Gerry Heffernan was in his office, feet up on the desk, looking totally relaxed. He patted his bulging stomach and grunted at Wesley to take a seat.

'Anything new, Wes?'

Wesley recounted his conversation with Caroline Tay, the news that a middle-aged man who wouldn't give his name had been enquiring about Nadia Lucas's whereabouts.

Gerry pondered the matter for a few moments. 'They seek her here, they seek her there, eh. I asked Trish to find out what she could about her but there's not much.'

'Caroline Tay says she never mentioned her family, which is odd.'

'They could all be dead or maybe they emigrated to Australia or something. Or they could be up in an isolated croft in the Highlands of Scotland. According to Trish she got her degree in Medieval History at York University so her relatives could be up there in the wilds of North Yorkshire,' Gerry added absentmindedly. 'Let's face it, they could be anywhere.'

'Did Trish find out anything else?'

'She's working on it.'

'We still don't know what she did between graduating and getting the job with Crace.'

'Eva Liversedge might be able to tell us.'

'Yes, there's bound to be references and that sort of thing.'

'If it's relevant.'

Wesley knew the boss had a point. He had a strong feeling that whatever was going on had its roots in the time Nadia worked for Crace, not in the distant past.

'We're talking as if this whole thing revolves round this Nadia. She could be a distraction. She could turn up at any minute.'

'Ian Rowe was e-mailing her. Ian Rowe had her car. Ian Rowe's dead and she's disappeared off the face of the earth.'

'Could she have killed him?'

Wesley sighed. 'I don't know what to think. Could Nadia be the woman in the field? I've asked Rachel to get some samples from her house for DNA matching.'

'Good.'

'We've no reason to believe that Rowe's death and the woman in the field are linked. But if it does turn out to be Nadia . . .'

Gerry Heffernan shook his head. 'My money's still on it being this Lithuanian lass. We need to talk to her mate but the interpreter's gone home and she's not available till tomorrow morning – some domestic crisis apparently.'

'Don't they know it's a murder inquiry?'

Gerry gave a dramatic shrug. There were some things that couldn't be rushed. 'And what about the Pure Sons of the West?' he continued. 'I've yet to be convinced that they're as pure as they try to make out. They've been sending letters to Sheryl Bright threatening to burn her alive. It seems too much of a coincidence that a woman just happens to be burned alive in the field owned by Sheryl's husband. And I don't like coincidences.'

The two men sat in amicable silence for a few moments. During the morning briefing, Gerry had scrawled his thoughts about the various suspects and other dramatis personae on the notice board, linking the names with crooked lines where he thought there was a link, however tentative. The board had ended up looking like the web of a drunken spider. It hadn't helped at all.

Wesley broke the silence. 'Grandal Field must be significant.'

'Go on.'

'It might be worth having another word with Professor Demancour. He's interested in Stephen de Grendalle, who owned the land back in the thirteenth century. There could be some link with the work Demancour did in France. Some Cathar connection.'

Gerry Heffernan smirked. 'You're not going to tell me it's some secret about the Holy Grail and hidden treasure? Come on, Wes, we're wandering into the realms of fantasy here.'

'As a matter of fact some treasure from the time of the Albigensian Crusade was found in a place called Saissac. It's on display in the town museum. Pam and I went to see it.'

He saw Gerry roll his eyes. 'Very nice. But do you think this Ian Rowe might have known where to get second helpings?'

Wesley shrugged. 'Gerry, I've really no idea. But I'm not ruling anything out at the moment. But it does seem odd that the victim was burned to death on a site connected with Demancour's research. And the Cathars were burned as heretics back in the thirteenth century.'

There was a light knock on the door, followed by the

152

appearance of DC Paul Johnson. 'Sir. I've just had Mrs Grogen on the phone ... Donna Grogen's mother.'

It took Wesley a few moments to place the name. Since the DNA tests had proved that Donna wasn't their victim in Grandal Field, he had put her out of his mind. 'Well? What did she say?'

'Donna's turned up.'

'Alive and well, I take it?'

'Yes. She went off with a lorry driver, only this particular lorry driver was an ex-boyfriend of Mrs Grogan's and that's why Donna kept so quiet about it all. It's been going on for a while apparently and she was using that Chas Ventisard as a smokescreen. Now it's all over Donna's come back with her tail between her legs. Do you want someone to have a word?'

Gerry sighed. 'I suppose we could do her for wasting police time. But then she didn't really know we'd be panicking and thinking she was lying dead in Colin's mortuary, did she? Rach saw the mother before so I suppose she should go and have a quick word when she's free. Just to put the lid on it.'

'And to see what Donna knows about Chas Ventisard and the Pure Sons of the West,' said Wesley. 'She was involved with Ventisard and she works for Jon Bright. She might still be up to her neck in it.'

Gerry Heffernan gave Wesley a sideways look. He was right, of course. Donna Grogen wasn't off the hook just yet.

Sheryl Bright parked her Mini Cooper in a passing place, some distance from the field's entrance, and walked the rest of the way. It was dusk now and she could see the lights of Tradmouth twinkling, reflected like jewels on the river's choppy waters.

She opened the gate to the field and the hinges gave a

153

complaining squeal, cutting through the silence. This place wouldn't be silent at night for much longer, she thought. Soon there would be car engines and sound systems and chattering televisions and children's screeching voices. Soon the quiet earth would be buried forever beneath bricks and concrete. And it was her husband, Jon, who would bring about its sterile death. Somehow that made everything worse.

In the distance Sheryl could hear the chugging engine of the passenger ferry, still plying to and fro from Queenswear to Tradmouth. She could see its lights as it glided across the water like some exotic pond-skating insect. She stood quite still and felt her eyes prickle with nascent tears. She had grown up in Queenswear. When she was a child she'd played with her brothers in the surrounding fields and she'd run across the cowpat-strewn grass to the trees by the water's edge on summer afternoons. And later she'd dug down and exposed its secrets ... but that was something she preferred to forget.

She wrestled a tissue from the pocket of her jeans and blew her nose. She was getting sentimental and that would never do. There was too much at stake.

She looked at her watch. He was late. She wished now that he hadn't suggested this place – not after what had happened. She had avoided looking at the corner of the field that was still cordoned off with police tape – the corner where the woman had been engulfed by the flames – but now she summoned the courage to turn and look. It seemed so ordinary now. Just a blackened patch, barely visible in the fading light. But her imagination still supplied that terrible picture of the flames and she thought she could still hear faint, terrified, screams wafting towards her on the breeze blowing in from the river.

She didn't hear him coming up behind her and when he touched her arm she jumped.

'You nearly gave me a heart attack,' she whispered. Somehow whispering seemed appropriate, even though there was nobody around to hear now that the archaeologists had all gone home.

She felt his arms engulfing her, holding her tight, secure.

'I've had a visit from the police.' The man's voice was serious, worried.

'And?'

'I said nothing, like we agreed. Perhaps we should— '

'No.' Sheryl Bright put a finger up to her companion's lips.

But he pushed her hand away gently before kissing her, tentatively at first and then more passionately. But he kept his eyes open, focused on the spot where the woman had burned to death on that awful Tuesday night the week before.

8

Unfortunately, there is little written evidence to back up my theory that Raymond Tresorer's daughter Jeanne is the same Jeanne whom Stephen de Grendalle brought back as his bride to his estates in Queenswear.

Tresorer was a knight in the household of Guillaume de Minerve. He was an important and trusted man and a prominent figure in the Cathar church. We do not know whether he was actually one of the Perfecti, *or* bons hommes *as the Cathars called them (good men or friends of God).* Perfecti *were men or women who lived in working communities but as members of a strict monastic order, eschewing sexual relations and eating no meat, as an animal might contain a soul waiting for revelation. The ordinary Cathar believer wasn't subject to these strict rules but he or she was required to have faith and prepare to attain knowledge through a spiritual baptism called the consolament which would be carried out by a member of the* Perfecti *on the believer's deathbed.*

But I digress. It is Jeanne who interests me more. A Jeanne de Minerve is mentioned in manorial records of the time and there is also a reference in the chronicles of Morre Abbey to a gift of a chalice from Stephen de Grendalle on the occasion of his wife Jeanne's baptism.

The question is, why would a woman be baptised twice into the Catholic church? Is it not likely that she was a convert from another faith? Catharism, for example? De Grendalle was clearly a devout man who was probably torn between love or infatuation for Jeanne and hatred for her supposed heresy.

However, as it turned out, religion was to be the least of his worries.

(From papers found in the possession of Professor Yves de Demancour)

After reading Michael a bedtime story and packing the dishwasher, Wesley poured himself and Pam a glass of wine and slumped in front of the television like millions of other overworked citizens. At that moment he didn't feel like thinking. Or doing much else, come to that.

Pam looked up at her husband and smiled shyly. 'Thanks for getting the wine.' She took a long drink and put the half-empty glass down on the coffee table with a satisfied sigh. 'How's the case going?'

'We're still trying to find Nadia Lucas but she seems to have vanished off the face of the earth. And Gerry and I went to see Sir Martin Crace today.'

'What was he like?'

'Very civil. Very charming. Told us bugger all, as Gerry would put it.' He hesitated. 'It looks are though there might be a people-trafficking connection.'

Pam raised her eyebrows. 'Really?'

Wesley cleared his throat, wondering whether he really wanted to go into the details, whether he wanted to bring the sordid business into the haven that was his home. But Pam was waiting eagerly. He didn't have much choice.

'A Lithuanian girl was found half naked wandering down Morbay promenade by some community support officers.

She'd escaped from a brothel. Poor girl was terrified and, once she was taken to Morbay nick and they'd got hold of a translator, the whole story came out. Apparently she'd paid these men to bring her here in a van and she'd been promised well-paid work as a waitress in London.'

'But when she got here she found out it wasn't food she was expected to serve up?'

'Precisely. She was brought to Morbay, kept prisoner in a brothel and . . . Anyway, she came here with a friend who's now disappeared. She tried to escape and now we fear the worst. Gerry and I are wondering whether the woman burned alive in Queenswear . . .'

Pam nodded, serious. 'Yes. It's exactly the kind of thing these bastards would do. Punishment – *pour encourager les autres.*'

To encourage the others – or to let them know what happened to those who tried to escape so that they were cowed into submission and obeyed their captors without question. Pam had probably got it right.

'Still doesn't get you any nearer finding out who killed Ian, though, does it?'

She was right again, Wesley thought. Ian Rowe might have been involved in some dodgy things in his time, but smuggling Eastern European girls into the country to work in brothels probably wasn't one of them.

Pam suddenly looked away and focused on the moving images on the TV screen. 'I keep thinking about Ian, you know,' she said softly. 'I can't get him out of my head. He was there one minute and . . .'

Before Wesley could answer, the doorbell rang.

Wesley was pleased to see Neil on the doorstep. Pam was in danger of getting maudlin and a bit of company would do her good. Besides, he'd been wondering how things were progressing at the Grandal Field site and now he had a chance to find out.

Neil sat down heavily on the sofa in the spot Wesley had kept warm, and accepted a glass of red wine. He was staying in Queenswear, at a place belonging to the parents of one of the archaeological team, conveniently empty as they were spending the summer in Spain, so that meant he could walk back into the centre of Tradmouth and catch the passenger ferry over the water. He slumped back, as if he was settled for the night.

'I had a visit from Boudicca today.'

Wesley knew he was referring to Una Gibson and not the queen of the Iceni. 'Why? You found some human bones?' he asked, suddenly interested. Where bones were, Una often followed.

'No. I wanted to ask her about Ian Rowe. She met him about six months ago, you know. In Exeter. He told her he was back for his mum's funeral and that he'd been working for Crace. Your name was mentioned, apparently. She told him you'd joined the Plods.'

Wesley smiled to himself. This solved the puzzle of how Rowe had known about his choice of career when they'd met in Carcassonne. 'What else did he say?'

'He mentioned a girlfriend who worked for some professor in France. And he asked her what she knew about the Cathars and she said sod all. She reckoned he was going to come up with some conspiracy theory or other . . . Holy Grail and all that. He hinted that he knew something that could make him rich.' He grinned. 'Cathar treasure maybe?'

Wesley rolled his eyes. 'How could he fancy himself as Indiana Jones when he failed the exams?'

'Anyway, by this time he was starting to get up Una's nose.'

'He always did.'

'I wasn't too keen on him myself,' said Pam quietly. 'But it's still a shock – him dying like that.'

'Have you been to see Martin Crace yet?' Neil asked eagerly, breaking the short, respectful silence that followed Pam's remark.

Wesley nodded.

'What was he like?'

'Cooperative,' Wesley replied noncommittally. 'So what else did Una have to say?'

'As a matter of fact Rowe told her that his mum had been a big pal of Crace's...implied that was how he got a job with him. But she thought this was a load of bullshit.'

Una could well be right, Wesley thought, wondering why Rowe hadn't told him about his mother's connections when they met in Carcassonne. It didn't seem the sort of thing Rowe would fail to mention out of modesty. And Crace hadn't mentioned it, which seemed to support Una's opinion.

Neil poured himself another drink. 'I'm still trying to track down the excavation reports for the Grandal Field dig in the nineteen eighties but I can't find them anywhere.' He frowned. 'I'm wondering whether Maggie March had them with her when she had the accident. Maplin said her car was burned out.'

'They'll probably turn up,' said Wesley, closing his eyes and taking a sip of wine, thankful that Neil's little problem wasn't likely to add to his workload.

Gerry Heffernan had wanted to speak to Yelena at the refuge first thing but the interpreter, who seemed to have recovered from her domestic crisis, had said she wouldn't be available till nine thirty at the earliest so they didn't really have much choice in the matter.

Wesley was silent as he drove out to Morbay.

'You look knackered, mate,' Gerry said, from the passenger seat.

'Neil came round last night. He's staying in

160

Queenswear and he caught the last ferry back. Cut it a bit fine but that's Neil.' He paused for a moment while he negotiated a roundabout. 'Paul Johnson's getting hold of Nadia's phone records and I was thinking about going through her things. I've asked Nick Tarnaby to look at the footage from a CCTV camera outside the bank a few doors away from Nadia's house. It's bound to have caught the mysterious visitor's car. Let's just hope we can get the registration number.'

'I'm not holding my breath.'

Wesley indicated and turned the corner into a street of red-brick Victorian terraced houses. The part of Morbay, well away from the promenade, that the tourists seldom if ever saw. 'This is it. Davenham Street.'

Wesley slowed the car down. The women's refuge wouldn't be easy to find. That was the point. It would look like any other house in the street. There would be no sign outside.

However, they had the house number and, once Wesley had found a parking space, they made for the front door, their warrant cards at the ready. The women who lived here would be wary of males.

They were expected, which made things easier, although Wesley couldn't help thinking that it might have been better if he'd gone there with Rachel rather than the boss. Gerry's intentions were good but sometimes he gave off the wrong signals.

A tall woman with spiky peroxide hair said little as she showed them into a room strewn with discarded toys and told them to take a seat. The interpreter, she said, had just arrived and was with Yelena, who seemed to be drawing some comfort from being able to talk to someone in her own tongue. Wesley thanked her politely and they sat down on a stained and sagging sofa.

After five minutes the door opened and two women

161

walked in. The taller of the pair was plump with wild, dark hair. She was dressed in a long skirt and baggy T-shirt and looked the comforting type. The other was a young woman in her early twenties, painfully thin with sharp features and fair hair scraped back into a tight ponytail. She looked at them with frightened, pale-blue eyes and her flesh had a pallid, pasty look, as though she hadn't seen the sunshine for a long time. Wesley had seen that look on prisoners serving a long sentence in jail. It was easy to tell which one was Yelena.

He gave the girl a reassuring smile and held out his warrant card for her to examine. He kept his movements slow and unthreatening, as if calming a terrified animal.

The tactic seemed to work. As soon as she realised Wesley was sympathetic, Yelena wanted to talk. In fact the plump interpreter was finding it hard to keep up with her nervous stream of chatter.

After twenty minutes they had the whole story. How Yelena and her friend Anya had longed to come to England to earn money and see the sights. They'd been offered the earth by a couple of men they met in a café in their home town. The men knew someone who was opening an upmarket restaurant in London and who was looking for reliable staff. He paid good wages and had a flat available for his staff to use. All the girls had to do was to find their fare. They had expected to fly but, when the mode of transport had been a battered blue transit van, they were disappointed but not suspicious, even when they'd been told to hide in the back when they were going through passport control. It was when they'd arrived in London that things turned bad. They were taken to a run-down building with bars on the windows and locked doors, where they were beaten and injected with drugs.

Wesley could guess the rest and he didn't really want

to hear it. But he sat there and listened to the interpreter speaking the words, hesitating sometimes, her voice cracking with emotion. After the beatings and the drugs came the men – sometimes ten or fifteen in a day. The girls were allowed to take their meagre meals together but each worked, as she put it, in their own shabby room. Little more than a prison cell. The drugs, she said, gave some relief from the pain. But not much.

'So what happened to Anya?' Wesley asked gently.

The interpreter asked the question and listened carefully to the answer before relaying it to the two policemen in English. 'One of the men left a door unlocked by accident one day. Anya took her chance and ran out. They chased after her. Yelena here says she never saw her again and when she asked what had happened to her, she was told she'd been punished.'

'Had Anya had any dental work? Fillings?' He looked at the interpreter anxiously but she seemed unfazed by the question. The answer was a shake of the head. Yelena didn't know. But she didn't think so.

Then Yelena spoke again and the interpreter hesitated before translating her words. 'Yelena is afraid that Anya might be dead,' she said, a slight tremor in her voice. 'They are very wicked men. Men without hearts or souls.'

Wesley caught Gerry's eye. They couldn't argue with that.

'We'll get you moved, love,' said Gerry slowly and clearly to Yelena, as though she was bound to understand. 'Somewhere out of Morbay. Somewhere safer. And if you can help us find the men who did this to you ... I'll send a woman officer round to take a statement and she'll need to ask you some more questions. We need to find the place you were kept and get a description of the men. That OK?'

The interpreter said her bit and Yelena nodded in reply.

Wesley was now beginning to suspect that it was Anya who had died in that field at Grandal Farm. As far as Yelena knew, Anya had had no dental work. Their victim had looked after her teeth – not that it had done her much good.

There was nothing more they could do for now. They smiled reassuringly and left. This was a job for uniform and Vice now – the brothel and the men had to be found and dealt with.

As they drove away Wesley felt a deep sadness and, when he glanced at the unusually silent Gerry Heffernan, he guessed he was feeling the same. But neither man spoke until they reached Morbay University. Wesley knew that it was best to put some things out of your mind. But he couldn't stop thinking about those two girls, full of excitement as they travelled to a new country – as his parents must have been when they travelled to England from Trinidad to study at medical school – only to find cruelty and evil in the place of hope. The thought almost made his eyes prick with tears.

Gerry's voice made him jump. 'What are we hoping to find here, Wes?'

'I want to see Nadia's colleagues, just in case anyone knows anything about her disappearance. We'll start with Professor Demancour. I'm sure he'll be able to point us in the right direction.'

'Unless he's got something to do with it,' Gerry observed. 'You've met him – what do you think?'

'I'm not sure,' Wesley answered. His mind was racing ahead. 'Perhaps we're looking at this thing from the wrong angle, Gerry. We've taken it for granted that Nadia is a potential victim but what if she killed Ian Rowe for some reason? What if she's our killer?'

164

'Tying up that woman in the field and burning her alive? Can you see a woman doing that, Wes?'

Wesley shook his head. 'Now we know about Anya it seems more and more likely that the two deaths aren't connected,' he said.

'That's true. Let's face it, Wes, it's just the fire bit that's making us link them.' He thought for a moment. 'Ian Rowe was using Nadia's car so they must have met when he arrived here.'

'Unless he knew where to pick it up.'

Gerry grunted. 'That's a possibility, I suppose.'

'I want to see if Nadia left anything at work. In her desk. Or her locker. I wonder if the uni staff have lockers.'

'Only one way to find out.'

They made straight for Professor Demancour's office and found him in, sitting at his desk studying a book of gargantuan proportions. He stood up when they entered and greeted Wesley with a handshake.

'It is good to see you again, Inspector. Are you digging for clues again?' He gave a little laugh and turned his gaze on Gerry. 'You have not brought your charming sergeant today.'

'I'm afraid she's busy,' Wesley answered, noting the look of disappointment on the professor's face. Rachel had clearly made an impression.

Wesley introduced Gerry Heffernan and the professor shook hands with exaggerated politeness, showing no sign of resentment about this second intrusion into his time.

'What can I do for you, gentlemen?' he began. 'I have already told you everything I know. There is nothing more I can ...'

It was Wesley who spoke. 'We were just wondering whether Nadia left any personal possessions here at the university. A diary or an electronic organiser, perhaps. Something that might help us to find her.' Wesley tilted his head to one side, awaiting a reply.

'If you can think of anything, professor, it'll be a help,' Gerry chipped in. 'We're getting very worried about her.'

'We are all worried about Nadia, Chief Inspector. You are, of course welcome to search her things but I do not know of anything she left here that might tell us where she is now.'

'When we last spoke you said you'd try to find her mobile phone number for us,' said Wesley.

Yves Demancour gave a small smile of triumph and raised his hand. 'Of course. I think it will be in her office. If you'll excuse me . . .'

Gerry was looking puzzled as the professor hurried out of the room. 'We know her number. We got it from Caroline Tay,' he whispered as soon as they were alone.

'Yes, but he doesn't know that,' Wesley answered with a wink as he began to examine the pile of papers on the cluttered desk. He didn't know what he hoped to find but there had been several times during his career when casual nosiness had paid off.

'Hurry up,' Gerry hissed, standing up to keep a look out.

Wesley examined the wooden letter rack at the back of the desk, stuffed with papers, letters and cards, and picked out a small card, pink and glossy, that was protruding between a couple of official-looking letters. He passed the card to Gerry who grinned knowingly.

'Aye, aye. I've seen this sort of thing pinned up in phone boxes.'

As soon as they heard a sound by the door they both sat down, Gerry shoving the card into his pocket and assuming an expression of cherubic innocence.

'I have her mobile number here, gentlemen. I have written it down for you,' Demancour said as he handed them a piece of paper with a set of neatly printed numbers.

'Thank you, sir,' said Wesley smoothly. 'That's very helpful.' There was a pause while he gathered his thoughts, pondering his next question. 'Professor, is there any chance Nadia's disappearance might be connected with the work you're doing? You see, someone who met Ian Rowe a while ago said he hinted that he knew something about Cathar treasure.'

'Really?' Demancour sounded wary.

'Could Nadia have been passing on the findings of your research to him for some reason?'

Demancour smiled. 'My interests do not lie with the trinkets men regard as treasure, gentlemen. As I told you before, Inspector, the research I have been undertaking with Nadia's help concerns Raymond de Tresorer and his daughter who came here to Devon.'

'Yeah,' Gerry interrupted, 'But there are stories of treasure connected with these Cathars, aren't there?'

'There are indeed many stories of treasure and mystery surrounding the Cathars, Chief Inspector. It has become quite a . . . how shall I put it? . . . an industry. The treasure from Montsegur, for instance, was reputed to be in a casket – or in some accounts a hessian bag – hidden by two Perfecti in a cave in Sabarthes and some say it is precious stones or gold or even the Holy Grail itself.' Suddenly Wesley saw Demancour's expression become guarded, as though a shutter had descended. 'But myself, I think the reality is quite different.'

'So there's no truth in the stories?'

Yves Demancour shrugged dramatically. 'Who knows? But as you see, I have studied the Cathars for many years and I am not a rich man so I leave you to draw your own conclusions.'

The professor gave another charming smile, but one that suggested he had said all he was going to say on the subject.

'You were going to let us have a look for anything she might have left here,' Wesley said. 'Would there be anything in her desk or . . .?'

'Her desk is in the next room. You are welcome to look. And there is a locker in the corridor she uses. I do not have the key but . . .'

Wesley thanked him and made straight for the desk in the adjoining room, Gerry Heffernan following behind. It was considerably smaller than the professor's and a good deal neater. The drawers were unlocked and contained very little of interest apart from a key and a university ID card with a coloured photograph. Rachel had had no luck obtaining a photograph from Caroline Tay so this was the first time they'd actually seen Nadia's likeness. Wesley held it out for his boss to see.

'At least we've got a photo of her at last,' said Gerry. 'Pretty girl.'

'She doesn't look like a murderer to me,' said Wesley, staring at Nadia's large brown eyes and dark curls, her freckled face with a slightly turned-up nose and her wide, generous mouth.

A faraway look appeared in Gerry's eyes. 'I arrested this lovely girl once who'd poisoned her husband and his sister. Gorgeous she was. Just goes to prove, Wes, you can never judge a pie by the packaging.'

Wesley didn't answer. He had seized the key and was making for the corridor outside. He had noticed a row of wooden lockers. If Nadia had left anything interesting, he would have put money on her leaving it somewhere more secure than her desk.

Gerry lumbered after him and watched while Wesley located locker number twenty-six, the number on the key fob, and turned the key smoothly in the lock. Both men stood back and looked at the open locker. There wasn't much inside. A sponge bag, a towel, a canvas shopping bag and a pad of lined A4 paper, unused. Wesley began his search but found nothing else apart from a compact umbrella. Nothing out of the ordinary.

Then Gerry pointed to a small shelf at the top. 'Anything up there?'

Wesley realised that he could easily have missed it. He reached up and felt round and he felt a glow of satisfaction when his fingers came into contact with something. Papers, perhaps. Some sort of package. His hand closed round it and he pulled it out.

'Photographs,' Gerry said eagerly as the brightly coloured packet fell to the floor. 'It's her holiday snaps. Let's have a shufti.'

Wesley picked the packet up from the floor and opened it. He flicked through the pile of photographs – about twelve in all – and handed them to the DCI.

'What are they? Is Ian Rowe on them?' Gerry asked as he fumbled with the packet.

'See for yourself. It doesn't really make much sense.'

Gerry examined them, a puzzled frown on his face. Then he handed them back to Wesley. 'Hardly beautiful views, are they? And these ones at the back look old. They're black and white. Who are the people, do you think?'

Wesley took another look. Most of the pictures featured groups of people posed, smiling for the camera, trowels and mattocks in hand, wearing shorts and sun hats, standing in front of deep trenches.

'It's an archaeological dig. Or rather several different ones by the look of it.'

'I guessed that much,' said Gerry. 'But what does it mean? Why has Nadia kept them in her locker? Does

169

she know those people? By the age of the photos, I'd imagine quite a lot of them are drawing their pensions by now.'

Wesley continued to examine the images, puzzled. 'I'd like to show them to Neil,' he said after a few moments. 'He might recognise some of the people and the locations. Or he might be able to point us in the direction of someone who does.'

Wesley put the photographs in his pocket, locked Nadia Lucas's locker and returned the key to her desk.

Professor Demancour was waiting for them in his room. 'Well, gentlemen, did you find anything that might help to find Nadia?'

Wesley showed him the photographs but he shook his head. He had never seen them before in his life. His only comment was that he didn't think the landscape and buildings looked French. In fact the countryside in the background reminded him very much of Devon. Wesley was inclined to agree but he said nothing.

After taking their leave, Gerry Heffernan touched Wesley's arm as they walked to the car. 'I'm going to ring this number,' he said in a stage whisper, pulling the pink card out of his pocket.

Wesley raised his eyebrows. 'As long as it's in the line of duty.'

Gerry Heffernan stood there in the university car park with his mobile phone pressed to his ear. He turned away from Wesley as though he didn't want to be overheard but Wesley could make out every word.

With a lot of umming and erring, Gerry made an appointment with Chantalle de Rose, giver of French lessons. For a split second Wesley experienced a moment of doubt – what if Chantalle was really a language teacher and Demancour had her business card because she was a fellow member of the French expat community? But one look at Gerry's face as he turned round told him his first instincts had been right.

'She said to go round at four. Asked me if I wanted to book anything special. Any ideas what she meant by that?'

Wesley tried to suppress a smile. 'Your guess is as good as mine. Want me to come and hold your hand?'

'I think you better had,' Gerry said as he began to make for the car.

DC Nick Tarnaby was starting to think that transferring to CID had been a bit of a mistake. He didn't like Gerry Heffernan with his putdowns and wisecracks and he wasn't that keen on Inspector Peterson either – the black man was too posh and Nick had the impression he was looking down on him. But then he felt that about a lot of people.

He had been trawling through CCTV tapes looking for the car belonging to the man who called on Caroline Tay asking for Nadia. The fact that he had such a mundane car made the job more difficult, of course, but at least it didn't demand too much effort.

He had been at it an hour when he spotted a dark-coloured Vauxhall Vectra drawing up and parking outside the bank on a single yellow line. And the man who climbed out fitted the description of Caroline Tay's visitor.

Nick smiled to himself. The registration number was easy to make out and he wrote it down on his note pad before returning to his desk and accessing the DVLC computer system. Bingo. There it was. Name and address of registered owner.

Mr Forsyte Wiley, whoever he was, had a few questions to answer.

*

Gerry kept looking at his watch and Wesley thought he seemed a little nervous.

'So how do you want to play it?' Wesley asked as they climbed the stairs to the CID office.

'How do you mean, Wes?'

'Well, do you want to tell her you're a policeman right away or do you want her to think you're a punter first?' Gerry was looking so terrified that he was finding it hard to keep a straight face. 'How far do you want to go?'

When he saw the look of horror on his boss's face, he couldn't keep up the pretence any longer. His lips turned upwards in a grin.

'Oh, very funny, Wesley. You're coming in with me. We don't want her making allegations of the police wanting something for nothing, do we? And it's no laughing matter: it happened to someone I knew in Morbay. Sergeant in the vice squad, he was and ...'

Wesley didn't really have time to listen to the boss's reminiscences. And besides, he wanted to go over what they had so far. As they swept into the office, he shouted over to Rachel who had just picked up her phone to make a call.

'Anything come in while we've been out?'

Rachel stood up. 'I was just about to ring the lab to see if they've got a match on that hair I took from Nadia Lucas's place. Mind you, it looks as if Anya could be our victim, don't you think?'

Wesley said nothing. He was keeping an open mind. He gave Rachel an encouraging smile before following Gerry into his office.

'Right, Wes, shut the door. What have we got so far?'

Wesley did as he was told and sat himself down. It was two thirty. Only an hour and a half to go before Gerry's encounter with Morbay's wild side. But if Wesley was any judge of traffic conditions in the holiday season,

172

they'd have to set off soon if they were to be on time for the appointment.

'The unidentified woman in Grandal Field was deliberately set on fire, so our killer must be a sadistic bastard. And then Ian Rowe was murdered and set on fire in Jack Plesance's holiday cottage. Is there a connection?'

'We can't establish one until we've got a positive ID on the first victim,' Gerry said with a sigh.

'There is one common denominator though. The Pure Sons of the West. We need to talk to Chas Ventisard and Jem Burrows again – and any more of their cronies we can round up.'

'What about Nadia Lucas? Any chance she could be the woman in the field?'

Gerry Heffernan picked up a pen and twirled it round in his fingers. 'The timings fit, I suppose, but my money's still on Anya.'

Wesley took the photographs they'd found in Nadia's locker out of his pocket and placed them on the table in front of him. 'I'm going to show these to Neil. He might recognise some of the faces and places.'

But Gerry wasn't paying attention. 'If Demancour is acquainted with one or more of Morbay's working girls then that gives us a tentative connection with Nadia too.' He pursed his lips, a picture of frustration 'It's all ifs and buts, Wes. Nothing I feel I can get my teeth into yet.'

Wesley saw Gerry pat his stomach. They'd had lunch early, just a sandwich on the move, and at that moment he looked as though he'd like to get his teeth into a good dinner.

There was a knock on the door, more a scrabbling than a bold tap. Gerry shouted, 'Come in,' and Nick Tarnaby shuffled over the threshold. He was holding a sheet of paper and his normally blank face looked unusually animated.

'I've think I've got a name for that person who called at Nadia Lucas's house in Neston, sir.' He said no more but hovered there expectantly.

'Well, aren't you going to let us in on the secret,' Gerry snapped.

'His name's Forsyte Wiley.'

Wesley caught the DCI's eye. 'Have you found out anything about him?'

'I Googled him.' Nick Tarnaby looked pleased with himself. Almost preening.

'And?'

'He's a private detective. He's just set up in Neston. Works on his own and advertises in the Yellow Pages.'

'The big time, eh,' Gerry chipped in. 'You've rung him, I take it? You've asked why he was looking for Nadia?'

Nick Tarnaby's face turned red. That was answer enough for Wesley. 'Ask Sergeant Tracey to do it, will you?' He made no effort to keep the impatience out of his voice. If Rachel dealt with it he was sure it would save time in the long run.

Once Nick had scurried out of the office like a frightened animal to relay the inspector's instructions to DS Tracey, both men realised that, if they wanted to be sure of being punctual for their appointment with Chantalle de Rose, it was time to go.

'The things I do in the course of duty,' Gerry mumbled to nobody in particular as he marched out, a determined expression on his face.

By the time they reached Chantalle's front door, any misgivings Gerry Heffernan might have felt about his deception had disappeared. He knew he might be

174

following the wrong trail altogether but he and Wesley wanted to know more about Yves Demancour, especially his dark side, if he had one. And Nadia had mentioned Yves' 'dirty little secret' in one of her e-mails to Rowe.

The house was in one of Morbay's seedier areas: not a red-light district as such but pretty close to it. Here large Victorian houses had been converted for multiple occupancy and their warren of flats and bedsits was filled with students and benefit claimants. The stucco on the house fronts crumbled, the paintwork flaked and the wheelie bins overflowed.

Chantalle was easy to find. A sign by the row of door-bells told them she was on the top floor. 'You'd be too knackered to do much by the time you got up there,' Gerry observed as he huffed and puffed up the narrow staircase.

'You should really get more exercise, Gerry,' Wesley replied.

'Don't you start. Joyce is always going on about it. Wants me to start swimming, of all things.'

Before Wesley could comment they'd reached the summit. The door to Chantalle's flat stood slightly ajar. Gerry put out a hand and pushed at it tentatively. It swung open to reveal a shabby interior, undecorated since the days when brown paint and large orange flowers were first in fashion.

He called out an experimental hello and a female voice responded with an unenthusiastic 'Come in'. The accent, Wesley thought, sounded foreign but probably not French.

As they entered the flat, Wesley's eyes began to adjust to the dim light – the thin floral curtains were closed. But he could see the woman sprawled across a large bed with a grubby red satin cover.

Wesley saw her eyes widen in alarm. 'Not two of you. I do not do two at once.'

'It's OK, love. Police,' Gerry said as they held out their warrant cards. 'Nothing to worry about. We'd just like a quick word, that's all. We won't keep you long.'

From the expression on the woman's thin, pinched face, Gerry's words did nothing to reassure her. In her world police were bad news. 'I don't know nothing. Why don't you piss off and leave me alone?'

The foreign accent had suddenly disappeared and they realised that Chantalle de Rose was definitely local. Gerry wasn't going to be deterred from his goal. He'd come across many Chantalles in the course of his career, most of them sad and drug-addicted, and he imagined this one was no different. 'We were wondering if you know a girl called Anya,' he began. 'She's in the same line of business as you. Has a friend called Yelena. They came over recently from Lithuania.'

Chantalle snorted in disgust. 'Bloody foreign girls, coming over here and taking our trade.'

'That's the free market for you,' said Wesley catching his boss's eye. 'What can you tell us about these foreign girls who are brought over? Do you know where they work?'

'God knows.' She lit a cigarette and took a long drag. Smoking in the workplace was banned but this obviously didn't bother Chantalle. 'Their pimps bring 'em over and keep 'em in some big building, so I've heard. Never let 'em out. They don't have nothing to do with the likes of me.'

Gerry coughed a little, wafting away the smoke with his hand. 'What do they say on the streets, love? Got any names for the pimps?'

She looked wary. 'I don't know and I'd never ask. I've heard they're vicious bastards. If a girl escapes and they find her, she doesn't survive for long.'

176

Wesley thought of Pam's words – *pour encourager les autres* – to encourage the others. They suddenly took on a sinister meaning. 'So you don't know where we can find this girl Anya?'

She shook her head. It had been a long shot and, if it hadn't been for the burned woman in the field, it was something they'd normally have left to the vice squad.

But Wesley had another question to ask. 'Do you know a man called Yves Demancour? He's a professor at the university.'

She suddenly looked wary. 'Yeah. I do as a matter of fact.'

'Any trouble?' Gerry asked.

There was a short pause. 'Nah.'

'Never?'

Her face clouded, as though she was reliving an uncomfortable memory.

'What is it?' Wesley said quietly.

The woman hesitated for a few seconds before answering. 'He was fine, no trouble but . . .'

'But what?'

She took a deep breath. 'I burned myself quite badly on the stove about three weeks ago. Had to go to A and E with it.' She rolled back her sleeve to expose a patch of shiny flesh on her left forearm, mottled and raw looking. 'It was really odd. He'd been quite normal but as soon as he saw it he seemed to get all excited. Then he wanted me to—'

'To what?' Gerry said, impatient.

Chantalle looked from one man to the other. 'He wanted me to scream. He wanted me to pretend I was caught in a fire . . . that I was burning. He watched me for a bit, getting all twitchy, then he goes and pretends to rescue me then he . . . well, he does the business if you know what I mean.' She frowned. It was clear the incident had disturbed her but now professional bravado took over. 'He paid me extra, mind,' she said defiantly.

'Has he asked you to do it again?'

She shook her head. 'I've not seen him since.' An uneasy look flitted across her face, there for a second then gone.

'Do you know whether he visits any other girls?' Wesley asked. 'The ones from Lithuania for example?' Perhaps, he thought Demancour had looked for someone other than Chantalle ... someone who'd take his fantasies a step further. Perhaps he'd met her in Grandal Field.

She shook her head. 'I don't know. It's not the sort of thing you ask. I'm not his bleeding wife, am I?'

Wesley's eyes met Gerry's but they didn't say a word.

Then she looked Wesley in the eye and smiled. He noticed that her teeth were stained with nicotine. 'Sure I can't do anything for the boys in blue? I must say you're gentlemen ... not like those sods from Vice.'

As they made a swift retreat, Wesley saw that Gerry Heffernan had a grin on his face. 'What do you make of that, eh, Wes?'

'I think it's worth checking out Professor Demancour a bit more thoroughly,' Wesley replied, deadly serious.

They said little on the journey back, both of them impatient to discover whether Demancour's fantasies had become reality in Grandal Field.

The first mention I found of Urien de Norton was in Stephen de Grendalle's will of 1232 in which he refers to Urien as 'my cousin'. He leaves Urien his share of a cog, the Saint Magdalen, *which plied between Tradmouth and Bordeaux.*

The bulk of Stephen's estate was left to the Morre Abbey, on condition the monks there pray for his immortal soul and for the forgiveness of his many and grievous sins. There was also a generous bequest to the Sisters of Stokeworthy Priory. There is no mention of Jeanne, which suggests that she was dead by the time he drew up the will. And I can't help wondering whether one of the sins mentioned in this will was her murder.

(From papers found in the possession of Professor Yves Demancour)

The small town of Neston wasn't home to many private detectives. Most residents of Neston who were in need of that sort of thing usually ventured into the nearby large seaside resort of Morbay where the choice was better and the surroundings more anonymous.

Rachel listened carefully to Forsyte Wiley's account of how, up till four months ago, he had been a member of this fraternity of Morbay sleuths. But, after a falling-out with his business partner, he had made the decision to set up on his own in a shabby office with woodchip walls and a garish carpet above a wholefood shop off Neston's main high street. So far business wasn't brilliant but the current fashion for divorce ensured that things ticked over nicely.

When Nadia Lucas had turned up unexpectedly in his office with an intriguing proposition, he'd thought all his birthdays had come at once. It wasn't the money, he claimed, but the fact that the task she set him was a challenge. It was a chance to do some real detective work for a change instead of recording the activities of unfaithful spouses. Something to get his brain working again.

As Rachel sat next to DC Paul Johnson, sipping tea, she watched the private detective, fascinated. She hadn't come across many private eyes outside the pages of detective novels and this one certainly didn't fit any of her preconceived ideas. Although he wore a wedding ring, he had an uncared-for look. His suit needed a good clean and his hair needed a wash. In some ways his appearance reminded her of what DCI Heffernan had been like before he had started seeing his lady friend, Joyce, and she wondered whether Wiley, like the boss, was a widower.

'So when did Ms Lucas visit you, Mr Wiley?'

'Must have been about six weeks back,' the man said. Rather than a world-weary gumshoe drawl, he had a homely Devon accent. 'She turned up at the office and said she wanted me to find out the truth about what happened to her mother.'

'And did you?'

Wiley nodded. 'I found out all right. Not that it was much help.'

Rachel caught Paul's eye. 'How do you mean?'

180

'It was all in the papers at the time. I'll show you.' He stood up, walked over to a large metal filing cabinet and after a few moments of fumbling, took out a cardboard folder. 'I had to go down to the *Tradmouth Echo* archives to get this lot,' he said as though he was recounting some tale of derring-do in some exotic and dangerous location.

He placed the folder on the desk in front of Rachel and she opened it. Inside were several photocopied newspaper cuttings which she studied before handing them to Paul. They were all reports of the same event, some dated soon after it happened, others later, after the inquest.

In September 1983 a car belonging to an archaeologist called Dr Wendy Haskel was found at the beach car park at Littlebury, unlocked and obviously abandoned. A note was found back at her house saying she was distressed about the death of her colleague, Dr Maggie March, and that she'd decided to end it all. Her body was never found but the currents are treacherous in that particular part of the coast so the coastguard wasn't particularly surprised.

'So this Wendy Haskel was Nadia's mother?' asked Rachel.

'That's right. She'd kept her maiden name after she married Nadia's father.'

Rachel read on. Wendy Haskel had been working on a dig in Queenswear and the woman in charge of the excavation, Maggie March, had died in a car accident the day before Wendy's disappearance. The two women must have been close, Rachel thought, for the death, however shocking, to have had that effect on Wendy. Or perhaps it had just been the thing that tipped her over the edge. The last straw.

Rachel looked up at Wiley. 'This all seems pretty

straightforward. She even left a note. Why did Nadia Lucas want you to investigate?'

Wiley shrugged. 'To tell you the truth I don't really know. She told me she thought there'd been some sort of cover-up. She said she suspected that her mother had been murdered ... or maybe even that she was still alive.'

'Any evidence of that?'

'Not that I could see, no.'

'Is her father around?'

'He died just over two years ago. Cancer. He'd brought Nadia up. It seems he accepted the Coroner's suicide verdict. He'd been living apart from Nadia's mother for a couple of years and he had custody of their daughter, which struck me as a bit odd. Nadia was only four when her mother died.' Wiley frowned. 'Who knows, perhaps Wendy Haskel couldn't cope with motherhood.'

'Could she have had post-natal depression?' Paul Johnson piped up helpfully.

'Possibly. We'll be charitable, eh.'

'Well some kind of depression would certainly explain her suicide,' said Rachel. She flicked through the cuttings again. 'To be honest, Mr Wiley, I don't see much here to contradict the inquest's verdict. Did you find out any more?'

'Not really. I found the address where Wendy was living when she disappeared but when I called round there was no reply.'

'Why did you call at Nadia's address?'

The man's face reddened. 'I wanted to bring her up to date. I happened to be passing and ...'

'And she hadn't paid you?'

'Well, er ... yes. That as well. A couple of weeks ago she stopped answering her phone and ... Well, I thought a personal visit ... Then her housemate said she'd gone and disappeared.' He took a deep breath. 'Yes, I admit I was worried that I wouldn't get paid for the work I'd done. In my position I can't afford to take charity cases.'

'And what is your position, Mr Wiley?' Rachel asked, giving the man an enquiring smile.

'My wife has MS. I look after her. Like I said, I can't afford to work for free.'

'I'm sorry,' said Rachel, and meant it. Her mother had a friend with MS so she knew the implications.

Wiley frowned as though he'd just remembered something. 'There was one thing that struck me as a bit odd,' he said, stroking his chin. 'Nadia said that her father destroyed some papers shortly before he died. Nadia didn't know what was in them but she said they looked like letters.'

'I don't suppose you've spoken to the people Wendy Haskel was working with before her death?' Paul asked. Rachel looked at him approvingly. It was a good question.

'Tracking them down would have been my next move,' Wiley said sadly. 'But, as I said, I can't afford to work for nothing.'

'And these letters her father destroyed ... did she get the impression they were important?'

'Oh, yes,' Forsyte Wiley said, sinking back in his seat. 'In fact she said she'd only just discovered one she thought her father must have missed. She found it stuffed underneath some old photographs in a box she'd taken from the family home when she was clearing out after her father's death. She'd never looked through them before ... you know how it is – you always intend to sort them out but never get round to it.'

Rachel sat forward. 'So what was in the letter?'

'Sorry, don't know. She never showed me the

contents. She just said that when she'd read it, she realised the implications and she had to find out the truth.'

'So this letter was important?'

'Oh, yes. She thought it could be the key to the whole thing.'

'Found anything?'

Neil looked up from his lowly position down in trench four and for a moment he couldn't see who was speaking because the figure was standing against the sun. He shielded his eyes and saw that Jon Bright was looking down at him.

Neil climbed out of the trench and wiped his soil-stained hands on his combat trousers. 'Plenty,' he replied in answer to the developer's enquiry. 'It's a good site. As you can see, we're uncovering some nice foundations. We'll soon have the entire layout of the manor house.'

'What about the ...?' Bright nodded towards the corner of the field still cordoned off with crime scene tape.

'We'll do that last. The Forensic people say they might need to do further examinations.'

Neil saw Bright fidgeting with his mobile phone and, by the expression on the developer's face, he could tell that the ins and outs of the manorial complex didn't really interest him. Not like money.

'I can give you a guided tour if you like,' Neil said innocently.

Bright took a deep, calming breath and Neil knew he was exercising iron self-control. He wanted to shout, to tell them to get on with it so that he could get the earth movers in and rip up the entire field, archaeology and all. He wanted to get his houses built so he could get

184

money in the bank. But Neil had a different agenda.

'I was thinking that when we've finished we could organise an exhibition, either in Tradmouth or Queenswear. The curator of Tradmouth Museum has already expressed an interest and—'

'I'll leave all that to you, Dr Watson. All I'm interested in is when my people can start work.'

Neil made a great show of considering the question. Then he looked at the developer and gave him what he knew was a maddening smile. 'How long's a piece of string? We don't know how long we'll be until we know exactly what's down there. It's always possible that there's something even earlier underneath the manor house. An important Iron Age site, for instance,' he added, enjoying the look of suppressed fury on Bright's face.

But before Bright could say anything his mobile phone rang. As he took the call his face clouded with worry.

'Call the police,' he barked. 'They've gone too far this time.' He pressed the button to end the call and swore under his breath.

'Problems?' Neil asked innocently.

Bright was breathing hard and Neil could tell that the call he'd just taken had really shaken him. 'Those bloody morons ... the Pure Sons or whatever they call themselves. They've only gone and set fire to our summerhouse.'

'That's bad,' said Neil with what sounded like sympathy.

'I'd better get home. Sheryl's in a terrible state. She was in the summer house and she'd just gone inside to make herself a drink when she saw the flames – some kind of fire bomb. Then she found a note pushed through the front door.'

Neil said nothing. As he watched Bright hurry back to

his car he harboured the uncharitable thought that at least the Pure Sons of the West had stopped Jon Bright breathing down his neck.

Gerry Heffernan had been impatient to return to the incident room to see whether anything new had come in. But Wesley had other ideas. While they happened to be in Morbay, he said, they might as well pop into the university again and have a word with Yves Demancour, just to get his side of the story. After all, he said, a woman being burned to death in a field and a man who got sexual thrills out of watching a woman pretending to be caught in a fire seemed too much of a coincidence to ignore. And besides, a visit to the professor now would save them a journey in the future – the queue for the car ferry was a nightmare this time of year.

The professor looked surprised to see them when they ran him to ground in his office again.

Wesley watched as Gerry produced Chantalle's pink card from his jacket pocket and threw it down on the desk. 'We've been to have a chat with a friend of yours,' he said. 'Chantalle. She told us all about your ... er ... tastes.'

'I don't know what you mean.'

'You asked her to pretend she was caught in a fire.' Wesley spoke quietly, watching Demancour's face.

The professor slumped in his chair, eyes lowered and his face turning a rich shade of scarlet. 'She had no right,' he muttered. 'These things, they are private.'

'I don't think prostitutes are bound to confidentiality like doctors and priests,' said Wesley. 'I can't help wondering if there's some connection between your preferences and the death of the woman in Grandal Field – not forgetting the death of Ian Rowe, who was a friend of your assistant, Nadia.' He paused for a moment to let

186

the words sink in. 'And you mentioned your interest in the wife of Stephen de Grendalle. Grandal Field is the site of the de Grendalle manor house. There are too many coincidences here, professor. Do you see that?'

Demancour nodded. 'And yet I am completely innocent,' he said quietly. 'Yes, I have certain needs but I would never ...'

Gerry looked as though he was about to say something but Wesley shot him a warning look. With any luck, if they left enough silence Demancour would feel the urge to fill it. Wesley's instincts told him that the man needed to unburden himself to someone. And he wanted that someone to be himself.

'I would never harm ... But I need to imagine ...'

'Go on,' Wesley prompted gently. 'Why don't you tell me about it?'

Demancour shook his head. 'I do not know why ...'

'I think you do,' Wesley whispered.

There was a long silence and Wesley could tell that Gerry was longing to ask some question or make some remark. But he managed to contain himself and eventually Demancour spoke. 'It is something I never discuss. Something I would tell no one.'

'You saw someone die in a fire, didn't you?' Wesley asked. It was a pure guess but when Demancour looked at him, his eyes wide with disbelief, he knew he'd struck lucky.

'You know?'

'Who was it?' Wesley pressed harder now he knew he was on the right track.

'It was my sister, Claudette. I was eight and she was four years older. We were playing with matches and her dress caught alight. I tried to help but ... I watched her die. When I close my eyes I can see ...'

To Wesley's dismay, the professor began to cry: loud,

body-shaking sobs. Wesley and Gerry stood watching him, uncertain what to say.

'When Chantalle played the role . . . When I watch her . . . I cannot explain it. It is like Claudette is there again with me. I try to put the fire out. I think one day I will put it out . . . . In my dreams – in my fantasy – I save her and everything is right again. I can't expect you to understand . . .'

He lapsed into deep, primitive sobs while Wesley looked on, unsure what to say. Then, when the sobs had subsided a little, he asked the question he'd been longing to ask. 'Where were you on the night that woman was burned to death in Grandal Field?'

He listened carefully for the answer, knowing that Demancour was probably too distressed to think up a lie.

'I was at home. You must believe me. I swear to you I had nothing to do with this horror.'

'Any witnesses?'

Demancour wiped his face with a pristine handkerchief and shook his head.

'Thank you. We'll be in touch,' said Wesley as they stood up to leave.

'Believe him?' asked Gerry once they were out of earshot.

'No idea,' was Wesley's reply.

'It was a fire bomb all right. A Molotov cocktail,' Paul Johnson said to Rachel with the confidence of an expert. 'Just put some petrol into a bottle, stuff a rag in the top, light the thing and chuck it in. The culprit could have done the deed and run in seconds.'

Rachel wasn't sufficiently well versed on the subject of home-made explosives to know whether Paul was right. But she'd never known him boast or exaggerate so she guessed that his conclusion was probably accurate.

They had been called to the Brights' place as soon as they'd returned from their chat with Forsyte Wiley in Neston. It was an emergency, they were told. And, as Rachel knew the background to the case – the threats Sheryl Bright had received from the Pure Sons of the West – she had been the one to answer the call.

She sat opposite Sheryl Bright in her living room while Paul went outside to inspect the charred remains of the summer house. This time Sheryl had had the presence of mind to keep the note that she'd found pushed through her front door. At least this was something, Rachel thought. But, looking at the sheet of A4 paper with the words and letters cut out crudely from one or more newspapers, she didn't think it would be much help. These days villains knew better than to oblige the police by leaving fingerprints. It was a shame but it was a fact of life.

She gave Sheryl a sympathetic smile. Having provided the woman with two cups of restorative tea already it was time to get down to business. 'Can you tell me exactly what happened, Sheryl? Take your time.'

Sheryl cleared her throat. 'I was in the summer house preparing a canvas. Then I came inside to make myself a drink and while I was filling the kettle I heard this whoosh sound. It seemed to come from outside so I went out to see what it was. I saw the summer house on fire and I just froze. I mean, I'd been in there a few minutes earlier. I could have been . . .' She put her hand to her mouth as though she'd just realised the potential horror of the situation.

'Go on,' Rachel prompted gently.

'I was in shock. I couldn't stop shaking. But I managed to call the fire brigade. When they put the fire out they told me they'd found glass on the floor and traces of accelerant. They said they thought it looked like

a Molotov cocktail – petrol in a bottle, that sort of thing.'
She shuddered.

'Anything else you can tell me? You didn't see anyone hanging around?'

Sheryl took a deep breath and shook her head. 'As soon as I'd called the fire brigade I ran to the front door. I wanted to see if there was anybody about but . . .'

'That was a bit dangerous,' said Rachel with a concerned frown. 'The attacker could have still been hanging around.'

'To be honest that didn't occur to me. I was thinking of a neighbour or a passer by . . . someone to help.'

Rachel nodded. Paul, she knew, had already investigated the possibility that a neighbour had seen something but had drawn a blank. The nearest houses were about a hundred yards away, well screened by trees and bushes, and there'd been nobody at home.

'When did you spot the note?'

'As soon as I went into the hall I saw it lying there on the floor. I read it and I knew . . .'

Rachel's eyes were drawn to the note, now protected by a plastic evidence bag.

'This will teach you to destroy our countryside,' it said. 'The Pure Sons of the West always keep their promises. Those who kill our communities deserve to die.'

The words sent a shiver through Rachel's body and she put a comforting hand on Sheryl's arm. 'Don't worry. They can't hope to get away with this. They can't claim it's just a warning any longer. Someone could have been killed.'

Sheryl looked up. 'Any sign of my husband yet? I called him half an hour ago. He said he'd come right over.'

'The traffic's bad at this time of the year. Holiday season,' Rachel said smoothly, sneaking a look at her watch. Jon Bright was certainly taking his time.

Suddenly she heard the sound of a key turning in the front door lock. Sheryl sat up straight, like an animal who'd just caught the scent of a predator. 'That'll be Jon,' she said. She didn't attempt to move but Rachel stood up to greet the man who was the target of the Pure Sons of the West's wrath.

Bright appeared in the doorway looking more angry than worried.

'What's been going on?' he said. 'What have those bastards been up to now?'

When Rachel told him, she could sense that he was reining in his temper – that if he let go of his emotions, his fury would explode.

'I want police protection for my wife,' he said through gritted teeth.

Rachel noticed that his hands were clenched, as though he were about to punch someone. So she didn't feel inclined to argue that, with two murders on their hands already, resources were a bit stretched.

But Sheryl saved her from this embarrassing admission.

'There's no way I'm going to have some policeman watching my every move,' she said angrily. 'Now they've had a go they won't try again. Anyway, why should we give in to them? Why should we be intimidated? I'll be quite safe now, I know I will. They've made their point.'

Rachel only hoped she was right.

It was almost dusk and Wesley knew that Pam wouldn't be expecting him home till well after the children had been put to bed.

Rachel had reported back from the Brights'. If their claims that they had nothing to do with the death of Ian

Rowe were to be believed, it looked as if the Pure Sons of the West had made their boldest move yet. However, the whereabouts of all the Sons they knew about had been checked and, so far, it looked as if they all had alibis. But alibis, Rachel thought, can be fragile things – if they don't have solid foundations, a little digging can make them collapse into dust.

In Rachel's opinion, Mrs Bright was bearing up well and it was her husband who was panicking for the pair of them. She'd observed that this wasn't unusual. The female of the species can often be stronger and more rational than the male. In the interests of good office relations, Wesley hadn't cared to contradict her.

He heard a voice behind him. 'You get off home, Wes. Busy day tomorrow.'

He turned and saw Gerry Heffernan behind him, arms stretching to the ceiling and mouth wide open in a yawn that wouldn't have shamed a gorilla.

'Tired, Gerry?'

The answer was a grunt. 'I'm getting off home myself and see if our Rosie has anything to report from the hostel in Neston – she did a stint there today and there's a note from Social Services that Yelena's been moved there from Morbay.'

'As long as the bastards who brought Yelena and Anya here don't find out where she is.' Wesley immediately regretted his words. Gerry was probably worried enough about Rosie's safety as it was.

Gerry didn't answer. It was possible that Yelena's friend had died horribly in Grandal Field and, if these men could do something like that, they were dangerous, capable of anything. He knew that Gerry found it hard to come to terms with the possibility of his daughter coming into contact with such things, however remote, and Wesley could hardly blame him.

Wesley walked home, the day's events running through his head, playing and replaying like a video. He was glad of the walk up the steep streets. Not only did it keep him fit, it provided him with valuable thinking time.

It was a lovely evening and he passed a few strolling tourists as he walked through the narrow thoroughfares, breathing in the scent of the flowers tumbling from well-kept window boxes. When he reached the top of the hill he turned to look at the town below. The passenger ferry was scuttling across the river, its windows glowing with light, and the fairy lights strung around the Memorial Gardens had just been lit. The pubs and restaurants were coming to life and the yachts bobbed contentedly at anchor on the swelling tide. If he hadn't been a policeman, he would have thought that all was well with the world.

But he knew otherwise. He focused his gaze on the other side of the river. Grandal Field wasn't visible from where he stood, not even in the daylight, and he felt somewhat relieved. But was it the Lithuanian girl, Anya, who'd died there, murdered horribly by one of the men who deceived and used her? Or was it someone else? Someone mistaken for Sheryl Bright perhaps? Or maybe it was the missing Nadia Lucas; the DNA results from the hairs taken from her room hadn't come back yet. He'd get someone to chase them up first thing in the morning.

Rachel and Paul had told him all about their conversation with Forsyte Wiley and the discovery of the letter that had sparked Nadia Lucas's search for the truth behind her mother's death. Rachel had called Caroline Tay to ask if the letter was at the house but Caroline couldn't find it. Perhaps it had been hidden somewhere. Wesley resolved to organise a proper search as soon as he could ... unless Nadia turned up in the meantime.

He turned into his cul de sac and was pleased to see Neil's old yellow Mini parked outside his house. He quickened his pace, taking his house key from his pocket.

When he entered the living room, Pam was sitting with her feet up, a glass of red wine in her hand. Neil looked comfortable in the armchair and his glass was almost empty.

'Have you heard about Jon Bright?' was Neil's first question. 'He had his summer house burned down. It was those Pure Sons of the West. They left a note.'

'I know,' said Wesley.

Neil looked vaguely disappointed, as though he'd been looking forward to breaking the news.

'The Brights reported it. They've been interviewed. So have the Pure Sons of the West. But they all have alibis and they're denying everything.'

Neil raised his eyebrows. 'Well, it can't be the husband because he was with me. Loth as I am to put the bugger in the clear. Think there could be a connection with the body in our field?'

Wesley never believed in lying to old friends. 'We don't know yet. We've not even got an ID on the body. The latest theory is that it was a punishment killing of an Eastern European prostitute.'

Neil wrinkled his nose. 'Wouldn't have thought you got that sort of thing in a place like Queenswear.'

Wesley gave him a rueful smile, pitying his naiveté. 'It's everywhere now. Can't get away from it.' He'd had enough of work and fancied a rapid change of subject. 'How's the dig going?'

'Not bad. How soon can we excavate the crime scene? There's a circular anomaly on the geophysics not too far from the spot where ... I'm sure there's something interesting down there.'

'Have you found out any more about the nineteen eighties dig yet?'

Neil shook his head. 'I'm coming to the conclusion that Dr March had all the notes and records with her when her car went up in flames, which is a shame. We could have done with those records.'

'Mmm.' Wesley thought for a few seconds. 'As a matter of fact Dr Maggie March's name cropped up in one of our investigations.'

Neil sat forward, suddenly interested. 'Really?'

'I told you Ian Rowe knew this girl called Nadia Lucas. She met him while they were both working for Sir Martin Crace.'

'Yeah. Go on,' Neil said, impatient to learn about the March connection.

'Well, it turns out Nadia Lucas is the daughter of Maggie March's second-in-command on the Grandal Farm dig, a Dr Wendy Haskel. Nadia lived with her father, who died a couple of years ago, but recently she's been trying to find out what happened to her mother.'

'Karl Maplin told me she'd killed herself.'

'That was the verdict at the inquest. She left a note and her things were found on the beach at Littlebury but her body was never found. Mind you, it's quite common for bodies to go into the water around that part of the coast and never emerge. According to Gerry it's something to do with the currents.'

'So Maplin's right. She did herself in – no mystery there. Except why she did it.'

'What if the two women were an item?' Pam said after a few moments. 'And Haskel killed herself out of grief when she heard her lesbian lover was dead?'

The two men looked at her, waiting for further pearls of wisdom.

'You need to talk to people who knew them,' she

continued. 'Archaeology's a small world so it shouldn't be too hard to track them down.'

Wesley smiled, feeling rather pleased that Pam's interest in the case, sparked by their little foray into mystery in Carcassonne, was continuing.

'Nadia hired a private detective to find out what really happened to her mother,' he said. 'Maybe he's the man she mentioned in those e-mails she sent to Rowe. But now she's vanished and the only thing we know is that Ian Rowe borrowed her car to drive to the cottage where he met his death. Or she drove him there and abandoned the car for some reason.'

'So let me get this straight,' said Neil. 'You think this Nadia might have killed Ian Rowe?'

Wesley suddenly experienced a feeling of hopelessness. Was Nadia a suspect or a potential victim? Or did she have nothing to do with the case at all? Had she merely gone off somewhere and lent Ian her car while she was away?

Suddenly he remembered that the photographs he had taken from Nadia's locker at the university were in his inside pocket. He took them out and handed them to Neil. 'Have a look through these and see whether you recognise any people and places.'

Pam got up and stood behind Neil's chair so she could see the images for herself but she gave up after a while as they meant nothing to her. Neil, on the other hand, was starting to look rather excited.

'I recognise some of these people. There's Karl Maplin. I mean, he's a lot younger and he's even got hair but it's him all right.' He pushed the photograph in Wesley's direction.

Wesley felt a little cross with himself. Of course it was a much younger Professor Maplin – why hadn't he recognised him? 'Anyone else?'

Neil frowned and studied the photographs in his hand again. 'Yeah. These were taken so long ago it's not easy to tell but I'm sure this is Bill Waites and this one's Chris Drifield. And that woman there, her face is familiar but I can't remember the name. I'm sure I've come across a couple more of them on various digs I've taken part in but I can't say there's anyone here I know well apart from Maplin. He'll be the one to ask. He'll know them all.'

'What about the locations? Anything familiar?'

Neil studied them again and after a while he looked up. There are some I don't recognise but I'm sure these are Grandal Field. The way you can see the river through those trees. Look.'

Wesley leaned over to get a better view. Neil was right. It did look like Grandal Field. He wondered whether any of the group pictures were of the team who carried out the excavations there back in the 1980s. And if so, which picture. He picked up the photographs of the people again. There were several of them – all of different teams. He studied the women in particular, wondering which of them were Maggie March and Wendy Haskel. But speculation was a waste of energy. He needed to speak to Karl Maplin.

'I discovered something rather interesting,' Neil said, interrupting Wesley's thoughts.

'What?'

'You know I told you that the site was connected with the de Grendalle family? Well, apparently there's a legend attached to the place.'

'Go on.'

'A knight went off to the crusades and brought back a bride. Anyway, he found out she was being unfaithful to him so he burned her alive because she'd been a heretic. Then he found out he'd made a mistake and she hadn't

197

been having it away with someone else after all. And he was so remorseful that he gave all his property to Morre Abbey.'

'I heard something similar from Professor Demancour at Morbay University. He and Nadia Lucas were researching the story. Mentioned a woman called Jeanne de Minerve.'

'I think the bloke who told me about it got it from a book of local legends. "The Burning Bride", the chapter was called.'

Wesley said nothing for a while then he looked up, his eyes glowing with excitement. 'So there's an old story about a woman being burned to death on the site and last week a woman was found burned to death in the same place. It can hardly be a coincidence, can it?'

'The killer must know the story,' said Pam. 'He must do; there's no other explanation. This burning bride business has some sort of significance. Maybe the victim was unfaithful to the murderer in some way.'

'I think we've cracked it,' Neil said, pouring himself another glass of wine. 'Mind if I leave the car here tonight?'

'Why not?' Wesley mumbled in reply.

Neil had ended up staying the night on the sofa. After the second bottle had been opened it had seemed rather churlish to chuck him out to walk down into the town and catch the late night ferry across the river.

The two men walked down to the centre of Tradmouth together, leaving Pam to give the children their breakfast. But for once she didn't seem to mind. It was the school holidays and, besides, the story of the burning bride seemed to have captured her imagination. She'd even asked Wesley to keep her up to date with developments.

Neil and Wesley parted on the waterfront and, when Wesley arrived at the CID office, he found that Gerry Heffernan was already there in his glass-fronted lair, sitting frowning at the report he was reading. He stood up when Wesley opened his office door. Something had happened.

'You've missed all the excitement, Wes. We've got a name for our body in Grandal Field.' He paused, as if he was announcing the winner of some film award, keeping his audience in suspense.

'And?'

'The DNA results have just come back. There's a match to the hairs Rachel took from Nadia Lucas's hairbrush.'

Wesley sat down heavily on the chair beside Gerry's desk. Somehow he hadn't expected this. Somehow he'd convinced himself that their dead girl was some unfortunate Eastern European prostitute, a victim of the times and the avaricious nature of man. But Nadia Lucas? What had she done to deserve such a fate?

10

Men have always been fascinated by the idea of lost treasure and, not surprisingly, the legend of the Burning Bride has its own mention of missing gold.

According to the tale, Jeanne brought some Cathar treasure over with her from her native France, but, needless to say, no such treasure has ever been found. Yet who knows, it might still lie beneath the Devon earth somewhere to be discovered by somebody wielding a trowel or a metal detector.

But I digress. It is just a tale, an irrelevance; part of the legend that has built up over the years acquiring additions like a boat acquires barnacles. I must return to the story. It is Jeanne's story that is important to me. It is Jeanne who was the forerunner.

I have found no mention of Jeanne in any records for the year after her arrival as a young bride, apart from the gift given by her husband, Stephen de Grendalle, to Morre Abbey on the occasion of her baptism. But perhaps during that year Urien de Norton was making his plans: his own twisted form of evil was growing like a maggot in his mind.

(From papers found in the possession of Professor Yves Demancour)

Wesley stared at the lab report, turning its implications over in his mind. Nadia Lucas was the victim. Nadia had been trying to discover the truth about her mother's death and now she herself was dead.

Gerry's voice interrupted his thoughts. 'So Ian Rowe must have borrowed her car after her death. How did he get hold of it?'

'Good question. But at least we know he couldn't have killed her. He had the best alibi of all. When Nadia was murdered in Grandal Field, Rowe was pestering me and Pam in Carcassonne.'

Gerry thought for a few moments, his chin resting on his hand. 'If Nadia and Rowe were killed by the same person it looks as if they might have been closer than we thought. He even knew where to find her car and the keys. You say he did a runner from Carcassonne. Maybe it wasn't that letter he received from Crace that made him take off like that. Maybe someone contacted him to say that Nadia was in danger.'

'Who?'

'Well, I don't think it was Nadia's housemate, Caroline Tay. If you ask me, she kept her distance. And it wasn't Forsyte Wiley, the private detective. He didn't even know Rowe.'

Wesley thought for a few moments then he picked up the phone. 'Jack Plesance, the owner of Owl Cottage. He might be able to throw some light on the matter.'

'He's worth a try and we've got to start somewhere.'

Wesley was about to call Plesance's mobile but he stopped and replaced the receiver carefully. 'There's another aspect to this case that we haven't considered yet, Gerry. Neil came round last night.'

'Oh aye,' said Gerry. Wesley could hear the impatience in his voice. He wanted to get on with the investigation, not listen to details of his inspector's social life.

'No, listen. There's a story about that field. A woman was burned alive there at the start of the thirteenth century.'

'Not our problem, Wes.'

Wesley ignored the note of flippancy in his voice and continued. 'Neil's been researching the site. The woman was murdered by her husband because he thought she was unfaithful but she wasn't. She'd once been a Cathar, a heretic, so he burned her alive, Gerry.'

'I've heard of copycat killings but not seven centuries apart. It's a coincidence. Or maybe someone read the old story and thought it would be a good location.'

'Or to make a point. Nadia was unfaithful. Or she betrayed someone.'

'So we're looking for a jealous boyfriend? Which brings us back to Rowe. Let's face it, we don't know that she was involved with anyone else.'

'What about Demancour with his fantasies about watching women being burned alive? They worked closely so who's to say they weren't an item? And he knows the story.'

Wesley sighed. Now it had been put into words, the theory of the historical connection somehow didn't sound quite so convincing. 'It's a start. We can ask everyone who knew her about her love life – someone's bound to know. And I want another word with Forsyte Wiley to see if she mentioned anything about a boyfriend.'

'Or someone who wants to be a boyfriend ... or a girlfriend. From the little we know of Nadia, it seems that Ian Rowe was the only man in her life but there could be someone else in the background.'

Wesley grabbed a piece of paper from Gerry's desk – a memo about crime statistics from Chief Superintendent Nutter that Wesley knew would inevitably be filed in the waste bin. He turned it over and began to write on the back. 'We need to talk to Forsyte Wiley, Jack Plesance, Caroline Tay and Professor Demancour for starters,' he said as he scribbled down the names. Then he looked up at Gerry. 'And we'll pay Sir Martin Crace and his entourage another visit.'

'Mmm. I reckon that PA might know more than she's letting on.'

They hadn't time for a wasted journey so Wesley asked Rachel to arrange another appointment with Sir Martin Crace. And they'd talk to his PA, Eva Liversedge, while they were at it.

But after a while Rachel poked her head round the door and reported that Sir Martin wasn't available to speak to the police until later that afternoon. He was closeted in a meeting with a government minister and they were having lunch together. 'That PA spoke to me as if I was a couple of rungs below the man who unblocked the drains,' she added, bristling with righteous indignation.

Once that was sorted out, Wesley made a short call to Forsyte Wiley, a simple enquiry about whether Nadia had mentioned any names they could follow up. When Wesley told him about the DNA identification he seemed genuinely stunned at the news, and assured him that he'd already told Rachel and Paul everything he knew. His relationship with Nadia had been on a purely business footing. He'd been hired to find out what he could about her mother's death, nothing more. And Nadia had revealed nothing to him about her private life.

Suddenly Wesley remembered something in Rachel's report, something he'd made a mental note of but had forgotten until that moment.

'You told my colleague that you'd traced Wendy Haskel's last known address, Mr Wiley.'

'That's right,' Wiley replied and recited it obligingly.

It was a Tradmouth address, one of the steep streets of small houses leading down to the harbour – somewhere he passed every day on his way to work.

'You also told Sergeant Tracey that you were going to trace the people Wendy Haskel worked with. Do you have any names?'

'Sorry, Inspector, but I didn't get that far.' To Wesley's surprise the man did sound genuinely sorry.

Wesley was about to end the call when he remembered one last question he wanted to ask. 'Did Nadia ever mention the name Ian Rowe?'

The answer was in the negative so Wesley thanked him and considered his next move. Somehow he'd imagined that, now they knew the identity of their victim, things might be more straightforward. But instead he felt more confused.

He looked up and saw Gerry Heffernan's bulky form bearing down on him. 'Any luck with our private eye?'

Wesley shook his head. 'I don't think he knows anything. He was shocked to hear about her death but that's only to be expected.'

Gerry grunted something Wesley couldn't quite make out. 'I've just asked Lee Parsons to trace her next of kin but it's not going to be an easy job. Mum topped herself, dad died and no brothers or sisters. Sad, eh.'

Wesley smiled. Gerry was showing his soft side.

'What about her phone records?'

'Not much luck there. There were a few calls to Ian Rowe in France. Several to and from Forsyte Wiley. A couple to Caroline Tay and a few to the university. And a pay-as-you-go number called her a couple of times in the days before her death and at four o'clock on the day itself.'

'Her killer arranging a meeting?'

'Possibly. But like I said, it's untraceable and it's also been switched off.'

Gerry looked up at the clock on his wall, always kept ten minutes fast so that he wouldn't be late for meetings with the Chief Superintendent. 'We'll go to Neston and have another word with Caroline Tay. Nadia's things'll need searching through and all. We need to find that letter Forsyte Wiley mentioned, the one she found with those old photos. He reckoned that's what triggered Nadia's search so it must be important.' He looked through his office window, scanning the faces in the CID office outside. 'We'll take Trish.'

Wesley nodded. He agreed that it would help if a woman went through Nadia's most intimate things and Trish could be trusted to sort the important from the irrelevant. He suddenly remembered something. 'When we first called round, Caroline Tay mentioned a break-in.' It was something he'd forgotten until that moment. Something routine that was dealt with by uniform. A crime number and an insurance claim.

Gerry caught on quickly. 'You think the break-in was connected with Nadia's murder? Her killer was searching for something?'

'Well, whoever broke in hasn't tried again so perhaps they found what they were looking for. That letter maybe?'

'Or maybe it was just a common or garden break-in. I suggest we get round there now and find out.' Gerry opened the office door and shouted over to Rachel. 'Rach. Get on to the university. If Caroline Tay's at work tell her we want to meet her back at her house a.s.a.p. Say it's urgent but don't tell her about Nadia yet. We'll break the sad news.'

Wesley saw Rachel pick up the phone and he turned to Gerry. 'When we've seen Caroline Tay there's someone else I want to visit. I think one of my old tutors might be able to help identify some of the people and places in

205

those pictures we found in Nadia's locker. According to Neil, there's not much he doesn't know about the archaeological fraternity in these parts.'

'You think there's a link with that old story Neil told you?' Gerry sounded sceptical.

'Nadia's mother was an archaeologist. Nadia was trying to find out the truth about what happened to her. Incidentally, Forsyte Wiley discovered Wendy Haskel's last known address. It's a long shot but there might be a neighbour there who remembers her.'

Gerry looked him in the eye. 'You reckon this mother's still alive and doesn't want to be found, do you?'

'No, and even if she was, surely she wouldn't kill her own daughter.'

'Stranger things have happened,' Gerry replied solemnly.

Wesley said nothing. It wasn't a possibility he wanted to consider.

Jem Burrows had watched the archaeologists for a full hour but he was certain they hadn't seen him. Somehow he had expected Bright to be there, causing the diggers grief. But it seemed he was leaving them to it.

He had thought that watching an archaeological dig would be interesting, like that programme on the telly where they had just three days to unearth all sorts of exciting treasures. But it looked quite boring really, painstaking and tedious, even though the footprint of a building was starting to emerge from the rich red earth.

Those low stone walls had been there for centuries, lying beneath the ground. And now they'd be destroyed by the foundations of Bright's nasty little boxes. Then those boxes would be filled with incomers and second-home owners.

But that wasn't his concern right now. His priority was to find out where Bright was. He needed to keep an eye on Jon Bright.

He took his mobile phone – pay-as-you-go and bought in a false name for cash – from his pocket, wondering whether it would be safe to make the call. He had to be careful, even though the police had checked out his alibi for the summer house fire and found it was rock-solid. He couldn't ruin it now. Not when everything was going so smoothly.

He thought of the burned-out summer house at Bright's place and smiled. Fire really was the best way.

Fire cleansed as well as destroyed.

Caroline Tay looked a little annoyed when Wesley, Gerry and Trish Walton first arrived at her house. She had been dragged away from work, she said, just when she was in the middle of something important. As she opened the door to let them in she eyed them warily, as though she felt outnumbered.

She invited them to sit, perching herself on the edge of an armchair, and Gerry gave Wesley a small nod. It was up to him to begin.

Wesley assumed his most solemn expression. 'I'm very sorry to bring bad news, Ms Tay, but I'm afraid Nadia is dead. She was murdered.'

He let this sink in for a few moments before continuing. 'You have heard about the woman who was burned to death in Queenswear?'

'The one in that field. It was horrible.' Caroline's voice was hoarse, barely audible. 'You don't think that was Nadia? Surely it couldn't be her. I thought it was some gangland thing. Nadia didn't mix with people like that.'

'You told us before that you didn't know much about her,' said Gerry.

207

Caroline frowned as she looked him in the eye. 'I know enough to be sure that she wouldn't get involved with anything violent. She just wasn't that type. She was an academic. She worked for a professor. And as far as I know she had no enemies.' She bit her lip. 'Is it something to do with the man who died in that cottage fire . . . that friend of hers? What was his name?'

'Ian Rowe. We're still pursuing enquiries.'

'What about that man who called here – the one I told you about? Is he—?'

'It turns out he was a private detective she'd hired to find out what happened to her mother,' Wesley answered. 'And we don't think he has anything to do with her death. Did she have any other visitors?'

Caroline shook her head. 'Nadia didn't seem to have many friends. She kept herself to herself.'

'Did she ever mention her mother's disappearance?'

Caroline raised her eyebrows. 'No, she didn't. Nothing like that. She never talked about her family. But then we weren't close. She was just my lodger.'

'Ian Rowe, the man who died, was driving her car. We've been assuming all along that she must have either driven him to the scene herself or met him to hand over the key. But now we know she was dead by then, so have you any idea how he might have got hold of it?'

'She kept her car in a lock-up garage just down the road. Only the lock was broken some time last year. Vandals.'

'So if Rowe knew where the car was and he had the key, he could have taken it without you knowing?'

She thought for a moment. 'She was always scared of losing her keys so she might have left a spare set somewhere. I know someone at work who keeps a spare key taped to her wheel arch. Nadia might have done something like that, I suppose. She never mentioned it to me but she might have told this Ian Rowe where to find it.'

Wesley caught Trish's eye. It seemed as likely an explanation as any. 'We'd like to look at her room. I take it you haven't found that letter my colleague phoned about?'

'No, I would have told you. But I didn't look very thoroughly. I mean she could have hidden it somewhere, I suppose.'

'When we first spoke to you, you told us you'd had a break-in. When was that exactly?'

Caroline seemed momentarily confused by the change of subject. 'Oh, er ... it was the day after I last saw Nadia.'

Wesley glanced at Gerry and saw that he was listening intently. The break-in had been reported but there was nothing much in the police files. No damage and apparently nothing much of value taken. But anything that was taken might now have acquired a new significance.

'So remind us,' he said. 'What did the burglar take?'

'I'm not sure ... I couldn't see anything missing. In fact he only went into Nadia's room – that's the only way I knew we'd been broken into. Nadia's room was in a bit of a mess. The drawers and wardrobe were open as though someone was looking for something. I just assumed he'd been disturbed before he could do the rest of the house or ...'

'Have you left the room how you found it?'

She shook her head. 'The mess wasn't that bad. It hadn't been trashed or anything. I just put the things back in the drawers and had a quick tidy round. I didn't want Nadia to come back and find—' She put her hand up to her mouth as though she'd suddenly realised that Nadia would never come back.

'We'll need to send a forensic team over,' said Wesley

gently. 'And take your fingerprints for elimination purposes.'

Caroline suddenly looked frightened. 'You think it was her killer who broke in? You think her killer has been in this house?'

'We don't know that for sure, love,' Gerry chipped in, trying to sound comforting. 'It might just have been kids looking for something to sell on. Like you say, they might have been disturbed.'

'The constable who called said that either I'd left the place unlocked or they'd used a credit card to get in. He asked me who had a key and I told him it was just me and Nadia.' She swallowed hard. 'She took hers with her when she went. I got the locks changed and had a new mortise fitted after he said that. I thought that if Nadia came back and couldn't get in, she'd come and find me at the university and I'd give her the new set.'

'Very wise, love,' said Gerry. 'I'm sure you'll have no more trouble. So you've no idea what might have been taken?'

Caroline thought for a while. 'I think Nadia had a few files in there – research papers, I think – but I don't think they're there now. Whether she left them at the university or whether they were taken by whoever broke in, I don't know.'

'The private detective Nadia saw mentioned a box of old photographs. He said Nadia took it from the family home but she'd only recently got round to looking through it. The letter we were asking about was hidden in the box.'

Caroline frowned. 'Yes, there was a carved wooden box. It looked quite old. She'd put it up in the loft with some stuff she'd taken from her dad's house and she went up there a few weeks ago and brought it down. I think it was in her room. I remember her saying it was quite pretty and she wondered if it was worth anything. But she didn't mention finding a letter.'

Trish stood up and gave Caroline a sympathetic smile. 'I'll just have a quick look through Nadia's things,' she said before disappearing upstairs.

Wesley didn't hold out much hope of Trish finding anything significant. If there'd been any clue up there to the killer's identity he would have taken it with him when he searched her room. Because he was as sure as he could be that it had been the killer who'd invaded the privacy of Nadia's room. When he'd killed Nadia, he had probably taken her house keys. Then he'd waited for Caroline to go out before conducting his search. He was glad that Caroline had had the presence of mind to change the locks. He wouldn't have liked to think of her being at the mercy of a killer who could come and go as he pleased.

Caroline stood and walked over to the pine dresser which stood against the far wall of the room. She opened the drawer and pulled out a small book with a tartan cover. A diary or address book.

'There is one thing I forgot to tell you. I found this stuffed down the side of the sofa a few days ago. It's Nadia's. It must have dropped out of her bag.' She handed the book to Wesley and he felt a sudden tingle of excitement. It was possible that the killer hadn't taken everything of interest.

He opened the book and leafed through the pages, aware of Gerry looking over his shoulder. It was half filled with scribbled notes and addresses. To Wesley at that moment it looked like newly discovered treasure. Surely her killer would be mentioned somewhere in this insignificant-looking book. Perhaps this was even what the intruder had been looking for.

'Thank you very much, Ms Tay,' he said trying to

keep the excitement out of his voice. 'Someone will go through this and trace everyone who gets a mention.'

He couldn't resist taking another look, just to see if there were any familiar names in there. And he wasn't disappointed.

They were all there: Ian Rowe's address in Carcassonne and his e-mail address; a number with the name M Crace next to it and, under that, the number of Eva Liversedge's direct line; Yves Demancour's home and work numbers and Forsyte Wiley's office phone. There were other names in the book too, most of them unfamiliar, but they would have to be contacted. Wesley was rather surprised to see Professor Karl Maplin's name amongst them. And there was a scribbled address at the back of the book with no name beside it: an address Wesley had come across before but it took him a few seconds to remember where. It was Wendy Haskel's last known address: the one Forsyte Wiley had discovered for her.

Someone had broken in to look for something and there was always the chance that this book was what they wanted.

At that moment Trish appeared again, walking slowly down the stairs. 'There's nothing much in her room,' she said. 'Just clothes, the usual. If she kept any papers up there, they've gone. No sign of any letters apart from official ones ... and no sign of a carved wooden box containing photographs, come to that.'

'Nicked by our burglar probably,' Gerry said. He had made himself comfortable on the sofa as though he intended to be there for the duration.

But Wesley began to make for the door. There was someone he wanted to see as a matter of urgency. When he reached Caroline Tay's front door he pulled his mobile phone from his pocket and dialled Neil Watson's number.

212

Tackling two problems at once would do wonders for police efficiency.

Gerry Heffernan wore the expression of a child who'd been told that his friend couldn't come out to play, Trish Walton thought as she sat beside him in the patrol car that was driving them back to Tradmouth.

As soon as they'd left Caroline Tay's house Wesley Peterson had driven off, saying something about seeing an archaeologist he knew and taking some of the photographs they'd found in Nadia Lucas's locker at the university with him. Gerry had reminded him not to be too long as they had a meeting with Sir Martin Crace at four that afternoon.

Trish would have liked to meet Sir Martin herself. When she'd seen him on the television talking about the Third World and the tragedy of AIDS in Africa, she'd thought he seemed like a man you could admire – and there weren't many of them about these days. But as she was a lowly detective constable she'd have to deal with more routine matters while her superiors dealt with the great and good.

She felt her arm being nudged gently and turned to face Gerry Heffernan, who now had an earnest frown on his face. 'Tell you what, Trish, we'll call at this Wendy Haskel's last known address in Tradmouth. I'm not expecting to find anyone there who knew her but, you never know, she might have been blessed with nosey neighbours.'

'This was back in the eighties, sir,' Trish said. She had been on many wild goose chases in her time and she suspected this might be another.

'Watch and learn, love. Watch and learn.' He tapped the side of his nose. 'If you can find yourself a pensioner who's lived there for years with too much time on their hands and a taste for gossip, you've cracked it.'

'And what if there's no one like that about?' she said, unable to hide her scepticism.

The chief inspector shrugged his large shoulders and Trish saw his shirt buttons straining dangerously across his stomach. 'They're the forgotten army, love. Loads of them around, only people don't notice. Specially you young people.'

Trish smiled to herself. In a couple of years she'd be hitting thirty and she didn't feel particularly young.

They'd just arrived in the police station car park and DCI Heffernan held the door open for her to get out. She mumbled her embarrassed thanks and they began to walk away from the station towards the centre of the town.

'Nice day,' the boss commented, making conversation. 'I fancied taking the boat out but . . .' He let the sentence trail off and they walked in silence around the side of St Margaret's church, where Trish knew he sang in the choir when work permitted. Once past the church, they climbed a flight of steps and found themselves on the street where Wendy Haskel had lived all those years ago.

The small, colourwashed houses on that steep, narrow little thoroughfare were all slightly different, which gave the street a pleasing and picturesque appearance. That was why Trish had a dreadful feeling that things might have changed since the 1980s. Now these houses would be second homes and holiday lets rather than the homes of the curious elderly. However, she said nothing to the boss. She didn't want to be labelled an incurable pessimist.

Gerry Heffernan didn't waste time. He lifted the anchor-shaped knocker on Wendy Haskel's old front door and banged it down hard several times. Inside the house it must have sounded like thunder, Trish thought.

The door was answered almost immediately by a

youngish woman in shorts with two toddlers clinging to her bare, pale legs.

Trish saw the DCI hold up his warrant card and she did likewise with an encouraging smile on her face to show they weren't intending to arrest the woman on the spot. 'Sorry to bother you, love. Police.'

A short conversation followed during which they learned that the house was now a holiday let but that the elderly couple who kept the key for the landlord lived next door. From Gerry Heffernan's triumphant smile as the door was shut on them, Trish knew he was bathing in the glorious satisfaction of being right.

Luckily the elderly couple were in. In fact it didn't look as if they managed to get out much. The small, bird-like woman who introduced herself as Mrs Mabel Cleary walked with the aid of a zimmer frame and her husband, who clearly used to be a large man but had now acquired the look of a burst balloon, sat slumped in a shabby armchair.

'We'd like to ask you if you remember a lady who lived next door back in the nineteen eighties,' Gerry began.

Trish perched on the edge of the tapestry sofa, listening for the answer, and when it came she had to concede defeat. The DCI had been on the right track all along.

'You mean Dr Haskel?' She turned to her husband. 'You remember Dr Haskel, Bert?'

'Peculiar one that,' was the man's growled and damning reply. 'Divorced.'

'A young woman came asking about her ... must have been about ten days ago. Said she was her daughter.'

Trish caught Gerry's eye. This was getting better.

'Was her name Nadia Lucas?'

The woman looked amazed, as if he'd just pulled off some extremely clever conjuring trick. 'That's right. How did you know?'

Trish saw the boss hesitate but after a few moments he seemed to decide against breaking the news of her death. That could come later.

'Can you tell us everything you told her, love? It'd be a great help,' he added encouragingly.

'It's a long time ago. That's what I told the daughter. But I remember Dr Haskel all right. She used to ask me to feed her cat. Ended up killing herself, she did. Walked into the sea and left her clothes on the beach. Terrible.'

'And she left you to look after the cat full time?' Gerry guessed.

'That's right. Not that we minded, did we, Bert?'

Bert shook his head.

'I'll tell you something for nothing – you could have knocked me down with a feather when I found out she had a daughter. The girl said she'd been brought up by her dad.' She shook her head in disbelief at Wendy Haskel's lack of maternal feelings. 'I never knew she had a kiddie. Fancy her killing herself like that when she had a kiddie. Selfish, that's what it is.' Mabel pressed her lips together disapprovingly.

So far Wendy Haskel had been described as peculiar, selfish and, by implication, an appalling mother. Trish wondered what other goodies they were about to uncover.

'So what else can you remember about Wendy Haskel?' Gerry prompted.

'She was a quiet woman. Apart from when the other one came round and they had rows.'

Trish saw the DCI sit forward, listening intently, and she held her breath.

'The other one? Which other one?'

Mabel gave another pout of disapproval. 'She lived alone but this other woman was there a lot. Older, she was. I thought she was a relative at first but then I wasn't so sure. And she wasn't the only one who visited her. There were men too. She lived on her own but she wasn't on her own much, if you know what I mean.'

Trish thought she saw Mabel wink but she could have been mistaken.

'So let's get this straight, love,' said Gerry. 'Wendy Haskel had lots of visitors, men and women.'

'A few men but just one woman. Just this particular one.'

'And she had rows with the woman. Did she row with the men as well?'

'Not that I heard.'

'Probably did other things with the men,' Bert chipped in. This time the wink was obvious.

'You thought they were her ...' Trish had been about to say sexual partners or lovers but she decided on something a little gentler. 'Boyfriends?'

'Can't say for sure but that's what we thought at the time, didn't we, Bert?'

'Any of them stop the night?' Gerry had decided on the straightforward approach.

'Not that I can remember. The woman did, I reckon – I sometimes used to see her coming out in the morning – but not the men. Can't accuse her of anything ... you know,' she added coyly.

Trish said nothing. Mabel and Bert obviously hadn't considered the possibility that Wendy Haskel's sexual tastes might not have included men but neither she nor the DCI were going to say anything to enlighten them.

'Did you know any of her visitors' names?'

She shook her head. 'I didn't know their names and I never asked.'

'Can you tell us what happened on the day Dr Haskel died? Did you see her at all?'

Mabel shook her head. 'We didn't see her all that day,

did we, Bert? But we heard her come in. Then we heard her moving about in the bedroom and then we heard the front door shutting. A couple of days after that a policeman came and told us she'd disappeared and that her clothes and bag had been found on the beach at Littlebury. We told him we'd heard her in the house that day but that's all we knew.'

'I saw her.'

Mabel turned to her husband in amazement. 'You saw her? Why didn't you tell the police? When did you see her?'

'I looked out of the window and I saw her disappearing down the road. She was wearing that big mac she sometimes wore. That white one with the hood. And I did tell the police.'

'You never told me.' Mabel sounded hurt.

'You weren't there. You were out at the shops when the bobby called first time – he had to come back later to talk to you. Remember?'

'No. I don't remember.' Mabel pouted. She looked annoyed, as though she'd missed out on something juicy.

Trish saw Gerry, in an effort to avoid a domestic incident, pull a photograph from his pocket and hand it to Mabel. 'Recognise anyone?'

Mabel examined the picture then she put on a pair of reading glasses and peered at it again. 'Yes. I reckon some of these used to come and see her. And that was her friend. The woman she used to argue with.'

Gerry Heffernan gave the woman one of his widest grins, the one that displayed all his teeth and made him look like a crocodile who'd just spotted a tasty snack.

Wesley arrived at Professor Karl Maplin's Victorian house on the outskirts of Exeter to find that Neil was just parking his yellow Mini on the street outside the front door. He watched his old friend climb out of the car, a smile of greeting fixed to his face.

'Well timed,' Neil said. 'I didn't realise you were keen to speak to Maplin as well. What's he done? Staged a hold-up at a bank, threatening the cashier with his trowel?'

Wesley's mental picture of the fussy archaeology professor demanding money with menaces was ridiculous enough to prompt a chuckle. 'I'm hoping he might be able to help us with our enquiries. Nadia Lucas had Maplin's name in her notebook.'

Neil raised his eyebrows. 'Didn't she work for a professor at Morbay University? Maybe she talked to Maplin in the course of her job. Come on. He's expecting us. I phoned ahead.'

Wesley didn't know whether to be pleased or annoyed. Gerry Heffernan had always favoured the element of surprise but, thanks to Neil, it was too late for that.

When Professor Maplin opened his front door beaming, as though delighted to welcome his two former students. But then Wesley remembered he always looked like that when he sensed the prospect of juicy gossip. Wesley glanced at his watch as he stepped into the cluttered drawing room. It was coming up to midday and he mustn't be late for his appointment with Sir Martin Crace. You couldn't keep National Treasures waiting.

'It's lovely to see you, boys,' the professor began as they took a seat. 'And I believe you're a police inspector now, Wesley.' He shook his head like a father whose child had turned out to be a disappointment to the family. 'I had high hopes that you'd stay on to do a doctorate.'

Wesley said nothing. He had copies of the photographs from Nadia's locker in his pocket. He took them out and spread them on the coffee table. 'I was hoping that you might be able to help me. Do you recognise any of these people?' He pointed to the picture in the middle. 'That's you, isn't it?'

The professor gave a little giggle. 'With more hair and less flesh. Where did you get these?'

'Wendy Haskel's daughter had them.' He paused. 'Her name's Nadia Lucas. Has she been in touch with you?'

'As a matter of fact she has. She came to see me. Rather nervous girl; very intense. A bit like her mother ... although physically she definitely favoured her father. Mind you, I only saw him the once so—'

'I'm afraid she's been murdered.'

The fixed smile vanished from Maplin's face and he looked stunned. 'Oh dear,' he kept repeating, shaking his head. 'Oh dear, that's awful.'

'You knew Wendy well?' He turned his head and saw that Neil, sitting beside him, was listening carefully.

'Yes,' Maplin said quietly. 'I knew Wendy. In fact we were rather close at one time,' he added in a whisper.

'You were, er ... lovers?' Wesley asked. It seemed strange to be questioning his old tutor on such intimate matters but he needed to know.

'No. We weren't lovers.'

'Was that because she was married?'

'No. She was living apart from her husband by then.' He pressed his lips tightly together as if to indicate he'd said all he was going to say on the subject.

'Do you recognise the other people in the photograph?'

'Yes. In fact Nadia showed me this very picture. I think this was taken on an excavation we did near Bloxham. A rather interesting Saxon farmstead, if I remember rightly.'

'This was before the dig at Grandal Farm outside Queenswear?'

'Yes. But not long before. Only a month or so. I was

doing post excavation work on the Bloxham site while Maggie and Wendy were starting in Queenswear.'

'Do you know where any of these people are now?'

'A few of them.' His finger came to rest beneath a pair of smiling faces. 'That's Charles and Hannah Whitling. Husband and wife team. They're retired now. Live outside Buckfastleigh. He's an old woman and she's got a bit of a temper.'

Wesley pointed to a teenage girl slouching at the edge of the group. 'Who's that?' Wesley didn't know why but the face seemed vaguely familiar.

Maplin screwed up his face in concentration. 'Oh, it's on the tip of my tongue. What was it now? She was a sixth-former. Volunteer. Used to wear low-cut tops. She wanted to study archaeology but . . .' He closed his eyes, his face contorted as though the effort of remembering was painful. 'It'll come to me. Nadia did ask me as well but I'm afraid I just couldn't recall . . .'

'Don't worry,' said Wesley hiding his disappointment. 'What about the others?'

The professor went on to recite some names, all with an accompanying comment, and Wesley wrote them down carefully in his notebook. Maplin had the current addresses of a few. The others he'd lost touch with long ago.

'You told Nadia all this?'

'Of course. She said she wanted to know more about her mother. She was only four when she died, you see.'

'Did she mention a letter she'd found recently . . . possibly something to do with her mother?'

Maplin shook his head.

'Maggie's accident and Wendy's disappearance must have been a terrible shock to you.' Wesley said once he'd put his notebook away, watching the man's face carefully.

'Yes. They were. Tragic. We were all devastated.'

'And all the records of the dig were destroyed?'

'I think we can assume Maggie had them with her in the car when she had the accident. As you no doubt know if you've been looking into the matter, Wesley, the car was burned out. Destroyed.' He looked away. 'As was the unfortunate Maggie.'

'Was Maggie March a close friend?'

'Maggie? Oh no, I wouldn't describe Maggie as a friend at all. I know you shouldn't speak ill of the dead, but I couldn't stand the woman ... unlike Wendy,' he added meaningfully. 'Now I didn't say too much about that to poor little Nadia.'

Wesley wanted to delve further but Neil interrupted.

'So you had no idea what they'd found at the Queenswear dig then?'

'Sorry, Neil. I can't add anything to what I told you before. I knew very little about that particular dig. Apart from the fact that, according to Wendy, Maggie was behaving rather oddly.'

Wesley sat forward. 'In what way?'

'Wendy wasn't specific. But I know Maggie's behaviour was giving her cause for concern. Maggie could be very – how shall I put it? – intense ... possessive. But as for the details, I'm afraid I don't know any.'

'What did you make of Wendy's disappearance?' Wesley asked.

'As I told Nadia, it was a shock ... totally unexpected. Of course I didn't see her after Maggie's accident the day before. Although I did give her a ring to tell her the news.'

'You spoke to her?'

'Yes, but she didn't say much. I must have said something like, "Have you heard there's been a terrible accident and Maggie's been killed?" but I remember she just mumbled something and put the phone down. Probably in shock, poor girl.' He paused. 'Perhaps, with hindsight, I was a little blunt.' He shook his head regretfully. 'After that we all presumed she'd locked herself away, overcome with shock or grief or whatever. Then that note was found ... and the clothes. I just hadn't realised that she felt that strongly for Maggie. Rather thought it was the other way round, actually. Just shows, you never can tell, eh?'

'You think they were in a lesbian relationship?'

Karl Maplin took a deep breath. 'It's the only explanation for Wendy's suicide, isn't it? She lost her lover in the accident and killed herself out of despair. It all fits.'

'What about Wendy's husband and daughter?'

'Wendy Haskel abandoned her family, Wesley. Never saw them as far as I know. But whether she abandoned them for Maggie, I can't tell you. Even my infallible radar for gossip didn't pick that one up. But I can tell you one thing for nothing. Wendy certainly didn't abandon her family for me. Of course I wasn't so blunt with that poor girl, Nadia. I tried to be sensitive but sometimes it's not easy, is it?' He suddenly looked up and smiled in triumph. 'Cher. That was her name.'

'Whose?'

'The sixth-former at the dig with the low-cut tops. Her name was Cher. Can't remember her second name, I'm afraid, but it was definitely Cher, like the singer. And before you ask, I've no idea what became of her, or even whether she went on to study archaeology at university.' He sat forward, suddenly remembering the laws of hospitality. 'Cup of tea, boys, or something stronger?'

Wesley made his excuses and left. His impending meeting with Sir Martin Crace was at the forefront of his mind. Much as he would have liked to stay for tea and scandal with his old tutor, there were some appointments that had to be kept.

223

Besides, he had the feeling he'd just learned something very important.

Colin Bowman pulled out the mortuary drawer housing Ian Rowe's charred remains and gently uncovered what was left of the face. He stared at the bared teeth, brown with smoke, and consulted the sheet of paper in his hand.

He hadn't held out much hope that any of the dentists in the area would have the dead man's dental records filed away but they'd struck lucky. A couple of years ago Ian Rowe had visited a dentist in Dukesbridge and had had four amalgam fillings. It was there in black and white on the chart. Seven fillings in all, three at some unspecified date in the past and the four more recent ones.

Ian Rowe clearly hadn't taken much care of his teeth and this left Colin with a dilemma. The man in the drawer had only had two fillings during his lifetime.

Colin looked from the chart to the corpse and frowned. What if the dentist had made a mistake and sent another patient's records? But when his assistant had telephoned, the chatty dentist had remembered Rowe and he'd recalled him saying that he worked for Sir Martin Crace.

As far as Colin knew, Rowe's mother had died around six months ago and there was no sign of a father so a DNA match was out of the question. It was a puzzle.

He had a corpse on his hands with the wrong ID and if it wasn't Ian Rowe lying there in the drawer, who was it? But it wasn't his problem. He replaced the sheet carefully over what was left of the cadaver's face, closed the drawer slowly and walked back to his office.

He'd have to call Gerry Heffernan. And he knew Gerry wouldn't be pleased.

Gerry Heffernan's phone rang just as they reached the

gates of Bewton Hall. As soon as Wesley heard the words 'Hi, Colin' he found himself straining to hear the conversation as he steered the car towards the drive. Colin Bowman might be a sociable man, but he never called just for a chat in working hours. Whatever he had to tell Gerry must be important.

Wesley was momentarily distracted when the two security men on the gates demanded their ID. It was a different set of heavily built men this time but they turned out to be as hostile as the pair they'd encountered on their last visit. Wesley flashed his warrant card and was about to drive off when one of them stepped in front of him and signalled him to wind the window down. But this time there was no argument and they were waved through just as Gerry finished his call.

'What did Colin want?' Wesley asked as they drove towards the house.

'You're not going to believe this.'

'Believe what? What did he say?'

'He reckons that the body in the cottage isn't Ian Rowe's. The dental records don't match. The corpse only has two fillings but apparently Rowe had a mouthful. You know what this means, don't you, Wes? Rowe might still be alive.'

Wesley began to back the car into a parking space, his mind racing. 'Is Colin absolutely certain? I mean, could the dentist have made a mistake?'

'According to Colin it seems pretty certain.'

'Jack Plesance didn't say anything about anyone else being in the house.'

'We need another word with Mr Plesance.'

'He's on our list. Sooner rather than later.'

As Wesley locked the car door he looked around, surveying the scene just as the lords of that particular manor must have done over the centuries. He could just see the strange little run-down cottage standing by the copse of trees. He hadn't noticed it as they'd driven up to the house but then his mind had been on other things. It still looked to him like the gingerbread house out of a children's fairy tale. But Sir Martin's mother's cousin from Zimbabwe lived there, not some wicked witch.

They made for the front door, which was opened, as before, by the housekeeper, Jane Verity. This time Wesley noticed that she looked tired, as though something – worry perhaps – was keeping her awake at night. Her manner was still calm and capable but a nervous twitch of her lips and her clenched fingers told him that there was some sort of emotional storm going on inside. He wondered why this was.

'Sir Martin's expecting you,' she said, sweeping up the staircase in front of them, as though she didn't want to make small talk. She showed them to Eva Liversedge's office and disappeared.

Eva stood up to greet them. She wore grey and had a businesslike expression on her face. No nonsense. She went before them into the inner sanctum and left as soon as Sir Martin invited them to sit.

'What can I do for you this time, gentlemen? I've already told you everything I know.'

'We'd just like to clarify a few things, sir,' said Wesley. 'Last time we talked we told you that Nadia Lucas was missing.' He paused. 'But now I'm afraid we have reason to believe she was murdered.'

Wesley found it hard to tell whether the look of shock on Crace's face was genuine or feigned. 'I really don't know what to say. That's absolutely awful. Of course I'll do anything I can to help to bring her killer to justice. How . . .?'

'A woman was murdered in Queenswear . . . burned alive. You might have heard about it on the news. We

226

now know the victim was Nadia Lucas.' He spoke bluntly.

Crace switched immediately into sympathetic benefactor mode. 'That's shocking ... really terrible. If her family need any help, of course I'll—'

'As far as I know she has no family.'

Sir Martin bowed his head.

'We found a notebook belonging to her and your phone number was in it.'

'That's hardly surprising, Inspector. She used to work here.'

'And you kept in touch with her?'

'No, I didn't. Look, I'm very sorry to hear she's dead, and in such appalling circumstances, but I really don't see how I can help you.'

Wesley caught Gerry's eye. There was something he wanted to try. 'We've just heard that Ian Rowe might not be dead after all.'

There was no mistaking the shock on Sir Martin's face, there for a split second then vanished. A shock akin to horror. 'You told me he'd died in a house fire.'

'I know but we now think there's been a case of mistaken identity. If he is alive, have you any idea where he might have gone? He has no passport so he can't have returned to France and we know that he intended to come here and see you.'

Sir Martin shook his head. 'As I told you before, Inspector, I haven't seen him since he worked for me. I'm afraid I can't help you.'

'He's been telling people you were a good friend of his mother's.'

Suddenly Crace looked a little wary. 'His mother worked in my parents' shop for a short time many years ago and that's one reason I felt obliged to employ him. But the truth is I didn't know her well.'

'Is there anybody else here who was friendly with him? Someone he might have kept in touch with?'

'I really can't say. You'll have to ask Eva.'

'Rowe sent Nadia an e-mail suggesting that he knew something about you – something he needed to prove. Any idea what that might be?'

Crace gave him a smile that was both charming and apologetic. 'I'm sorry, I have no idea.'

Wesley began to notice small tell-tale signs – glances at his Rolex, fingers drumming on the desk – that they had begun to try Crace's patience. He knew they'd get nothing more out of him for the moment. He stood up and Gerry did likewise, slowly and reluctantly. Wesley guessed that he'd been comfortable. 'We'll speak to Ms Liversedge. Thank you for your time.'

As they left, Wesley couldn't help feeling they'd had a wasted journey. Only the momentary look of horror on Sir Martin's face when he'd found out Ian Rowe might still be alive, and the slight trace of wariness when Rowe's mother was mentioned, told Wesley that there might be something to discover if they had the opportunity to dig deep enough.

Their interrogation of Eva Liversedge didn't prove any more productive but, as they were about to take their leave of her, things started to look up.

'So you've really no idea where Ian Rowe might be?' Wesley asked, almost as an afterthought, expecting the answer to be in the negative.

'No but—'

Wesley leapt on the hesitation like a cat on a mouse. 'But what? If there's anything you know, however trivial it may seem, you have to tell us.'

'We're investigating a murder, love,' Gerry chipped in, not too helpfully in Wesley's opinion.

There was a long pause while the PA decided how

much to reveal. Eventually she spoke, her words careful and measured. 'I don't wish to betray confidences or speak out of turn, Inspector, but when he was working here I saw Rowe with Jane Verity, the housekeeper. On one occasion . . .'

'Go on,' Wesley prompted.

'On one occasion they were kissing. I said nothing, of course. It was none of my business but . . .'

Wesley saw that Gerry was grinning as he stood up. 'Thanks, love. I could give you a kiss for that.'

Eva looked horrified.

'Thank you, Ms Liversedge. We'll see ourselves out,' said Wesley, rescuing the situation.

As they hurried down the stairs they saw Jane Verity crossing the entrance hall. They hadn't expected it to be that easy.

'Can we have a word, love?' Gerry called out in a voice that could probably be heard at the gatehouse. 'In private.'

Jane Verity stopped and stared at them, frozen like a statue. But after a few moments she relaxed. 'Of course.'

She led the way through the swing door that had once separated upstairs from downstairs in the social hierarchy and they ended up in a comfortable, if slightly old-fashioned, sitting room. The housekeeper's room in the past and in the present. She invited them to sit, her hands still clenched.

'We believe you were friendly with Ian Rowe. Why did nobody tell us this before?'

'It was a long time ago. And he's dead, isn't he? What's the point of raking it all up again now he's dead?' She fixed her eyes firmly on the threadbare carpet at her feet, as though she didn't dare to meet the policemen's eyes in case she gave away some precious secret.

229

'Tell me about Ian,' Wesley said gently. 'What was he like?'

A smile flickered on her lips then disappeared. 'Full of big ideas. Big talk. He used to—'

'Used to what?'

She turned her head away. 'Nothing.'

'What was his relationship with Nadia Lucas?'

'He always used to say there was nothing between them, that I was the only one. But I didn't believe him.'

'Did Nadia mention anything about trying to find out what happened to her mother when she was working here?'

Jane shook her head. 'No, but Ian said she was a bit crazy. I think her mum killed herself when she was a kid and her dad had just died of cancer. I felt a bit sorry for her at one time if you must know. Then she went to France to get a job with some professor and Ian stayed on for a while. Till he got caught drinking and driving.'

'Did you love him?' Wesley wasn't quite sure why he asked the question.

'I don't really know what love is,' she replied after a long pause. 'We had sex. It lasted a while but, by the time he left, it was over. End of story. Like I said, he was full of stories – mostly fiction,' she added with a hint of bitterness.

'Any stories you remember in particular?'

'He said his mum was a close friend of Sir Martin's. He never said how she knew him; just implied that she had this wonderful relationship with the boss that made him untouchable. Then he got sacked for drink driving so it must all have been rubbish. Ian told me his mother was ill, but Sir Martin never went to see her or sent her anything. And he would have done if she was an old friend. He's that sort of man.'

'He never told you how his mother knew Sir Martin?'

230

'He might have told Nadia but he never told me.' There was a suggestion of bitterness behind the words. Perhaps Jane Verity had been jealous, Wesley thought to himself.

'I think I'd better tell you that Nadia Lucas is dead,' Gerry said bluntly. 'She was burned to death in Queenswear.'

Jane Verity's hand went to her mouth. 'Oh, my God. I heard about it but I'd no idea it was her.'

'She's only just been identified.'

'So both Ian and Nadia have died in the same way. They must be linked. Have you any idea who—?'

'Afraid not. And there's a possibility that Ian might still be alive,' Wesley said, watching her reaction carefully.

Her surprise was genuine. If someone was harbouring Ian Rowe, it wasn't Jane Verity.

As they took their leave, Jane made no attempt to show them out. She sat in her armchair, staring ahead. Perhaps she had fallen for Rowe's charm – she was a good ten years older than him and she wouldn't be the first plain, middle-aged woman to fall for someone like Rowe. It had probably been happening since the Iron Age, Wesley thought to himself with a smile.

'Who's that?' Gerry said as Wesley started the car.

An elderly woman with unruly grey hair was making her way down the drive. She walked with a slight limp and a baggy beige cardigan was pulled tightly around her shoulders.

'I wonder if it's the woman from the cottage. Crace's aunt from Zimbabwe. Shall we have a word with her?' said Wesley suddenly.

'Why?'

'She might have seen something.'

'Well, I'd rather find out what Ian Rowe wanted to see Sir Martin about.'

Wesley shook his head. 'Rowe was a fantasist. He's got nothing on Sir Martin or anyone else for that matter. I think it was all in his head. Come on. Let's have a word with the aunt.'

Gerry sighed. 'OK, but let's make it quick. There's a load of paperwork on my desk. And I want a proper ID on that body from the cottage. And we need to get all patrols looking out for Ian Rowe.'

Wesley got out of the car. 'This won't take a moment. And, who knows, Nadia and Rowe might have spent cosy afternoons at her cottage sipping tea and sharing confidences.'

Gerry emerged slowly from the passenger seat. The cottage stood at the edge of the copse, small and cosy-looking with red-brick walls, small-paned windows and tall chimneys. But as they drew closer they could see the flaking green paintwork and the weeds in the tiny front garden, separated from the grounds by a low picket fence.

Wesley knocked at the cottage door.

'She won't know anything,' Gerry whispered as they stood waiting for the door to open. 'Bet you a fiver.'

'You're on.' Wesley wasn't a gambling man but at that moment he'd say anything to stop his boss moaning about the delay. Besides, he wasn't altogether sure he'd lose the bet.

The door opened slowly to reveal a tall woman with steel grey hair, worn longish for her age. She had taken off her cardigan to reveal a baggy blue shirt and her only concession to any form of vanity was a colourful silk scarf tied around her neck. Her hair flopped forward, hiding half her face in its shadow.

Wesley showed his warrant card. 'Sorry to bother you, Mrs . . . er . . .'

She stepped back further into the shadows. 'Trent.

232

Bertha Trent. And it's Miss.' Her voice was low and bore the trace of some kind of accent. Probably that of her native Zimbabwe. And she sounded wary, possibly resentful at being disturbed.

'We'd just like to ask you a few questions if we may,' Wesley continued, aware of Gerry standing behind him, shifting from foot to foot. He still couldn't see the woman's face properly and he suddenly wished that he could push the hair back to get a proper look.

'What about?'

'Did you know a young woman called Nadia Lucas who used to work for Sir Martin?'

'I hardly know anyone who works up there. I live a self-contained life here, Detective Inspector. I don't bother Martin and he doesn't bother me.'

'What about a man called Ian Rowe? He used to drive for Sir Martin.'

'I'm sorry. I can't help you.'

As she was about to close the front door her shirt sleeve fell back to reveal a hand that was little more than a claw, a mess of red flesh, shiny and mottled. He lifted his eyes to her face. The sun had just emerged from behind the clouds and in the brighter light he caught a glimpse of the side of her face she had been so careful to keep hidden behind the strands of hair. Like the hand it was a mess.

Wesley put his hand on the door to stop her closing it. 'I'm sorry, Miss Trent, but can you tell me about your accident?'

'What accident?' She sounded defensive.

'What happened to your face ... and your hand?'

She froze and he could feel the hatred in her eyes as she looked at him. 'It was no accident and anyway, it's none of your business.' She almost spat the words out and Wesley was rather taken aback by the vehemence of her reaction.

'Please.' He could feel Gerry's hand nudging his back, as if to say, 'Leave it.'

The woman took a deep, shuddering breath. 'If you must know it was Mugabe's thugs ... the ones who call themselves war veterans. I had a farm ... a successful farm I took over from my parents. They set fire to the house with me in it and they laughed while they did it. Three of my staff died. They burned me out of my home. Satisfied?'

Wesley saw the hatred in her eyes. She was scowling at him as though he himself was one of her attackers, returned to torment her. Maybe, he thought, it was because of the colour of his skin. But then during her time in Zimbabwe she must have known a lot of good and decent Africans.

'I'm really sorry,' he said softly. 'And I apologise for disturbing you,' he added, feeling Gerry's hand in his ribs again.

The DCI was right. It was time to go. And it looked as if he owed the boss a fiver.

After the archaeological team had gone home Neil Watson remained behind to tidy up and ponder that day's discoveries in solitude.

He perched himself on an upturned feed trough that had been left in the corner of the field and studied the contents of one of the finds trays. Lots of medieval pottery of exactly the right date to have been used by the household of Stephen de Grendalle.

He'd now managed to learn quite a lot about Stephen from the archives. He'd sailed from Tradmouth to San Diego de Compostela on a ship carrying pilgrims in 1209. Then, fuelled with piety, he'd travelled north to fight with Simon de Montfort against the Cathars. Early in the summer of that year a crusading army had been raised in Burgundy at the request of Pope Innocent III and, for some reason best known to himself, maybe in penitence for some sin, Stephen, the lord of a Devon manor, had joined up. But while he was there, witnessing the terrible punishments meted out to the unrepentant heretics, he'd apparently fallen in love with a young woman called Jeanne who'd been sentenced to be burned alive with her fellow inhabitants of Minerve.

There was no clue to how Stephen had managed to rescue Jeanne from her gruesome fate but it was clear that they fled back to England to avoid her capture and execution. Once back in Devon she was baptised and she lived with her new husband until the legends took over: vague tales of how she betrayed Stephen with another man and, as a consequence, became the burning bride of local folklore. But did that local folklore have any basis in fact?

Neil looked at the corner of the field where the unfortunate murder victim had died. There had been some interesting geophysics results a few yards from the spot. Quite intriguing. He now had permission from the police to start digging in that area and he planned to begin work the next day. But part of him felt a little squeamish about disturbing that particular place.

His thoughts were so immersed in the past that a sudden noise made him jump. Hollow footsteps on the planking laid around some of the trenches. He looked up and saw a woman walking across the site. She was looking around, taking an interest, but there was something clandestine in her manner that made him stay silent rather than shout a greeting.

She hadn't seen him, that much was clear. But then he was sitting in shadow shielded by some low tree branches. If he wanted, if he just stepped back a little towards the trees, he could watch with no danger of being seen and find out what she was going to do. Then he suddenly felt guilty. It wasn't really his style to watch people unobserved. But it was his site and watching in silence for a minute or so would do no harm.

But as he stood up he knocked over a wheelbarrow, which fell to the earth with a crash. The woman looked round. She wasn't dressed for an archaeological site: she wore summer sandals, a floral skirt and a guilty expression on her face, as though she'd just been caught doing something she shouldn't. However, this woman didn't look like any nighthawk he'd come across in the course of his career, and she was carrying a raffia handbag rather than a metal detector.

'Hi,' Neil said, raising a hand. 'Can I help you?'

The woman seemed to take a few moments to gather her thoughts. 'Er, I just thought I'd have a look. I'm Sheryl Bright. My husband's the developer who owns this field. He's not around by any chance, is he?'

Neil shook his head. 'Haven't seen him today. Sorry.'

'Well, like I said, I was just passing and I thought . . . Thanks.' She turned to go, took a few steps, then turned back to face Neil. 'I took part in a dig once. It was fun.'

'If you're at a loose end, come and give us a hand,' said Neil, trying to hide his surprise. Somehow he couldn't see this woman with Jon Bright. She was far too good for him.

Sheryl Bright's heart was pounding. She hadn't expected anybody to be at Grandal Field. When she'd taken part in the dig there all those years ago, they'd knocked off at five or five thirty. Some of them had gone off to the pub but she'd been too young to join them, something she'd resented at the time.

Unsure what to do, she walked away, back to where her Mini Cooper was parked down the lane from an older, scruffier yellow model and some way away from the familiar battered grey Ford. If she waited till the tall and rather attractive archaeologist with the longish fair hair had gone it might be OK. But he hadn't shown any sign of being ready to leave so she knew she could be in for a long and frustrating wait.

She looked at her watch. It was almost seven and she was hungry. Then she got back into her car and sat there for ten long minutes, ducking down as the archaeologist climbed into the yellow Mini and drove away. The last thing she wanted was for him to come over, knock on her car window and strike up another conversation.

As soon as she was sure he'd gone she got out of the car and walked back to the field. This had to be sorted out once and for all.

She skirted the field, sticking close to the trees so that she wouldn't be seen by any casual passer-by. When she got to the spot where the police tape hung like tattered bunting, she heard a noise behind her and froze.

'Is that you?' she said in a loud whisper.

But as she turned her head to look round, she felt strong arms around her pulling her towards the dark shelter of the trees.

11

I have already mentioned Walter Fitzallen, local entre-preneur and founder of Tradmouth's fortunes. Some letters that passed between Fitzallen and Stephen de Grendalle still exist, buried deep in various archives, but the one that Urien de Norton sent to de Grendalle is by far the most interesting. However, I'll deal with that later.

From the correspondence between Fitzallen and de Grendalle, it is obvious that the two men were on fairly amicable, if businesslike, terms. They write of ships and cargoes, of the sale of land and of gifts to the church for the salvation of their souls. There is one in particular from de Grendalle to Fitzallen which contains the follow-ing passage (I paraphrase because the language is somewhat obscure to the modern reader).

'Your gift to the priest at Townton was most generous and I am minded to do likewise in gratitude for my most felicitous union. I thank you for your kind invita-tion to dine on the feast of Saint Matthew. I urge you to show kindness to my wife as our land and society are most strange to her.'

A letter dated a month later mentions Fitzallen paying

another visit to the de Grendalles. And some time after that Walter's heiress wife, Isabelle Fitzallen, writes to her father expressing her displeasure at the news that her husband has been seen by Urien de Norton out riding with Jeanne de Grendalle, lately called Jeanne de Minerve.

We can only assume that Jeanne and Fitzallen had hit it off at their first meeting and had arranged another encounter. But was everything as it seemed to those suspicious minds?

(From papers found in the possession of Professor Yves Demancour)

Wesley was surprised that Neil hadn't turned up the night before, and a little disappointed. He'd been looking forward to telling him the unexpected news that Ian Rowe could still be alive. Since Neil had started working at Queenswear, he'd taken to using the Petersons' house as a base, spending his evenings there and sometimes even sleeping on the sofa when he'd missed the last ferry. Pam had even fed him on a couple of occasions; as it was the school holidays she didn't mind too much – in term time he would certainly have been pushing his luck.

When Wesley arrived in the CID office first thing that morning, listing in his mind his tasks for the day ahead, he met Gerry Heffernan on the way out. Gerry looked worried, which wasn't like him. Something was wrong and Wesley asked him what it was.

'ACC Cuthbert wants to see me – he's come all the way down from his ivory tower in Exeter to cane my backside. There's been a complaint about us.'

'What are we supposed to have done?'

'I'll give you three guesses.'

'Sir Martin Crace?'

'See what you get by interrogating the great and the good. They have friends in lofty places.'

Wesley thought for a few seconds. 'You know what this means, Gerry?'

'We're up to our necks in manure?'

'No. It means we've got Crace rattled about something. Which in turn means that he may not be as pure and perfect as he likes to make out. He knows that if we dig too deeply we might unearth something unpleasant.'

Gerry's expression didn't change. 'You could well be right, Wes, but it'll be hard convincing the ACC of that.'

Wesley knew he had a point. What they needed was proof that Sir Martin had some involvement in the deaths of Nadia Lucas and the unknown man found in Owl Cottage. But the proof might be hard to obtain now that Crace had put the shutters up.

'Would you like me to come up with you, Gerry?' Wesley knew only too well how these things worked. As a member of an ethnic minority, his support for Gerry would count for a lot. It wasn't something he was particularly happy about, in fact he found it patronising, but the powers that be seemed to worry about that sort of thing a great deal.

Gerry grinned and their eyes met in understanding. 'Might not be a bad idea.'

Wesley followed him out. If they were to be hauled in front of the ACC for daring to do their job, they might as well face it together.

Once in Chief Superintendent Nutter's office, they stood in front of Nutter and the ACC like a pair of naughty schoolboys. The ACC, a thin, dapper man in an immaculate uniform, looked from one to the other.

'There was really no reason for you to come up here, Detective Inspector Peterson,' he began.

'I visited Sir Martin and I felt I should be involved, sir.'

The ACC arched his fingers. 'Sir Martin says that you've been harassing him and his staff. And he said that your attitude to the security staff on the gate on your first visit was arrogant and confrontational.'

Gerry was about to open his mouth to speak but Wesley got in first.

'I deny that wholeheartedly, sir. We've been asking questions about his former employees; one has been murdered and another is suspected of involvement in a murder. Those security men were rude and obstructive and I think we were rather lenient with them. Perhaps Sir Martin isn't quite aware of how his staff behave towards visitors they consider, er ... unsuitable,' he added reasonably.

This seemed to stump the ACC. He cleared his throat and shot a glance at CS Nutter. 'Well, sometimes these security people can get a bit above themselves, I admit. But the fact that the complaint comes from Sir Martin himself ...'

'I'm sure Sir Martin, like any good employer, believes in supporting his staff,' said Wesley smoothly. He was looking straight ahead so he didn't catch the glint of satisfaction in Gerry's eyes. 'However, he wasn't present so he can't possibly know how his employees behaved. But we do. We were on the receiving end.'

The ACC grunted something Wesley couldn't quite hear. The bit about supporting staff was good, he thought to himself. He felt rather proud of that.

'I shall speak to Sir Martin and tell him I've had a word with you. I assume you won't be calling on him again.'

'That depends, sir. This is a murder inquiry and I'm sure the public wouldn't like to think that we shy away

241

from interviewing witnesses just because they have wealth and position.'

This time Wesley stole a glance at his boss.

Then the ACC spoke again. 'Well, Sir Martin did say that his security staff have been under a bit of pressure lately. It seems that one of them walked out unexpectedly some days ago so the others have had to cover for him. I know it sounds like an excuse but . . .'

Wesley and Gerry looked at each other before Gerry spoke for the first time. 'When you say walked out, sir, did he storm out or did he simply not turn up? And when was this exactly?'

When the ACC admitted that he had no idea, Gerry broke the bad news. 'We may have to pay another visit to Bewton Hall after all, sir. But we'll be on our very best behaviour. We won't frighten the horses this time. Promise.'

A momentary look of horror flashed over the ACC's face before he said, 'Just make sure you don't. No more complaints. Is that clear?'

'Yes, sir,' Wesley and Gerry said in unison.

'I thought we were going to get six of the best,' Gerry said as they hurried down the stairs back to the CID office.

'Are you thinking what I'm thinking about that security guard?'

'If he suddenly disappeared around the time of the fire at Owl Cottage, it might not be a coincidence? We'll send someone round to have a word with Eva Liversedge – I bet she knows everything that goes on in that place and we have to find out if he just walked out in a huff or if he's vanished with no explanation.' He gave Wesley a wink. 'No need to bother Sir Martin this time. And we'll send Rachel and Paul. Just routine enquiries.'

Once they reached the office, Gerry gathered the

troops for the morning briefing. They faced the notice-board with its photographs of the dead captioned by Gerry's scrawled comments and Wesley began to go over the new developments.

Dental records had proved that the corpse in Owl Cottage on the outskirts of Whitely wasn't that of Ian Rowe, which meant that the dead man was still unidentified and that Rowe was still out there somewhere. And he needed to be found.

They'd discovered that Nadia Lucas's mother had disappeared and was assumed to have committed suicide after her colleague, and possibly her lover, had died in a car accident in 1983. And before she met her gruesome death in Grandal Field, Nadia herself had engaged a private detective, Forsyte Wiley, to discover all he could about her mother's fate – an investigation apparently triggered by the discovery of a letter. Then, shortly after her death, Nadia's room at the house she shared with Caroline Tay had been searched, possibly by her killer. As there was no sign of the letter Nadia had told Wiley about, it was safe to assume that the thief had taken it.

It was possible that Nadia's boss, Professor Yves Demancour, was involved in her death somehow because he found the idea of women being caught in flames sexually gratifying. And, as well as this, a connection with Sir Martin Crace and his entourage was starting to look increasingly likely, especially now they'd been politely warned off.

Of course they couldn't forget the threats to Sheryl Bright and the arson attack at her home either, although the only surviving threatening letter she'd received had yielded no forensic clues.

When the briefing was over and the day's tasks allotted, Wesley followed Gerry into his office. 'I want to speak to that couple from Buckfastleigh who were on the dig with Nadia's mother and Dr Maggie March. I'll take Trish if that's OK.'

'Fair enough. Nadia had their pictures in her locker and it's possible that she went to see them so it's time we had a word,' said Gerry. 'You still think this business with Nadia's mum has something to do with her murder?'

Wesley thought for a while. 'I don't know, Gerry. It's just ...'

'A good, old-fashioned hunch?'

'Something like that.'

'Well, I don't see anything wrong in following your instincts now and then. I want another word with Jack Plesance. According to Uniform he's still down here. I need to ask him who else was likely to have been in that cottage. And where we should start looking for Ian Rowe. Your old mate's in this up to his neck if you ask me.'

This time Wesley couldn't be bothered pointing out that Rowe had been no mate of his. But he couldn't argue with the DCI's logic. This had all started with Rowe and now all roads seemed to lead to the man.

But he'd leave that to Gerry. Somehow he never wanted to see or hear of Ian Rowe again.

Charles and Hannah Whitling – the husband and wife team – lived in a small cottage which stood on a lane between Buckfastleigh and the famous Benedictine abbey of Buckfast.

'This is nice,' said Wesley to Trish Walton as they drove down Buckfastleigh's high street. 'I don't think I've been here before. The DCI mentioned that there's a pub here that hasn't changed since the war.'

Trish said nothing. She was too busy looking for the right road to indulge in small talk. Eventually she turned off the main road and it wasn't long before they came to a halt outside the Whitlings' cottage.

They'd rung ahead so they were expected. And Wesley could tell from the lavish choice of cakes and biscuits laid out on the coffee table that visitors of any kind were a rare and welcome treat.

The couple were still recognisable from that old photograph Wesley had found in Nadia Lucas's locker. Hannah Whitling was a sensible-looking woman, still favouring the checked shirt and long khaki shorts she probably wore during her digging years. Her husband was a tall, suntanned man with a shock of white hair. He too wore khaki and check. Wesley found himself wondering whether the pair still helped out at digs. But Neil hadn't seemed to recognise their names and the world of archaeology was notoriously small.

Wesley thought it best to establish his credentials before the questioning started. He sensed that the Whitlings would be more likely to confide in a fellow archaeologist than a detective inspector so he chatted for a while about his time at Exeter studying with Karl Maplin and his friendship with Neil, while Trish sipped tea and listened politely.

Eventually he steered the conversation round to Maggie March and Wendy Haskel.

'I remember Maggie and Wendy were very close,' Charles Whitling said. 'I told Wendy's daughter that when she came round.'

'She came here to see you?'

'Oh, yes.'

His wife gave a snort of derision. 'Close. Maggie and Wendy were having an affair, darling.' He smiled at her husband fondly. 'Really, you can be so innocent sometimes.' She gave Trish a conspiratorial look as if to say, 'Men . . . what can you do with them?'

'Let me get this clear,' said Wesley. 'Maggie and Wendy were having a lesbian relationship? You're absolutely certain?'

She shifted in her seat. 'Oh, yes. I could tell by the way they were with each other. Intense. Even passionate. And the looks that passed between them. They were more than friends all right. Funny they both had children. Not that I said any of this to Nadia, mind.'

This was something new. Wesley sat forward. 'You're saying Maggie March had children too?'

'Just the one, I think.' She frowned. 'But I can't remember . . .'

Charles Whitling screwed up his face in concentration. 'It was a boy, I think. Or rather a young man. She must have had him when she was quite young.'

'What about his father?'

'Not around and Maggie never mentioned him. Of course Wendy had Nadia. Not that she saw her much because I know for a fact she lived with her father. Wendy showed me a picture of her once and I sensed she was sad that she didn't have much of a relationship with her daughter.' She hesitated for a moment. 'There was something sad about Wendy, you know, and it didn't surprise me that much when I heard she'd left her clothes on the beach and walked into the sea. Don't you agree, darling? I said that to Nadia. I don't think your mother was very happy, dear, I said.'

But Charles wasn't toeing the line. 'I thought Wendy was rather a nice girl. Always friendly. Not like Maggie. Maggie could be a tartar. Tragic the way she died though.'

'Do you remember much about the dig at Queenswear? The one Maggie March directed just before her death?'

'Oh, yes. It was rather a good one . . . some fascinating finds but we had neither the time nor the resources to dig the whole site. I remember Maggie being particularly excited about the foundations of a round dovecot. There are several examples in Devon, you know, but this one had been burned to the ground at some point in its history and apparently never rebuilt.' She smiled. 'There are legends about the lord of some manor in Queenswear locking his unfaithful wife in a dovecot and burning it to the ground with her inside it. And presumably the unfortunate doves. The location, of course, isn't specified but this particular find did seem to fit the story. Strange, don't you think?'

'Do you remember who else took part in the dig?'

'Of course,' said Charles and proceeded to recite some names Wesley had heard before from Professor Maplin. 'And then there was little Cherry. Well, I called her Cherry – she called herself Cher in those days. Probably thought it was more ...' He paused, searching for the appropriate word. 'More trendy. She wanted to study archaeology at university but I don't know whether she did.'

'What was her surname? Do you remember?'

'It was Bakewell. I remember we laughed because that's the name of a cake round Derbyshire where I grew up. That's why we called her Cherry, isn't it, dear? Cherry Bakewell.' Hannah gave a tinkling little giggle and looked at her husband for confirmation.

'That's right,' he said. 'Little Cherry Bakewell. And we saw her in the paper not long ago, didn't we?'

'Did we?' Hannah looked confused.

'Remember. It must have been last year. I pointed it out to you. That's Cherry Bakewell, I said.'

'Oh, I remember now. It was something to do with an art exhibition.'

'She was twenty-five years older, of course, and she was using her married name, but I never forget a face,' Charles said proudly.

247

'And what was her married name? Can you remember?'

Charles shook his head. 'Sorry.'

But Hannah rose from her seat and hurried over to the large mahogany sideboard that took up one wall of the small room. After rummaging inside one of the drawers for a minute or so, she returned triumphant, carrying a yellowed newspaper cutting in her hand. 'This is it. I cut it out.'

She handed the cutting to Wesley and when he'd read it, he handed it to Trish. 'Did you tell Nadia about this?'

'I did, yes.'

'May we keep this, Mrs Whitling? It could be important.'

'Of course. Another cup of tea?'

Wesley accepted. He thought he deserved it.

He'd just made the discovery that Cherry Bakewell was now Sheryl Bright – wife of the developer of Grandal Field.

Rachel felt a little overawed by being in the home of Sir Martin Crace. She was not usually given to self-doubt but she felt rather nervous at the prospect of meeting the great man, and she'd been somewhat relieved when Eva Liversedge had told her over the phone that he was in London that day for a meeting at the House of Commons.

When she entered Eva's office with Paul Johnson by her side she gave the PA her most charming smile. She knew she had to watch her step.

'So sorry to bother you again, Ms Liversedge, but I assure you we wouldn't be here unless it was important.' She made no mention of DCI Heffernan's encounter with the ACC concerning Sir Martin's complaint: it was probably better, she thought, to ignore it for now.

Eva Liversedge pressed her lips together. She didn't look pleased. 'You'd better get on with it then.'

Rachel glanced at Paul and cleared her throat. 'It's come to our attention that a member of your security staff has gone missing.' She tilted her head to one side expectantly and watched Eva's face.

But her expression gave nothing away. 'That's right. But I don't see how it concerns—'

'Has anybody heard from him?'

Eva shook her head.

'Has he been reported missing?'

Eva gave an exasperated sigh. 'I understand that his partner's been to the head of security kicking up a bit of a fuss. She's asked to see Sir Martin but I had to say he wasn't available.'

'I thought he took a personal interest in all his staff,' Paul said with studied innocence.

'He does but ... He has a lot on his plate at the moment. He can't concern himself with every junior staff member who walks out on his girlfriend and—'

'You don't know for certain that he's walked out,' Rachel said. She was getting sick of tiptoeing around. This woman was annoying her. 'Something could have happened to him. We'll need his name and address. We'd like to talk to his partner ourselves.'

'You'll be wasting your time. She's a hysterical woman and—'

'If we could just have those details we won't bother you any further,' said Rachel calmly.

Eva Liversedge walked over to a large filing cabinet and took out a file. She handed it to Rachel who copied the details into her notebook.

The missing man's name was Denis Wade and the partner who was causing Eva grief was called Linda Potts. And, as the address wasn't far away Rachel decided, with Paul's agreement, that it would do no harm to display a bit of initiative and pay Ms Potts a visit.

The address was in Dukesbridge itself, in a block of modern flats behind the main shopping street. It didn't have views of the river, or much else for that matter apart from the backside of a supermarket – pretty views would have doubled the flat's value.

The woman who answered the door was stick-thin with a pasty complexion and her mousy hair was pushed back behind her ears. She looked at Rachel suspiciously as she held up her warrant card, almost as though she was used to unwanted visits from the boys and girls in blue.

'I believe your partner's gone missing, Ms Potts. Mind if we come in for a chat?'

This was the open sesame. Linda Potts stood aside and let them into a flat which was small but immaculately neat.

'I didn't know whether to report it officially,' she said in a rush of anxiety. 'Miss Liversedge told me to wait a bit but—'

'Why was that?'

Linda gave an exasperated shrug. 'I don't think she wanted it to get into the papers. Sir Martin's a very important man, she said. It wouldn't do for him to be associated with . . .'

Rachel knew she was repeating verbatim what Eva Liversedge had told her and she suddenly felt angry on this woman's behalf. 'Well, we know about it now but we'll need some details. When did you last see him? Can you think of any reason he might have chosen to go off without telling you?'

Once Linda got going it was as if a cork had been pulled out of a bottle. It was hard to stop her going into every detail of their last week together, some so intimate that Rachel noticed that Paul was blushing.

Denis enjoyed his job at Bewton Hall and his

disappearance was quite unexpected. Linda had spoken to his colleagues in security and they seemed as puzzled as she was. Denis had worked there two years and Sir Martin thought highly of him and trusted him. In fact he was sometimes asked to do special jobs for Sir Martin, she said proudly.

But it was when Linda told her the exact date of Denis's disappearance that Rachel asked for the name of his dentist and whether there was anything in the flat that might provide them with a sample of his DNA.

She saw the anguished look on Linda's face as she hurried off to fetch Denis Wade's toothbrush but she resolved to stay professional and focussed. Especially now she'd learned that Denis had disappeared on the night of the fire at Owl Cottage. Someone had met their end in that cottage and, now they knew it hadn't been Ian Rowe, she feared very much that that someone was Denis Wade.

Wesley slumped down at his desk, his notepad set in front of him. Maggie March had had a son, but he had no idea whether this fact was relevant.

After a while he picked up the phone and dialled Sheryl Bright's number. He needed to talk to her. She'd been there on that dig. She'd been around when Maggie March had died in the car accident and Wendy Haskel had killed herself. She'd only been a schoolgirl, helping out in her summer holidays, but she might have seen or heard something relevant. She might even hold the key to the riddle of Nadia Lucas's death.

When there was no answer, he put the phone down. He'd try again later. But then he remembered the threatening letters she'd been receiving and he suddenly felt worried for her. Perhaps he'd send a patrol car round. Just to make sure she was all right.

He heard Gerry Heffernan's voice booming across the office. 'Hey, Wes, I've just spoken to Jack Plesance – he says that, as far as he knows, Ian Rowe was the only one in that cottage. Of course he was miles away in Birmingham at the time so he couldn't know who Rowe might have met up with which is a fat lot of use. Let's hope this lead of Rachel's about the missing security guard comes to something.'

'If it does, I reckon our Saint Martin could be in this up to his neck,' said Wesley quietly as he picked up the phone and tried Sheryl Bright's number again.

But there was still no reply.

Neil hesitated before sinking his trowel into the area the police had cordoned off – the strange round shape which had given such a strong signal on the geophys. He was trying hard to ignore the fact that a woman had burned to death a few yards from this particular spot, telling himself that they'd been kept waiting long enough for access and he needed to find out what was causing that geophys anomaly. But when he looked round at his colleagues, he noticed that they too were holding back, almost as though they shared his misgivings.

The digger had stripped off the top layer of soil with the delicacy of a chef slicing the skin off a fillet of fish and Neil stood for a moment looking at the result before taking a deep breath and squatting down to make a few exploratory scrapes with his trowel.

But a commotion at the other end of the field interrupted his efforts. Voices chanting, people shouting slogans.

'Save our countryside. Save our Devon. Save our countryside. Save our Devon.'

He straightened up to see what was happening and his heart began to race. They were all over his trenches.

They could destroy the archaeology if they carried on like that. He began to march towards them, fists clenched, face set in anger. Neil didn't get angry very often but the sight of people who knew nothing about his work trampling all over the site like a herd of undisciplined elephants did the trick.

'Oi. Get off there,' he heard himself shouting, surprised at the strength and violence of his own voice. 'Get off this site . . . now.'

He stood there, knees slightly bent like a Wild West gunfighter waiting for a shootout. A long-haired young man in combat gear was swaggering towards him and the rest of the invaders had fallen silent.

Neil could see his team out of the corner of his eye. They were watching, breath held. This was High Noon. Neil's opponent faced him, a determined look on his face.

The invader spoke first. 'Jem Burrows – spokesperson for the Pure Sons of the West. We're here to protest peacefully about the rape of our Devon countryside. You'll know this is an important site as well as a place of outstanding natural beauty so I'm inviting you and your team to join us in our objections to this development which is motivated purely by greed and the bottom line.' The speech had obviously been prepared and rehearsed. When it was over, he looked at Neil, awaiting a response.

Burrows's words had the desired effect. Neil's anger had subsided, leaving only a small niggle of irritation.

'I can't say I disagree with you, mate. Only thing is, can you tell your comrades not to go near our trenches? They might destroy valuable archaeology. Why don't they stick to the edge of the field?'

Jem Burrows leaned forward, offering his hand. Neil took it and they shook hands to the cheers of the Pure

Sons of the West and the puzzlement of the archaeological team before Burrows turned and issued orders to his protesters who scurried to their positions and stood awkwardly, as though, with this sudden lack of opposition, they felt rather lost.

Burrows sidled up to Neil. 'Er, have you any idea when Bright's due to turn up?'

Neil shook his head, trying to hide a smile. It looked as though Jem Burrows had miscalculated his protest badly. 'Sorry, mate. He doesn't show up every day. Only when he wants to hassle us for digging too slowly. Look, I'm on your side but I really don't think there's much point hanging round.'

Burrows gave Neil a conspiratorial smile. 'It's a nice day and there's a lovely view of the river so we might stay around for a bit ... just in case. Promise we won't get in your way.'

'Fair enough,' said Neil.

If Jem Burrows wanted to waste his time, that was up to him.

Jon Bright parked his wife's Mini Cooper in front of the garage and watched the automatic door open slowly, almost lazily. He'd told Sheryl that he intended to work from home that afternoon but his own car wasn't in its usual spot on the gravel drive, which meant she must have gone out already without waiting to say hello. No doubt she'd borrowed the Range Rover because she'd needed to transport her easel and the rest of her art paraphernalia. Anyway, he enjoyed driving the Mini from time to time. But, looking at the empty drive, he felt a little uneasy, knowing that Sheryl would be driving around the countryside alone in search of some picturesque spot to capture on canvas without a thought for her personal safety. After everything that had happened she still wasn't taking adequate precautions against the lunatics who called themselves the Pure Sons of the West. She'd even refused police protection after they'd firebombed the summerhouse. Sometimes she was too laid back for her own good.

Sheryl was an artist so she tended to see things differently from other people. Until quite recently he'd found her mildly bohemian ways attractive, a refreshing contrast to his own world of business. But in the last few months this aspect of her nature had begun to get on his nerves – especially now that she seemed to have retreated into a world of her own and was taking the threats of those lunatics so lightly. They were dangerous and now they'd proved it. He'd really hoped that after the destruction of the summerhouse she'd start to take things more seriously.

He pressed the accelerator gently and the car moved forward into the shadows of the double garage that stood some twenty yards from the house. Once he was inside, the door closed slowly behind him with a low-pitched electronic hum and he was left in silent darkness. As he climbed out of the car and locked it with the remote control, he smiled to himself. Tomorrow he'd go and put the fear of God into those archaeologists but in the meantime he had work to catch up with, away from the constant interruptions of the office.

He walked over to the side door with his briefcase in his hand and was about to let himself out of the garage when he heard a sound somewhere behind him. A scrabbling in the dark, an animal maybe.

But before he could turn round the blow came and he slumped to the ground. Then the stench of petrol began to fill the air.

12

If someone rescues you from certain death, you owe them your loyalty at the very least, so Jeanne committing adultery with another man must have seemed to Stephen de Grendalle like the ultimate betrayal.

We know little about de Grendalle as a man, except that he was a devout son of the church, as so many were in those far-off days. I wonder whether Jeanne was also devout in her own way. The Cathars believed that our 'tunics of flesh', as they described our bodies, were bound to fall prey to impurity and sin. It was only the soul that was pure.

Walter Fitzallen, founder of Tradmouth's fortunes, must have been a dynamic and powerful man and such men are attractive to women as I know from experience. So when Urien de Norton saw Fitzallen and Jeanne together, he jumped to the worst conclusion, a conclusion that was to lead to Jeanne's agonising death.

(From papers found in the possession of Professor Yves Demancour)

Wesley put the phone down. 'There's been a fire at Jon Bright's place. His garage has been burned to the ground.'

Gerry scratched his head. 'Anyone hurt?'

'Don't know yet. The fire investigators are still combing through the wreckage. Sheryl Bright's car was inside, apparently, and a note was pushed through the letterbox. Looks like it's our friends the Pure Sons of the West again.'

'Is Mrs Bright at home?'

'Yes. Apparently she's OK.' He paused. 'Cherry Bakewell.'

'You what?'

'I haven't had a chance to tell you yet but when Trish and I went to see Charles and Hannah Whitling, those archaeologists who worked with Nadia's mother, they told us that Sheryl took part in the 1983 dig at Grandal Field. She was a sixth-former at the time and before she was married her name was Bakewell – usually known as Cher but the Whitlings called her Cherry. I've been intending to speak to her. I want to find out what she remembers about Maggie March and Wendy Haskel. The Whitlings told Nadia about her so she might even have got round to paying her a visit.'

Gerry looked interested. 'You still think Nadia Lucas's death is connected with what happened to her mother?'

Wesley nodded. 'I'm sure it is. Don't know why or how but ...'

'A hunch. I've had a few of those in my time,' said the older copper.

'And fire. It's all connected with fire.' He saw Gerry raise his eyebrows. 'Nadia was burned to death. So was the man we thought was Ian Rowe – it'll be interesting to see whether that really was Denis Wade. Dr Maggie March was killed in a burning car back in 1983 and now we've got another fire at the Brights' place.' He paused for a moment. 'You know, Gerry, I can't get this story of the Burning Bride out of my head. It's like some sort of motif, always there in the background. Nadia was killed in

257

Grandal Field. According to legend, the bride in question was married to the lord who owned that land.'

'Coincidence?'

Wesley shrugged his shoulders. He could see the scepticism in Gerry's eyes. Maybe the boss was right to be sceptical. Maybe he was getting too imaginative. 'Right, we'd better get out to the Brights' place and see what's going on, and while we're at it we can ask Sheryl Bright about March, Haskel and Nadia.'

'The Nutter's always banging on about efficiency,' Gerry said with a grin that verged on the wicked.

Half an hour later they were sitting in the Brights' living room. Through the window they could see the fire fighters outside, sifting their way through the wreckage of the garage. Sheryl chose to sit with her back to the French windows so she couldn't see what was going on and Wesley couldn't blame her. He could sense her anxiety as she fidgeted with the fringes of the cushion she was hugging to her body, as if for comfort. Her husband had borrowed her car that day because she needed the Range Rover. Her car had been in that garage so he must have come home. But, as yet, the fire investigators had found no trace of him.

'Can you tell me what happened, Mrs Bright?' Wesley began.

She nodded. 'I was out painting. Not far away really – just four hundred yards or so up the lane. I took the Range Rover because it's easier to transport my easel in the bigger car and there's a handy lay-by to park in. I grabbed a quick sandwich before I went out and I set up my easel in the field around one o'clock. Then I found that I hadn't brought any water for my brushes so I called at a cottage nearby – I know the woman who lives there from an evening class I taught a couple of years ago and I see her from time to time. We chatted for a while on the doorstep then I turned round and saw smoke coming from the direction of our house so I ran all the way up the lane to investigate and I saw ... I knocked on my neighbour's door and she called the fire brigade. It was terrible.' She tore a tissue from the box on the coffee table and blew her nose. She was on the verge of tears.

'I believe you found another note.'

'It was lying in the hall so they must have pushed it through the letterbox like before. It's in the kitchen.'

Wesley looked at the DCI who gave a small nod of approval. He walked through into the kitchen where he found the note lying on the worktop. Someone, probably the constable who first attended the scene, had had the presence of mind to place it in a protective plastic bag. Not, Wesley thought, that this would do any good. If it was like the other he'd seen, the writer would have left no trace of his or her identity.

He picked it up and read the words through the veil of plastic. 'You wouldn't listen, would you? You've been tried in your absence and the death of your wife is your just punishment for the rape of our land. There is only one way of dealing with those who murder communities. If it continues, you'll be next.' It was signed 'The Pure Sons of the West'. Wesley reread it, thinking that the author of the note had a good command of English. Just like Jem Burrows.

He carried the note back into the living room and gave it to Gerry. Then he looked Sheryl Bright in the eye. She looked frightened and his next words weren't going to make her feel any better.

'The note implies that you were the intended victim, Mrs Bright.'

She looked up at Wesley, her eyes desperate. 'They must have thought I was driving the Mini and that I'd be in the garage. Do you think I'm in danger? Do you think they'll try again?'

'Don't worry, love,' Gerry said comfortingly. 'I reckon we'll be able to make an arrest pretty soon. Now all we have to do is find out where your husband's got to. Any ideas where he might be?'

Sheryl shook her head. 'If the car was in the garage, that means he must have come home. Maybe he went out for a walk or . . .'

Wesley looked at her sharply. 'Is he in the habit of going for country walks?' Somehow Jon Bright hadn't struck him as the type to appreciate the beauties of the countryside.

'Sometimes. I don't know.' She didn't sound very convincing.

Wesley leaned forward. 'Leaving that for the moment, I'd like to ask you about an archaeological dig you took part in back in the nineteen eighties.'

Sheryl looked surprised, and a little relieved as if she was glad of the change of subject. 'Yes. I remember. It was in Queenswear. I was living over that side of the river at the time and I was thinking of doing archaeology at university but . . .'

'Did you?'

'No. I decided on art instead. I don't know whether the dig put me off.'

'How do you mean?' Wesley asked quietly.

'Well, some of the people were nice enough – like the couple. Oh, what were their names?'

'Charles and Hannah Whitling.'

'That's right. How did you know?'

'I've spoken to them recently. They remember you. In fact they saw your picture in the local paper . . . an art exhibition?'

She managed a weak smile. 'Fancy them remembering.'

'What about the woman in charge, Maggie March?'

'Dr March. I didn't like her much, which is an awful thing to say because she died in a terrible accident just after I left. She was pretty nasty to me a couple of times. I was only young and I didn't think of answering her back, telling her where she could stick her job. I would now but I thought that if I wanted a place at uni . . .'

Wesley nodded. Being able to say in a university interview that she'd worked with Maggie March would have given her a few brownie points. 'What about Wendy Haskel?'

Sheryl thought for a few moments. 'She was quite nice even if she did seem a bit neurotic. And I'm sure there was something between her and March. Wendy used to chat to me quite a bit during breaks and she'd make sure I was helping in her trenches, that sort of thing. She seemed really keen to encourage me and I had the feeling that March didn't like it. She used to give me really evil looks and a few times I saw her and Wendy arguing. I can't swear that it was about me but that's the impression I got.'

'Do you think they were lovers?'

Sheryl raised her eyebrows then considered the question. 'Well, it never occurred to me at the time. I mean, I was only seventeen and I'd led quite a conventional life . . . and this was twenty-five years ago, don't forget. But, looking back, I think they probably were. But they both had children. Wendy had a little girl who lived with her estranged husband. She showed me a photo of her once. I think she missed her.'

'What was her name?'

Sheryl shook her head. 'Sorry. Can't remember.'

'So you haven't had a visit from a woman called Nadia Lucas?'

Sheryl looked up, puzzled. 'No. Why?'

261

'Nadia Lucas was Wendy's daughter and she was visiting people who'd known her mother.'

'Well, she never came here.'

'What can you tell us about Maggie March?'

'Someone said she had a grown-up son but there was never any mention of him or any partner. That was a bit of a mystery.'

'Have you been back to have a look at the site?'

'Briefly. Just a flying visit,' she said quickly. 'I've got an exhibition on in Neston next month so I've been rather busy.'

'Do you remember anything strange happening on that dig in 1983? Anything at all out of the ordinary?'

She gave Wesley a weak smile. 'Well, it was the first dig I'd ever been on so I wouldn't really have known what was normal, would I?' She hesitated. 'The only odd thing happened just after I'd finished. But that was nothing to do with—'

'What was it?' Wesley asked. 'What happened?'

'It was nothing. Just a mistake, that's all.'

'What was?'

'My mum got into a bit of a state about it. Tradmouth Hospital sent a letter asking me to go to Outpatients and when I rang them to ask why, I was told that someone had been admitted and they'd given my name for some reason – all my details. My mother contacted them and they said that the woman who'd given her name as Sheryl Bakewell had discharged herself. That's all really. We never got to the bottom of it.'

'Did they tell you anything about this woman?'

'No. Nothing. We never heard any more about it. I thought at the time that it might have been someone I knew from school who didn't want their family to know what they'd been up to for some reason but . . .'

'A bit of a mystery, then,' said Gerry. 'But, like you

say, probably nothing to do with your archaeological dig.'

'That's right.'

Wesley seemed to have lost interest in this unexplained case of mistaken identity. 'Strange that your husband should be building on the very field you were excavating,' he said.

'Yes,' she replied. 'I suppose it is. Not that I remember much about what was found.' She hesitated. 'I heard somewhere that it's an important site. Jon won't be too pleased if they stop his development.'

'Have you tried his mobile, love?' Gerry asked.

Sheryl looked a little irritated. 'What do you think I've been doing? Until you arrived I was trying it every few minutes.' She picked up her own phone and pressed a button. But after a few moments she shook her head. 'Voice mail again. And when I called the office his secretary just said he'd gone home early to catch up on some work.'

When she'd been talking about the Queenswear dig she had started to look more relaxed, Wesley thought. But now that her mind had returned to the reality of her present situation, her face showed signs of strain again.

'All our patrols are on the lookout for your husband, Mrs Bright. We'll find him.'

She glanced over her shoulder towards the window. The fire crew were still damping down and combing what was left of the garage. 'But what if he was in there? What if he—?'

'Best not to think about that till we have to,' Wesley said quickly.

'You look as if you could do with a brandy, love,' Gerry Heffernan said. He walked over to the drinks cabinet in the corner of the room and poured a large measure of cognac into a crystal glass.

While Sheryl was sipping the comforting liquid, Wesley took out his mobile phone and speed-dialled Neil's number. There was always a slim chance that Jon Bright had decided to visit the site of his development in an attempt to chivvy the archaeologists along and had cadged a lift in someone's car. When Neil answered he stepped out into the hall. Sheryl would hardly want to hear negative news.

'I was thinking of calling you,' were Neil's first words. 'We've got a bit of a situation here. We've been joined by the Pure Sons of the West who are staging what they call a peaceful protest. I've cleared them out of our trenches now so they're not really causing too much of a nuisance. But if Bright shows his face I've got a nasty feeling that might change.'

'Any sign of Bright?'

'No. I think they were expecting him to be here keeping a beady eye on us. But we've not seen him since yesterday.'

'How many protesters are there?'

Neil didn't answer for a few moments, as though he was doing a swift head count. 'Around thirty. Their leader seems to have them under control so they've caused no damage.'

'Is that Jem Burrows?'

'That's right. How did you—?'

'He's come to our attention. Is there someone called Chas Ventisard there too?'

'There is one called Chas, yeah. Don't know his second name.'

'What time did they arrive?'

'Ages ago. Late this morning.'

'And none of them have left?'

'Don't think so. No.'

'You've not called the police, have you?'

264

'I thought I'd better let them know. They sent a patrol car round to keep an eye on things but . . .'

'Thanks, Neil. If Bright shows his face, call me.'

As soon as he ended the call he heard a thunderous knocking on the front door. He fumbled with the lock, impatient to see who it was. He hoped, for Sheryl's sake that it was Jon Bright returning home to find his garage burned to the ground and his wife's car destroyed. But when the door swung open he saw a fire officer standing there.

Wesley quickly introduced himself and showed his warrant card. 'Any news?' he said, keeping his voice down. He didn't want Sheryl to overhear anything bad.

'Afraid so,' said the fire officer. We've found a body in the debris. Badly burned. Clutching car keys in the right hand. Just thought you'd want to know, Inspector. You could have a murder on your hands. Can't be sure yet but the fire investigator thinks it looks like arson.'

He gave Wesley a businesslike smile and turned away. It looked as if Jon Bright might have turned up after all.

Professor Yves Demancour let himself into his flat. He had had a free afternoon and that evening he was due for an assignation with Chantalle. There had been many times when he'd promised himself he'd give up their meetings, but it never seemed to happen.

He was about to make for the kitchen when he stopped. He stood there perfectly still, listening, but all he could hear was the faint twitter of birdsong outside in the garden, the sound of distant traffic and an ambulance siren wailing as some unfortunate soul was conveyed to the hospital nearby. And yet something wasn't right. He was a fastidious man, almost obsessively neat, and within those few seconds he could tell something had been moved.

He told himself he must be imagining things. Recent events had made him jumpy. Nadia had died a hideous death and he couldn't help wondering whether he himself was in danger.

Over the past week there had been times when he'd seen assassins in every shadow. The intrusion of the police into the darkest crevices of his private life had shaken him. And sometimes when he closed his eyes he could see the flames and hear his sister's cries, which, in his mind, became Nadia's. He would ask Chantalle to play the part again tonight, he thought, wiping the sweat off his forehead with the back of his hand. If he re-enacted his fantasies again it might just conquer his dark pangs of fear. Or it might make things even worse.

He took a deep breath and carried his bulging brief-case into the living room, where he dumped it on one of the armchairs. He needed a drink. Then he'd feel better and he'd be able to get on with reading over some of his students' essays before his evening meal and his appointment with Chantalle. The cognac bottle on the bookcase was almost beckoning to him, so he fetched a glass from his tiny kitchen, grabbed the bottle by the neck and poured himself a generous measure.

As he raised the glass to his lips, he heard a noise from the bedroom. He swung round, his heart racing. There was someone there with him in the flat. An intruder.

Yves Demancour was a man who hated danger and the threat of violence. He had seen the results of suffering, the raw flesh and the agonising pain. He closed his eyes. Perhaps whoever it was had come to kill him. Or, worse, to torture him for pleasure or to get him to give away the secret he kept closest to his heart. His treasure.

What was the best course of action? He weighed all the options in his mind. The most sensible would be to call the police. But would they get there in time?

There it was again, another sound. Footsteps creeping out into the hall. Demancour stood quite still, toying with the idea of concealing himself behind the sofa with the telephone. But when he tried to move, he found he was frozen to the spot. And the footsteps were getting nearer. Too late for action now.

When the figure loomed in the doorway, he stared like a terrified wild beast caught in the headlights of some monstrous lorry.

The Pure Sons of the West were the obvious suspects. Someone had been burned to death in that garage and they had more or less claimed responsibility in the note that had been pushed through the door so they had to be brought in. But Wesley had always worked on the assumption, against all the standard rules of policing, that obvious isn't necessarily correct.

'You're very quiet,' Gerry said as they drove out to Queenswear.

'I've been thinking. Don't you think all this business with the Pure Sons of the West is a bit . . .' He searched for the word. 'Theatrical. There's something not quite right about it.'

'Evidence?'

Wesley kept his eyes fixed on the road ahead. 'Haven't got any.'

'Then I suggest we get some. But I agree. No murderer I've ever known has drawn attention to himself like that.'

'Unless he knew he had an unbreakable alibi.'

'Exactly. And your mate Neil's given him one. However, it might not have been Jem Burrows himself who did the dirty work. Let's face it, it could be any of them. Burrows looks bright enough to know the value of delegation.'

Of course Wesley had thought of all this. Since he'd talked to Sheryl Bright he'd thought of little else. It was just a matter of finding out which of the Pure Sons of the West were absent from the protest at the appropriate time. Simple really.

When they reached Grandal Field Neil looked pleased to see them and Wesley guessed the protesters were starting to get on his nerves. Two uniformed constables who'd been leaning against their patrol car straightened themselves up when they saw the two CID men arrive, in an effort to make it look as if they were doing something useful rather than enjoying the sunshine.

While Gerry went over for a chat with the officers, Wesley was swept off by Neil for a tour of his trenches.

'There's been a development,' he said quietly as they walked. 'Two as a matter of fact.'

'What do you mean?'

'The dental records of the corpse found in Owl Cottage don't match Ian Rowe's.'

Neil stopped, his mouth gaping open. 'You mean he could still be alive?'

'It looks that way.'

'Any idea where he is?'

'We're working on it. And there's something else.' He looked around. There was nobody to overhear what he was about to say. 'We think Bright might have turned up.'

Neil grunted. It was clear he didn't have a high opinion of Bright and Wesley wondered how he'd take the news of his death.

'There was a fire in his garage at home. The firemen found a body. We can only assume it's Bright.'

Neil's eyes widened. 'Was it accidental or—?'

'We're treating it as suspicious. And a note was found from your friends the Pure Sons of the West saying they'd carried out their threat to kill his wife and he'd be next.'

'You think she was the intended victim?'

Wesley shrugged. 'He was driving her car so it certainly looks that way.'

'Well, I can tell you they've been here all day. None of them have budged. And before you ask, this is all of them. The lot. They made a great point of saying that. Important protest – full turn-out.'

Wesley smiled. 'Thanks. That's just what I expected. I don't reckon this is a protest as much as an elaborate alibi.'

'You mean I'm being used?' he said with mock horror.

'Something like that. They all had to be seen to be miles away from the action.'

'How's Bright's wife taking it? I met her yesterday, you know.'

'Really? Where?'

'She came to have a look at the site.'

'Yes. She mentioned that she'd paid a quick visit.'

'Nice woman,' Neil continued. 'She's done some digging.'

'We know all about that. She actually helped Maggie March on this site when she was a teenager.'

'She never mentioned that.' Neil looked a little disappointed. 'Where was she when her husband ...?'

'Painting in a nearby field. But she was chatting to a neighbour when the place actually went up.'

Neil thought for a few moments. 'When I met her here I don't think she was expecting to see me.'

'How do you mean?'

'I think she was expecting to see someone else.'

'Any idea who?'

Neil shook his head. 'Your guess is as good as mine.' He thought for a moment. 'If she was having an affair, might her husband have been sending her the threatening letters? Perhaps he intended to kill her but he ended up setting himself on fire.'

As a theory it was as good as any – but his conversation with Neil was due to be interrupted. Gerry Heffernan was marching across the field towards them, avoiding the trenches with the sure-footed elegance of a hippopotamus in a maze. Wesley saw him wave. He looked as if he had some news.

'Hi, Neil,' he said as reached them. 'How are you doing?' He didn't wait for a reply. 'Wes, I've just had Colin Bowman on the phone. He's had a quick look at the body in the garage and he reckons it's suspicious. Victim's got a ruddy great head wound. He was bashed before the garage was torched. Proverbial blunt instrument.'

'Like the victim in Owl Cottage?'

Gerry shrugged. 'Possibly.'

Wesley looked at Neil apologetically. 'That's put paid to your theory.'

'I reckon it's the coroner after overtime payments,' mumbled Gerry as he turned to go back to the car.

Wesley examined his note book before taking his mobile phone from his pocket and punching out Rachel Tracey's number. He needed a few names checked out and Rachel was the person to do it swiftly and efficiently.

When he'd finished the call he turned back to Neil and gave his old friend an apologetic smile. 'See you soon then,' he said before raising a hand in farewell.

'So what's going on?' Neil asked, curious.

'The Pure Sons of the West have some explaining to do,' Wesley replied before making for the car.

'I thought you were dead,' Demancour said softly.

Ian Rowe didn't answer. He looked dishevelled and scared. Not the cocksure man Demancour had once met back in France.

'How did you get in?'

Ian Rowe held up an old credit card, scratched and undoubtedly out of date. His pass key. 'Sorry. Didn't have much choice. I need help.'

There was a desperation in the man's eyes that made the professor nervous. 'Where have you been?'

'Lying low. Hostel in Morbay that doesn't ask too many questions. Thought I'd stay there till the fuss died down.'

'You've heard about Nadia?'

Rowe hesitated before he replied. 'I heard it on the news. Fucking shock it was. But Nadia was a worried lady. She was scared of something and I reckon you know what it was.'

There was a pause and Demancour looked into his visitor's eyes. Nadia had introduced Rowe to him when they'd worked in Toulouse. He hadn't trusted him then and he certainly didn't trust him now.

'Yes, she seemed to have something on her mind.'

'I thought she might have been frightened of you.'

Demancour shook his head vigorously. 'Whatever was worrying her, it was nothing to do with me. I told that to the police. Why should I harm Nadia?' He eyed Rowe suspiciously. 'What about you? You had her car. Maybe you know who killed her.'

'She said I could borrow her car. Told me the garage lock was broken and she kept a set of spare keys taped to the wheel arch. Not very hot on security, our Nadia. But I had to abandon it because I'd left the bloody keys inside the cottage when it was torched.'

'You saw who started the fire?'

Rowe shook his head. 'Whoever it was made sure they

weren't seen and I didn't hang round to say hello. Look, I need to get away before they come looking for me again. I need money.'

Demancour gave a high-pitched laugh, almost a giggle. 'You think I have money? I have no money.'

'But you've got the treasure. Nadia said you'd found something fantastic. Where is it, Yves? Have you got it here? Or have you sold it to some collector already and pocketed the cash?'

Yves Demancour began to laugh. He couldn't stop himself and soon his whole body was shaking. 'You want to see the treasure?' he spluttered after a few seconds. 'You really want to see my treasure of the Cathars?'

Rowe stepped forward, threatening, towering over Demancour like a bird of prey over some hapless rodent. 'I haven't time to play fucking games. I need money. I need to get away.'

'I will show you the treasure. Wait.' Chuckling to himself and ignoring the urgency in Rowe's voice, the professor shuffled across the room and reached up to the top shelf of his bookcase. He took down a plain oak box and opened it carefully, almost reverently. Then he slipped on a pair of white cotton gloves and took out a small oblong object wrapped in white tissue paper which he carried over to his desk and laid down with exaggerated gentleness.

'Let me see.' Rowe made to push the professor out of the way but Demancour stood firm.

'Patience.' He folded the tissue paper aside carefully to reveal a small leather-bound book, ancient and mottled with the centuries.

Rowe reached for the thing but Demancour brushed his hand away. 'One touch could do immense damage. It is eight hundred years old and extremely fragile. When I have collated all my research I shall present it to a suitable museum or library. But until then I am the guardian of this treasure and I must ensure that no harm comes to it while it is in my care.'

He could sense Rowe's impatience as he opened the book gently at a random page. The language was familiar to the professor, who had made a study of it. But he knew Rowe had no idea what it meant. Occitan, the ancient language of the Languedoc, was a mystery to him.

'Is this it? Is this the fucking treasure?' Rowe almost spat the bitter words.

Demancour knew only too well that he had expected coins or jewels, something that could be converted into ready cash. Not a treasure of scholarship. He leaned over the delicate book protectively, half afraid that Rowe, in his fury, would seize the thing and fling it across the room.

'Did Nadia lead you to believe it would be of some monetary value? Is that what she said? Did you think it would be something like that gold found at Saissac? Or did you expect the Holy Grail?' Demancour smiled as he shook his head. 'No. This is the Cathar litany, their beliefs and their way of worship. A thing so precious that it is beyond price. Nadia did not lie to you. She merely overestimated you.'

Demancour rewrapped the book carefully and replaced it in its box. 'I think you'd better go. I will give you what money I have in my wallet but you will find it isn't much.'

He saw Rowe's hand form into a fist but he did his best to maintain his cool exterior. If you showed fear, that was when predators were at their most dangerous.

The fist tightened. 'Nadia used to say how she was scared you'd say her research was yours. She didn't trust you, Demancour.' Rowe stepped forward and stood so close that Demancour could feel his hot breath on his face. 'I think you killed her. She told me your little secret, you know.' His lips formed into an unpleasant grin. 'You like the idea of burning flesh, don't you?'

Demancour opened his mouth to speak but no sound came out.

'Nadia told me all about it. It was a student back in Toulouse, wasn't it? Took her out and plied her with drink and got her to pretend she was on fire. Then you got a cigarette lighter out and she screamed the place down. Caused a bit of a scandal, didn't it? That's why you came over here. Did you ever try it on with Nadia? Maybe you did. Maybe your nasty little fantasies went a step too far. Maybe you took her to that field and ended up killing her. Maybe you wanted to keep your precious treasure all to yourself and pass her research off as your own. She told me she was on to something. Something about a woman who came to Devon from France. Jeanne de Minerve, isn't it? She was getting obsessed and she said she was going to write a book about her. Where are all her notes and her papers? That's what I want to know.'

Demancour shook his head. 'I know nothing of this matter. Now leave me alone.'

'You're lying. I know you are.'

He took a step towards him but Demancour picked up the phone on his desk. 'I'm calling the police,' he said.

'You wouldn't dare. And if you do, I might just tell them you're a murderer,' Rowe hissed as he backed away.

Jem Burrows sat in the interview room with a beatific smile on his face and all the confidence of someone who knows they're completely in the clear. He had witnesses – dozens of them, so he couldn't possibly have killed Jon

Bright. The Sons hadn't sent any anonymous notes to his missus, and they had absolutely nothing to do with the fire in the summer house. Someone had set them up. A man like Bright was bound to have a lot of enemies and the Sons were useful scapegoats. Maybe he'd even set the summer house on fire himself and blamed them to get them off his back. And as for murder . . . even a greedy bastard like Bright whose main aim in life was to ruin the natural environment, didn't deserve that.

'Ever met Mrs Bright?'

'I don't think so,' Burrows said quickly.

At that moment, as if on cue, the door opened and Trish Walton scurried in, trying to look unobtrusive. She bent and whispered something in Wesley's ear but all the time he kept his eyes fixed on Jem Burrows' face.

When she had finished Wesley looked up. 'We've been making a few enquiries, Mr Burrows.' He paused to let the idea sink in and saw a flash of wariness in Jem's eyes, there for a second then swiftly concealed. 'You worked for a gardening company for a while. Tradmouth Landscapes.' Wesley knew the company – Gerry Heffernan's son, Sam, had once worked for them during his university vacation. 'One of our officers has spoken to Tradmouth Landscapes and they told us where you worked.'

'How very thorough,' Burrows said with a hint of sarcasm.

'You worked at the Brights' place. Regular maintenance contract. Until you quit your job three months ago, you went there every week.' Wesley looked expectantly at the man on the other side of the desk. In the silence he could hear the faint sound of the tapes whirring in the recording machine. He imagined he could hear Jem's brain working at the same time, thinking up some excuse, some story.

After a few moments he seemed to come to a decision. 'OK, I admit I worked in the garden but I never saw the Brights because they paid the firm direct. Our paths never crossed.'

'We can ask Mrs Bright.'

'She'll back me up.'

Wesley looked into his eyes. 'You seem very sure of that.'

'I am 'cause it's the truth. There's no way I, or any of my comrades, set that garage alight. We were all in Queenswear in full view of the police and a dozen archaeologists. We're all innocent and I'd like to go now.' He folded his arms and stared at Wesley defiantly. The outraged law-abiding citizen wrongly accused.

But somehow Wesley Peterson didn't believe a word of it.

It was Rachel who suggested that they pay a visit to Jon Bright's place of work. Wesley had intended leaving it until the following morning and using what remained of the afternoon to catch up on the mountain of paperwork that the murders of Nadia Lucas, Denis Wade and now Jon Bright had generated. But he knew Rachel was right. It was best to speak to Bright's colleagues while the shock was still fresh and they were off their guard. The paperwork could wait.

Jem Burrows was still in custody and Gerry had said that he wanted to interview him again before they went home for the night. He had guilt written all over him, Gerry had observed, but as for how he – or one of his followers – had managed to do the dirty deed while they were all under observation in Grandal Field, that was anybody's guess.

When Wesley and Rachel reached the offices of Tradford Developments, they were greeted by Donna

Grogen, who was sobbing inconsolably into a tissue while Bright's secretary, a well-built, motherly woman in early middle age, rested a comforting arm around her shoulders.

'It's a terrible business. Terrible,' the secretary said when they'd introduced themselves. 'Was it an accident or . . .?'

'I'm afraid we're treating Mr Bright's death as suspicious,' said Rachel, her words causing a further outpouring of grief from Donna.

'He was so nice. He was so good to me,' Donna sobbed.

Wesley watched her, wondering whether this could be the same girl who didn't bother coming into work when her mother's ex-boyfriend made her a better offer. Her grief for Bright, he thought, could hardly be that deep. Unlike her colleague's: the motherly secretary, Liz Ruben, looked genuinely shocked.

'I wonder if you could tell us about Mr Bright's movements yesterday.' Wesley addressed Liz as she looked the more reliable of the pair.

'He was here all morning then he said he had some paperwork to do so he went home for the afternoon. He said he'd have more peace and quiet there.'

'Did he often work from home?'

'Sometimes. When he wanted to get something done without being interrupted. And he had a lot to catch up with – all the correspondence and reports connected with the planning application for the Grandal Field site. Some archaeologists were working there. He wanted to see whether he could get round the requirements for a full archaeological investigation. The delays were starting to annoy him. Then there were these environmental protesters but they were just a nuisance, not a real problem. How's Mrs Bright?'

277

Wesley sensed that the question was rather unenthusiastic, as if Liz was only making an enquiry into the widow's wellbeing for form's sake.

'Shocked but bearing up,' Rachel said. 'She's gone to stay with a friend.'

Liz looked away and Wesley wondered whether there'd been something between the secretary and the boss, something that caused her to resent his wife. Liz Ruben was hardly mistress material, he thought. Although sometimes it was hard to tell. His time in the police force investigating the muddy depths of people's lives had taught him that the most unlikely people can sometimes end up in bed together.

'You know Mrs Bright well?' Rachel asked. She'd obviously sensed the undercurrents too.

'Not very. Well, we used to pass the time of day but recently ... well, she's been very offhand. As though she doesn't want to talk. I thought I might have said something to offend her.'

'Why do you think she was being like that?'

Liz shrugged. 'No idea. I've racked my brains but I can't think of anything ... apart from these threats, of course.' Her hand went up to her mouth. 'I hope she didn't think they were anything to do with me. I mean ...'

Donna began to make reassuring noises, muttering that nobody in their right mind would connect Liz with that sort of thing.

Wesley leaned forward. 'What can you tell us about Mr and Mrs Bright's relationship? In confidence of course.' His instincts told him that Liz was just about ready to dish the dirt on the Brights.

Liz appeared to consider the question for a few moments. 'You don't really know what goes on in other people's marriages, do you, Inspector? I mean, she has

278

her painting and her gardening and I don't think he was particularly interested in either. She's a professional artist, you know. Has exhibitions and everything.'

'I know. Are you saying that they didn't have much in common?'

She pressed her lips together. 'I don't think it's my place to say. But I reckon that recently they've been living separate lives, so to speak.'

He decided to change tack. 'Firm doing well, is it?'

'Not bad.'

'So she'll be a wealthy woman?'

Liz didn't answer but Donna piped up. 'I reckon she will. I reckon he'll have been very well insured,' she said with a meaningful look.

'Pity Sheryl Bright's got an alibi,' Rachel said as they left the office.

'There's too many unbreakable alibis in this case if you ask me. Makes me suspicious.'

There was a smile on Rachel's lips as she started the car.

So, according to Liz Ruben, Sheryl Bright was interested in gardening. But Jem Burrows had said that she never had anything to do with the firm of gardeners she employed. These two opposing facts rang alarm bells in Wesley's head.

But the untimely death of Jon Bright was only one of his problems. He couldn't forget about Nadia Lucas. She was the hub around which everything else revolved.

Nadia had been on a quest to find out what really happened to the mother who had disappeared off the face of the earth twenty-five years ago. What if, Wesley thought, Wendy Haskel had faked her own death and was still alive somewhere? What if she didn't want to be found, for some reason? But surely no mother could kill her own daughter in that terrible way, pouring petrol on her and setting her alight, then watching her body being consumed by flames. Surely he was on the wrong track here. Unless Wendy was ill or seriously disturbed. He had to consider every possibility.

He picked up a couple of files from his desk: the reports of Maggie March's fatal accident and the details of Wendy Haskel's apparent suicide. The accident seemed fairly straightforward. The car had veered off an isolated road between Queenswear and Bloxham and hurtled into some woodland, hitting a large oak full on before bursting into flames. Maggie had been killed by the impact before being burned. No traces of soot were found in her lungs so the pathologist had concluded that her death was mercifully sudden. She was identified by what was left of her jewellery, as well as the fact that she never let anybody else drive her car. Wendy, presumably shocked by the news of her friend's death, broken so brutally by Karl Maplin, left a note in her cottage the following day and drove out to Littlebury, where she left her car in the car park and her clothes and handbag on the beach before, presumably, wading into the water until the waves covered her head.

So why did he feel there was something wrong?

He noticed an envelope on the far corner of his desk that hadn't been there before. He reached across and opened it and found that it was a copy of a birth certificate. He had asked Paul to see what he could find out about Maggie March's elusive son and it looked as though he'd made a start.

Margaret Ursula March had given birth to a son, John Martin March, on 3 May 1958 but the space for the father's name had been left blank. The child would be in his early fifties now. At the time of the dig he would have been twenty-five, more than old enough to have left home. But who had cared for John Martin when he was a child, Wesley wondered, while Maggie March was pursuing her career? Grandparents maybe? Or a nanny? He wanted to find out everything about the set-up with Maggie and Wendy and their respective children. Of course he already knew what had become of Wendy's daughter, Nadia: she was lying in a drawer in Tradmouth Hospital's mortuary awaiting her funeral, which hadn't yet been arranged. But where was John Martin March now? And what had become of him when his mother had met her tragic death?

Two children scarred by the past. Wesley visualised them, standing hand in hand, the young man and the tiny girl. Both lost and motherless. He shuddered and looked at his watch, suddenly longing to see his own children. Time with them suddenly seemed so precious . . . and so fragile.

He could see Gerry Heffernan through his office window, feet up on his desk and totally relaxed as he flung budget forms towards his rubbish bin. Wesley left his desk and opened the boss's door.

'I've just been thinking about Maggie March's accident and Wendy Haskel's suicide.'

'And?'

'It all seems straightforward but I've still got a funny feeling about it. Maggie died of head injuries and she was dead before the fire started. What if the injuries weren't caused by the crash? What if the whole thing was staged? Paul found Maggie's son's birth certificate and there's no father mentioned.' He saw Gerry raise his eyebrows. 'His name was John Martin March and he'd be in his fifties now. I'd like to find out what happened to him. And I've asked Trish to contact Tradmouth Hospital to see if they have any record of the person who was admitted using Sheryl Bright's name.'

'What's this?'

'Around the time March and Haskel died a woman was admitted to hospital using Sheryl's name and address. Odd, don't you think?'

'What was she in hospital for?'

'Don't know. All we know is that Sheryl received a letter from the hospital telling her to go for an outpatients appointment a couple of weeks later. She rang them and they told her that someone had been using her name and address.'

The DCI frowned. 'It could be nothing but it's certainly worth looking into,' he said. 'Let's hope they keep records that far back.' He examined his watch. 'Well, it's almost eight o'clock so we won't get any joy with any of that tonight. We've got Jem Burrows contemplating the error of his ways in the cells so why don't you get off home?'

'What about you?'

'Sam's off out with some veterinary nurse from his practice and Rosie's doing her stint at the refuge in Neston so she won't be home till later. And it's Joyce's night for Weightwatchers,' he added coyly. 'I'll give it an hour to see if anything new comes in and hit the road myself.'

'Has Rosie come across Yelena at the refuge?'

Gerry shook his head. 'She's been moved on again. It was reckoned that she'd be safer in Exeter.'

Wesley said goodnight. As he walked home a sudden thought struck him. John Martin March. What if he was in the habit of using his middle name and he'd adopted the name of Crace for some reason? Sir Martin was around the right age, after all. But the idea seemed so outrageous that he decided to say nothing, not even to Gerry. He needed proof and that wasn't available until tomorrow. He'd just have to be patient.

*

Pam knew that Wesley would be late again. It was the same every time there was a major murder investigation. She was almost getting used to it. But that didn't mean she liked it.

She had half expected Neil to turn up and she'd been rather relieved when the doorbell had stayed silent. She'd had to get the children to bed and Uncle Neil's presence always proved a little disruptive. He really had no idea about routine and discipline.

Just as she was clearing up in the kitchen, placing Wesley's congealing dinner carefully in the microwave, the doorbell rang. Neil again. She filled the kettle and flicked it on. They'd have tea. Wine would come later when Wesley was home.

She hurried out into the hall but when she opened the front door there was nobody there. However, Neil knew them well enough to try round the back if he didn't get an answer. She called his name a couple of times but when there was no response she closed the door again and returned to the kitchen, half expecting to see Neil's face grinning at the back door, waiting to be let in. But there was nobody there.

The kettle had just switched itself off and a plume of steam was rising from the spout. She took a mug from the cupboard but when she heard a loud crash from the direction of the utility room, the shock made her drop the mug on to the worktop. It bounced on to the floor and shattered into pieces as a dark figure appeared in the doorway.

13

The letter from Urien de Norton which planted the seed of suspicion in Stephen de Grendalle's mind is ambiguous to say the least.

I can picture de Norton as a weasel of a man, smooth and softly spoken. He would have written the letter by his own hand then instructed a servant to ride over to Queenswear to deliver his poisonous morsel of news.

'On market day I did see your wife speaking most privily with Master Fitzallen. I approached to speak with her, to convey my greetings to your lordship, but she and Master Fitzallen left the market place with great haste in each other's company.'

The letter went on to deal with some routine estate business but by the time de Grendalle had finished reading, the seed must have been sown. And when the second letter was delivered, written in de Norton's hand but left unsigned, de Grendalle's jealousy must have reached danger point.

(From papers found in the possession of Professor Yves Demancour)

It was still light and Neil didn't feel like leaving the site even though the rest of his team had gone some time ago. He stood there alone in Grandal Field feeling rather

284

furtive, as though he'd just stepped through his own private gateway into the thirteenth century.

It was all there set out in front of him: the whole manorial complex outlined on the ground. He could see the remains of an oven in the kitchen; the great hall with its central hearth to keep the whole household, from the highest to the lowest, warm in winter. The outbuildings were all there: the buttery, the stables, the barns and the brewhouse. Stephen de Grendalle had been a man of substance. But, as far as Neil could tell, he hadn't bothered to rebuild his dovecot when it had been burned to the ground.

Once the police had taken their crime scene tape away, he had supervised the digging of the dovecot area himself and it had been clear from the start that the strong geophysics signal had been caused by a thick layer of burned material. He had come across such things before in the course of his work. The remains of a building, burned to the ground and abandoned. Only this particular building had been circular, the sort of medieval dovecot he had seen several times before in Devon. And in just the right place, close to the house but not too close.

He found this discovery particularly exciting because the physical evidence seemed to fit in with all those strange local legends about the burning bride: the French wife of Stephen de Grendalle who had been punished for her infidelity; who had been locked in the dovecot while her loving husband set it alight. There were many animal activists, Neil knew, who would have been more worried about the unfortunate doves than the woman, but a shudder of horror passed through his body as he stood alone on the very spot where she must have met her agonising end. And the girl who'd died there a couple of weeks ago had been burned to death near that very spot.

He looked at his watch and realised it was time he was going. He'd already locked up at the church hall and he knew his colleagues would be in the pub. There'd be a lot of speculation about the future of the site now Jon Bright was dead, and he felt he wanted to join in.

He was just locking the gate leading to Grandal Field when he spotted a battered grey car parked up against the hedgerow. He'd seen it before. In fact he was sure it had been there on the evening he'd bumped into Sheryl Bright.

Then he remembered. He'd seen its owner get out of it much earlier that day. And he'd also seen the owner taken away by the police.

It was Jem Burrows's car, he was sure of it.

Perhaps Wesley would be interested to know that Burrows' car had been parked there just as Sheryl happened to be wandering around the site. He tried his number but it was engaged.

'You're looking well, Pam,' Ian Rowe said with a smug smile that made Pam want to slap his face.

'What the hell are you doing here?' she said, taking a step back.

'You really shouldn't leave your back door unlocked, you know. I'm surprised Wesley didn't tell you that. Or maybe you thought that being married to a policeman puts you in some sort of protective bubble. Sorry to have startled you and all that but you'll really have to learn to be more careful.'

'What are you doing here?' she repeated. 'And how did you find out where we lived?'

'You're not ex-directory. Very careless. Not like Wesley at all.'

'What do you want?' Her heart was thumping as she looked Rowe in the eye, her fists clenched in both fear

286

and pent-up fury. She wanted him out of her kitchen and out of her life. He was trouble.

She took a deep breath. 'Wesley's due back any minute.'

'Good. I need to see him.'

She was tempted to tell him to get lost but she sensed that he wouldn't take no for an answer. He wasn't going to leave until he got what he wanted. Whatever that was.

'The police thought you were dead,' she said, watching him suspiciously.

'I nearly was,' he answered quickly. 'And if a certain person finds out I'm still alive I don't reckon I'll last long.'

Pam's curiosity got the better of her. 'What are you talking about?'

Rowe hesitated. 'I'll wait for Wesley. I need to tell him the whole story.'

He slumped on to a stool and ran his fingers through his hair, leaving furrows in the greasy locks. He looked as though he needed a good bath and a meal. Pam's charitable side fought with her anger and eventually scored a little victory.

'Do you want something to eat?'

Rowe looked up and gave her a smile that verged on the dazzling. Through the dirt and hunger, he still clung on to a vestige of his charm. 'I don't want to put you to any trouble.'

She didn't answer. Considering that a man who intruded into her home uninvited didn't deserve much effort, she put some bread in the toaster and opened a can of beans. Beans on toast. Student food to keep body and soul together. And keep Ian Rowe occupied until Wesley turned up. Then she sat down on the stool opposite her unwelcome visitor, sending up a silent prayer that Amelia wouldn't call down as she sometimes did, wanting an extra bedtime story or a drink. She didn't want to leave Rowe on his own. She felt she couldn't trust him not to rifle through their private belongings in search of money or credit cards.

'What time does Wesley usually get in?' Rowe asked.

'That depends,' she answered quickly. 'Where have you been living since ... since the fire?'

'At a hostel for the homeless in Morbay, keeping my head down. They tried to bloody kill me so I'm taking no chances.'

'Who did?'

He hesitated and shook his head.

'Does anybody know you're here?'

'Only Demancour, Nadia's boss. I paid him a visit earlier. Don't worry. I left him in one piece.' He smiled. 'I got it all wrong about him. I was led to believe he'd got his hands on some valuable treasure, something he'd pinched from some museum or archaeological site. I thought he'd hand over some of his ill-gotten gains in return for my silence. How wrong can you be?'

He began to laugh and the laughter gradually grew louder, almost uncontrollable. Pam watched him and felt a thrill of fear. Could he be mad? Had he set fire to the cottage himself because of some sort of paranoid fear that 'they' were after him? Could a lot of this be in his head?

The sound of a key in the front door made her jump. She hadn't realised she was so tense. She felt a rush of relief that Wesley was home and she called out to him loudly. 'Wes. We've got a visitor. Ian Rowe's here.'

She watched Rowe stand up and turn to face the door, drawing himself up to his full height.

Wesley appeared in the doorway. There was a look of shocked disbelief on his face, there for a moment then swiftly suppressed. As he walked into the kitchen Pam caught his eye and gave him a slight nod, as if to say, 'I'm OK,' before starting to butter Rowe's toast. If Rowe was planning anything, he could hardly act while he was eating.

Wesley stared at Rowe for a few moments before speaking. 'Where have you been?' he said. 'We've been looking for you. We thought you were dead, until we got hold of your dental records.'

'Ah, yes. I can explain that.'

'Go on then.'

Wesley sat down on the stool beside Rowe and leaned towards him expectantly.

'I don't suppose there's any chance of a bath, is there?' Rowe asked. 'The world of the homeless is fine if you want to disappear for a while but it's almost impossible to keep up the usual standards, if you see what I mean.'

'Maybe later,' Wesley said in a voice that told Pam he wasn't falling for Rowe's smooth talk a second time. 'What made you come here?'

'I need to know what's going on. And a bit of police protection wouldn't come amiss.'

'We'll see,' Wesley said firmly. He wasn't going to make Rowe any promises. 'Look, Ian, I want to know everything. The lot. And don't leave anything out.'

Pam spooned the beans on to the toast and pushed the plate under Rowe's nose. He began to shovel the food into his mouth like a man who hadn't eaten for a while. When the plate was clean he sat back, satisfied, and gave Wesley a smile.

'I've made a bit of an ass of myself, Wesley. And now I think I'm in the proverbial shit.'

'Go on.' Wesley spoke softly, inviting confidences.

'I've just been round to Yves Demancour's place. And if he tells you I threatened or assaulted him, he's lying.

I just wanted to find out what happened to Nadia.'

'You told me you asked Demancour for money.' Pam couldn't let him get away with that one.

'OK. Nadia told me he'd found some treasure, something fantastic, so I thought he'd be OK for a few quid. Anyway ...' He gave a bitter laugh. 'Anyway this fantastic treasure turned out to be some mouldy old book.'

'You asked him about Nadia?'

'He claims he knows no more than I do.'

'Believe him?'

'No. He's lying. I think he could have killed her. He's weird enough to set light to her like that. You've met him, I presume?'

Wesley didn't answer the question. 'Tell me what happened.'

Pam watched Rowe's face. She guessed that this was what suspects looked like when they were about to tell all. She sat quite still, not wanting to distract Rowe from his revelations.

'I came back to Devon to see Martin Crace.'

'We know about that. We found the letter in your holdall. You made the appointment through Eva Liversedge.'

'Of course. She deals with all his appointments. He's always saying he's got no secrets from her. Not altogether true but—'

'And did Eva know where you were staying?'

'Yes. I told her I was at Jack's cottage. I feel a bit bad about taking off like that after the fire. Jack's been good to me, letting me stay there, but I reckoned that, if someone was trying to kill me, it might not be wise to hang around. Mind you, I suppose he's insured. Jack likes to do things properly.' He focused the charming smile on Pam again. 'Not like me. Wing and a prayer, me.'

'Why did you want to see Crace?' Wesley asked.

'That's my business.'

'Ian, people have been killed,' Pam heard herself say, rather to her surprise. 'You've got to tell Wes everything you know.'

'Truth is, I don't reckon I know very much. I thought I did but—'

'You haven't answered my question,' said Wesley. 'Why did you want to see Sir Martin? You can either talk here or we can go back to the police station and you'll be interviewed properly under caution with the tapes running.'

Rowe raised his hands in mock surrender. 'OK, OK. Don't go all Mr Plod on me.' He paused for a few moments, gathering his thoughts. 'I wanted to confront him.'

'Confront him?'

'I wanted him to take a DNA test. Martin Crace is my father.'

Pam glanced at Wesley and saw that he looked as surprised as she was.

'He edged me out of my job there ... said I'd been drinking when I hadn't. At first I wondered whether he thought I'd stumbled on something he didn't want known, like some scam or ... I asked Nadia to keep an eye out for anything unusual but she drew a blank.'

'So what makes you think he's your father?' Pam asked.

'I needed a blood transfusion once when I had an accident. I found out then that the man I'd thought was my father wasn't. My mother would never say who my real father was, only that I'd be proud of him. She used to say how she'd known Crace when he was young. She'd worked for his dad or something. I could tell he meant a lot to her but I didn't know why till after she died six months ago and I read through some old diaries she'd left locked away in an old suitcase in the loft. It was all there.'

'What was?'

'Like I said, they were old diaries and it was all teenage stuff about how she was in love with him and how they used to meet. When I was working for him I told him who my mum was and he said he remembered her but he was sort of cagey – made out she was just a Saturday girl in his dad's shop and he hardly knew her.'

'Teenage girls have been known to have fantasies ... and write them down in their diaries,' said Pam as though she knew what she was talking about.

But Rowe ignored her. 'Everything was OK for a while then I got the feeling I was being edged out, as if he didn't want me around, and I started to ask myself why he wanted rid of me. Then six months ago, when I found the diaries, I knew.'

'Where are the diaries now?'

Rowe put his head in his hands. 'I left them on the coffee table in the living room of that bloody cottage, didn't I? I was going to look through them before the meeting ... prepare my case. But everything in that room went up in smoke. Nothing left.'

Pam was tempted to say, 'How convenient,' but she decided to keep silent.

'Who else knew about this?' Wesley asked.

'Nadia ... and Jack. I mentioned it to Jack but he told me to leave it. He reckoned Crace'd never admit it.' He thought for a moment. 'Crace is a clever man, Wes.'

'I can't understand why you didn't just ask your mother straight out about her relationship with Crace when she was alive,' Pam said.

Rowe looked away. 'Like I said, she died six months

ago. But she'd spent the last couple of years of her life away with the fairies in a haze of vodka.'

'I'm sorry.'

'Don't be. We never really got on.'

'You didn't think of asking Sir Martin straight out if he'd had an affair with your mother?' she continued.

'Pam's right, Ian. I don't really understand.'

'Image, dear boy. If it's one thing Sir Martin Crace doesn't want, it's a scandal.'

Pam snorted. 'In this day and age. So he got a girl pregnant when he was young. Big deal. He could even have turned it to his advantage. Tearful father and son reunion.'

She saw Wesley give her an admiring glance. He knew she was right.

'Ah . . . that's the awkward bit. When my mum died I discovered that she was only just fifteen when she had me. Getting a fourteen-year-old girl pregnant when he must have been around twenty wouldn't have looked good on Crace's CV, would it?'

'That's more like it,' Wesley whispered.

'Since I read those stupid teenage diaries I've been wondering what to do about it. The dates were right, you see. Then I plucked up the courage to ask for an appointment and when the letter came from Eva I admit I was surprised. I'd expected to be fobbed off. In fact I rang Eva when I arrived in Devon and dropped a few hints.' He smiled. 'Something like "Some papers left by my late mother contain some interesting facts." I thought she'd tell Crace and it might get him worried. Soften him up. Then I spelled out a few home truths and I said that once it was proved who my father was, she'd treat me with a bit more respect. She'd treated me like shit in the past so I couldn't resist it.'

Pam looked at Wesley. The thing about Sir Martin Crace being Rowe's father could well be a figment of his vivid imagination, she thought. That was the trouble with people like Rowe: it was hard to know what to believe.

'I presume Nadia knew about all this?' said Wesley. 'We saw the e-mail she sent warning you to be careful.'

'Oh, yes. She knew everything and she agreed that I had a right to know the truth – just like she wanted to know the truth about her own mum.'

'Perhaps she confronted Crace herself?' Pam suggested.

Rowe hesitated. 'I don't . . . No. She'd have told me. After all, it's almost like heresy to say anything against Martin Crace, isn't it? She wouldn't have acted on her own. Surely.' Somehow he didn't sound too sure of himself.

Pam was starting to feel confused and one look at Wesley told her that he was too. Either Sir Martin was the bad guy or he wasn't. But if Rowe's story was true, his reputation might never recover.

'What about the cottage? One of Sir Martin Crace's security men was found dead inside.'

Rowe gave a low whistle. 'Was that who it was?'

'His name was Denis Wade. He was knocked unconscious then the cottage was set on fire. You were there at the time. Did you kill him?'

Rowe looked outraged. 'Absolutely not. I had nothing to do with it. I might not be a saint but I draw the line at murder.'

'So tell me what happened.'

'OK. I'm upstairs and I hear someone smash the window. I creep to the top of the stairs and see this guy going into the living room so I make my way downstairs and I stand by the door. I can hear him opening drawers and searching the place, so while he's busy I manage to get outside, intending to get in Nadia's car and drive off. But I've left the bloody car keys upstairs, haven't I?

Stupid. Anyway, I'm just wondering what to do when this car drives up so I hide behind some trees but it's pitch dark and I can't see much so don't ask me to tell you the make or number or anything like that. Someone gets out and I hear them going up to the front door and ... there's no sound of glass breaking or anything so maybe I'd not closed it properly. Anyway, I wait there for a while until whoever it is has driven away then I see flames at the windows and I think, bloody hell, they've set the place on fire. They must have really wanted rid of me. I thought they were together, you see. I thought the second one had joined the first. Then I make for the main road and I manage to hitch a lift to Morbay and that's where I've been, lying low.'

'What made you think they were together? Did you hear them talking at all or ...?'

Rowe shook his head. 'I just assumed they were. No particular reason.'

Wesley took his phone from his pocket. 'Sorry, Ian, but I really need you to make a proper statement down at the station and we might need to ask you some more questions.'

Rowe stood up, sending his stool flying back.

'You don't believe me. You think I killed that bloke at the cottage.'

'You ran away from the scene.'

'I was scared. I thought they might be looking for Mum's diaries and they'd torched the place to destroy any evidence. And I'm here now, aren't I?'

Wesley raised his hands in a gesture of appeasement. 'OK, OK. But we need to find out who killed the man in the cottage and you're our only witness. We need your help.'

Wesley's words seemed to work. Rowe sat down again and Pam gave him a weak smile. She asked him if he wanted a cup of tea but he shook his head.

Wesley had gone out into the hall to make the call to Gerry. Rowe was trusting him, she thought. Just like people trusted Sir Martin Crace. But then she realised she'd misjudged the situation. Rowe was perched on the edge of his seat, as if preparing for another quick getaway.

Wesley returned to the kitchen and sat down. But Ian Rowe stood up.

'I've changed my mind. I'm going,' he said. 'Thanks for the . . .' He nodded towards his empty plate.

'Don't you want to establish if Sir Martin's your father?' said Pam. 'If he takes a DNA test—'

'You know, Pam, I'm starting to wonder if it's worth the hassle.' He grinned. 'And there's always another time, eh. Wait till the dust settles.'

'I thought you wanted police protection,' said Pam.

Rowe looked at Wesley. 'I did but I don't think I fancy being banged up in a cell for the night. I should have known better than to trust a copper.'

Wesley stood up and took a step towards him. 'Ian, if you're really in danger, we can help you. And if you're telling the truth you have nothing to fear.'

'Now where have I heard that one before?' He began to make for the back door. 'I'm off back to France. I'll be safe there.'

Pam opened her mouth to ask how he planned to get there without money or passport but thought better of it. Tradmouth harbour was packed with yachts ready and able to glide over the Channel. It would just be a matter of hitching a ride, and Rowe had the smooth talk to pull it off.

But Wesley had other ideas. He rushed over to the door and blocked the way. 'Sorry, Ian. I can't just let you go off like this. You're a vital witness in a murder inquiry.'

Pam saw Rowe square up to her husband and she was suddenly afraid. Rowe was slightly taller and better built, and, although Wesley was probably the fitter of the two, Rowe had the look of a street fighter who didn't care about playing by the rules.

The two men stood there for a few moments, staring each other down, before the spell was broken by the sound of the doorbell. Pam dashed out to answer it, her heart thumping, hoping that it would be Gerry and not Neil, who would, she knew, be useless when it came to any form of physical conflict.

When the door swung open, she saw Gerry standing there, a uniformed constable behind him. 'Where is he?' he asked as he stepped in. Then he looked at her. 'You OK, love?'

'I'm fine. But if I were you, I'd get in there quick,' she said, nodding towards the kitchen. 'Wes is trying to stop him leaving.'

Gerry gave the constable an 'after you' look and the pair disappeared into the kitchen. She stayed in the hall. This was police business, she thought, and if Rowe was going to put up any resistance, she didn't want to be there to witness it.

Five minutes later the constable led Rowe out to the car with Wesley and Gerry following behind. Pam caught her husband's eye and he paused, an apologetic look on his face.

'I'll try not to be long,' he said, touching her hand.

'You haven't eaten yet.'

He gave her a rueful smile. 'I'll have it when I get back.'

'Whenever that is,' she mumbled under her breath.

Wesley didn't hear, or he chose to ignore it. As she stood in the hall she could hear Ian Rowe's raised voice quite clearly as they left the house.

'By the way, Nadia told me she didn't die, you know. She said it was the other way round.'

But Pam had no idea what he meant.

The mobile phone belonging to Jem Burrows had been placed in a plastic box in the custody suite. When it began to ring, the custody sergeant stared at it, wondering whether to ignore it or give in to the temptation of answering. After a while the overly cheerful ring tone – a lively electronic salsa – started to get on his nerves and he pressed the button that would silence the tiny instrument.

'Hello,' said a female voice on the other end of the line. 'Where are you? Have the police spoken to you again?'

The custody sergeant hesitated. 'Er, yes.'

'What did they say?'

'Nothing much.'

There was a long pause. 'Jem, are you all right?' He could hear suspicion in her voice. He'd been rumbled.

The line went dead. But when he called up the details of the last call he found it was in Jem Burrows's list of numbers.

He smiled when he saw the name, picked up the phone on his desk and punched out DCI Heffernan's number.

14

I'm rather surprised that the fatal letter still exists. I thought that Stephen de Grendalle would have destroyed it, torn it to pieces in a fury. And yet he might have kept it as evidence, something tangible to confront Jeanne with, and it somehow became lost amongst his other papers. Here is the text (translated from Norman French, so we can surmise that the writer was a man of some status and education).

'Your adulterous heretic wife met with Walter Fitzallen on the morning of the Feast of St Mary Magdalene in the wood behind your estate. I myself saw them together. One who wishes you well.'

To a man like de Grendalle, this anonymous note must have been devastating. How he must have loved the woman he rescued from the flames of Minerve. How this accusation of infidelity must have eaten away at him like a worm in his heart.

(From papers found in the possession of Professor Yves Demancour)

Wesley turned over, wrapping the duvet around his body, and kissed Pam on the nose. She stirred a little and reclaimed the duvet with surprising violence.

'I'm going into the office early,' he whispered in her ear.

She opened her eyes wide and sat up. 'You were there half the night. Your dinner's still congealing in the microwave.'

'Gerry and I got ourselves a takeaway from the Golden Dragon. We didn't starve.'

'I never thought you would. So where's Ian Rowe?'

'Enjoying the lavish hospitality of our luxury custody suite.'

'Is he being charged?'

'He's just being held for questioning at the moment but I reckon a charge of withholding evidence and breaking into Professor Demancour's flat will do to be going on with. Demancour reported the break-in – it seems Rowe put the wind up him badly.'

'Well, at least we know Rowe didn't kill Nadia Lucas. It happened when we were in France.'

'Mmm. That's one thing we can be sure of.' He thought for a few moments. 'But I'm still not sure he's telling the whole truth about what happened at the cottage. He says he saw this mysterious figure. I tend not to believe in mysterious figures. They're far too convenient in my opinion. Far more likely he killed Wade himself and did a runner, panicking when he found he'd left the car keys in the burning building along with all his stuff. It's just a matter of proving it.'

Pam didn't answer. A small voice had just broken the early morning peace. Amelia was awake and hungry.

Wesley dressed and grabbed a quick breakfast of cereal and orange juice. He felt impatient to get to the station that morning although he wasn't sure why.

As he was about to leave, Pam came downstairs to make breakfast for herself and the children. He put his arms around her and kissed the top of her head. Her hair smelled of shampoo, something herbal and wholesome.

'I'd better go,' he whispered. 'See you this evening. Not sure what time.'

She gave him a resigned smile, the smile of a policeman's wife who had heard it all before. At that moment their days in Carcassonne seemed a whole world away.

The walk down the hill to the centre of Tradmouth gave him a chance to think. Denis Wade had broken into the cottage, possibly on the orders of Sir Martin Crace or Eva Liversedge. It was easy to imagine Rowe, frightened and panicking, hitting the security man over the head and setting the cottage alight to hide his crime, only realising later that he'd left his belongings and the keys to Nadia's car upstairs – and by then the fire had spread to the staircase, making it impossible to retrieve them.

It would have been unplanned, a spur-of-the-moment crime like so many others. And yet a little voice in Wesley's head was telling him that it was more complicated than that; that there was some connection to Nadia's gruesome death in Grandal Field. Although he couldn't see what that connection could be.

His mobile rang and he looked at the name of the caller. Neil. It wasn't like him to call so early in the morning so it must be important.

'Wes. I was trying to get hold of you last night.'

'Sorry. I was a bit tied up. Last night was, er ... interesting. Ian Rowe turned up at our house unexpectedly. He's been taken in for questioning.'

Neil swore softly. 'So what's he done exactly? Did he kill that bloke in the cottage or what?'

'I'll tell you about it when I see you. It's a long story,' said Wesley, not quite sure how to answer. What exactly *had* Ian Rowe done? He still had the feeling he hadn't learned the truth.

Neil cleared his throat. 'Er, I don't know if it's important but Jem Burrows's car is still parked on the lane near Grandal Field.'

Wesley's heart sank. Traffic matters were hardly his concern.

'I thought I'd better tell you because I saw it there when Sheryl Bright turned up after everyone had gone home a couple of nights ago. I never saw any sign of Burrows but it's odd, isn't it?'

'Very odd. You didn't see them meeting or ...?'

'Can't say I did, mate. Sorry.'

Wesley ended the call, pondering the implications of Neil's revelation. It was possible that Sheryl Bright had been meeting the leader of the group who'd allegedly threatened her; a man she must have met before because he'd worked in her garden. Things were coming into focus at last and he couldn't help smiling to himself, hoping that people he passed as he walked wouldn't think he was mad.

It was a beautiful day and the tourists were out in force, ambling along the esplanade, staring out over the river to Queenswear, while cars circled the boat float in search of a precious parking space. The Memorial Gardens looked positively tropical with their glossy palm trees. On the surface it seemed that all was right with the world but Wesley knew otherwise. A sergeant in summer shirt sleeves greeted him as he entered the police station and Wesley raised his hand in acknowledgement. But there would be no holiday atmosphere in the CID office. Not with their current workload.

Nevertheless, Gerry Heffernan looked remarkably cheerful when he arrived, positively bubbly, with a twinkle in his eye that told Wesley there'd been a development in his absence.

He beckoned Wesley into his office and there was a wide grin on his face as Wesley cleared a pile of forms off a chair before making himself comfortable.

302

'You'll never guess,' the DCI said, leaning forward conspiratorially.

'Surprise me.'

'Sheryl Bright made a call to Jem Burrows's mobile phone last night while he was in the cells contemplating the error of his ways and I got someone to check out Bright's life insurance. If he pops off, the wife cops for a fortune.'

Wesley raised his eyebrows. 'I've just had an interesting call from Neil.' He told Gerry the gist of Neil's revelations and the DCI gave a low whistle. 'So can we assume that they'd arranged an assignation? That all the threats and anonymous letters were meant to put us off the scent?'

'I always thought there was something a bit theatrical about them,' Wesley said. 'All those letters cut out of newspapers. And why did she burn the first few she got? Looking back, that should have rung alarm bells.'

'But both Sheryl and Burrows have solid alibis for Jon Bright's murder.'

Wesley said nothing. At that moment those alibis were the only reason that both Jem Burrows and Sheryl Bright weren't in the interview room being questioned about Jon Bright's murder. And the situation was starting to annoy him. Once they had the Bright case wrapped up, they could concentrate on the murders of Nadia Lucas and Denis Wade. Although the similarity of the three deaths hadn't escaped his notice. Death by fire. Was there a connection? It was a question he kept asking himself but, as yet, he had no answer.

Ian Rowe and the death of Nadia Lucas had been on his mind since the previous night. In fact he hadn't slept well because he'd been turning over all the possibilities in his mind.

Nadia had met her death by fire near the spot where a

young woman was said to have died back in the thirteenth century. Nadia's mother had been involved in the excavation of that particular site thirty years ago and Maggie March, the woman in charge of the dig, had died in a burning car. Fire. The same motif again and again. Death by fire. Just like Jon Bright.

The ruins Neil had uncovered at Grandal Field dated from a time when heretics were burned because the fire was meant to purify their souls. He didn't know why this thought suddenly occurred to him but he couldn't help feeling it was significant in some way. But how and why, he still had no idea.

Wesley had been so deep in his own thoughts that the ringing of Gerry's phone made him jump. The DCI picked up the receiver and listened to the person on the other end of the line. Gerry had never been one to conceal his feelings so Wesley could tell at once that the news was exciting.

'That was the fire investigator,' he said as he put the receiver down. 'They've found some unusual things at the seat of the fire in the Brights' garage. He thinks the smashed bottle was to make us think that a Molotov cocktail had been used again, the same as in the shed.'

'So what were these unusual things? What does it mean?'

Gerry grinned as though he was enjoying keeping his colleague guessing. 'You'll see. We've got Jem Burrows here on the premises and I'm going to have Sheryl Bright brought in.'

The phone rang again. As Gerry spoke his smile widened, showing a set of uneven teeth. If the fire investigator had brought good news, this was even better.

'Guess what, Wes,' he said when the call was over. 'I asked someone from Forensic to take a look at Jem Burrows's computer. It seems he's been looking at some interesting websites – one of them telling you how to make a device that delays the start of a fire, using a plastic bottle full of petrol suspended above a couple of candles.' He paused, the storyteller building up to the punch line. 'Traces of melted plastic and candle wax were found in the Brights' garage and I reckon that once Sheryl had knocked her husband over the head and set that little lot up, she'd have had plenty of time to go off painting and chat up the neighbours before the place went up, apparently because the killer chucked a Molotov cocktail through the window. Clever. Only she made one very bad error. The glass from the broken window was all over the ground outside.'

'Which means she broke the window on the inside when she was setting it all up.' He shook his head. 'Silly mistake.'

'Conspiracy to murder.' Gerry savoured the words. 'When we've brought her in, we can charge them.' He suddenly frowned. 'Can't have our usual celebratory drink tonight though. We might have cracked this one but there are two more to go.'

Wesley knew the boss was right. Once Jem and Sheryl had been interviewed again and charged, there was still the matter of who killed Nadia Lucas and Denis Wade.

It had all started with Nadia's death. Death by fire.

The charges had been made but Sheryl and Jem were sticking to a policy of 'no comment' as suggested by their respective solicitors. They had witnesses who'd swear that they were elsewhere when the garage caught fire and it would be up to the police to prove otherwise.

'It's just a matter of waiting for the forensic reports,' Gerry observed as they walked down the corridor away from the interview room. 'And I'll bet that Sheryl set fire to her own summer house and all. All an elaborate smoke-screen,' he added with a grin.

But Wesley's mind wasn't on the Bright case. 'I'd like another word with Ian Rowe,' he said.

'Well, he's on the premises. Help yourself. But he's been over what happened in that cottage I don't know how many times. No inconsistencies as yet.' He put a large paw on Wesley's shoulder. 'Look, Wes, why don't you get someone else to question him? Fresh approach? How about Rach and Trish? The female touch. Rowe looks the type who'd respond to that,' he added with a wink.

Wesley saw the wisdom of Gerry's suggestion. Besides, he'd had enough of Rowe capitalising on their tenuous student relationship. But something Rowe had said the night before was baffling him and he hadn't been able to get it out of his head. 'She told me she didn't die. It was the other way round.' What was? And who didn't die? Only Ian Rowe could enlighten him.

Twenty minutes later he was back in the interview room. Gerry had decided to keep him company and sat back on his chair, completely relaxed, with an 'all's well with the world' expression on his face, like a man who'd just enjoyed a good dinner.

Rowe seemed nervous, as if the reality of his situation had just hit him. He wore a blue disposable jump suit which made him look thinner than when Wesley had met him in Carcassonne. And he looked deflated, as though the fight had gone out of him.

When the tape had been set running Wesley started the questioning, keeping it formal. 'Why did you return to England from France?' he asked.

'I've told you.'

'Tell me again.'

'I wanted to see Crace. I'd managed to get an

appointment with him. I was going to confront him once and for all with what I knew about him and my mum. I was going to ask him to take a DNA test.'

'Is that why you went to work with him in the first place, because your mother talked about knowing him?'

'You know all this. I've told you.'

'So remind me, how did you make the appointment?'

'I told you. I wrote a letter. But when I arrived I phoned up and Eva answered. I told you about it last night, Wes. Remember?'

'Did you talk to Sir Martin?' Gerry asked.

'No, only to Eva. I couldn't resist teasing her. I hinted that I knew something really bad about Crace ... something he'd done in his past that I knew he'd pay good money to hush up. I said my mother had left papers that contained some interesting facts, that sort of thing. She's got no bloody sense of humour, that woman. But she'd have treated me a bit different once Crace had taken the DNA test and it came out who I really was.'

'You're sure Crace is your father, aren't you?'

'Of course.' There was a hint of desperation in Rowe's voice, as though he was trying to convince himself as much as the two policemen sitting opposite him. 'Once it's all sorted, I'll be out of here,' he said, looking at Wesley defiantly.

'What about Nadia?'

'I called her to tell her I was hoping to get an appointment with Crace and I asked if I could borrow her car when I came over. Must have been the day before she died.'

'Did she talk about her mother?'

'Yeah – really heavy stuff. She'd hired a private eye but I don't think he was much use and she said she couldn't afford to keep him on for much longer. She'd started talking to some people who knew her mum and she was getting in really deep, I could tell. That's why I wanted you to see those e-mails she sent me. I was worried about her.'

Wesley leaned forward, as though he was about to share a confidence. 'You said something when you were arrested. Something about someone not dying and it being the other way round. What was all that about?'

Ian shrugged. 'It was just something Nadia said when I called her about the car.'

'What exactly did she say?' Wesley asked patiently.

'I can't remember the exact words but it was something like. "I don't think she died – it was the other way round." A while ago she said she'd been wondering whether her mother might still be alive so that's probably what she meant. Her body was never found, you see. And people have been known to fake their own deaths by leaving their clothes on a beach, haven't they? I wonder if she went off and started a new life.'

'And abandoned her daughter?'

'That's what bothered Nadia. She said her mother wasn't like that but that could have been wishful thinking on her part. After all, she'd left it to her ex-husband to bring Nadia up, hadn't she?'

'Did Nadia mention a letter she'd found? Something her dad had failed to destroy before he died?'

'She did as a matter of fact. But she didn't say what was in it. She said she'd show it me when she saw me.'

'You think she could have been on to something when she said it was the other way round?'

A smile spread across Rowe's lips. 'Maybe. Who knows?'

Sir Martin Crace was at Bewton Hall that morning. Eva Liversedge had told Gerry on the phone that he wasn't receiving visitors but then Gerry had pointed out that he

308

wasn't a visitor, he was the police. And Sir Martin would receive him whether he liked it or not.

Wesley, who would have put it more tactfully, listened to the one-sided phone call with creeping embarrassment but the DCI's straightforward approach seemed to work and Eva yielded without much argument. But when they arrived at the hall she had a face like a gorgon with a bad hair day as she showed them into Sir Martin's presence, enough to turn any man to stone.

However, Sir Martin himself seemed almost welcoming, eager to help the police with their enquiries. Last time they'd met, Wesley had sensed that he'd been annoyed at their persistence, but now all seemed to have been forgiven as he invited them to sit and ordered tea.

Sir Martin arched his fingers and assumed an expression of polite enquiry. 'How can I help you, gentlemen? I assure you, I've already told you everything I know and I really don't think—'

'You'll know that one of your security staff was murdered. Denis Wade.'

'I know all about it, I'm afraid. Everyone here has given statements and I assure you that his death, regrettable though it is, has absolutely nothing to do with me.'

'Strange though,' said Wesley. 'How all these people who used to work for you seem to be either dying or disappearing.'

'Ian Rowe and Nadia Lucas hadn't worked for me for some years. And I understand Rowe has been found alive. I don't want to teach you your job, Inspector, but perhaps you ought to be making enquiries into his activities.'

'That's already in hand,' Wesley said quickly. 'In fact he told us something rather interesting. He told us that he thinks you might be his biological father. He says that's why he wanted to see you. You did know his mother many years ago, I understand?'

Sir Martin smiled. 'I knew her slightly but there was never anything between us because she was only fourteen at the time and I must have been about nineteen or twenty. She worked in my parents' shop. Saturday girl. She got into trouble, as they used to say – delightfully old-fashioned phrase that, don't you think? – but I assure you that she didn't tell me who the father was. I understand she married later so all's well that ends well, I suppose.'

'The marriage didn't last and she became an alcoholic. Died six months ago,' Wesley said quietly.

There was a slight pause. 'I'm very sorry to hear that but I'm not sure what it has to do with me if someone mistakenly thinks I'm his father.'

'Would you be willing to take a DNA test?' Gerry asked.

Sir Martin shot him a hostile glance. 'I really don't see why I should. My word should be enough.'

'It would settle the matter once and for all.'

'It would but—'

'So you're willing?'

Crace hesitated. 'I'll think about it. Now if that's all—'

'Not quite,' said Wesley. He wasn't going to be dismissed until he'd learned everything he came to learn. 'I've been looking at your website. I understand you were adopted yourself.'

'I make no secret of it.'

'Have you ever tried to contact your biological mother?'

'Yes. But I'm afraid I discovered that she'd died a few years ago. Cancer. It's one of the great regrets of my life that I never met her, Inspector. I'm sure you can understand that.'

'Of course. Do you happen to know her name or any details of her life?'

310

There was a long silence, as though Crace was making a decision. 'Her name was Elizabeth Crowley and she was a university student who got pregnant and gave me up for adoption. She thought it was for the best. She went on to marry and have two more children. And before you ask, I haven't contacted my two half-sisters. Perhaps I will one day but ... but when I found out Elizabeth had died, it just didn't seem appropriate somehow, intruding into their grief.'

'But you must have contacted her family or you wouldn't know how she'd died or ...'

Crace gave Wesley a knowing smile. 'If you must know I employed a private detective. I didn't wish to make the initial approach, if you see what I mean.'

'Quite. The detective wasn't called Forsyte Wiley, was he?'

Crace shook his head. 'No. Why? Who's Forsyte Wiley?'

'Just someone Nadia Lucas employed to find out what happened to her mother.'

'Really? I employed a man from London who's well known for his discretion. I'm afraid I've never heard of this Mr Wiley.'

'What about your adoptive parents?'

'Both dead, alas.'

Wesley watched Crace's face carefully. It was time to test the waters and see the reaction. 'You're quite sure that your biological mother's name wasn't Maggie March?'

But there was no tell-tale sign of recognition. Crace merely looked puzzled. 'No. I've told you. It was Elizabeth Crowley. You're barking up the wrong tree, Inspector, and if I were you, I'd go home and check my facts. Ian Rowe is obviously a fantasist. I'm afraid, like all people in the public eye, I attract that sort of attention from time to time.'

Crace wore an expression of irritated innocence. The man was either a good actor, Wesley thought, or he was telling the truth.

'Can you give us the name of the private detective you employed to find your mother, sir?'

Crace hesitated before taking his wallet from his inside pocket and extracting a business card. 'I'm afraid you won't be able to contact him. He left that agency and now he's working in the States.'

He said the words apologetically but Wesley was sure he could detect a tiny note of triumph.

'And you can't tell me what your security guard, Denis Wade, was doing in the cottage where Ian Rowe was staying?' Gerry asked unexpectedly.

Crace looked a little startled by the sudden change of subject. 'I assure you I've no idea.' He leaned forward and looked Wesley in the eye. 'He certainly wasn't there under my orders if that's what you're thinking.'

'I never said he was,' said Gerry innocently. 'But your staff are very loyal, aren't they? I've noticed that. You must be a good boss,' he added. A spot of flattery never went amiss with powerful men.

'I try to be,' Crace replied with what sounded like humility.

They took their leave, shown off the premises by a silent Eva Liversedge. If Sir Martin Crace was involved in any way with the deaths of Nadia Lucas and Denis Wade, it wasn't going to be easy getting him to admit it.

As they drove away, Wesley found himself feeling quite depressed.

Eva Liversedge watched from the office window as the policemen departed. They'd asked her why she hadn't mentioned that Ian Rowe had telephoned her when he arrived in England. She said it had slipped her mind and

312

she was certain they'd believed her. After all, she couldn't be expected to remember every phone call she'd fielded over the past few weeks, could she?

She stood there for a while, staring as their car disappeared round the bend in the drive near Bertha's cottage. They'd been snooping around asking more questions. She wished they'd go away and leave them all in peace.

The telephone on her desk began to ring, an insistent, businesslike drone. Eva put on her working face, tight-lipped and efficient, and hurried over to answer it.

When she heard the voice on the other end of the line she frowned. This was the last thing she needed.

'Miss Liversedge. It's Linda Potts – Denis Wade's partner.'

'What can I do for you, Miss Potts?'

'I need to talk to you about something Denis told me.'

Eva's heart began to beat a little faster. 'And what's that?'

'Something about the night he died. He said something about meeting you and—'

'Let me stop you there, Miss Potts,' she said in a voice intended to freeze the blood in Linda's veins. 'What passed between myself, Sir Martin and Mr Wade was strictly confidential and if you were to break the confidentiality agreement signed by your late partner, there might be unfortunate consequences, legal and financial. Do I make myself clear?'

There was a long silence. Then Linda Potts spoke. 'Are you telling me I won't get that pay-out Sir Martin promised me?'

'Take my advice, Miss Potts. Say nothing. Do nothing. Or, as I said, the consequences could be rather unpleasant. Good day.'

Eva Liversedge replaced the receiver carefully and

stared at the telephone as though it had offended her in some way.

Linda Potts was a loose cannon. And loose cannons had to be controlled if disaster was to be averted.

'Good job it was insured, sir,' the constable said, looking at the blackened windows of Owl Cottage with a slightly smug expression on his face.

Jack Plesance scowled. The last thing he needed was a policeman trying to be clever.

He looked at the cottage, still standing strong and upright although the areas around some of the windows had been flicked with flames at the height of the fire, leaving blackened patches of soot on the shabby pink-washed walls. The structural engineer had assured him that the fire damage was confined to the interior of the central section, including the staircase. It would cost a fair bit of money to put that right and the smoke-damaged rooms would need redecorating, but Jack wasn't too bothered. The place had needed gutting anyway if it was to become a desirable second home. In some ways the fire, and the resulting insurance money, had solved a few problems.

Jack nodded towards the crime scene tape. 'When can I arrange to start work?'

The young constable drew himself up to his full height. 'You'll have to ask DCI Heffernan, sir. He's in charge.'

Jack felt a sudden stab of irritation. DCI Heffernan again. He was the one who had Ian Rowe in custody. Ian had phoned him when he'd first been arrested, wanting to know if he could fund a decent solicitor. Jack had recommended someone and reluctantly agreed to pay when Ian had pleaded poverty. He'd been tempted to tell him to use the duty solicitor and get legal aid but something had stopped him.

314

The constable's voice interrupted his thoughts. 'Nice motor, sir,' he said, casting an admiring glance at Jack's new Land Rover Discovery. 'Bet it costs a fortune to run, eh, what with petrol prices these days.'

Jack made a noncommittal noise. He'd only come to make a quick assessment of the damage to his property and he didn't feel inclined to get involved in a cosy male chat about motor vehicles.

He was about to return to the car when he noticed the young constable was watching him. 'Big engine, that model. Bet it goes like the clappers, eh, sir.' He smirked. 'In fact we know it does, don't we?'

'It's not bad.'

'But like I said, you have to take care on these roads. And we don't want any more points on that licence, do we?'

Jack didn't reply. He wasn't going to let some cocky little copper spoil his day. He drove away but when he came to a convenient passing place he stopped the Discovery and took out his phone.

When his call was ended he swore softly under his breath. He needed to see Ian Rowe but the police said it wasn't possible. Rowe was in the cells. Safely locked away.

Wesley was driving back towards Tradmouth, stuck behind a slow-moving caravan on a narrow Devon A road that left no room at all for overtaking, when a call came in from the police station.

Gerry answered it and, from the one-sided monosyllabic conversation, Wesley couldn't tell what type of news was being conveyed. But when the call ended Gerry told him to turn the car around. They were going back to Dukesbridge. Linda Potts had telephoned Tradmouth police station saying that she had important information and she wanted to speak to the officer in charge of the investigation as soon as possible.

'Hope it's worth the journey,' Gerry said as Wesley found a farm entrance and turned the car back to face Dukesbridge. 'My stomach thinks my throat's been cut. Think we should stop somewhere on the way? There's a place that does nice pub lunches just outside—'

'Let's find out what Linda Potts has to tell us first,' Wesley said quickly. Some instinct told him that they shouldn't let the call of Gerry's stomach delay things. There would be a chance to grab a sandwich later.

'OK. But you won't be able to hear what she says for the rumbling of my guts.'

Wesley couldn't help smiling. 'I'll take the risk.'

When they reached Dukesbridge Wesley found a parking space in front of Linda's flat and sent up a swift prayer of thanks. He hadn't fancied driving round in circles for ages, wasting valuable time.

When Linda Potts greeted them Wesley could tell she hadn't slept. There were dark rings beneath her eyes and she had the pale, drawn look of the ill or the grieving. She wore a baggy T-shirt that hung off her thin frame, giving her the appearance of a child dressing up in adult clothes that are far too big for her.

Gerry hung back at the flat door and Wesley realised that it would be up to him to do the talking. He held out his hand. 'Ms Potts, I'm DI Peterson and this is DCI Heffernan. I believe you've already spoken to our colleagues DS Tracey and DC Johnson.'

She nodded. 'Yes. But I wanted someone in charge this time. I've got something very important to tell you.' She looked round as though she was afraid of being overheard and invited them inside. Wesley knew she was nervous. She fidgeted with the hem of her T-shirt, twisting it out of shape with her restless fingers as she invited them to sit.

'I phoned Sir Martin's secretary but she told me not to say anything. She said that if I talked to anyone I might not get the pay-out Sir Martin promised me. He's very generous, you know. Good to his employees.'

'So I've heard. What is it you're not supposed to say?'

She hesitated and Wesley was concerned that she might be having second thoughts. To Linda Potts Sir Martin's generous pay-out would mean the difference between keeping her head above the waters of debt or going under. She was probably wondering if talking to the police was worth the risk. And it was his job to persuade her that it was.

'Have you evidence that Sir Martin's committed some criminal offence?' he asked softly.

The answer was a shake of the head. 'Not directly, no.'

'Then why don't you tell us what you know and let us judge for ourselves?' He looked at Gerry for confirmation and the DCI nodded enthusiastically.

'That's right, love. And I promise we'll do our best to keep your name out of it. You'll be an anonymous informant and all that.' His stomach gave a gurgle of complaint. 'Pardon me,' he said, patting his gut.

This seemed to lighten the atmosphere and even elicited the ghost of a smile from Linda. She sat silent for a while, staring at her hands, trying to come to a decision. Wesley only hoped it would be the right one.

'OK,' she said at last. 'On the night Den was killed he had a phone call. He said it was from Eva – Sir Martin's PA. Then he said he had to go out 'cause there was something she wanted doing.'

'Did he tell you what it was?'

She hesitated. 'Not exactly. But he said she was going

to meet him and drive him somewhere. She wanted someone warning off.'

'Who?'

'Bloke called Rowe. He said this bloke used to work for Sir Martin and now he was threatening to make trouble.'

It was Gerry who spoke next. 'How exactly was your Den going to warn him off? Did he take any weapons with him or—?'

Linda shook her head vigorously. 'No. Den wasn't like that. He wouldn't hurt a fly. He was probably just going to have a quiet word, like.'

Wesley caught Gerry's eye. In the real world people who threatened to make trouble weren't warned off with a friendly word in their ears. An iron bar had been found near Denis Wade's body and Wesley couldn't help wondering whether the security man had brought it with him with the intention of doing Ian Rowe some serious injury.

'Do you know why Eva wanted Ian Rowe warned off?'

She shook her head again. 'But whatever it is, it must be serious because Miss Liversedge told me to keep quiet. It must be something bad, mustn't it?' she said, looking from one man to the other.

'Yes. It must be,' Wesley said gently.

The next move was obvious. They needed to speak to Eva Liversedge again. But first Gerry insisted on buying a sandwich from the Dukesbridge branch of Winterleas, fortuitously situated two hundred yards from Linda's flat.

Once Gerry's hunger had been satisfied, Wesley drove to Bewton Hall. They had no trouble with the security men on the gate this time. They were recognised and allowed through with a threateningly polite 'good afternoon'. It was amazing how much menace they

318

managed to convey in those two harmless words, Wesley thought.

When they arrived at the hall Jane Verity greeted them. She looked nervous, as though she knew something was wrong.

'How's Ian?' she asked quietly as she led them up the staircase to Eva's office.

'Still in custody. You didn't tell us about his claim that he was Sir Martin's son last time we spoke,' said Wesley. He watched her face carefully.

'That was because I didn't believe it for a moment. It was just wishful thinking if you ask me.'

Wesley nodded. This seemed to be what everyone thought. Ian Rowe was a fantasist. And from what he knew of Rowe, he felt he would probably agree. But in these days of DNA testing, claiming something like that was more risky than it would have been in times gone by. He wondered how Rowe intended to get around the scientific evidence.

Eva was waiting for them, an expression of cool indifference on her face, but beneath the mask Wesley suspected she was worried.

'If you want to see Sir Martin again you can't. He's engaged. Some visitors arrived by helicopter half an hour ago and he's not to be disturbed.' She looked from one man to the other, daring them to challenge her.

'We don't need to see him this time,' Wesley said. 'We'd like a chat with you.'

She looked at her watch. 'It's not convenient.'

'Oh, I think it is, love,' Gerry said, earning himself a look that would curdle milk. 'It was you who ordered Denis Wade to put the frighteners on Ian Rowe, wasn't it? Were you doing Sir Martin's dirty work or were you acting off your own bat? I think it might be the second and when Sir Martin finds out . . .'

319

'We want to know why you thought Ian Rowe needed silencing, Ms Liversedge,' Wesley put in. 'Was it about Rowe's claims that Sir Martin was his father?'

Eva seemed to wince at the words. 'Ian Rowe is a liar.'

'But Sir Martin was willing to give him an appointment. If he was such a nuisance, he'd have made some excuse not to see him. He's a busy man after all.' Wesley looked her in the eye. He had the feeling he was getting somewhere. 'It was you who tried to make sure he didn't get to see Sir Martin, wasn't it?'

'I've told you everything I know. Now if that's all, gentlemen ...'

She sat down and began to turn the pages of the large diary on her desk. But Wesley wasn't going to leave it there.

'Why did you drive Denis Wade to the cottage where Rowe was staying? Why did you tell Wade's partner to say nothing about it? Come on, Ms Liversedge, we're waiting for an answer. And if we don't get one we can continue this conversation down at the police station if you wish.'

For the first time, Eva Liversedge looked unsure of herself. 'That won't be necessary. If you must know it was about Rowe's claims to be Sir Martin's son. I wanted to ensure that he didn't go to the press. He told me on the phone that his mother had died recently and left some papers. He implied they were rather ... incriminating. But he could have been lying to cause trouble. I asked Denis to search the place where he was staying to see if he could find them.'

'Was that on Sir Martin's orders?'

She looked up and Wesley could see a new honesty in her eyes, as though she'd realised that lying was pointless. 'No. He knew nothing about it. I was just trying to protect him. You know what the press are like, if they get a sniff of something like this. Rowe was claiming that his mother was only fourteen when she had a brief relationship with Martin so you can imagine the headlines, can't you? Saint Martin Crace has sex with underage girl. All lies, of course, but mud always sticks.'

'You drove him there. Did you hang around?'

'No. I just dropped him off and told him to call me if he needed picking up. I didn't hear from him again that night.'

'That's because he was dead.'

'I wasn't to know that.'

'You didn't feel you should go back to check whether he was OK?'

She shrugged. 'For all I knew he'd taken a taxi back home or met friends in some pub. It wasn't my place to enquire about his social arrangements.'

Wesley glanced at the DCI who was listening, apparently fascinated. 'How far did you tell Wade to go to shut Rowe up?'

'I just asked him to have a word, that's all. And I challenge you to prove otherwise.'

'This was before Rowe had a chance to see Sir Martin? Why didn't you wait to see what he had to say? He might have been quite reasonable. He might have believed Sir Martin when he told him he wasn't his father.'

Eva gave what sounded like a snort of disbelief. 'You forget, Inspector. Rowe worked here. I knew him. He wasn't going to give up if he thought he could get a few quid out of it. Martin's too soft for his own good.'

'A DNA test would have disproved it.'

'Perhaps. But I didn't want it to get that far. Now, if that's all.'

Wesley's eyes were drawn to Eva's desk and a brightly coloured stamp on a thick white envelope on top of her in-tray caught his attention. A foreign stamp. South Africa. He felt Gerry nudge his arm.

'We might need to ask you some more questions,' he heard the DCI say, a veiled threat behind the words. 'And we'll get a search warrant if we have to.'

Eva didn't react. 'Very well,' she said as though she didn't care one way or the other. 'If you'll excuse me, I have work to do,' she added coolly.

As they were about to leave there was a sudden commotion outside, a thunderous noise so loud that Wesley almost felt he had to cover his ears. They looked out of the window and saw a helicopter rise up gracefully and swoop off over the trees behind the house.

'Might be worth hanging around for another quick word with Sir Martin if his visitors are going,' Gerry said in a voice loud enough to be heard over the relentless clatter of the engine.

Wesley noticed that Eva was brushing imaginary bits off her businesslike black suit in preparation for her boss's entrance. She looked at them and scowled. 'You only saw him earlier today. This is beginning to look like police harassment. If I were you I'd get going before a complaint's put in to your superiors.'

But Wesley and Gerry weren't going to be intimidated.

'I'm sure he won't mind if we just hang round to say hello,' said Gerry cheerfully. 'It'd seem rude not to, wouldn't it, Inspector Peterson?'

Wesley nodded, straight-faced, as Gerry sat himself down to wait. It was only five minutes before Sir Martin Crace put in an appearance but, sitting there under Eva's hostile stare, to Wesley it seemed longer.

The great man looked surprised to see them. 'I hadn't expected you back so soon, gentlemen,' he said politely. Wesley guessed that he was exercising considerable self-control.

'So sorry to bother you again, sir,' Wesley said smoothly as they followed him into his office, closing the

322

door behind them. 'It's just that we've just been talking to Denis Wade's partner.'

'How is she?' Crace sounded genuinely concerned. Saint Martin at his most saintly.

'Still very shocked.' He paused. 'And she was even more shaken when she received a call from your PA telling her to keep her mouth shut.'

Crace opened his mouth to speak then shut it again, lost for words. 'Why should Eva say that?'

'That's what we were wondering. She says it's connected with Ian Rowe's claim that you're his father.'

'That's nonsense.'

'Is it?'

'Look, I'm not Ian Rowe's father. I admit that I didn't have a high opinion of Rowe but I was quite happy to see him and put him straight.'

'You knew his mother. You were around when she got pregnant.'

Crace sighed. 'If it helps to settle the matter once and for all, I'd be willing to take a DNA test, just to allay all suspicion. This is getting beyond a joke.' He hesitated. 'Now if that's all, I really am very busy.'

As they left they passed Eva. She was emerging from her office laden with files and letters and she looked away, avoiding their eyes.

Frustration was a dreadful thing. Wesley's GP sister would have told him that it was bad for the blood pressure and probably a lot else besides. They'd cleared up Jon Bright's murder but those of Nadia Lucas and Denis Wade still remained unsolved and the smiling images of the victims gazed down at him from the CID office noticeboard, mocking his inability to bring their killer or killers to justice.

Gerry had been summoned upstairs to bring Chief

Superintendent Nutter up to date with developments. Wesley sat at his desk going through what they had so far, searching for inspiration. What had happened to Maggie March's son – John Martin March? If he could only find him, he had the feeling that he would get some answers.

He'd have been a young adult when his mother had met her tragic end. Surely he would have attended his mother's funeral. But, unlike at weddings, people didn't take pictures at funerals. It just wasn't done. If it had been, at least they'd have had a chance of knowing what John Martin March looked like.

There was nobody of that name and age on any records they had. Nobody who had a driving licence, a national insurance number or a criminal conviction was a match for that name and date of birth. It seemed as though John Martin March had disappeared off the face of the earth. March had been Maggie's name at birth so it was always possible that John Martin had met up with his biological father later on and was using his name. But what that name was, he hadn't a clue.

He glanced over at Rachel who was sifting through witness statements and when their eyes met she smiled.

'Anything new?' he asked, making conversation.

She shook her head. 'All Denis Wade's known associates have been interviewed but they haven't said anything particularly interesting.'

'Any luck with tracing John Martin March?'

'No trace. It's as though he disappeared off the face of the earth. Maybe he went abroad after his mother was killed in the car accident. Or he might have changed his name.'

'Maybe. It's five o'clock. Why don't you get off home a bit earlier tonight?' he said gently.

'I think I will. I'm going out for a meal with Barty this evening. It's his birthday.'

324

'Good.' Wesley looked away. It seemed that Rachel had tamed Barty Carter, the man who had threatened her with a shotgun on their first encounter. He tried to tell himself he was glad for her.

He began to go through the files again. Statements and forensic reports. After a while the typed words began to swim before his eyes and he looked up to see Rachel examining her watch.

She caught his eye again and frowned. 'I can't help feeling sorry for that Nadia, you know. Imagine what it must be like to know that your mother committed suicide like that. I mean, she didn't even mention her in that note she left, did she? How can someone do that to a kid?'

Wesley sat there quite still for a few moments before looking for the file on Wendy Haskel's suicide. When he found it, he stared at the photocopy of the suicide note before picking up his phone and tapping out the number of Neil's mobile.

Neil answered after several rings, his voice excited. 'Hi, Wes. You should see the pottery we're getting out. And we've just found a brilliant coin. King John, would you believe.'

'Great. I'll have to come and have another look when I've got a moment. In the meantime, I want you to do me a favour. Do you keep records of old digs at your Exeter office?'

'Yeah. There are boxes full of old files down in the basement. Why?'

'Could you ask someone to go through them to see if there are any examples of Wendy Haskel's handwriting? I wouldn't normally ask but it's rather urgent.'

Neil hesitated, as though Wesley had just asked him to undertake a particularly onerous task. 'I'll give Paula a ring. She looks after our filing system. Hope she hasn't gone home. You still holding Ian Rowe?'

'For questioning, yes. Can you contact Paula? Like I say, it's really important. If she can find something ask her to fax me a copy. You know the number.'

Wesley put the phone down, hoping that Neil would move quickly for a change. And hoping that his hunch would be proved right.

Sir Martin Crace went through the post that Eva had left on his desk. There seemed to be a lot of it today. But then the post hadn't arrived until after lunch and he'd been tied up in meetings most of the day.

There was the usual batch of requests, ranging from approaches from major charities to straightforward begging letters from individuals on hard times. Then there was the other letter that had arrived in the envelope with the colourful stamp, the one he read over and over again before walking to the drinks cabinet and pouring himself a measure of single malt.

This was something that needed some thought.

15

There is no further mention of Urien de Norton. He was a bit player in history, a catalyst. How gossip and rumour can cause damage, almost like fire running out of control.

I sometimes wonder whether my own mother's death was brought about by whispers and the judgement of others. I know now that there was talk surrounding her relationship with Dr March. Did that make her take her own life? I wonder. Or was it Dr March's death in that dreadful accident?

There are people I must talk to – people who can help me get at the truth. But I digress. This book is not about me or my mother. It is about Jeanne de Minerve. Jeanne who died in that dreadful way. Her husband must have been consumed by jealousy to trap her like that in the dovecot and set fire to it. He must have listened to her screams as she died in agony.

How could he have turned from her rescuer to her torturer? Perhaps he justified it to himself. Perhaps he reasoned that, as he had saved her from the flames, he had a right to return her to them.

(From papers found in the possession of Professor
Yves Demancour)

Over the many years Wesley had known Neil, the last thing he had come to expect from his old friend was efficiency. But it seemed that this time Neil had mended his ways. When Wesley returned from Gerry Heffernan's morning briefing at nine o'clock, there was a fax on his desk, compliments of Paula at the County Archaeological Unit in Exeter. It was a copy of a handwritten report dated April 1981 concerning a Roman section of Exeter's city walls, probably a preliminary draft of something that would have been typed up later on. And the name at the top was Wendy Haskel, Field Archaeologist. As Wesley read it, his heart started to beat faster and he was surprised to feel his hand shaking a little as he reached for the file that contained a photocopy of Wendy's suicide note. He had a feeling that this was the moment of truth, something that would confirm or disprove his worst suspicions.

For a few seconds he hardly dared look in case he was wrong. Then, his heart still pounding, he hurried to Gerry's office, clutching the two sheets of paper tightly in his hand.

'Wendy Haskel didn't kill herself,' he said as he pushed the door open.

Gerry looked up. 'So where the hell is she then?'

'Nadia Lucas told Ian Rowe that it was the other way round and now I think I know what she meant. It wasn't Maggie March who died in that burning car, it was Wendy. Nobody saw Wendy after that accident. Professor Maplin spoke to someone on the phone but he said the voice just muttered something incomprehensible – he presumed that Wendy was too shocked by the news to speak. But what if it wasn't Wendy on the other end of the line? From what Maplin told me, it could have been anyone. The neighbours heard someone going into her house and saw somebody disappearing down the road in Wendy's distinctive coat. But nobody actually saw or spoke to her. Wendy's things were found on the beach the day after and a short note was found in the house. But that note wasn't written by Wendy. I've compared the handwriting with a report she wrote. Someone's tried to copy her writing but when you examine it carefully you can tell that it wasn't written by the same person. The suicide note was a fake and nobody thought to check it at the time. Maggie March faked it all and disappeared. No wonder no body was found. Wendy's body was burned beyond recognition in Maggie's car in the days before DNA and Maggie, now officially dead, could skip off into the wild blue yonder with a new identity. And maybe a joyful reunion with her long-lost son.'

Gerry picked up a pencil and turned it over in his fingers, deep in thought. After a few seconds he looked up. 'You got any proof of all this?'

'Only the difference between the handwriting on the suicide note and the report . . . and what Nadia told Ian about it being the other way around.'

'Her writing could have been shaky because she was so distressed. It's not enough, Wes,' the DCI said, shaking his head. Then the ghost of a smile appeared on his lips. 'But it's a start. How are we going to prove it, eh?'

'I've got an idea. But it'll mean a trip to Exeter.'

Gerry watched while Wesley made a phone call. The last thing they wanted was a wasted journey.

Sir Martin Crace had always acknowledged the wisdom of sleeping on a problem. But somehow a night spent lying awake, twisting his body restlessly from side to side in a futile attempt to blot out the thoughts in his head and drift into unconsciousness, had done nothing to make his dilemma any clearer.

And the thought that Eva might have overstepped the mark didn't make him feel any better. He relied on Eva almost as other men relied on their wives. Theirs had been a sort of sexless marriage and, if it was proved that she had committed some crime, it would almost be like learning of the infidelity of a beloved wife. He'd been through that once before and he didn't think he could face that particular situation again. That's why he'd never remarried. He'd always thought he could trust Eva but she couldn't fool him. She looked worried sick.

He sat in his office sipping the morning coffee she had silently brought him, reading and rereading the letter. Then he picked up the phone. He had to check if there had been some sort of mistake.

But when the call was ended he realised this had only made things worse. He had no choice now but to act.

But how was he going to approach the problem?

'This is DCI Gerry Heffernan,' Wesley said with a smile as Karl Maplin held out his hand.

'Delighted to meet you,' Maplin said, glancing at the clock on the mantelpiece. 'I have a lecture in an hour but if I'm late I'm sure it will amuse my students no end to hear that I've been helping the police with their enquiries. Now how can I help you, gentlemen?'

'You said on the phone that you've kept a lot of photographs of digs you've worked at over the years.'

'Indeed I have.'

'You also said that Maggie's son helped on one occasion.'

'Just the once if I remember rightly – in the late seventies, I think it was. He'd have been in his teens and his mother was trying to get him interested in something constructive. He was a difficult young man, not one of nature's archaeologists as I recall. And unfortunately it wasn't a particularly spectacular site – just a couple of pieces of Iron Age pottery. Quite disappointing from his point of view, I should imagine.'

'I take it he lived with Maggie.'

'No, as a matter of fact he didn't. I remember that quite clearly and it didn't really surprise me as I would never have thought of Maggie as the maternal type. Maggie had given birth to him when she was a student and left it to her sister to bring him up. As far as I know, the sister was a good deal older and had a large family of her own so I don't suppose an extra one was too much of an inconvenience. But really, that's all I know.'

'What about the boy's father?'

Maplin leaned forward confidentially. 'I've no idea. Even my radar for gossip couldn't detect that one,' he added with a mischievous smirk. 'I was always convinced that Maggie was otherwise inclined sexually speaking so maybe the son was the result of an experiment of some kind. We all make mistakes, don't we?'

'Do you remember the boy's name?'

Maplin closed his eyes. 'Matthew ... Martin ... Michael. I'm sure it was something beginning with M. But I can't be sure after all these years.'

'You don't happen to know the sister's surname, do you?'

'Sorry.'

'But you do have a photo of the boy?' Wesley felt they were getting so near. Just a few more steps and they'd be there.

'I very much doubt it.'

'I mean a group photograph taken at the dig he was on.'

Maplin hesitated. 'I'll see what I can do,' he said and left the room. After a few minutes he returned with an armful of battered photograph albums and let them fall on the dining table with a clatter. 'Now which dig was it?' he mumbled to himself, flicking through the pages.

Wesley and Gerry could do nothing but watch as he studied photograph after photograph, punctuating the silence with small chuckles of delight when he came across some particularly rewarding memory.

'Oh, there's Cher Bakewell,' he said, pointing to a picture of a pretty teenage girl. Wesley hardly liked to tell him that Sheryl Bright, née Bakewell, was now languishing in the cells, accused of murdering her husband.

'And here's one of Maggie with . . . yes, that's him. Nineteen seventy-seven, that was – site near Exmouth. As I said, it was the only time he came with her on a dig.'

Wesley took the album and studied the photograph, Gerry looking over his shoulder.

They stared at the image in silence for a minute or so. There was something vaguely familiar about the boy. But had Wesley seen him recently, over thirty years older and with considerably less hair? Or was it his imagination? He caught Gerry's eye and knew that the DCI was as puzzled as he was.

Perhaps if he stared at the face of that nondescript young man long enough it might come to him.

Sir Martin didn't know whether to take anyone with him when he tackled the problem. To take one of his security staff might seem rather heavy-handed. Eva was the obvious choice, of course, but he was no longer sure whether he could trust her.

No, this needed delicate handling. Discretion. He would go alone.

He was expecting a telephone call from his Paris

headquarters in ten minutes. When he'd dealt with that he'd act.

The visit couldn't be put off much longer. Not after what he'd just learned.

'Why don't you have another word with Sheryl Bright?' Gerry asked as he took his jacket off and flung it on to his coat stand, where by some miracle it stayed hanging.

Wesley watched him, his mind elsewhere, still wondering whether he had really seen Maggie's son somewhere recently, many years older now, middle-aged in fact, with all the inevitable changes wrought by time on his face and body. Or perhaps it was just his imagination.

Gerry interrupted his thoughts. 'Tell you what, let's both speak to Sheryl. I want to know what really went on at that dig of Maggie March's at Grandal Field. If you're right and it was Wendy in that burning car—'

'It means Maggie killed her then stopped any questions being asked by faking her suicide. And it means that Maggie probably assumed a new identity.'

'Unless she killed herself out of remorse.'

'Then there'd be no point in the charade of the suicide note and the burning car. No, Maggie March wanted to survive.'

'She could be anywhere.'

'Not if she killed Nadia Lucas when she was getting too close to the truth.'

'We know that private detective, Forsyte Wiley, didn't have much luck.'

'But Nadia carried on the investigation on her own, remember. She had all those photos in her locker. She'd been round to some of the people involved in the dig asking questions.'

'But nobody knew anything.'

'What if she stumbled on Maggie, the woman who was supposed to be dead? Or Maggie's son? We need to find out about Maggie's sister. What was her name and where are her children now? The family are our best bet, I'm sure of it.'

Wesley suddenly felt despondent. Tracing Maggie March's unnamed sister and her brood might take some time. They didn't even know whereabouts in the country they lived. In fact by now they could be anywhere in the world.

After issuing his orders and receiving a groan from Nick Tarnaby, who complained that tracing family trees wasn't his idea of modern policing, Wesley arranged for Sheryl Bright to be brought to the interview room. He was probably doing her a favour, he thought. After spending hour upon hour in those cells in the station basement, she'd be glad of a change of scene.

As she took a seat opposite him, she looked defiant and demanded her solicitor.

'I don't want to talk about your husband's murder this time, Mrs Bright,' Wesley said quietly. He wanted her to regard him as a sympathetic ear. He wanted her to remember. 'I want to talk about that dig you took part in at Queenswear in 1983.'

'Oh, that again,' she said impatiently. 'I've told you everything I know already. I can't help you.'

'You thought Maggie March and Wendy Haskel were an item?'

She nodded. 'I suppose so.'

'Do you remember Karl Maplin?'

'Yes. I remember him.'

'Why are you smiling?'

'Oh, he was a terrible gossip, always stirring it. Men can be worse than women sometimes. And he was the worst of the lot.'

334

'Could he have told Maggie that Wendy and you . . .?'

'That'd be nonsense. But I wouldn't have put it past him. I think he got his kicks out of making mischief. He saw it as entertainment.'

'But what if Maggie had believed him?'

Sheryl thought for a moment, screwing up her face in an effort to recall something. 'You know, you could be on to something there. Maggie March was fine with me at first then suddenly she turned really bitchy, giving me all the worst jobs and . . . It's probably what put me off the idea of archaeology for life. She was such a bitch.'

'And that letter you had from the hospital shortly after Maggie March's death – you don't happen to remember what department the appointment was for, do you?'

'I think it was for the burns unit. Why?'

Wesley felt like kissing her. But she was under arrest for murder so it would have been inappropriate, to say the least.

'Hi, Neil, how's it going?'

Neil sat at his desk in his site office cum church hall and pressed his mobile phone to his ear. If Annabel, who worked in the county archives, had taken the trouble to call, it meant she'd discovered something interesting.

'Dig's going brilliantly but things are a bit uncertain. The developer's been killed. Wes won't tell me much but rumour has it he was murdered.'

'Wasn't you, was it?'

He could hear the giggle in Annabel's voice.

'No, it wasn't. Not that I wasn't tempted at times. Anything to report?'

'There certainly is. I found a chronicle relating to Stokeworthy Priory in the Cathedral records.' She paused for dramatic effect. Neil knew this tactic of old.

Something juicy was coming. 'And it looks as if your lady from Minerve didn't die after all. There's a record of her joining the sisters at Stokeworthy Priory. And her husband – Stephen de Grendalle isn't it? – gave them a bloody great donation. Guilt money perhaps.'

'Are you absolutely sure it's the same woman?'

'Jeanne, lately known as Jeanne de Minerve, wife of Stephen de Grendalle. She took the veil and brought a thumping great dowry to the priory.'

'But all the other evidence points to the fact that she died – she burned to death in the dovecot. We've even found the burnt layer.'

'Well, sorry to disappoint you, Neil, but it looks as though she survived and got her to a nunnery.'

'So much for local legends then.'

'People like a good story.' There was a long pause. Neil could almost hear Annabel's brain working. 'Just because she survived it doesn't mean she wasn't caught in the fire. Perhaps she was disfigured. Perhaps that's why she chose to be locked away. Just a thought.'

Neil ended the call and walked outside. It was time to get back to the dig. And he wondered, in view of the young woman burned to death near the site of the dovecot, whether Wesley would be interested in this new development.

The cottage on the edge of the woods. It had always reminded Martin Crace of something out of a fairy tale, pretty but vaguely sinister.

He suddenly realised that nobody knew where he was. Eva normally kept track of his comings and goings but he had crept out of the office without telling her where he was headed.

But it didn't matter. He only wanted a discreet chat with his mother's cousin, just to clarify a few things. He looked down at the letter in his hand. There was probably a perfectly simple explanation.

He lifted the door knocker and let it fall three times.

Gerry Heffernan couldn't think of any grounds to hold Ian Rowe for much longer, even though he wanted to, so he'd been released on bail. Free to go ... for the time being.

Wesley went down to the custody suite to say goodbye. He didn't much like the man but he still had a sneaking feeling that he should keep tabs on him. He had been the one Rowe had sought out to share his worries about Nadia Lucas with, after all. He had been the one who'd started the whole business.

Rowe was just collecting his possessions when Wesley arrived and he turned to give the inspector a weary smile.

'Well, well, Wesley. I'm being released on bail. Nice one, eh.'

'Only because Pam and I aren't pressing charges for breaking and entering and neither is Professor Demancour.'

'Oh, come on, Wesley, don't be such a prig.'

'You will stick around. We'll need to ask you some more questions.'

'Yeah. Your friend here just said.' He nodded towards the custody sergeant, who was busying himself with his paperwork. 'I was going to get in touch with Jack and see if any of his properties are free, but apparently I've got to go back to the hostel in Morbay so they know where to find me. You've still got my passport. When can I have it back?'

'In due course,' Wesley said in official tones. If he wasn't careful Rowe would play the old pal card and he wasn't falling for that again. And besides, he didn't want

Rowe skipping the country while there were still questions to be answered.

'Any nearer finding out what happened to Nadia?' Rowe asked as Wesley turned away.

'Not yet.' He saw a look of derision on Rowe's face. Fine detective you are, it said. 'By the way, we've talked to Sir Martin Crace. He utterly denies being your father. He's even said he'd consider taking a DNA test. If I were you, I wouldn't bother him again.'

'But you're not me, are you, Wesley?'

'Pity those diaries you said your mother wrote got burned in the cottage.'

Rowe shrugged. 'It makes no difference. I know what I know.'

Wesley walked out of the custody suite. If Rowe wanted to make a fool of himself by harassing Crace, that was up to him. He'd had enough of Rowe. In fact he would be quite happy if they never met again.

As he walked down the corridor his mobile began to ring. From the display he saw that it was Neil and he answered it, hoping he'd learn something relevant to a case that he still found frustrating and confusing. But that was too much to hope. Neil's mind, as usual, was on archaeology.

He'd just made an exciting discovery about the history of his site. The woman who had supposedly been burned to death near the spot where Nadia Lucas had met her end hadn't died after all. She'd retired to Stokeworthy Priory and lived the rest of her life as a nun. Neil had a theory that she'd been caught in the burning dovecot and suffered disfiguring injuries.

But fascinating though this was, it didn't help Wesley bring Nadia's killer to justice. But it jogged something in the recesses of his mind. Around the time of Maggie March's supposed accident someone had used Sheryl

338

Bright's name at the hospital burns unit. Could it have been Maggie herself using the first name that came into her head, the name of the young girl she knew from the Queenswear excavation? Could she have been injured when she set fire to the car with Wendy Haskel in it? But it was still just a theory. He only wished he had some proof.

He told Neil he'd see him soon and ended the call just as Gerry Heffernan loomed into view down the corridor.

'I need to get out of the office,' Gerry said wearily. 'Preferably somewhere the Nutter won't find me. Fancy a coffee in the canteen?'

Gerry looked like a man who needed company. It would have been churlish to refuse the invitation. They sat down at a table in the corner with two steaming mugs of coffee and sat in amicable silence for a while.

It was Gerry who spoke first. 'So where are we up to? We've got Cherry Bakewell and Jem Burrows charged and your mate Rowe's been released on bail because, dodgy though he undoubtedly is, we can't actually prove he's done anything illegal. He's not even tried to extort money out of our friend Crace . . . although I suspect that was his ultimate intention.'

Wesley sighed. 'But what had Nadia discovered, that's what I want to know.'

'Her long-lost mum?'

'No. She told Rowe over the phone that it was the other way around. Wendy Haskel died in Maggie March's place and March faked Haskel's suicide so that she could disappear. I think Nadia was killed because she was about to find out the truth.'

'By someone who knew all about the site and the story associated with it? By Maggie March? She could still be around here somewhere with a new identity.'

'And her son. Don't forget the son. Maybe Nadia

found Maggie. Maybe she told her she knew her secret. She knew she was a murderer. Who knew Ian Rowe was back here?'

'Crace himself. Eva. Jane Verity. Denis Wade.'

'And?'

'Excuse me, sir.' Wesley looked up and saw DC Nick Tarnaby standing by the table, shifting from foot to foot. His eyes were fixed on Gerry as though he feared he would spring up and devour him at any moment.

'What is it?'

'I don't know if it's important or ...'

'Go on,' said Wesley encouragingly.

'Someone from uniform's just been up to the CID office. He says he bumped into a bloke yesterday at that cottage near Whitely that got burned down ... the one where that man was killed.'

'Did this bloke he bumped into have a name?' Wesley asked, glancing at Gerry, who was watching Tarnaby with barely disguised impatience.

Tarnaby studied the notebook in his hand. 'Bloke with a Discovery he'd nicked for speeding. He said it got him thinking so he checked the date he issued the ticket. It was on the night of the fire and this bloke in the Discovery was going like the clappers on the road to Neston. Away from Whitely. His name was ...' He turned over the page. 'Hang on ... I wrote it down somewhere ... .'

Wesley caught Gerry's eye. Suddenly he knew why the youthful face of Maggie March's son on those old photographs had seemed so familiar. 'Let me guess,' he said. 'It was the owner of Owl Cottage. It was Jack Plesance.'

Nick Tarnaby's mouth gaped open. 'That's right. You must be psychic, sir.'

*

Sir Martin Crace stared at the woman he knew as Bertha Trent, his eyes drawn to the disfiguring scarring on the left side of her face, the side she always kept hidden.

He'd always believed she'd suffered those burns when Mugabe's so-called war veterans had set fire to her farmhouse out in Zimbabwe. She'd described her experience in vivid and heart-rending detail. How they broke the door down. How they bayoneted her cowering maid. How they laughed when they locked her in a bedroom and set the property alight. But now he couldn't be sure of anything.

'I've just received a letter from a solicitor in South Africa,' he said quietly.

'Oh yes.' Bertha showed no sign of unease.

'The solicitor – a Mr Kronje – said he was very sorry to have to inform me that my mother's cousin, Miss Bertha Trent, died in a Cape Town nursing home recently. I had dealings with Kronje some years ago when Bertha's farm was attacked and she was reported missing, presumed dead. But now he's telling me that she somehow managed to escape to Cape Town. He says that the trauma she'd suffered brought about a loss of mcmory and it was only on her death that someone went through the few possessions she'd brought out of Zimbabwe with her and found items that confirmed her identity.' He looked at the woman expectantly but she turned her face away. 'So if you're not the real Bertha Trent, who are you?'

There was no answer. But Crace heard a sound behind him. Someone opening a door. He swung round.

'Hello,' he said to the newcomer. 'I've not seen you for a long time. What are you doing here?'

Jack Plesance didn't answer. But with a smile he produced an iron bar from behind his back.

*

Eva Liversedge trod the thickly carpeted path to her office. A phone was ringing so she hurried her pace.

The call was from London. Someone from Number Ten wanting to speak to Sir Martin urgently. He wasn't in his office so she dialled his mobile number.

After a few rings it was answered and she heard what sounded like a muffled cry before the call was ended abruptly. She stared at the phone for a few moments then tried the number again. This time it rang out and she knew that something was wrong.

Hurrying out into the hall she felt panic rising inside her. 'Has anyone seen Sir Martin?' she asked Jane Verity, who was walking with her customary serenity towards the green baize door.

'I saw him go outside,' Jane said. 'He had something in his hand. Looked like a letter. He was walking down the drive.'

Eva suddenly remembered the letter he'd received, the one from South Africa. The one she'd assumed was just a misunderstanding. As Jane disappeared into the cosy depths of the servants' quarters, she stood there, wondering what to do. Was it really worth ringing the police or was she panicking about nothing?'

The woman turned to face Jack Plesance and he could see the shiny, mottled scarring on the side of her face, vivid red and pulling her features out of alignment.

'I didn't know Bertha Trent was still alive,' she said breathlessly. 'You said she'd disappeared.'

'That's what they told Crace. That's why I asked you to come back. I knew that all you had to do was turn up and say you were Bertha. Crace had never even met her. Mum, please. How was I to know she'd got away to South Africa? I thought there'd be no problem.'

Jack put a hand on his mother's arm but she pulled it away.

'That's what you always think. I sometimes wish—'

'What?'

'That I'd not come back here. I'd made myself a life in Africa after ...' She looked into her son's eyes and saw that they were brimming with tears. Why did he always have to be so emotional? Why did he have to feel things so deeply?

But she knew why. She had been like that herself, especially when Wendy, her lovely, beautiful Wendy, had betrayed her by flirting with that silly Cherry girl. She'd seen them together, laughing and giggling, and she began to fear that she was losing her. Then that silly, bitchy little man Karl Maplin had told her he'd seen them kissing. Wendy and Cherry. He'd taken such a delight in telling her. Wendy had denied it, of course. She'd said that she'd just been friendly towards Cherry; that there'd been nothing in it.

But sometimes jealousy, once roused, won't lie down. It had preyed on her mind, burrowed like a worm into her soul until she convinced herself that Wendy couldn't be trusted.

Then they had quarrelled and she'd struck Wendy so hard that she'd fallen and struck her head. She had known from those blank, open eyes that her beloved Wendy was dead and she'd stood there staring in horror at the result of her terrible, tempestuous emotions. She hadn't meant to kill her, but who'd believe her? That was when she knew she'd have to keep a cool head and devise some sort of plan. She needed everyone to believe that it was her who'd died in the car, and then she had to make it look as if Wendy had killed herself out of grief. Then she'd disappeared to Africa where nobody knew her past, intending never to return. And for so many years it worked.

Until her son had found her, until he had traced her through a letter she'd written to her sister, and told her he needed her.

She heard a groan. Martin Crace was lying face down on the floor, partially shielded by Jack's body. He moved his arm; he was coming round.

'What are we going to do?' she asked. Since they'd been reunited Jack had become her rock, she thought. Even after all those years when she had rejected him.

'He knows now. There's nothing else for it.'

'How?'

He smiled. 'Same as before. Fire purifies. Fire destroys evidence.'

Maggie March shuddered. She hated fire. Fire had terrified her ever since she'd tried to rescue those excavation reports from her burning car and the flames had touched her face, leaving her scarred for life. She'd forgotten those important reports had been there on the back seat until it was too late and she'd tried instinctively to retrieve them, even though she could never have used them. It had been automatic, something she did without thinking. So stupid.

She had covered her ears when Jack told her how he'd poured petrol over the unconscious body of Nadia Lucas. At first he had told her that Nadia had become an investigative journalist, searching for the truth about Wendy's disappearance, and that he'd lured her to the field with the promise of a story. The field where Maggie had last worked with Wendy: the field connected with that strange legend of the burning bride. She'd once shared that legend with Jack and he'd been so interested when she told him about the burned foundations of the circular dovecot she'd discovered during the dig – the spot where the bride was supposed to have died.

Then later he confessed that he'd lied to her. Nadia had

really been Wendy's daughter. He'd met her in Neston and told her he was taking her to meet someone who knew the truth about her mother. He'd driven her to the meeting place, Grandal Field, and Nadia had trusted him enough – or been desperate enough – to go with him. When she learned this, Maggie cried. Wendy had been so precious to her – and Nadia had been Wendy's flesh and blood.

That man Rowe, who'd once driven for Crace, had told Jack all about Nadia's search for Wendy and Jack had encouraged his confidences. Through Rowe he knew about the letter Nadia had found amongst her father's things, spelling out Maggie's relationship with her mother . . . a letter Maggie had written in the hot fires of jealousy, threatening to kill her beloved. After he'd killed Nadia, Jack had taken her keys and let himself into her house to retrieve the letter. Nadia had been getting close to the truth so, if Maggie was to be kept safe, Nadia had to be silenced. But Maggie wished that Jack had found a kinder way.

'Have we got to kill Martin? He's been so kind to me.'

'Don't get sentimental, Mum,' he snapped. 'We can't afford sentimentality.'

She looked at her son's eyes and saw that they were cold, devoid of any pity or emotion. 'What about that man you told me about? Ian Rowe? You killed the wrong man in your cottage. Rowe's still about and he—'

'I don't think he knows the truth. I thought he was on to it but now I'm not so sure. But I might have to deal with him even so.'

'I've had enough of killing,' Maggie whispered. She felt her son's arm around her shoulder as he kissed the top of her head.

'It'll be all right, Mum. We'll go away, just you and me. Somewhere nice, eh.' He took her in his arms and kissed her again. 'It'll be fine, you'll see.'

She turned away, fingering the scarred flesh of her face, listening to the sound of liquid gurgling from the petrol can. It was as though it meant nothing to him now. They say murder is easy with practice. In a second he would light the purifying flames. Then it would be over.

But when she heard the distant sound of police car sirens her body froze.

Wesley climbed out of the car and looked up at the elegant façade of Bewton Hall. Everything looked normal. But Eva Liversedge had made that panicked phone call. She'd said she thought Sir Martin was in some sort of trouble. She'd sounded upset and Eva didn't seem the kind of woman who upset easily.

'Has she no idea where he's gone?' Gerry asked as he squeezed out of the passenger door.

'She said he was on foot and she said something about a letter from South Africa – she kept saying it must be a misunderstanding. She mentioned Bertha so there's a chance that Crace might have headed for Bertha Trent's cottage. I just hope we're not too late.'

The patrol cars were pulling up, crunching gravel beneath their tyres. Wesley took it upon himself to organise the search of the grounds. Crace would still be on the premises, he was sure of that. The security guards at the gate had told him that nobody had left the estate in the past hour. Wesley himself began to walk down the drive towards the woods.

'So let me get this clear: you think that woman in the cottage calling herself Bertha Trent is really Maggie March?' Gerry said as he trotted to keep up.

'I can't be absolutely sure yet but—'

'And Jack Plesance is her son?'

'He lied to us. He wasn't up in the Midlands when his cottage was torched. He was here in Devon. Breaking the speed limit on the main road leading away from Whitely.'

'Maybe he just torched the place for the insurance,' Gerry suggested.

'I keep looking at that photograph. He's John Martin March. I'm sure of it,' said Wesley hurrying his pace.

Gerry said nothing. The cottage had come into view at last.

Crace lay face down on the floor, his arms cradling his head as though he was defending himself from attack. Jack hadn't poured the petrol directly on to his body, but had flicked it around the room. He stood there with the box of matches in his hand. His mother put her hand on his shoulder.

'Is he dead?'

'If he's not he will be soon.'

The words made Maggie shudder. He took her in his arms and bent to kiss her scarred cheek. John had always been a strange, cold child. Her sister had told her how hard it was to cope with him but she'd had no choice in the matter when Maggie had abdicated her responsibility to pursue her own interests. Perhaps it was her rejection of him all those years ago that had made him difficult, she thought. He had sometimes been violent towards his cousins, her sister had told her. Then later his obsession with her began; his smothering love.

John was working for Crace when he contacted her and asked her to come back to England. Sir Martin's mother's cousin in Zimbabwe had just been reported missing, and, as Crace had never met her, Jack reckoned that, if she took on Bertha Trent's identity, they could be reunited, be mother and son again. It was what he wanted more than anything, he said. When her sister's husband died Maggie encouraged him to return to the

Midlands, to leave Sir Martin's employment and start his own business: she was sure he wouldn't be able to keep their secret if he stayed there in such close proximity. But he still spent half his time in Devon, playing the devoted son in secret.

For a long time the plan worked: Sir Martin didn't suspect a thing when she arrived with tales of how she had suffered under Mugabe's brutal regime. He believed every word and gave her a house and financial support. And now, looking at him lying helpless on the floor, she felt sorry. He didn't deserve to have his generosity repaid like this.

'I can't let you do this, John,' she heard herself saying. The words came out quietly, almost apologetically.

'We've got no choice, Mum. He knows about you now.'

She placed a hand on the bare flesh of his arm, imploring. The other deaths had been wrong and so was this.

'Do you want the truth to come out, Mum? Do you want to go to prison for killing that Wendy woman? It's for the best. If Crace dies in a house fire, they'll think it was an accident.'

'They didn't think Nadia was an accident.'

'I had no choice, Mum. She was on to you. I couldn't let her . . .'

She felt the tears streaming down the mottled, shiny flesh of her scarred face. 'You killed that man at your cottage.'

'I thought it was Rowe. It was dark and I hit him. How was I to know it was the wrong man?' he said in a self-pitying whine. 'I had to get rid of Rowe because he was close to Nadia – she'd confided in him. I didn't know how much he knew so I couldn't take the risk.'

'When's it going to stop, John? I've had enough,' she

sobbed, wiping the tears and mucus from her face. 'Let's just go.' She began to tug at his T-shirt, but he pulled away, opening the matchbox. 'Leave it, John. Let's go.'

He swung round and took her in his arms so roughly that she gasped. 'I can't let you rot in prison, Mum. We've got no choice.'

He released her from his grip and she stumbled to the ground, clawing at him, trying to stop the inevitable. She could see the match in his fingers, poised over the matchbox edge, and she could smell the choking petrol fumes. Crace was still lying there motionless although she was sure he was still breathing.

As she launched herself at her son, there was a thunderous banging on the door. Jack made use of the distraction to shake his mother off and light the match. When he threw it, the room ignited with a sound like rushing wind.

Jack grabbed her arm and began to pull her away from the blaze but she wriggled out of his grasp and lunged at Crace.

She caught hold of his ankles and started to drag him away from danger as she heard her son's voice calling, desperate, like a frightened child. 'Mummy. Mummy. Come back. We need to get out.'

He was fighting his way towards her and she had to act. The iron bar he'd used to render Crace unconscious was still lying there on the floor by the sofa. She picked it up awkwardly and swung it at his head.

He collapsed to the floor, a look of utter amazement on his face as his lips formed the word 'Mummy' and his eyes closed.

Suddenly she saw two figures looming through the smoke, masking their faces, coughing and gasping.

'Help me,' she called to them feebly. Crace seemed to be getting heavier. She couldn't manage on her own.

She recognised her two helpers. They were the police-men who'd visited her. She heard the older one shouting as the young black inspector darted forward, shielding his face with his sleeve against the billowing smoke. The flames were licking round Crace's limp body as he came closer.

'Help him.' The words came out in a splutter as the smoke caught the back of her throat.

She heard the older man shouting again as the inspect-or, with a massive effort, relieved her of her burden and dragged Crace out of the room, dropping his body for a second as the heat began scorch his hands and face. Coughing, he caught hold of Crace's shoulders again and began to move faster, pulling the dead weight towards the door and safety, leaving her staring at the flames.

She sank to her knees, calling Jack's name. She could just see him through the smoke. His eyes were closed and the flames were approaching him. When the inspect-or returned for her, grabbing her firmly to drag her away from danger, she slithered from his grasp and threw herself towards the flames. She heard his hoarse voice shouting to her as she reached for her son's body, holding on to him firmly, as though protecting him from the conflagration.

She closed her eyes and blocked out the sound of the flames and the voices of her rescuers. It would be better this way. She knew the inspector was close, still trying to save her. But she didn't choose to be saved.

There was another whooshing sound as the sofa caught alight. It was almost over. She could hear shouting in the distance. And a scream of pain before everything went bright and she felt a deep and numbing peace.

16

All my assumptions have been proved wrong. I have actually found her grave. And I was astounded to discover that she died some ten years after her marriage – in fact she outlived her husband by two years.

The chronicles of Stokeworthy Priory (fragments of which still exist in the Diocesan archives) say that the sister lately known as Jeanne de Minerve was buried in the priory burial ground. How could this fact have been missed over all these centuries?

Stephen de Grendalle's burial at Morre Abbey, where he was a generous benefactor, is recorded in 1218. He left his lands to the Abbey and not to his wife, who we now know was still alive. From this I assume that the couple were separated and that she took the veil immediately after the fire.

But there is no mention of her in his will, which makes me wonder whether he knew of her survival. Perhaps she escaped from the burning dovecot and took refuge with the sisters. But there is mention of her bringing a dowry to the Priory so perhaps she entered the cloistered life with her husband's blessing and financial support.

I shall try and discover more about Jeanne's story in

due course. But first I have a search of my own to complete – the search for my mother.

(From papers found in the possession of Professor Yves Demancour)

Pam hoped that Wesley wouldn't always bear the scars of his foolhardy but heroic attempt to save the lives of a pair of murderers. Gerry had told her that Wesley had already managed to get Sir Martin Crace out of the burning cottage when he'd insisted on going back in to rescue Crace's two would-be assassins.

Why Wesley had done it, Gerry didn't know, although he'd probably get a commendation for his trouble. But in spite of his best efforts, he'd failed. Maggie March and her son, Jack Plesance, had both perished in the blaze.

Pam felt angry with him for risking his life. More than angry, furious. He had young children who needed their father. He might have left her widowed. As she walked into the ward at Tradmouth Hospital, she thought she was going to find it hard to forgive him.

When she spotted him lying there, propped up on hospital pillows with a transparent oxygen mask dangling around his neck and his left arm bandaged, she hesitated for a moment. Neil was already sitting there by his side, popping grapes into his mouth as he talked and looking quite unconcerned. After a few seconds she carried on walking, her eyes fixed on her husband's face. He didn't look too bad, considering what he'd been through. But that wasn't the point.

She felt tempted to turn round and go home. Wesley had Neil to keep him company, after all. It would only take a visit from Gerry Heffernan and some of his CID colleagues to make it quite a party. But it was too late for a retreat. He had seen her and he'd raised himself up on his pillows, coughing with the effort. He looked pleased to see her and she suddenly felt a stab of conscience.

'How are you?' she asked as she sat down on the bed. She'd brought nothing with her. She'd left the children with a neighbour and hurried straight to the hospital so she hadn't had time.

'The doctor said I'll be fine. I inhaled some smoke and there are some superficial burns to my arm but—'

'He'll get time off work,' Neil chipped in. 'So it's not all bad.'

Wesley ignored his friend and grasped Pam's hand. 'I'll be out of here in a day or so. How are the kids?'

Neil offered her a grape but she shook her head and leaned forward. What she had to say wasn't for the whole ward to hear. 'You risked your bloody life. What about me and the kids, eh? What about your family?'

'I was only doing my job.'

'That's right, Pam,' said Neil. 'He was only doing his job. You should be proud of him. I've never done anything heroic like that.' He popped another grape into his mouth. They were almost finished. He looked into her eyes, a mischievous smile on his lips. 'So you won't be interested in the reward then?'

'What reward?'

'You don't save the life of an extremely rich man like Crace and come away empty-handed. He's offered to give you and Wes a luxury holiday. All expenses paid to anywhere you fancy. Your choice.'

Pam hesitated, lost for words. Perhaps she'd been too hasty. She forced a smile. 'That's nice.'

'I'd go for the ruins of Pompeii myself,' Neil said.

Pam saw the temptation on Wesley's face but before she had a chance to make her objections to any holiday that involved too many archaeological sites, another figure appeared, hovering at the end of the bed as though unsure how he'd be received.

353

'Hello Wesley. Hello Neil, long time no see,' Ian Rowe said. 'Sorry about,er . . .'

Wesley and Neil looked at the newcomer expectantly. 'I heard what happened and I just came to say goodbye. I'm off back to France. Back to Carcassonne.'

'What about Sir Martin? What about this thing about the DNA test?'

Rowe shrugged. 'He says he'll take one if I insist but he keeps making excuses – he's off to some summit or he's got a meeting with the Prime Minister. He keeps denying that he's my dad . . .' He hesitated. 'Sometimes it seems more trouble than it's worth. And he's dropped hints about his team of expensive lawyers who'll no doubt take me to the cleaners if I breathe a word to the press so . . .'

'So you're thinking of giving up?'

'I don't know. Perhaps I haven't got much choice if he keeps stalling. I can't force him to take a DNA test, can I? And if any questions are asked he'll just say he's willing but the time's not right. Maybe when he's dead I'll prove it once and for all.'

Pam looked at him, shocked. Her husband and his colleagues had gone to so much trouble to rescue Crace and now this man was standing there wishing him dead.

'At least you know who killed Nadia now. At least she's had justice.' He looked at Wesley. 'So what exactly happened? Why did they kill her?'

Wesley took a deep breath which brought on a coughing fit. Pam put her arms around his shoulder, suddenly protective. He shouldn't be bothered like this. She gave Rowe a hostile look.

But once Wesley had recovered, he seemed quite happy to talk. 'Nadia pieced the facts together and she'd worked out that Wendy Haskel might not have committed suicide. That thing she said to you – "What if it's the other way round?"'

Rowe's eyes widened in horror. 'It could be my fault she was killed. I phoned Jack one day and we got chatting. He'd known Nadia and he seemed really interested so I told him all about her trying to find out what happened to her mother and the letter she'd found and everything. If it wasn't for me she might still be alive. Why couldn't I have kept my bloody mouth shut?'

'You weren't to know,' Pam said gently. She'd never seen Ian Rowe genuinely upset before.

'Come to think of it,' Rowe continued, 'Jack was always a bit obsessed with his mother. He used to talk about her a lot ... said she was wonderful. He never gave any hint that she was actually living at Bewton Hall. They kept up a good act.'

'She'd rejected him as a child,' said Wesley. 'Maybe that's why he became obsessed with her. I think he'd have done anything to hide what she'd done all those years ago. Maggie would have known all about the site at Queenswear. She'd been in charge of the excavation and she'd have known the legend of the burning bride and how it fitted in with the burned layer found at the dovecot. I wonder if she went there with Jack and pointed out the spot. I wonder if she watched him kill Nadia and set her body alight.'

'And me?' Rowe said almost in a whisper. 'Why did he try to kill me? I was supposed to be his friend.'

'Because you were trying to find out what happened to Nadia,' Wesley replied. 'Only Eva sent Denis Wade to warn you off about Crace and try to get hold of that evidence you told her you had. When you heard him break in, you left the house and hid outside. It was dark and Jack didn't expect anyone else to be in there. Wade was just unlucky. He died in your place, Ian. That fire was meant for you.'

'I know.'

Pam watched Ian as he walked out of the ward. If she never saw him again in her life, it wouldn't bother her in the least.

Wesley never thought he'd miss work so much. The buzz of the CID office, Rachel Tracey organising the younger DCs like a mother hen, Gerry Heffernan's wisecracks. He felt helpless and somewhat useless as he convalesced at home. He'd tried to persuade Pam that he was fine to go back but she'd put her foot down. It was good to be home together in the school holidays, she said. He tried hard to agree with her and felt guilty when he failed.

He was sitting outside in the garden, feet up on the sunlounger watching the children playing in their plastic sandpit, when he heard the telephone ring inside the house. A few moments later Pam emerged from the French windows, carrying the handset as if it was something dirty. 'It's for you. A Professor Demancour. The station gave him your home number,' she said with obvious disapproval.

Wesley took the handset, suddenly feeling a burst of new energy rushing through his body. 'Hello, Professor. What can I do for you?'

'There is something I should have told you. Something that troubles me. Can we meet?'

When Wesley ended the call he stood up stiffly and called to Pam that he was going out. Before she could raise any objections, he had climbed into the car and backed out of the drive. Demancour was at home and was expecting him.

The professor seemed subdued and rather preoccupied as he admitted Wesley to his flat. He said nothing as he led him through to the living room and Wesley felt impatient to know what it was that he wanted to tell him.

'I've kept something from you,' Demancour began. 'I know I should have told you when you questioned me but—'

'What is it?'

There was a long pause. Then he walked across the room to the cupboard where he'd kept his precious book and took out a file.

'The manuscript Nadia was working on when she died,' he said, placing it in front of Wesley. 'It's about Jeanne de Grendalle. She did a great deal of research and made some interesting discoveries. This is just the first draft.'

'Why didn't you tell me about this before?'

Demancour's face turned red. 'Please don't think badly of me but I was tempted to use her discoveries in my own work. But I realise now that it would be wrong.'

Wesley said nothing. He opened the file and began to read through the sheets of paper.

The manuscript was typed, double-spaced. It was all there, the story of how Jeanne and Stephen had met and fled France. Of how he had brought her to his estates at Queenswear and how she had been baptised into the Catholic church, rejecting her Cathar faith. Some of it came from Nadia's imagination, some from historical records. But the letters from Urien de Norton had been real enough. They had been found amongst other papers in the archives. Urien de Norton had planted seeds of jealousy in Stephen's mind by telling him that Jeanne had been seen with Walter Fitzallen, the local entrepreneur and the man who had begun the rise in Tradmouth's prosperity by turning the town from a small fishing community into an international port.

There seemed to be no solid evidence of Jeanne's infidelity but that was clearly what de Norton was hinting at. She had been seen with Fitzallen meeting in secret, whispering in corners. Wesley wondered what de Norton's motives were. He was obviously some distant relative of de Grendalle's so did he hope for an inheritance? Then he thought of Karl Maplin and his love of gossip, stirring the pot for his own entertainment, feeding emotions that had led to murder. Some people just got their kicks that way.

'Did you know that Jeanne survived the fire?' said Demancour. 'Records exist that indicate she entered the convent at Stokeworthy. She became a nun.'

'What year?'

'1212. Stephen died in 1218. He was buried at Morre Abbey. It wasn't uncommon for widows to enter a religious house, but a married woman .... Perhaps he did try to kill her and then she chose to take the veil.'

Wesley smiled. The explanation seemed far-fetched but, taken together with all the other facts, it also seemed likely. He knew that the dovecot had burned down at some point in its history – the archaeology confirmed that much. But perhaps some imaginative person in the past had put two and two together and come up with completely the wrong conclusion. Perhaps it was just a case of a married couple separating. Perhaps the fire had nothing to do with it.

'We'll never know for sure,' said Wesley.

'But you know who killed Nadia?'

'Oh, yes. We know that. But he's dead.'

'Why did he . . .?'

Wesley took a deep breath and recited the facts. 'He also tried to kill Ian Rowe,' he added. 'But he got the wrong man.'

'Now that wouldn't have been a great loss to the world,' Demancour said bitterly.

Wesley didn't answer. 'If there's nothing else you want to tell me . . .'

'No. I just felt you should know about Nadia's manuscript. I'm sorry if I've wasted your time.'

'Oh, you haven't,' Wesley said. 'In fact, you've done me a favour.'

On his way home he called in to the police station. He needed to get back to normal.

Epilogue

Sir Martin Crace had asked to see DI Peterson. He wanted to thank him personally for saving his life.

Eva Liversedge had been replaced by another PA. She had taken early retirement, Wesley was told, as the replacement, a younger version of the original, led him to the inner sanctum. The words 'on a very generous pension' were left unsaid but Wesley was certain that Eva's loyalty, however over-enthusiastic and ill-judged, wouldn't have gone unrewarded.

Sir Martin looked well. But then, like Wesley, he'd had a month to recover from his ordeal. Wesley felt that his own recovery was now complete. It was only the scarring on his arm that remained, ugly and disfiguring. From now on he'd feel self-conscious about wearing short sleeves in the summer, although Pam had come round to saying that he should be proud of his marks of battle.

Sir Martin bore no scars. He'd been fortunate. He stood up as Wesley entered and held out his hand. Wesley took it and shook it firmly.

'I felt I had to thank you personally, Inspector. You were a hero. I believe you're to receive a commendation for bravery.'

Wesley smiled modestly but didn't answer. The truth

was, he had come to find the whole thing rather embarrassing. He didn't feel like a hero. He felt scared and angry and frustrated with the system. In short, he felt as he supposed everyone else felt. He was tempted to say he felt like a fraud but he decided against it.

Eva's replacement brought coffee – a cafetière and two cups. Wesley breathed in the aroma. For ages he'd only been able to smell smoke, and fresh-ground coffee was a treat.

'When I was coming up the drive I noticed that you've had the cottage demolished.'

'I thought it best,' Crace said as he poured the coffee. There was a long silence, as though he was wondering how to tackle a thorny subject. When Wesley was sipping his coffee he finally spoke.

'I've been wondering whether to confide in you, Wesley. I may call you Wesley, may I? Inspector sounds so formal.'

Wesley nodded, wondering what was coming.

'Do I have your assurance that what I'm about to tell you stays within these four walls?'

'If it doesn't involve a criminal offence, yes.'

'You knew Ian Rowe from university, I believe.'

'Yes, but we were never friends.'

'And you know about his claims … that I was his father?'

'Yes.'

'Did you wonder why I avoided taking a DNA test?'

Wesley didn't answer.

'The truth is, if you have any influence with him at all, I'd appreciate it if you could persuade him to drop the matter.'

Wesley stared at Crace for a few seconds. 'May I ask why?'

Crace arched his fingers. He was thinking. After a

long silence he spoke. 'Can I rely on your discretion, Wesley? Can you assure me that you won't pass on anything I say even if you might consider it a technical breach of the law?'

'I can be discreet but I can't make any promises.' He looked Crace in the eye. 'You are Rowe's father, aren't you? I can even see the resemblance.'

Crace sighed and sank back in his chair. 'Look, Wesley, the last thing I want is for the press to get hold of it. Ian's mother was fourteen at the time. A very mature fourteen and she assured me she was older. All I want is to ensure that Ian doesn't come back and try to rake over the whole business again. Can you imagine what would happen if the tabloids got a whiff of the story? I have my reputation to think about, Wesley. And that's so important to my charitable work. How could I stand up at a UNICEF meeting when it was plastered over the front pages that I'd made a fourteen-year-old girl pregnant?'

'It was a long time ago. And the woman's dead. It would never come to court.'

'What does that matter to a tabloid editor? I want you to keep in touch with Rowe and if he ever attempts to revive his accusations, I want you to persuade him that he's wasting his time. You could remind him that I won't hesitate to sue for slander if he persists.'

Wesley said nothing. He could see Crace watching him anxiously, waiting for his agreement.

Crace gave him a forced smile. 'Now, have you thought about where you and your family would like to go for that holiday? I'd make sure no expense was spared, of course, that goes without saying.' He smiled. 'How about the Caribbean? The best hotels, of course. Or perhaps a cruise?'

Wesley stood up. 'Thank you for the coffee, Sir

Martin,' he said. 'But I think I'll have to decline your offer.'

He knew Crace was watching him as he walked the long walk across the Turkish carpet. He'd often wondered what it was like to be bribed and now he knew. It was strangely tempting. But he couldn't live with himself if he caved in. However, he wasn't sure how he was going to explain his decision to Pam. Or what he'd do if Ian Rowe appeared in his life again. He'd just have to hope and pray that the situation never arose.

He drove back to Tradmouth, a smile on his lips. The moral high ground was a good place to be.

The CID office was fairly quiet on his return. The tourist season was drawing to an end but valuables were still disappearing from yachts berthed in the harbour and there was a spate of burglaries at holiday apartments to clear up, so some of the team were out conducting interviews.

But as soon as he walked into the office Gerry Heffernan bore down on him, a worried look on his face. Something had happened. Without a word the two men hurried to Gerry's office and sat down.

'Just had a call from the coastguard,' Gerry began. 'A body's been washed up near Bloxham. Been in the water a month or so, Colin reckons. Young woman. Not very recognisable but what's left of her fits the description of that missing Lithuanian lass. Anya.'

Wesley bowed his head.

'I told Colin we'd get over there.'

Wesley followed the DCI out. It was best not to mention Crace's little dilemma. Not when there was murder to deal with.